STRONG CONVICTIONS

An Emmett Strong Western

To Rob,
So great to have
worked with you
at SCS. I really
enjoyed getting
to know you!
God bless you
richly!
GP Hutchinson

G P Hutchinson

Strong Convictions: An Emmett Strong Western
GP Hutchinson

ISBN-13: 978-1499151022
ISBN-10: 1499151020
Library of Congress Control Number: 2014915119
CreateSpace Independent Publishing Platform
North Charleston, South Carolina

The author would like to thank Karla Van Horne of
Purdy Gear Custom Leather Goods (www.purdygear.com)
for her gracious permission to incorporate the image of
"Phil's Gun Rig" into the cover art for this novel.

Cover design by Steven Novak (www.novakillustration.com).

Strong Convictions: An Emmett Strong Western

GP Hutchinson

CHAPTER ONE

San Antonio, Texas, July 1876

Gabriela gasped. Emmett whipped his head around.

One minute the two of them had been peering into the window of Dalton's custom boot shop. She had placed her hand on his shoulder and whispered, "I'll be right next door at Baldwin's Millinery." Next thing he knew, she was in the grasp of a seedy-looking Mexican tough, bracketed by two of his equally coarse compadres.

Emmett pivoted as he sized up the situation. His gaze darted from Gabriela—her eyes wide—to each of the three threats.

The one clutching her was the biggest of the three. Paunchy. Thick lipped. A week's growth of dark whiskers. "So you like to play with our girls, eh, cowboy?" he said.

Gabriela, her satin dress rustling, struggled against the sweaty troublemaker. The Mexican sneered. "Well, they're not for you."

"Let go of my wife." Emmett kept his voice low and firm. "Now." Though his heart hammered in his chest, he was holding himself together—for Gabriela's sake. He was determined to let neither rage nor fear get the best of him. Either would only dull his senses.

"Wife?" the tough said. "What made you think you could take her from her own people? Have her all to yourself?"

"I never belonged to you," Gabriela hissed. She jabbed her elbow into the troublemaker's gut but was ineffective in wriggling free.

"Let go of my wife," Emmett said. "I won't tell you again." He shifted his stance.

The big man's amigos picked up on Emmett's subtle movement. Their hands now hovered over their holstered six-guns.

A half second more, Emmett thought. That's all he'd give him. His senses were alive with uncanny clarity. His body felt charged.

The Mexican didn't let go. "We don't give our pretty girls to gringos. Maybe I'll carve up her face. Make her look like a gringo woman."

He and his compadres laughed.

Emmett's skin prickled. *Threatening to hurt my wife now? This little tête-à-tête's over.*

He drew first, hoping that simply thumbing back the hammer of his Colt would be sufficient to get this no-count to release Gabriela.

Didn't look like it was going to turn out that way.

The fellow on the left cleared leather. Emmett let him have it right in the hand. No problem from eight feet away. Hadn't thought or aimed. Pure instinct. The fellow's gun kicked out into the street. He grabbed what remained of his bloody thumb and howled.

Both of the others drew at the same time, one pistol coming up from around Gabriela's waist, the other from near her arm.

The fellow on the far side of Gabriela sidled toward the one holding her. He fired at Emmett and missed.

Emmett ignored him and went for the instigator of the whole affair. Without blinking he squeezed the trigger, certain he would hit his mark.

If he had feared anything, it was that one of the Mexicans might put a bullet in his wife—inadvertently or on purpose—before he could stop him.

But it was his own finger that killed her. His own overconfidence.

The fellow sliding toward the instigator stumbled. When he did so he bumped his compadre just hard enough to turn Gabi into the trajectory of the bullet.

She slumped in the Mexican's arms, dark blood seeping out of her chest and down the silver-gray satin of her bodice.

The Mexican dropped her like a rag doll onto the plank porch. Then he and his amigos cut and ran.

Emmett grew dizzy. He fell to his knees and crawled to Gabi. He scooped up her limp body and cradled her in his arms. She wasn't breathing. His heart pounded.

I killed my wife. His hands trembled. *My God, I've killed my Gabi.*

He tried to cry out for help, but his cry only broke into jagged weeping. All he could manage was to murmur, "Come back, Gabi. Please come back."

But she didn't come back. His Texian beauty was gone. He held her for a very long time, stroking her soft black hair, caressing her youthful but lifeless cheek.

Townspeople gathered around. At first just a couple, then a dozen or more.

In a voice just loud enough that Emmett could hear it, a tactless yokel in the crowd said, "Say, that's Emmett Strong, ain't it? He can shoot a rattlesnake right between the teeth at twenty yards—"

"And shove his Colt back in the holster before the snake ever twitches," his equally indiscreet companion added.

"Wonder how them Mexicans got the drop on Strong's woman and lived to walk away from it."

A fellow with a graying long-handle mustache said, "It didn't go down like that. And it weren't Strong's fault." His voice quavered on his last couple words.

Though it was probably only a few long minutes, it seemed like an hour before somebody brought a doctor.

Emmett looked at the doc through a blur of tears. "She's gone, isn't she?"

The doctor shook his head as he examined Gabriela's wound, checked her pulse, and finally patted Emmett's shoulder. He muttered how sorry he was.

At last Gabriela's brother, Juan Carlos Galvez, arrived. His eyes were already red and swollen. He squatted beside Emmett. Squeezed Gabi's shoulder. Put a hand to his forehead and let a flood of tears flow.

As Juan Carlos's shoulders heaved, Emmett Strong stared numbly down the long, dusty street into the growing darkness.

—⁂—

Emmett and Juan Carlos eventually chased down the Mexican—a nasty piece of work named Victorio Sanchez. Caught up with him in a cheap cantina in Laredo—but not until after they'd joined the Texas Rangers and spent eleven months in the saddle, riding from this burg to that, following up on one person or another's recollections.

Although Emmett still went about heeled, he found himself reluctant to draw his Colt. Fact was, during those eleven months, he never once unholstered it to point it at another human being, outlaw or otherwise.

Yet when he and Juanito finally cornered Sanchez, Emmett put on quite the fandango.

"Today," he said, his gaze cutting through the harsh glare that painted street, adobe, and clapboard alike the same acrid white. He peered into the dark, rectangular void of the cantina's open front doors

Juanito nodded. "You don't have to talk me into it, *hermano*. I'd have gone in yesterday…or the day before."

"Too sober yesterday. Too quick."

"Drunk or sober, dull or slick, you'd have taken him."

Emmett shook his head. "Waited this long. Why let him make it a contest?"

"Well…" Juanito rubbed his chin. "The muchacho you sent in says he's stinking drunk today."

Emmett nodded and nudged his horse forward.

As had become his method, he wasted no time between the hitching rail and the front doors of the watering hole. A quick glance at Juanito, then he breezed right on in. Allowing only moments for his eyes to adjust to the dim light of the windowless adobe, he scanned the cantina.

There was Victorio Sanchez, draped over the left end of the plain plank bar. No mistaking that ugly profile.

Emmett charged.

As expected, the Mexican drew on him. But Emmett had already closed to within arm's reach. Giving the desperado no further time to react, he locked his hands on Sanchez's thumb and wrist. He gave a mean twist and wrenched the six-gun away.

For a split second, he had a mind to pistol-whip the outlaw. Instead he tossed the gun to the floor and proceeded to beat the tar out of the man with his bare fists. Even without the pistol, he made a bloody mess of him. And when he finished, he dragged Sanchez out of the place by the boot.

Juanito had covered the whole affair with a twelve gauge.

Emmett was in the courtroom the day the jury declared Sanchez guilty of manslaughter. The bailiff read the decision. The judge's gavel came down. It was official. Justice had been served.

Not certain precisely what he had expected to feel once Sanchez had been sentenced, Emmett was unsettled to experience no sense of relief. No sense of accomplishment in having tracked down and arrested the man responsible for his wife's death. No release from the notion that, at least in part, he too was to blame. Everything felt empty. Pointless.

Emmett's brooding was cut short when, on the way out the door, Victorio Sanchez jammed his feet against the doorframe and began to flail and shout.

"You still lose, gringo."

The door slammed against the wall and the bailiff joined the marshal in grappling with the prisoner.

"You couldn't even protect your woman." A smirk twisted his lips. "She belonged in the arms of a better man than you."

Emmett found himself on his feet with Juanito restraining him.

The marshal shot an elbow to Sanchez's mouth—still split from the slogging Emmett had given him—and at last wrangled him out of the courtroom.

The buzz in the gallery eventually died down. Folks began to file out.

Before Emmett knew it, only he and Juanito remained. There he stood, behind the lawyers' table—right where he'd been when Sanchez had taken his last verbal potshots. His gaze drifted to the window. He had no interest in accompanying the marshal to deliver Sanchez to the penitentiary at Huntsville. He'd seen enough of the man whose needless intrusion had led to Gabriela's death.

After several silent minutes, Juanito spoke. Though he kept his tone low, his voice reverberated from the high ceiling and the polished wood and marble walls. "You satisfied now, brother-in-law?"

Emmett shifted his gaze to the now-closed door where they had hauled out Sanchez. "Taking him away won't bring her back."

Juanito put a hand on Emmett's shoulder and gave a firm squeeze.

"What about you?" Emmett asked. "She was your sister before she was ever my wife."

"I wanted to shoot him down in Laredo."

"It's what you wanted to do. But I know you. You and I are cut from the same cloth. And you couldn't live with yourself if you stooped to brute revenge."

Juanito leaned against the rail behind the lawyer's table. "You make me sound nobler than I am."

After another pause, Emmett said, "I can't just go home now, you know. I'll see her everywhere."

"What are you going to do then?"

His fingers drifted to the badge on his chest. "Ride with the Rangers, I guess. Run down hard cases like Sanchez—men who go about ruining other folks' lives."

"Sorry, *hermano*, but to me that doesn't sound like the best plan for getting over all this."

"Don't know whether I want to get over it."

Juanito lowered his gaze and kicked his heel on the floor. "We both loved her. In different ways, but we both loved her. Now we need to move on, Emmett. You're young still. There's still plenty of time for you to—"

"Hobble your lip," Emmett snapped. "I'm not ready for that yet. Maybe never will be."

Juanito picked up his hat from the table. He kept his gaze on Emmett. "OK, it's hobbled."

Emmett drew a heavy breath and looked one final time around the empty courtroom. At last, turning toward the door, he asked, "You coming with me? I'm going to hunt desperados."

Juanito took his own quick glance around, then nodded. "*Sí, hermano*. Let's go."

CHAPTER TWO

March 1881

The Jeffersonian was as grand a restaurant as any in Austin—a top-notch place for a celebration. Crystal chandeliers above, fine china and sterling flatware on the tables, everything from oysters to steak on the menu.

Emmett clapped his brother, Eli, on the shoulder and took a seat next to him. His brother went on talking.

Today was Eli's day, and Emmett was proud of him. Having just been sworn in as a Texas state senator, he would be filling the seat of an incumbent who had sadly succumbed to heart problems.

Emmett wasn't paying particular attention to what Eli was saying. Instead he was musing over how often that day people had commented that the two of them looked so much alike. Both stood about five feet ten. Both had dark-brown hair, hazel eyes, and strong chins. But to Emmett, that's about where the similarities ended—especially since, as an adult, Eli had always sported a long, full mustache. Emmett—who typically kept himself shaved—thought the facial hair gave Eli an aura completely different from his own.

Though only thirty-two, Eli seemed to Emmett like a man old before his time. Perhaps that impression of age—and along with it an air of respectability—had helped Eli gain that senate seat. One way or the other, Emmett thought, his brother looked ace-high today in his pinstriped black suit.

To Eli's right at the circular table sat his pretty wife, Nan. Eli was older than Emmett. Nan was younger. Much to Emmett's chagrin, Nan had a roving eye…which sometimes landed on him. On occasion she had placed her hand on his and spoken of how lonely he must be without Gabriela. With a twinkle in her bright blue eyes, she'd said she wished she could somehow help ease his loneliness. He hadn't liked the way she'd done that, but he'd kept it to himself.

Attractive as she was, Nan was no temptation to Emmett. He still clung too dearly to Gabi's memory. Besides, he believed in the sanctity of matrimony and loyalty to kin.

Emmett couldn't figure out Eli's blindness to Nan's flirtations. Worse yet, he wondered whether it was only Nan's gaze that wandered. And then he felt like a cad for thinking such a thing.

At least today Nan was fixed on her accomplished husband, as well she should be.

Along with Eli, Nan, and Emmett at the table sat another couple—Senator Edward Lattimer and his wife, Elizabeth. Ed Lattimer, who wore spectacles and sported a full beard, had served with Eli in the cavalry a few years before. After military service they remained close friends. Ed was the one who had gotten Eli into law and now into politics.

Emmett smiled to himself. His big brother had made it to the statehouse. He was just as much a big fish as Ed Lattimer, even without the prestigious pedigree.

Almost as if she'd read his mind, Elizabeth Lattimer said, "Nan, you must be so proud of Eli." Emmett didn't know Mrs. Lattimer well. His impression was that her gracious manner was genuine.

Nan giggled and responded, but Emmett missed what she said. The conversation between Ed Lattimer and the waiter at his elbow had distracted him. They were going back and forth over the virtues of various labels and vintages of wine.

A few minutes later the waiter returned, opened a bottle, and began to pour for each person in their party. When he at last approached Emmett, he asked whether they were still waiting for one last guest to fill the table's vacant sixth chair.

Emmett placed a hand on the chair back, looked off toward the restaurant's front windows, and paused briefly. "No," he said. "She won't be joining us today. She's been away for some time now."

"Very well, sir," he said. And with a slight bow of the head, he retired.

Conversation over the luncheon soon evolved into two separate dialogues—one between Nan and Elizabeth, the other between Eli and Ed. Emmett listened to bits and pieces of each, adding little to either.

Halfway through the meal's main course—just as he had pierced another juicy slice of steak—Emmett sensed someone drawing near the table at a brisk pace from behind him. The person's voice boomed so loudly and cantankerously that it prompted him first to twist to see who it was, then to rise to his feet in anticipation of trouble.

"Eli Strong," the man roared, "you reckon you're gonna be my state senator? Like hell you are!"

The restaurant grew silent. Men and women alike turned and stared. The intruder could've been anyone from the streets of Austin. Tall and thin. A few days' whiskers. His range clothes were all of faded browns and tans. Topped with a well-worn Stetson and hooved with boots a little short of dry and cracked, the uninvited guest could've been a cattleman, a mule skinner, a stagecoach driver, or a sodbuster.

"You know what you are, Eli Strong?" the intruder continued. "You ain't nothin' more'n a murderer." He pounded a vacant table, rattling the place settings.

"Here now, man," Ed Lattimer said, rising. "Let's be civil. Show some respect."

Eyes bulged from the man's beet-red face. His voice modulated up an octave. "I ain't got no respect for the likes of Eli Strong."

Emmett caught a whiff of whiskey off the man. He impulsively felt for the weight of his holstered Colt Peacemaker, then recalled he'd been walking around all morning unarmed. After all, Austin was a civilized town.

"What's your name, sir?" he asked calmly.

The intruder kept his eyes fixed on Eli. "Only name that matters much right now is Thomas Blaylock. He was my brother. And you yourself as good as killed him when you and that cavalry you commanded didn't do nothin' about them damned Comanches up at Adobe Walls."

"Adobe Walls?" Eli said. "That was seven years ago—"

Blaylock's brother kicked the vacant chair next to Emmett and sent it tumbling. Emmett tensed for action. Even if he'd been carrying his Colt he wouldn't have drawn on the man. But his fists were ready to let fly.

"Yeah, it was seven years ago," the man hollered. "I didn't have no pa. My brother Thomas was like a pa to me."

Eli held up a hand. "Listen, I'm truly sorry about your brother—"

The man jabbed a finger at Eli. "You refused to listen to what everybody kept sayin' was gonna happen. And you refusin' is what got him killed."

Again Eli tried to apologize, but Blaylock's brother wouldn't let up.

"Then to add insult to injury, instead of hangin' that bastard Chief Quanah Parker, y'all went and give him a nice big ranch over across the Red River."

About that time, the bouncer from the saloon next door came lumbering in along with the restaurant owner, a waiter, and a big black man whose hands were still dripping dish suds. Without a word, the bouncer grabbed Blaylock's brother by the back of the collar and tiptoed him, struggling and protesting, all the way to the front door.

"I ain't finished with you, Senator Strong," the man bellowed. "You got my brother killed."

The dishwasher opened the door, and the bouncer flung the nuisance into the street.

"Senators, ladies…" The restaurant owner, face flushed, looked from one to the other. "I don't know how I can apologize enough for this embarrassing disruption."

"Think nothing of it." Eli patted the man on the shoulder. "The fellow just had a bit too much to drink. He'll go home and sleep it off."

"No, I insist. This establishment has a reputation to maintain—and not for that kind of behavior. Let me offer you this meal on the house."

Ed Lattimer shook his head as he took his seat. "There's no need for that. Besides, what will the rest of these fine folks think?" He swept his arm across the room where most of the other patrons were getting back to their meals. "Their luncheons were interrupted too. You've got a full house here. We shouldn't get special treatment just because we're senators. And I fear buying lunch for the entire crowd would put too big a strain on your profits today."

Visibly relieved, the restaurateur said, "You're too kind. Let me at least offer you a second bottle of wine." He mopped his brow with a starched white napkin.

"That'll be fine. Thank you." Eli nodded and sat again as well.

Once a waiter had righted the fallen chair and the timidly smiling restaurateur had shepherded away his staff, Ed Lattimer said in a low voice, "Always have to watch what we accept in front of the voting public." He half covered his mouth and leaned toward Eli. "At the same time, being a senator does come with some rather nice perks." He then erupted in a less-than-dignified guffaw.

Eli smiled and took a sip of wine.

Emmett glanced around the dining room, took his seat, and turned to his brother. "Eli," he asked, "did you recognize that fella?"

Eli pursed his lips and shook his head. "Not at all."

"He's never come calling on you before? Never shouted at you out of a crowd you might've been speaking to?"

"Not that I can remember."

"Well, do you recognize the name Thomas Blaylock? From the siege up at Adobe Walls?"

Again Eli shook his head. "Don't let it bother you, Emmett. It was nothing. Really."

He turned back to Nan and Elizabeth. "Now where was I? Ah, yes." He resumed recounting an anecdote about a Texas Supreme Court justice and a one-legged widow from Galveston. The women were all smiles and giggles.

Emmett, meanwhile, stared at the door where the bouncer had unceremoniously tossed out Thomas Blaylock's brother. He wondered how the fellow knew to find Eli here. Had to have read in the newspaper about the swearing in. Must've followed them over from the courthouse. It troubled Emmett. Elbow on the table, he rubbed his finger across his lips. *Fella's been nursing a grudge for a long time.*

Luncheon went on for another hour. By the time pecan pie and coffee had been served, Emmett had grown weary of political talk and war stories about people he didn't know. He was glad when somebody suggested they should all head back to their hotel rooms for naps.

When Emmett stood, he left his glass of wine half-full—the same glass the waiter had poured him before the meal. The others had imbibed quite a bit more.

They stepped out of the restaurant onto the walkway and then into bright afternoon sunlight.

"Oh my!" Nan said, shading her eyes. "The glare out here…"

The words had hardly left her lips when, from out of that glare, a voice bellowed, "I was waitin' on you, you murderin' politician." It was Blaylock's brother again, now mounted on a tall bay horse.

Emmett squinted into the sun. He sidestepped so it wouldn't blaze from directly behind Blaylock's face.

"The law won't carry out justice for my brother," Blaylock said. "Well, I will. Finally."

At that, he reached over his horse, pointed a Schofield revolver at Eli, and fired.

The gunshot resounded off the closely set brick and wood buildings. For a frozen moment everyone stared in stunned silence.

Emmett then reacted, rushing Blaylock. But Blaylock twisted his reins, spurred his horse viciously, and tore off in a mad gallop. A few buildings over, he cut into an alley and disappeared from sight.

Only then did Emmett stop running. In the middle of College Avenue, forty yards from the Jeffersonian, he spun and looked for Eli. His brother was down. Ed Lattimer was holding him.

Emmett sprinted to Eli's side. His brother's eyes were rolled back. His breathing was labored. Where his white shirt showed between his vest and his trousers…Well, there was little white to be seen. Blaylock had gotten him right in the belly.

Nan, all color drained from her face, patted his cheek. "Eli," she said, her voice throaty. "No, Eli."

"Ed," Emmett said, "my friend is waiting for me in the saloon right across the street. Let me get him to find us a doctor."

Ed nodded. But before Emmett could even cross the avenue, his brother-in-law, Juanito, came running. A round-faced stranger with dark eyes and short-cropped hair trotted alongside him.

A crowd was gathering.

As Emmett stepped down into the street to meet Juanito, a bearded fellow with a satchel practically bowled him over.

"Make way," the man said.

Emmett eyed the man's bag. "You a doctor?"

"Yep. Office just a few doors down."

Emmett followed him back to where Eli lay.

"Heard the gunshot and came out as fast as I could," the doctor said. "Don't get much of this type of thing in Austin anymore, thank goodness."

He went to one knee and began blotting Eli's stomach with a cloth, trying to get a good look at the wound.

"How bad is it, Doc?" Emmett asked.

"Not sure. We need to get him over to my office where I can work on him properly. Might make it."

"Might make it" didn't sound very promising. But the doctor was there. He and the good Lord were the only ones who could offer Eli any real help at this point. Meanwhile, Emmett didn't want the madman who'd shot his brother to get away clean.

"Ed, can you stay with Eli and the doc?" he asked the senator. "I'm going to see if I can catch up with that shooter before he gets too far away."

Nan looked up at Emmett, panic on her face. She clutched his sleeve. "Emmett, you can't leave us."

"Ed'll take good care of you, Nan. And the doc'll take good care of Eli. I can't do anything for him myself. But if I don't go now, that Blaylock fellow may get away for good."

"We won't leave you, Nan," Ed said. "Let Emmett go."

As Nan loosened her grip, she began to sob.

Emmett squatted and took his brother's hand. He looked into his half-closed eyes. "Be strong, Eli. You hear? You hang in there. This doctor's gonna take real good care of you."

Eli managed a weak nod but said nothing.

A couple of men pulled up a buckboard wagon and began to spread a quilt in the back for Eli.

"Horses, Juanito?" Emmett asked.

His brother-in-law pointed back across the street. "Right over there."

The round-faced fellow who had come from the saloon with Juanito said, "I don't have anything better to do. Might I possibly be of help?"

The fellow caught Emmett by surprise—both with his offer and his unique accent.

"Granville Sikes," the man said, offering his hand. "Recently of Her Majesty's Twenty-Fourth of Foot in South Africa."

Emmett looked the Brit in the eye, gave him a quick handshake, and said, "Thanks. That'd be kind of you."

As the doctor and a few bystanders gingerly lifted Eli and carried him to the wagon bed, three badged lawmen trotted up.

"Who did the shooting?" the tall one in front asked.

"Don't know his given name," Emmett answered. "Family name is Blaylock."

The bouncer who had earlier pitched Blaylock from the restaurant spoke from the boardwalk. "It was Charlie Blaylock, Sheriff."

"Aw, hell!" The lawman took his hat off and slapped it across his thigh.

"I'm the victim's brother. Name's Emmett Strong. Sounds like you've dealt with Charlie Blaylock before."

The sheriff nodded. "If he's headed back up to his place, we're probably in for a pitched battle. Won't be any picnic tryin' to roust him out of there."

Emmett and Juanito showed the sheriff their Texas Ranger badges.

"I'm sure you boys have taken care of this kind of business before then," the sheriff said.

"Home would be the last place I'd go if I'd just shot a state legislator," Emmett said.

The sheriff motioned for his deputies to follow him. "He very well may've headed off elsewhere. But I figure the fastest way to find out precisely where is to start at the Blaylock homestead. There's always somebody up there."

Emmett glanced back at Eli, then set off alongside the sheriff. "Wherever he went—I assure you—we'll flush him out. Whatever it takes."

CHAPTER THREE

The sun was hanging just above the distant trees by the time Emmett and the others arrived at Charlie Blaylock's place in the hill country just outside of Austin. Gathering horses and weapons had taken longer than Emmett had figured on. The sheriff had had to make an arrest up here once before. He'd expended a great deal of ammunition on that occasion.

The two-story raw-wood house sat on a rise. Very few trees round about for cover. A couple of oaks here and there.

"Reckon Charlie's up there?" Juanito asked.

"That's what we're here to find out," Emmett said.

He turned to the sheriff. "It'll be nice if we can get this done before dark." He wanted to get back to Eli as soon as possible.

"Don't count on it," the sheriff said. "Blaylock and his cousins stick together like cold grits."

"I'm not interested in Blaylock's cousins, neighbors, or pet goats. I only want the one that shot my brother."

The sheriff thumbed a few more rounds into his Winchester. "You know the old saying, 'over my dead body'? Blaylock clan motto."

"I'd rather not…But I'll oblige 'em if I have to."

Emmett observed Sikes looking things over quite apart from the rest of the group. "What's on your mind, Mr. Sikes?"

"This isn't totally unlike the lay of the land at Isandlwana," he said. "Actually a few more trees than we had there."

"Isandl-what?" the sheriff asked.

"Isandlwana…in Africa. A place where we faced the Zulus two years ago."

Emmett's eyebrow went up. "I read about that in the papers. Didn't think there were any British survivors."

"The papers don't always get things right. I was left for dead, along with one other chap. Took us quite some time, but we crawled out."

Emmett and Juanito looked at one another.

"And if you're wondering whether I'm a deserter, I didn't desert the British Army. They deserted me."

Emmett shrugged. "Another story for another day. The more pressing matter is getting Charlie Blaylock outta that house up there."

The sheriff said, "Best to take it from two sides at once."

"I don't mean to boast," Sikes said, "but I'm quite good with a rifle, even at long range."

"How good?" Emmett asked.

"I've hit a whiskey bottle at two hundred yards."

"On purpose?" Emmett cocked his head.

Sikes gave a half grin.

Emmett returned to his horse and drew a Sharps Model 1874—a "Little Fifty"—out of his rifle scabbard. "If you're as good as you say you are, you may be able to hold down one side of the house all by your lonesome with this." He shucked the cartridge belt from his shoulder and handed it to the Englishman. "Go ahead. Find yourself a spot and get comfortable."

Sikes hefted the buffalo rifle. "If they surrender?"

"Taking 'em alive'd be good."

He turned to his brother-in-law. "Why don't you take your Winchester and go with Sikes till things start up. If he lives up to billing, maybe you can slip around and lay down some cross fire."

Juanito nodded.

"Just don't mistake me and the sheriff's boys for Blaylocks," Emmett said. He turned to Sikes. "Or Zulus."

"You keep your head down," Juanito said.

Emmett and the sheriff decided they'd go together as far as the barn to be sure the Blaylocks didn't make a run for their horses. From there, they'd each take one of the deputies and split up. The sheriff would start the music, seeing that he'd been there before.

Armed with a twelve-gauge coach gun and his Colt revolver, Emmett walked in silence. He pondered as he'd done so many times since Gabriela's death: five years now, and he'd never again pointed his Colt at anyone. A shotgun, yes—but never the Colt. Tonight he might have to use it, even if he wasn't sure of himself. He didn't plan on letting his brother's would-be assassin vamoose.

A quarter hour later the sun had set. The four men had made it to within about seventy yards of the barn when a shot rang out. Then two more. Everyone hit the ground.

"Dang!" one of the deputies said. "We been spotted."

"Well, go on then, boys," the sheriff said. "Now that they know we're here." He shouldered his Winchester and started shooting at windows.

Emmett's weapons were better suited for up-close work. He wanted to get to the barn, maybe twenty yards from the house.

"You coming with me?" he asked the nearer of the deputies.

The deputy clung to the ground. "Too hot for me just yet."

"Bluebonnets won't stop a bullet."

"That's OK. Them fellas' aim don't seem so good at this range. I'll wait."

Emmett paused only long enough for the sheriff and both deputies to reload and resume peppering the windows before he hopped up and ran a zigzag path toward the cowshed.

The Blaylocks' aim proved better at closer range. Emmett's stomach tightened and lightning flew down his spine when a couple of bullets whizzed by a hair too close.

He made it to the barn and stumbled inside. Now he had the Blaylocks' back door covered. Nobody was going to get out without his permission—or a burst of buckshot.

The first cry from the house coincided with a report from the buffalo gun. Emmett figured Sikes had caught somebody lingering a breath too long in the front upstairs window. The moaning from inside the house died away quickly.

Emmett hoped Charlie Blaylock—down a man already—would go ahead and call it a night. He soon gave up on that notion. While the folks inside mostly held their fire, every now and then—almost certainly when the sheriff and his deputies were trying to advance on the house—they'd unleash a hot fusillade. Sheriff had been right. This was no picnic.

Next time they opened fire, Emmett sprayed a couple of windows with blasts from the twelve gauge. His angle on the openings wasn't great. But he figured he'd let them know the law was closer at hand than they might have realized.

Even as dusk turned to dark, a full moon and clear skies made for pretty good visibility. After a fashion, a second cry came from within the house. Angry shouting followed.

"Well, get him the hell away from the window," a voice yelled.

"You shut the hell up," another shouted. "I'll get him when things cool down a bit."

Emmett decided to take advantage of their frazzling nerves. He'd rush the back door, both barrels blazing, if he had to. But if there was another way…

"Hey," he called out from the barn. "Let's end this dance early so nobody else gets hurt up there."

No one answered—by word or by gunfire.

"Send out Charlie Blaylock, and we'll leave the rest of you alone," he shouted.

Everyone held their fire. Emmett could hear bumping and shuffling up in the homestead. Then all went quiet for a few moments.

All of a sudden, someone flung open the door on the far side of the house. It slammed against the front porch wall. There were hurried footfalls on the wood plank flooring. Both the buffalo rifle and a Winchester sounded, almost simultaneously. The footsteps stopped and a string of tumbling thuds followed.

"That's three of yours down," Emmett called out. "How long do you—"

"Shut up, lawman," a voice from inside the house cut him off. "You'll get yours when you try to come in and take Charlie."

Somebody had tried to run for it. Somebody else seemed determined to stay and make the lawmen pay. So what would going in cost him?

Emmett looked around the barn for something of the right weight and size. He spotted a few horseshoes, picked one up, and returned to the barn door. Holding the coach gun with one hand, he tossed the horseshoe onto the back porch with the other. Instantly a shotgun boomed from inside, ripping a hole in the back door.

Blazes! Might cost a lot to go in.

The standoff dragged on. During the lulls Emmett wondered whether his brother would pull through. In his mind he saw Charlie Blaylock, pistol pointed at Eli. Heard the shot. Saw his brother on the ground, bleeding. He was tired of this game. It was time to break the stalemate.

The eastern sky had just barely begun to brighten when Emmett sensed someone outside, tight up against the wall, approaching the barn door. His pulsed quickened. Had he dozed off for a minute, just long enough for Charlie Blaylock to slip out of the house? He readied the coach gun.

"Emmett, it's me," came the whisper. "Sheriff Haywood."

"Glad you said something," Emmett murmured. He took a step back.

The sheriff slid in through the narrow opening. "Don't know about you, but I'm ready to end this thing."

Emmett nodded. "Been ready. Wanna send your deputies down to fetch Juanito and Sikes? We can kick in the door as soon as they get back."

The sheriff wasted no time. With a quick, "Sure 'nough," he slipped out of the barn again to set things in motion.

Emmett wanted to hurry for another reason. The sun would be coming up at his back. If they timed things right, they could hit the door with the glare of the rising sun behind them—directly in the eyes of the waiting Blaylocks. Might help a little.

But when the sun began to bathe the weathered gray backside of the Blaylock house in golden brilliance, Emmett was still alone. This was the critical moment. He squeezed the grips of the shotgun and stole a peek out the barn door. Where were the others?

Maybe five minutes later, cautious footfalls broke the silence along the north side of the barn.

"Loaded and ready, *hermano*," Juanito said in a hoarse whisper. He was just outside and to the right.

"I'm bettin' at least one of 'em will try to run," the sheriff murmured from behind Juanito.

"Can't let anybody run," Emmett said. "Now let's do this."

His stomach knotted up on him; he knew that as soon as they heard his boots hit the porch, they'd likely send another blast of buckshot through the already shot-up back door.

To blazes with it! Drawing a deep breath, he led the charge.

A couple yards shy of the porch, he leveled his coach gun, unleashed one barrel, and took another nice-sized chunk out of the door. Didn't need to kick it in now. It swung back from the force of the blast.

He rushed the doorway and pulled the other trigger. The second barrel roared. No sense waiting for them to reply. They'd had all night.

Only one of Blaylock's people was in the kitchen—a bloody mess sprawled on the floor. Emmett broke his coach gun, popped out the spent shell casings, and inserted two more.

Juanito arrived at his elbow.

From the kitchen, Emmett saw that the front door was blocked open by a corpse. The fellow lay on his back in an awkward position, a big, dark hole in his chest.

"Throw down your weapons," the sheriff roared from alongside Juanito. "All of you."

The air smelled of gun smoke. All was quiet for a moment.

"You're all shot up," Emmett yelled. "Now call it quits."

Again it was quiet.

Wood flooring creaked beyond the wall to the right.

"Bedroom," the sheriff mouthed.

Emmett motioned for the whole bunch to ready their weapons. He was just about to squeeze off another shot when an old navy-model revolver came tumbling out onto the sitting room floor.

"OK, that's good," he said. "Anybody else wants to live oughta do the same thing. Right now."

"Ain't nobody else in here can shoot 'cept me," said the voice. "And I just tossed you my gun."

"Is that so?" the sheriff said. "Well, come on out. Show us you're unarmed."

The floorboards creaked again, and a black man—probably in his thirties—emerged from the side room into the doorway. He held his hands high, palms forward.

Emmett gestured for him to come into the kitchen.

He did, and one of the deputies grabbed his arm while the other patted him down.

The deputy looked to the sheriff. "No weapons."

Emmett cocked his head as if to say, "Don't lie to me now," and asked, "Anybody else alive in here?"

"Last one can shoot—you got him right there," the black man said, nodding to the fellow on the kitchen floor. "Mr. Cyrus is alive." He pointed to the side room. "But he ain't gonna be shootin' nobody no time soon."

With a Colt ready in each hand, Juanito pushed past everyone to the side door. "Like the man said, Cyrus won't be shooting anyone soon."

Emmett followed and saw that Cyrus lay propped up against the wall, half-conscious, bleeding from both arms.

"And Mr. Matthew's upstairs. But he don't look good either."

The two deputies looked to Sheriff Haywood. With a raised thumb he sent them to check.

"What's your name?" Emmett asked the black man.

"Timothy, sir. Timothy Frey. I'm just a hand around here. I ain't got no special attachment to the Blaylock family."

"Where's Charlie Blaylock?" Emmett asked.

Cyrus Blaylock tried to say something. His face contorted. All that emerged was a moan followed by spasms of coughing.

"He's gone, sir. Been gone since yesterday," Frey said.

Emmett's eyebrows shot up. *What?* "Are you telling me you all have been shooting at us all night—and taking shots from us—and all the while Charlie Blaylock hasn't even been here?"

"That's right, sir."

"Aw, hell!" the sheriff said.

Emmett took in the blown-out windows, the holes in the walls, and—most troubling of all—the blood all over the place. All he could do was shake his head.

"I's tryin' not to shoot, but the other folks here was all tryin' to keep y'all occupied so's Mr. Charlie could make good his getaway."

"Where'd Charlie Blaylock go, Timothy? Did anybody say?"

"Oh, we know where he's headed, sir." Timothy looked tired. "Mr. Charlie got a brother name Seth out in Nevada. Mr. Seth's a rich man. Rich and powerful. Got him some of that silver money from Virginia City. That's where Mr. Charlie's gone."

"And he's got a fifteen-hour jump on us," Emmett said.

More coughing erupted from Cyrus. He wheezed, "You black son-of-a—" Spasms of coughing gripped him again.

"What do you think, Sheriff?" Emmett asked. "You think Timothy's telling the truth? Or would Timothy lie to cover for Charlie Blaylock?"

"I think you'd better get a move on if you want to keep things simple. Catch Charlie Blaylock before he makes his way out of Texas. Me and my deputies, we'll clean things up here."

Emmett glanced at Juanito and Sikes. "Long as we're this far behind, I'd like to check in on Eli."

"And I'd like to take a quick look around outside," Juanito said. "See if I can cut sign. Figure out which way Charlie Blaylock rode."

Emmett asked Timothy, "Anybody happen to say exactly how he'd be traveling to Nevada?"

"No, sir," Timothy answered. "He took his horse and left 'bout four o'clock yesterday. Headed north. That's all I know."

"North," Emmett said. He rubbed his forehead. Even as he considered Charlie Blaylock's travel options, he wondered whether his brother was still alive.

CHAPTER FOUR

E li hadn't made it through the night.

Emmett waited in the lobby of Austin's Greentree Hotel while Elizabeth Lattimer went upstairs to get Nan. His mood was dark. Out at the Blaylock place, he hadn't had much time to dwell on what his brother's death would mean to him. And there had been hope that he might survive. But now, as far as this life went, it was all over for Eli.

Staring through the lace-curtained windows, he said to Juanito, "A few short years ago, who'd have ever figured I'd end up losing a wife *and* a brother to gunplay?"

When he turned, it looked as though Juanito was going to say something but then decided against it. He simply shook his head, then dropped his gaze.

"Nan's not gonna take this well, but I can't stay here," Emmett said. "I'll start thinking about Gabriela again, and between her and Eli, I fear I'll slide into a despair I can't climb out of."

"Will running down Charlie Blaylock keep you from that kind of despair?" Juanito asked.

"Doing something—anything—has got to help. I can't just sit and think."

Sikes spoke up. "Wouldn't it be better to at least stay for the funeral? To say good-bye?"

"Just be spotting Charlie Blaylock a bigger lead on me. I'll mourn my brother better once justice has been served. Then I'll be able to stand beside his grave and say my good-byes properly."

"I'm obviously not a Texas Ranger," Sikes said. "But I've been on campaign in the wilderness. I'd like to lend a hand in catching Blaylock...if you wouldn't mind me riding along with you."

Emmett studied the Englishman. "You handled yourself well last night. I'm sure we could use you. But this can't be what you came to Texas for."

"I came to Texas for a new start."

The novelty of Sikes's accent took the edge off Emmett's somber mood for a moment. "A new start doing what?"

"I wanted no further part of Her Majesty's army. And considering where I've been and what I've seen, England's too tame for me. The American West seemed like a good fit. Wasn't really sure what I'd do once I arrived, but here I am. You've got a need, and I'd be glad to throw in with you."

"What do you think, Juanito?"

"I hate to mention it at a time like this, but we don't have much dinero. I don't know how we'd pay Señor Sikes."

Sikes hurried to speak. "Oh, I can pay for my own needs. I've got a bit of money."

"Wouldn't be right," Emmett said.

"Sure it would. Whether I ride with you or stay here, I'd have to support myself."

"You sure?"

"I am."

Emmett shook his head. "Now I feel beholden to you."

"Not at all."

Just then Elizabeth Lattimer and Nan reached the lobby. As soon as Nan saw Emmett, her tears began to flow again. She took his hand and led him to a fancy settee in the corner.

He found it hard to meet her gaze.

She put an arm around his neck, buried her face in his shoulder, and let herself bawl.

"I'm so sorry, Nan," he said. He swallowed hard.

"What are we going to do now, Emmett?" she asked between sobs.

Unable to imagine Nan living alone for even a short time, he said, "You should probably go stay with your family for a while."

"And what about you?"

Since Nan sat almost on Emmett's lap, there was plenty of space left on the settee. Elizabeth Lattimer, who had been standing, now sat beside the two.

"Emmett, stay with me," Nan said. "Otherwise I don't think I'll be able to get through this."

He tried to ease her tight embrace. "I can't stay, Nan. It'll kill me."

She pushed away from his shoulder just far enough to look him full in the face. Though her eyes were red from crying, her blue irises still shone, clear and youthful. Tears glimmered like diamonds on her lashes and cheeks. "You know how to mourn," she said. "You lost your dear wife and you got over it."

"I never got over it," he said. "And grieving for Gabriela nearly broke me."

"Please help me, Emmett," she whispered. "It'll break *me* if you don't." She returned her head to his chest and clung tighter.

If he'd had any doubt before, it had evaporated now. He was gentle, but he took her by the shoulders and held her away from him. "I love you like a sister, Nan. But I have to do this for Eli—go after his murderer, that is."

She kept her hands on his arms. Tears still streamed down her cheeks.

"And every hour I wait gives Charlie Blaylock a better chance of getting away for good," he said. "Your folks and the Lattimers will take good care of you, I'm sure."

"We will, Nan," Elizabeth said.

Nan shook her head. She blotted her eyes with a handkerchief. "But you'll come back to look after me once you've caught Charlie Blaylock, won't you, Emmett?"

It wouldn't be like that between him and Nan. Of that he was completely sure. He squeezed her hand and said, "You won't be alone."

After a brief embrace, he stood and turned for the door, determined not to look back.

CHAPTER FIVE

The American River, just outside Sacramento, California

C harlie Blaylock's brother, Seth, leaned forward in his saddle, watching a girl and her young man playfully splashing about in the shallows of the river.

The young woman, slim and caramel complexioned, clutched her skirt and petticoat, only halfheartedly attempting to keep them dry as she waded barefoot in water just shy of knee deep. She scooped a handful of water back at the boy. With a broad grin that revealed bright teeth and winsome dimples, she said, "You ain't nothing but a tease, William Stanton."

Water dripping from his blond hair, William laughed aloud and doused her again. She squealed but still smiled as she made her way to the bank.

"Whatcha gonna tell your pa when you arrive home all soakin' wet?" he said.

"I'll tell him you tried to drown me, that's what."

Screened from the pair by a cluster of willows, Seth shifted toward the rider next to him and murmured, "She don't look Mexican, does she?"

The wispy rider adjusted a paisley neckerchief and said, "No. Doesn't look Indian either. She's a pretty one, though."

Just a hair too loudly, the rider on the other side of Seth said, "Hell yeah, she's pretty."

Seth scowled and held a gloved finger to his lips.

A serious-faced fellow whose horse stood just behind Seth's said quietly, "Mr. McIntosh could pass her off as an Egyptian beauty. That should fit his style."

Seth nodded and flicked the leather loop off the hammer of his pistol. "I like that," he said. "An Egyptian beauty."

He admired her graceful form and dark locks as her boyfriend gave mock chase to her on the riverbank. When the young man slipped on the mud and plopped unceremoniously to the ground, the girl put a hand to her mouth and laughed aloud.

Seth looked up and down the waterway. As far as he could see and hear, no one else was around.

"OK," he said. "Are we ready?"

The wispy rider to his right nodded.

"Let's go then."

At that Seth and his five hands walked their horses out into the river and fanned out around the youthful couple.

"Having fun, are we?" Seth asked with a wry smile.

The boy shaded his eyes from the sun. "Yeah, Mister. Just havin' a little fun. We weren't doin' nothin' wrong."

The girl's grin faded. She edged toward the young man.

Up close, Seth thought she looked maybe seventeen or eighteen and even prettier than from a distance.

"Well, young William," he said, "my friends here"—he nodded to the three riders closest to him—"are gonna have you follow them a little ways down the river. Y'all are gonna have a little chat."

William was frowning now. "Wha—what're y'all gonna do?"

Seth observed William's fists tighten. The girl now stood almost behind him.

One of the three men Seth had designated already had a lasso in hand. He tossed it skillfully over William's shoulders. The young man fought to wriggle free. Before the girl could do anything about it, the rider on the opposite end of the arc roped her.

She screamed, "No, William. Don't let 'em do this to me." She too struggled against the rope and began to cry.

"William," the one who had lassoed him said, "if you don't want to get dragged down underneath the water, you'll come along with me." He started his horse downstream.

The young man began to slosh along, laboring to maintain his footing. He kept looking back helplessly. "Just don't y'all hurt her," he called out, fighting back tears. "Ain't no reason to hurt her."

The wispy rider led a spare, saddled horse to the girl.

"You ride?" Seth asked the girl.

She stared down the river toward William. Although the afternoon air was warm, she shivered.

"Help her up," Seth said to the wispy rider.

The rider dismounted and waded to the girl. "Foot in the stirrup. Go on."

The girl obeyed. Once she was in the saddle, Seth's companion tied her hands to the saddle horn.

Seth glanced around. He nodded toward the east. In response, the ones who had helped him lasso and secure the girl led her off in that direction.

She peered over her shoulder, tears rolling down her cheeks. "Where we goin'?" she barely managed to say.

"We'll be riding awhile," the one who had helped her into the saddle said.

"I can't. My pa'll be waitin' for me." She began to cry more vocally. "My pa'll be waitin'."

No one replied.

Seth wheeled his horse and rode downstream. Just around a bend and behind a copse of cottonwoods, he found the other three hands and William. One of the three had gagged the boy. Seth gave the bottom of his vest a tug with both hands, tilted his head, and sized up the young man.

William's eyes were red and tear-rimmed.

"Oh, we could make such sport of this, couldn't we, boys?" Seth said, a crooked grin reappearing.

The three chuckled.

A long-haired rider with a dark stubble chin asked, "How we gonna play this, boss?"

Seth reseated the hat on his head. "Quick and quiet."

The stubble-chinned fellow raised an eyebrow and rested his hand on the big, antler-handled knife that hung from his belt.

Seth nodded. He glanced at William.

The boy went pale.

"Leave him in the bushes when you're done. And hurry to catch up with us," Seth said. He reined his horse around. Then giving a little spur, he galloped off in a cloud of dust.

CHAPTER SIX

From his saddle, Emmett patted the neck of his tobiano pinto—a horse he loved dearly—and scanned the broad horizon. Pancake-flat land, dotted here and there with stunted cedars, stretched out miles and miles in front of them. Only off to one side did a few low hills break the monotony of the plain. Although it was late March, the grass remained mostly straw colored with just a hint of new green.

The sun shone brightly and the air was already quite warm, so Emmett appreciated the steady breeze. His stomach fluttered just a bit as he contemplated closing in on his brother's killer.

Juanito, Sikes, and he had spent a solid week on horseback, heading northwest from Austin in pursuit of Charlie Blaylock. Now, straight ahead—maybe a mile away—lay the brand-new railroad town they believed the outlaw had been headed for.

"Hard as heck to read sign on roads and trails as heavy traveled as the ones we've covered," Emmett said. "You've done a fine job, Juanito."

"Glad Blaylock's horse had that one bad shoe," Juanito said. "Tracking him would've been a whole lot tougher without it."

"Had to have slowed him down some too."

Sikes's saddle leather creaked as he shifted his weight. "If he has any sense at all, he's got to assume you're on his tail, Strong. He didn't risk stopping to get the animal reshod. You think he'll risk it to wait on a train?"

Emmett nodded. "This has got to be the end of the line. Press that horse much farther like that and it'll end up buzzard bait."

"Doubtful he ever planned on riding all the way to Nevada anyway," Juanito said. "Not all alone. Not on just one horse."

Sikes squinted toward the town. "How often does a westbound train pass through?"

"Not sure," Emmett said. "At least daily, I hope. Blaylock gets to El Paso more than a day ahead of us, and the whole game changes."

Sikes undid a few of the buttons of his bib-front shirt, pulled up the edge of his loose neckerchief, and mopped his brow. "So that's where a Texas Ranger's jurisdiction ends then—at the next state's border?"

"That's where it ends—officially."

"Ever chase a man outside your jurisdiction?"

"I have," Emmett said. "Way outside."

"People respect your badge out there?"

"Sometimes yes, sometimes no. Couple times it resulted in a whole new set of problems." Emmett glanced back and decided the horses and pack mule had been spelled long enough.

Sikes asked, "Ever go as far as Nevada?"

"Nope."

"Will you this time? If that's what it takes?"

In his mind, Emmett could just about see Sikes wearing his pith helmet and red British Army tunic. It made him grin slightly for the first time in days. "Yep. If that's what it takes. However," he continued, "depending on what time the train comes through, this thing could be over inside the next hour. Charlie Blaylock might be right ahead of us—right there in Sweetwater. You gentlemen ready for action if it comes to it?"

Sikes patted his holstered Colt. "Ready enough."

Juanito broke his coach gun, took a look, and whipped it closed again. "*Listo, hermano.*"

"OK then," Emmett said. And with that, he gave a chirk that set his horse trotting toward the town.

Sweetwater was a busy place. The Texas and Pacific Railroad had only recently established service there. Townspeople were building as though it was going to be the new Abilene or Dodge City. The pounding of hammers and rasping of saws emanated from all quarters. New livestock pens, stores, hotels, and places of entertainment were going up everywhere.

"Save ourselves a lot of time if we go straight to the rail station, *sí*?" Juanito asked.

Emmett gazed up and down what seemed to be the main avenue. Horses stood flicking their tails in front of a number of establishments. He wouldn't know Charlie Blaylock's mount from any other without checking the shoes of each. "I suppose you're right," he answered.

The train station's raw lumber siding hadn't yet begun to weather. A graying fellow in shirtsleeves and suspenders whistled as he energetically applied the first coat of forest-green paint to the building.

"Afternoon," Emmett said to him.

He turned around, brush in hand, and pushed back his hat. "Yes, sir. What can I do for you?"

Emmett rested his hands on his pommel. "Nice little burg you've got here. Looks like the railroad's been a boon to you."

The man smiled broadly. "Oh, it is. It is indeed."

"What time's the westbound come through?"

The man set his brush down on the edge of the paint pail, pulled out a pocket watch, and took a look at it. Shaking his head, he said, "Afraid you fellas just missed it by...an hour and fourteen minutes. Next one won't come through till tomorrow. Eleven fifteen a.m."

Emmett thought for a moment. He didn't figure Blaylock could have made it to Sweetwater in time for yesterday's train. He had to have just purchased a ticket today. "You sell the tickets here in Sweetwater, right?"

"I do," the man said. "Just got out of my ticket office clothes to come out here and get this started. Thought it'd make the town look fine as cream gravy to have a pretty painted railroad station. And the Texas and Pacific's payin' for the paint."

"Mighty nice," Emmett said. "Anybody buy tickets this morning?"

The railroad man nodded, beaming. "Yes, sir, sold six tickets this morning. Won't be any time before Sweetwater'll be a real hoppin' town."

Sikes chuckled. "A veritable London on the prairie."

Emmett wiped the lower half of his face to hide his grin.

"Name's Emmett Strong. Texas Ranger. We're trailing a man who shot a state senator down in Austin a few days ago." Just saying the words turned Emmett all business once again. "It'd be tough to describe the fella in a way that he'd stand out from others. Looks pretty ordinary. Tall and thin. Whiskers." Emmett visualized Charlie Blaylock back at the fine restaurant in Austin. "Thin nose," he added.

The railroad man nodded. "You're lucky. Five tickets went to one family this mornin'—husband, wife, and three kids. The other one I sold to a tall, thin fella. Looked as dusty as you three—like as if he'd been on the trail a few days. Brown pants and coat. And a Stetson, of course."

"Packin' iron?"

"Two pistolos and a long iron."

"Don't reckon you got a name from him?"

The railroad man shook his head. "He wasn't in a real friendly frame of mind, that one."

"I expect not." Emmett blew out a long breath. His gaze followed the parallel rails west to the horizon.

"Bought a ticket to El Paso," the railroad man said. He bent over and stirred the paint with his brush. "If you decide to follow him by train, I'll be happy to sell you gentlemen some tickets in the morning. Meanwhile, the Palacio over there on Broadway Street is a real nice hotel."

Emmett cleared his throat. *Sam Hill! Missed him by less than an hour and a quarter. And that throws us almost a day behind now.*

He peered at the railroad man once again. "Accommodations for horses on the trains each day?"

"There's a livestock car, yes. Costs extra, of course."

"And did the outlaw we're talking about take his horse?"

"No, sir. Must've left it or sold it in town."

Emmett nodded. "Much obliged, sir. Let us confer."

He touched the brim of his hat, wheeled his horse around, and headed for the Palacio. Juanito and Sikes pulled up on either side of him.

"Left his horse here," Sikes said.

Emmett nodded. "Money from even a mediocre horse could pay for passage all the way up there. A little left over for food, too."

"He's got another one-day jump on us," Juanito said.

Sikes looked back toward the station. "Any other options for us? Other than waiting till tomorrow for the next train?"

"There's a stagecoach route pretty much parallel to the railroad," Emmett said. "The Bidwell Overland Mail Road."

"The stagecoach will never catch up with the train." Juanito said. "Not even if it comes through town this afternoon."

Emmett reined in his horse. "There is one thing we can do," he said. "Let's find the telegraph office and send word to the marshal in El Paso. He can be waiting for Blaylock when the train stops there. If that murderer sold his horse, he won't hop off the train anywhere before El Paso."

"Telegram—brilliant idea," Sikes said. "He can't outrun electricity."

At the telegraph office, all three men dismounted. It felt good for Emmett to stretch his legs. As frustrated as he was to have so narrowly missed bagging Blaylock in Sweetwater, his hopes rebounded at the prospect of having Blaylock caught, jailed, and waiting for pickup by the time he and his compañeros arrived in El Paso.

A short, balding man attended the window in the telegraph office. He wore garters on his sleeves and leather bracers on his forearms. With a pinched voice he asked, "What can I do for you gentlemen?"

Leaning on the counter at the window, Emmett said, "I need to send a message to the town marshal of El Paso, please."

"Ah, official business, is it?"

"Actually," Sikes said with a straight face, "we'd like to invite him to a soiree we'll be throwing over at the Palacio right here in Sweetwater."

The telegraph employee stopped in his tracks, pencil and paper in hand, eyes fixed on the Englishman. "You must be from back East," he finally said.

"Quite so," Sikes said with a mischievous smile.

Emmett chuckled. He took the pencil and paper and wrote down his message. Sliding it back across the counter along with the fee, he said, "My friend was just funnin' you. But if the marshal sends a reply, the Palacio is where you'll find us."

Juanito grinned on the way out.

CHAPTER SEVEN

The train ground to a halt and released a loud hiss of steam at the station in El Paso. Onboard, Charlie Blaylock pulled his Stetson a little lower over his eyes. His nerves were as tight as banjo strings. He scanned the platform for armed men with stars or shields on their chests. There were none.

Never know who you can trust these days, he thought. *Never know who'll stab you in the back even after you've paid handsome.*

He waited till the aisle was clear, then rose and stretched, trying to look as nonchalant as any other passenger. Before stepping down he bent and peered out the railcar windows again, scouring not only the platform but also building fronts along both sides of the tracks. Good. Still no sign of wary lawmen.

As he passed the conductor, he asked, "How long now till the train rolls on?"

The blue-uniformed railroad man squinted at a large clock on the outside wall of the station. "About twenty minutes, sir. They've got to top off the water and load some more firewood."

"So I've got time to go send a telegram?"

The conductor gave a sharp nod. "I would think so." He pointed catty-cornered across the way. "Telegraph office is right over there."

"Much obliged," Blaylock said.

He rested his Winchester on his shoulder and strolled casually, eyeing folks of every walk going about their daily business.

Charlie Blaylock was beginning to feel pretty clever. He hadn't wasted the week he'd spent in the saddle making the dash from Austin to Sweetwater. Neither had he written off as sapheads the lawmen who'd certainly be on his tail. Texas being a big state, it would take some time for him to make good an escape. In a flat-out horserace to the state line, the law dogs would most assuredly catch him, especially since his own mount had come so close to throwing a shoe. The railroad was the only smart choice. But getting on and getting out of the state before the law nabbed him in one rail town or another—that was the trick. Now here he was in El Paso—the last stop before leaving Texas.

Yeah, Charlie, he thought, *some folks take you for stupid, but you ain't stupid.* He smiled to himself for choosing a town that had only just gotten railroad service two weeks earlier. Figured a lot of lawmen might not be aware yet that Sweetwater even had a train station.

But there had been one more consideration, just in case the law did follow him to Sweetwater: wherever there was a railroad station, there was bound to be a telegraph office. And they could always telegraph ahead. So Charlie Blaylock had paid off the telegraph operator in Sweetwater. Paid him plenty not to send any message about him to the law in El Paso. He'd told him to accidently send it to Fort Worth.

Seems like the ballast I offered the telegraph man was enough.

Blaylock paused just outside the door of El Paso's telegraph office, looked back and forth, and proceeded in.

Only now did he feel safe enough to wire his brother, Seth, up in Nevada to let him know he was coming.

Once again he couldn't hold back a grin. *Told them boys back home in Austin I was headed to Virginia City. Seth ain't in Virginia City. He's in Carson City. And from what I hear, he's rich and powerful up there. Law dogs won't be able to touch me.*

To the operator behind the counter he said with a smile, "How much to send a telegram to Carson City, Nevada? I wanna let my baby brother know I aim to pay him a visit."

And I can't wait to see Seth's face when I tell him I've finally vindicated our big brother by killin' that Eli Strong.

CHAPTER EIGHT

The Next Day

Emmett was the last person off the railcar. He gazed at the brown hills to the north and recalled catching and arresting old Horace Thompson—a cutthroat stagecoach robber—in those very hills. If luck was on his side, he wouldn't have to do the catching and arresting this time. He and his pardners could pay the marshal a visit, let Charlie Blaylock spend one more night in El Paso's crowbar hotel, pass a relaxing evening on the town, and begin to escort Mr. Blaylock back to Austin tomorrow.

The jailhouse in El Paso was an adobe brick affair with few windows. Must've been hot as blazes in the summer. It'd be a few years before the trees planted around the building would offer any appreciable shade.

Emmett rapped on the front door and let himself in. Juanito and Sikes followed.

A deputy marshal in shirtsleeves and vest stood up as they entered. His hands hung easy by his sides, not too far from his twin holstered Colt Navy revolvers. "How can I help you all?" he said.

"Emmett Strong's the name. Texas Ranger. The day before yesterday, I sent the marshal a telegram asking about a fugitive on the run from Austin—a murderer by the name of Charlie Blaylock. I believe Blaylock was on the westbound yesterday when it rolled into El Paso."

The deputy frowned and shook his head. "I'm sorry, Mr. Strong, but I don't believe Marshal Perry received such a telegram. If he had, I'm real sure he would've let me know..." He looked from Emmett to Sikes then to Juanito.

Emmett cocked his head. "So there's no Charlie Blaylock locked up in the hoosegow back there then?"

"Got three guests back there right now—two locals that got drunk and tore up a cantina last night and one out-o'-towner who's been with us for about a week now."

Dangit! What could've happened to that telegram? Emmett rubbed his forehead. "Is the marshal here in El Paso today?"

"Yes, he's out ridin' 'round the town somewhere. I'm not sure precisely when he'll be back." He wiped his nose with the back of his hand.

Emmett sighed. "I think I remember where the telegraph office is. Over by the Wild Hog Saloon, right?"

"Still there." The deputy nodded.

"Let me go check with them—and see if there's some reason why they might not have gotten my message."

"All right," the deputy said. "I'm real sorry. I'll tell the marshal y'all came in. If you'd like to come back later, I'm sure he'd be pleased to talk with you. And we can always offer y'all some hot coffee."

Emmett thanked the deputy and led his friends out. The unseasonably hot afternoon air only added to the souring of his mood.

Beneath the skimpy shade of a young oak he stopped and faced Juanito and Sikes. "We don't have much time to make up our minds on this, so tell me your gut-level feeling. We know Blaylock bought a ticket back in Sweetwater. That ticket would take him at least as far as El Paso. Nothing says he had to stay on the train all the way here, though. Since he left his horse in Sweetwater, you think he might've doubled back on us?"

"You mean got off the train somewhere west of Sweetwater, waited for an eastbound, and then got back on to go reclaim his horse?" Sikes asked, rubbing the back of his neck.

"Something like that."

Juanito shook his head. "Why spend so much dinero on a ticket all the way to El Paso then? If that's what he planned to do, he could've bought a ticket to Colorado City, just one county over. Much cheaper."

"Maybe he wanted to send us on a wild goose chase. Give himself plenty of time to ride off elsewhere. Might value time more than money right now," Emmett said.

"Then you think the black fellow back at the Blaylock place outside of Austin…What was his name? Timothy?" Sikes said. "You think he lied to us when he said Charlie was heading to Nevada?"

Emmett toed a small, half-buried rock. "No. I think he thought he was telling the truth."

Juanito looked around. "Texas may be big," he said, "but if I shot a senator in this state, I'd want to get as far away as possible, as fast as possible."

"Nevada's pretty far away."

"My guess?" Sikes said. "I don't think he's doubled back. I think he's pressing on ahead of us. To Nevada and to his brother."

Juanito said, "That's what I'm thinking, too."

Hearing the locomotive's bell clanging, Emmett glanced in the direction of the train station. If they were to buy tickets, load their horses, and board the train once again today, they'd have to act immediately. "Then do we even need to check with the telegraph office?" he thought aloud. "If the marshal didn't get the telegram, he didn't get the telegram. That's all there is to it."

Juanito too stared toward the sounding locomotive bell. "What difference would a lost telegram make to us now?"

"I don't know. But I think I'd rather play it safe than step off a train a thousand miles from here only to find Charlie Blaylock never went that way after all."

Juanito nodded. "There'll be another westbound tomorrow."

"Better to err on the side of caution," Sikes said. "If Blaylock is already outside your jurisdiction and on his way to Nevada, one extra day in El Paso won't matter anyway."

"Shouldn't." Emmett took off his hat and wiped his brow with his sleeve. "Let's go see what we can find out then."

Juanito and Sikes went on into the Wild Hog Saloon to get a table while Emmett went to the telegraph office directly across the street. The telegraph operator there was younger than the one he'd dealt with back in Sweetwater. After showing his badge and identifying himself to the gangly redhead, he asked, "In the past couple days, have you had any telegrams coming in from Sweetwater? Or have you sent any out to Nevada? Comstock region in particular?"

"Matter of fact, there was a fella come in here yesterday to send a message up to Nevada—Virginia City or Carson City, one or the other," he said, pivoting to thumb through a neat stack of paper forms in a wooden box. "Let's see…Here you go. To a Mr. Seth Blaylock of Carson City, Nevada." The young man offered Emmett the paper.

Emmett accepted it and silently read Charlie Blaylock's brief message announcing to Seth that he'd be paying him a visit.

"Hmm. Carson City," he said to himself, rubbing his chin. "Thought for sure Timothy said it was Virginia City."

The telegraph employee waited patiently.

"Well…this is the Simon pure." Emmett slapped the paper back down on the counter. "But nothing from Sweetwater?"

The young fellow searched through the entire stack once again. "No, sir. Nothin'."

"Telegrams ever get delayed for some reason? Come in a day or two after they were sent?"

"Never heard of such. That'd be peculiar."

"Peculiar indeed." Emmett shoved off from the counter, touched the brim of his hat, and said, "Even so, you've saved me a lot of second-guessing. Thanks for your help."

Minutes later he joined his compadres in the Wild Hog Saloon—a much more civilized establishment than its name might have suggested. Papered walls. A rich, polished hardwood bar with brass footrails. Beside the left-hand wall stood an upright piano, but at the moment, nobody sat on the piano bench.

The place wasn't crowded yet. Three men leaned against the bar, and patrons occupied a few scattered tables. Occasional laughter punctuated the quiet buzz of conversations around the room.

Juanito and Sikes had gotten a corner table in the cooler, more shaded half of the place. Both men were already nursing beers.

Sikes had lit up a cigar. "Pretty señoritas in here, Strong."

"Angelicas," Juanito said, wiggling his eyebrows.

Emmett glanced at the three ladies of the line posing at the foot of the stairs on the other side of the room. "Well, two of them are pretty anyway," he said. He turned back to his pardners. "Here's the news: Charlie Blaylock came through yesterday. Sent a telegram ahead to Seth Blaylock up in Nevada. Said he's coming to stay for a while."

"No telegram from Sweetwater?" Juanito said.

"Nope. Don't know what happened to that one."

Juanito clumped down his near-empty glass. "Too bad. Would have been nice to catch him before he got out of Texas."

Emmett nodded. "Missed another break."

"Are we dragging our feet?" Juanito asked. "Should we have stayed with today's train?"

Emmett at last got the attention of the barkeeper. He pointed at Juanito's beer and held up three fingers. "No," he said. "Checking with the telegraph office was actually a good choice."

"Oh?"

"Yep. Turns out Seth Blaylock is in Carson City, not Virginia City…according to the telegram Charlie sent, anyway."

"That's worth knowing."

Emmett's mind was already up in Nevada. "Virginia City, Carson City… The law up there should cooperate. But you never know."

"Wild and woolly country from what I've heard," Sikes said. "The world-famous Comstock Lode." He admired his cigar. "People get their hands on the kind of fortunes coming out of those silver mines, some of them seem to think they can buy anything—or anyone—they want, including constables and such."

"The richest town in America," Emmett said. "That's what Virginia City boasts."

"More money, more buying. I wonder whether that's why Charlie Blaylock thinks he'll be so safe up there."

Emmett nodded. "Maybe."

"Back on Blaylock's tail tomorrow then?" Juanito asked.

"Tomorrow," Emmett said.

Elbows on the table, Juanito steepled his fingers. "Out to California, up to Sacramento, and then back over the Sierra to Nevada, right?"

"That's right."

Sikes blew out a slow stream of cigar smoke. "Never thought I'd get to see the whole continent so quickly."

"You'll see quite a lot," Emmett said. "Colorful country."

"Been there before?"

"Not that far north."

The bartender set three glasses of beer on the table and picked up Sikes's and Juanito's empties. "If you gentlemen decide you're interested in some sportin', there's entertainment available for you." He tipped his head in the direction of the staircase. There were now five calico queens smiling back at them. "Just let me know. I'll have the madam make arrangements for you."

Sikes's eyes widened. "Speaking of colorful country, the scenery right here is positively delightful." He smiled. "A bit of heaven on earth."

Emmett glanced back. "They may be pretty, but I'm not sure how many skirted demons like those you'll find flitting about in heaven." He chuckled quietly. "You'd better watch out, Sikes. One of 'em just might snatch your soul away to someplace a lot less comfortable."

"What?" Sikes was still grinning. "You don't partake?"

Juanito leaned back in his chair and eyed the ladies.

"It's been a while," Emmett said. He took a swallow of beer.

"Come on, Strong. That blonde looks absolutely delicious."

Emmett followed Sikes's gaze across the room. The blonde was indeed attractive. Slender yet shapely. Fair of face. Prettier than most women of any station in life. Yet he felt no desire for her. "Sad truth is," he said, "if she stays in this trade, you won't even recognize her inside of two or three years."

Sikes's smile faded. "You're a cheerful chap." He turned to Juanito. "Is he always this jovial?"

Juanito cringed.

Emmett pulled a silver dollar from his vest pocket and laid it on the table. He stood, emptied his beer in one gulp, and said, "I'm gonna stable the horses. You gents stay as long as you like. I'll see you at the Hotel Rio Grande when you're done. Across the street and down two blocks."

CHAPTER NINE

"**D**id I offend him?" Sikes said once Emmett had left. "Rather thin-skinned for a lawman, isn't he?"

"No, you didn't offend him." Juanito paused. "This talk of women and heaven…Some time ago Emmett suffered a very difficult loss. I think when she left this world she took his heart along with her."

Of all the sappy…Sikes considered giving Juanito a hard time, but something told him to hold up. There might be an interesting story behind all this. Tossing his chin toward the girls near the stairs, he asked, "Was she a…?"

Juanito shook his head. "Nothing like that. Nothing at all like that. She was my sister."

Sikes felt his face redden. "Well." He cleared his throat. "What an absolute ass I am!"

"*No hay problema*. You didn't know."

"I'm truly sorry, old chap."

Juanito nodded and took a sip of beer.

Just then the blonde Sikes had been eyeing sashayed from the stairs to the table. With one hand on a chair back, she hovered over the two. A smile appeared.

Sikes waited for her to proposition him, though he now felt conflicted. He looked her full in the face and wondered how such a young and pretty woman could end up doing what she did for a living. Plenty of men would line up for the chance to marry a girl with her looks…were she not a soiled dove. Even so, there had to be some decent bloke out there who'd be all too happy to snatch her out of this shady business, cherish her, and provide for her.

"Your friend," the girl said. "The one with the broad shoulders. Why'd he leave so soon? The place has hardly even begun to get lively."

It surprised Sikes, but he was actually relieved that she asked about Strong rather than about whether he was game to take her to bed. "Can we buy you a drink?" he offered. "Perhaps my friend Juanito here could tell us both the story of that broad-shouldered fellow you're asking about."

That's exactly what Sikes realized he wanted—to have this pretty girl sit close beside him while he learned the history of Emmett Strong and Juan Carlos Galvez—the two men he'd signed on with for this unforeseen adventure across the American West.

She glanced over her shoulder. The madam wasn't out with the girls, and the bartender was busy polishing glasses.

"I suppose they wouldn't mind if I had a quick drink with you," she said, "since it's early yet."

Sikes took in her scanty attire. Lots of black lace tulle. A corset that squeezed her where it ought and lifted where—in truth—it needn't have bothered. Bare arms. Legs showing from the knees down. Her bustle rustled when she sat.

She scooched her chair close to his and hung on his arm. Following another glance over her shoulder, she said in a low voice, "Miss Lindsey may not fuss at me if I act like you and I might end up upstairs after all."

He considered asking her how she wound up in this line of work, but decided he'd wait. "What do you like to drink, Miss…?"

"Geneve," she said. "But you can dispense with the 'Miss.' Just call me Geneve."

"Pleased to meet you," Sikes said, inclining his head. "Sikes is the name." He extended a hand across the table. "And this is my friend, Juanito."

"*Encantado*," Juanito said, tipping his hat.

"Nice to meet you both. I'll just have a beer since that's what you gents are drinkin'," she said.

Sikes signaled for the barkeeper.

"So like I asked before," she said, "why'd your friend leave so early?"

Sikes gave a sly grin. "Perhaps I should be jealous. You keep asking about my friend, but not about me."

"Now whose arm am I holdin' on to?" Her blue eyes sparkled. "If I didn't find you appealin' at all, Mr. Sikes—believe me, I'd be hangin' onto the banister over there with the other girls."

Was this trade talk, he wondered, or was she really pleased with what she saw?

The barkeep stopped by the table.

"Mr. Sikes wants to buy me a beer, Gus," she said to him.

He cocked his head. "If Miss Lindsey comes around with her dander all up, don't you go blamin' me."

Sikes patted Geneve's knee. "If Miss Lindsey is out of sorts, just direct her to me," he said. "Miss Geneve and I may be together here at the table for a while. There's more than one kind of female companionship a man needs."

"True enough," Gus said. "Be right back with the beer." He tossed a wink at Geneve.

"Now, Juanito," Sikes said, "this may be the first time you and I have had the chance to talk about Emmett without Emmett being right alongside to object. So Miss Geneve and I would like to hear his story. If you don't mind."

She slapped Sikes's arm playfully and said, "I told you it's just Geneve, not Miss Geneve." Then turning to Juanito, she said, "And yes, I am interested in Mr. Emmett's story."

Juanito leaned forward and folded his hands on the table. "Perhaps the best start," he said, "is to tell you that Emmett hasn't always been the serious-minded man you see today. Back when he first met my little sister, he was full of mischief. He laughed a lot more."

"What happened?" Geneve asked.

Sikes sat back in his chair and let Geneve rest against him.

"Emmett and his brother, Eli, are grandsons of one of the founders of Texas. My grandfather was one of the original Texians too. Our grandfathers fought side by side against Santa Anna at San Jacinto."

"And formed the great nation of Texas as a result," Sikes said, smiling over his beer.

"That's right. And then Emmett's father was a military man—a West Point man. He's the one who taught his sons to shoot, only he didn't have to do much teaching when it came to Emmett."

"So Emmett and his brother joined the army?" Geneve asked.

Juanito shook his head. "Eli Strong was the disciplined one. He went to West Point. Emmett was too—how do I say this?—too distracted."

Sikes flicked cigar ashes. "And what did Emmett do? You said his father didn't have to teach him much about guns. Always a lawman? A gun for hire?"

"No, my father would never have let Emmett anywhere close to Gabriela if Emmett had been—as you say—a gun for hire. Even as close as our families have been since the eighteen thirties."

"So not a hired gun. What then?"

"Emmett fell in love with my sister when she was maybe fourteen. He was sixteen. All he wanted to do—all day, every day—was show up at my father's dry goods store and tease my sister. This was down in San Antonio."

Sikes chuckled. "I don't see it."

"No, it's true," Juanito said. He too was grinning now. "So my father and his father got together and decided that if they couldn't keep him away from Gabriela, they'd at least make him work to gain her hand."

"I like this story," Geneve said, resting her elbow on the table and her chin in her hand. "It sounds romantic."

"Oh, that's Emmett," Sikes said. "Ever the romantic." He chuckled.

"Shush," Geneve said, giving Sikes a playful smile.

"Emmett worked very hard," Juanito said. "He had a natural sense for business. Even as young as he was, he helped make my father a wealthy man."

"And he won a place in your family tree," Sikes said.

Juanito nodded.

"Did she love him back?" Geneve asked. "I know she must have."

Juanito's gaze drifted. "*Ay, sí*. They made each other very, very happy. I have never seen such love between a man and a woman."

Sikes wiped a palm across his face. "All right. Enough. This is far too saccharine, even for a ladies' man like me. Tell me about Emmett, the natural pistolero. Was it only handguns? Or the rifle as well?"

"Oh, he can handle a rifle just fine," Juanito said, looking as though his mind had transported him to some open field where he and Emmett might have engaged in a friendly shooting match. "But it was the *pistola* in his hand that was like magic."

Geneve edged forward, eyes fixed on Juanito.

"Nobody—not even our fathers or grandfathers—could remember anyone who could use a revolver so effortlessly and with such incredible results."

"Fast?" Sikes asked.

"Like a bullet itself."

"Accurate, I assume."

"Without even thinking about it. Up close. Fifty yards away. It still doesn't fit in my head how he could do it. He could hit bottles, tiny rocks, coins."

"What about moving objects?" Sikes asked.

"Jackrabbit? No problem. Rattlesnake? No problem."

Sikes had no delusions about firearms. He knew firsthand that there was no glory in taking a human life. Yet he had to know. "Did he ever have to use those talents against another man?"

"Not until the day my sister died."

It was quiet at the table for a moment. Sikes heard Gus pouring drinks at the bar. Laughter floated on the air from other tables.

"He never had to use his talents against other men," Juanito continued. "People knew his reputation. And nobody ever challenged him."

Juanito snapped his fingers. "Oh, one day these three hombres came into my father's store and decided they might rob him. They were from out of town. Didn't know about Emmett. They had guns out, pointed at my father. Emmett walked in from the storage room in the back."

"I thought you said he never used his talents against people until—"

Juanito cut Sikes off. "One of the customers told the robbers, 'Hey, I'm not kidding you hombres. You will all three be dead before you reach the door if you don't leave now. That young man who just walked in, that's Emmett Strong.'"

"And they listened to him?"

"That customer's face was so white when he said it. The robbers all turned to Emmett. Emmett just kept walking—right up to the robbers. No hesitation. His hand right above his holster. His face as calm as if he were walking into church. Those *ladrones* backed out pronto. We never saw them again."

"And then," Geneve said, her eyebrows upturned, "that day with his wife? Your sister?"

Juanito lowered his gaze. "An accident."

"Emmett?" Sikes asked soberly.

"Witnesses say these men had their hands all over Gabriela. Emmett got the first one that drew on him. Shot his thumb off."

"And then?" Sikes asked.

Juanito was having difficulty going on with his story.

"How'd he miss?" Geneve whispered, wiping her moist eyes.

"They say the third man stumbled unexpectedly. Accidentally pushed Gabriela into the line of fire."

Juanito stared in silence.

Sikes didn't know what to say. He'd been around death—on the battlefield, up at Blaylock's place outside of Austin. But he'd never been in a situation where someone that dear to him was in imminent, personal danger, and his marksmanship would make the sole difference between sorrow and solace.

"What then?" he finally asked.

"Emmett joined the Texas Rangers to hunt down the man who started the incident."

"So that's how he became a lawman."

Juanito nodded. "Him and me together. We run down men who ruin other people's lives. It's what we do."

Sikes lifted his glass. "Must be reassuring to ride with a man so capable with a handgun."

"Never has been the same," Juanito said. "Somewhere inside him, he's probably as good as he ever was with the *pistola*. But he has lost his confidence. He won't draw his Colt unless he has to. And he almost never uses it. If he can do the job with his fists, he'll handle it that way. If a gun is necessary, he prefers a shotgun now."

"Is the word out on him?" Sikes said. "Do outlaws know he's lost his touch?"

Juanito shook his head. "Almost everybody still thinks he's the deadly pistolero."

"And Gabriela?" Geneve said. "Does he still pine over her?"

"Five years," Juanito said. "I've never seen him look at another woman the same way." At that, Juanito's gaze rose to meet Geneve's. "So please don't be offended if he doesn't look at you with desire."

Juanito turned to Sikes. "That's what I meant: his body still walks around on this earth, but his heart is in heaven."

"Shame," Geneve said, staring out the saloon's half doors. "Handsome man. Rugged handsome. Clean handsome."

About then, Sikes felt someone standing over his shoulder. He turned and looked up.

"You gonna take this girl upstairs or not, Mister?" It was a crusty-looking cowhand type. "'Cause I had my eyes fixed on her for near 'bout an hour now. Been waitin' my turn all polite like. And all you been doin' is sittin' here at the table with her. This here woman's goin' to waste tonight 'cause of you."

Sikes turned his back to the cowhand and said, "The lady's busy just now."

"She don't look busy."

"When she becomes available, I'm sure she'll let you know, all right?" Sikes's eyes searched Geneve's questioningly.

She shook her head ever so slightly.

The cowboy shifted to the side and leaned, one hand on the table. "Mister, you need to take this girl on upstairs and get done with her now. Else give her up and let me have my turn with her."

Sikes shoved his chair back from the table.

Geneve clutched his arm.

"What difference is it to you whether I pay her to lie in a bed with me or to sit at a table with me?" Sikes said.

"Like I said, you're wastin' her time. These kind of women ain't for talkin'. They're for—"

Sikes sprang to his feet and clamped his hand over the cowhand's jaw and squeezed hard. Through his own gritted teeth he said, "Whatever her profession, she's a person, not a thing. You hear?"

Three other equally dirty cowhands jumped to their feet two tables over, knocking down a chair in the process.

The fellow in Sikes's grip went for his six-gun. Sikes jerked his knee up into the man's privates, then head butted him. He melted to the floor.

The other three cowboys cleared leather. A shotgun blast roared through the room, and everybody froze in place. Gus leaned over the bar, the scattergun pressed against his shoulder.

"You three get the hell outta here," he yelled at the cowhands as he thumbed back the other hammer of the double-barrel twelve gauge. "And take your troublemakin' pardner with you." He tipped the business end of the shotgun toward the man Sikes had dropped.

"But what you gonna do 'bout that fella?" one of the three ventured, pointing at Sikes.

"He ain't done nothin'," Gus said. "Now get out like I told you."

Sikes turned to Gus and touched the brim of his hat. He slipped his fingers into his pocket and drew out a single coin—a ten-dollar eagle. "For the beer and for the lady's services," he said. "You and Miss Lindsey work it out, will you?"

"Got you covered," Gus said.

The cowboys holstered their smoke wagons under Gus's watchful eye.

Juanito, still seated—back to the wall—on the other side of the table, discreetly showed Sikes the butt of his revolver as he slipped it back into its holster.

Once the cowhands had dragged their friend out of the saloon, Geneve looked up at Sikes. "You wanna take me upstairs now?"

He glanced at Juanito.

Juanito spread his hands and shrugged.

Sikes said to Geneve, "You go on up and dream of a man like Emmett Strong. I suppose Juanito and I had better head over to the hotel. We have a long way to travel tomorrow." He squeezed her hand and gave her a kiss on the forehead. "You're a sweet girl, Geneve. It's been a pleasure."

She stood up beside him, her lips slightly parted.

CHAPTER TEN

Carson City, Nevada

Charlie Blaylock breathed a sigh of relief as he got off the train in Nevada's capital city. It had been a long trip, but he was happier than he was tired. In fact, he felt happier than he had in years. In killing Eli Strong, he had at last avenged the death of his big brother, Thomas. He had made good on an oath. And he had made a clean getaway from Texas.

Don't care if I never step foot in that godforsaken state again, he thought. *And let's see them Texas law dogs just try to touch me up here.*

He mused over what he'd heard about his little brother's fortune here in mining country. Money and power. Not that he planned to lean on Seth forever. Maybe he could start a dig of his own. Enjoy the good things in life. Have people bowing and scraping to him for a change.

Taking in a deep breath of the cool, dry air, he picked up his war bag. A railroad employee was loading luggage onto a hand truck nearby. Charlie ambled over.

"Where might I find the post office in this town?" he asked.

"Thataway." The porter pointed. "Just across the street on the next corner."

Charlie thanked the fellow and strolled on.

Inside the post office, he waited for two men to finish up their business at the counter. Each looked to be in his thirties. Both wore new-looking clothes powdered with a bit of trail dust. When they turned toward the door, Charlie stepped aside to let them pass. He heard the door close behind him as he strode up to the desk.

"I just arrived in town," he said. "And I'm looking for Seth Blaylock. Reckoned if anyone would know where to find him, you might."

The postal clerk's gaze went from Charlie to the front window. Charlie followed the clerk's line of sight and through the glass saw the two men who had just concluded their business there. They were talking to a third fellow—a younger, shorter hombre. Had the look about him. Almost certainly a gunhand.

"M-maybe you should ask those gentlemen right outside," the clerk stuttered. "They can probably help you better than I can."

Charlie frowned. What could've drawn that kind of reaction from the postal clerk? He stared at the visored employee momentarily, then nodded and pushed away from the counter.

Outside, he paused, waiting for a break in the three men's conversation. He paid particular attention to the one he figured to be the gunhand. Shiny, tall-shanked boots. Silk vest. Nice hat—low crown and broad brim. It wasn't the way the fellow wore his gun that made him look so dangerous. It was more a matter of his stance—the way his hand hung. Looked like a man you'd never catch off guard.

Before long the three noticed Charlie staring.

"What're you lookin' at?" the oldest of the three asked.

Charlie shifted his weight. "Clerk inside…said I ought to talk to you gentlemen. I'm looking for Seth Blaylock."

"You are?" the one who looked like a gunhand said. His steely gaze seemed to bore right through Charlie.

Charlie Blaylock licked his lips. An old feeling welled up from somewhere deep inside. People often seemed to look down on him—and talk down to him. He was so used to folks writing him off as a no-count good-for-nothing that he could only assume these men had jumped to the same uncalled-for conclusion.

His gaze never left the gunhand. He reasoned that even if he managed to drop his war bag, he'd never get both hands on his Winchester before this little bantam would gun him down right where he stood.

"You gonna stare at me all day, fella?" the gunhand asked. "Or you got something you wanna ask about Seth Blaylock?"

"Well," Charlie said, "I heard Mr. Seth has some, uh…" He swallowed. "I may be mistaken—bein' new around here and all—but, uh, I heard Mr. Seth might be hirin' some new help. And I'm lookin' for a job."

The two men who had been inside the post office pivoted to face Charlie more squarely. They both chortled. The gunhand smirked.

"You come with a recommendation?" the gunhand asked. The fingers of his right hand twitched just a hair.

Charlie's thoughts raced. *Who are these cusses?*

"'Cause Seth Blaylock don't hire just anybody off the streets," the oldest one said.

Again the men chuckled.

Now wait a minute. Charlie shook his head. How would they know who Seth would or wouldn't hire? He finally got ahold of himself, stuck out his chest just a little, and said, "My name's Charlie Blaylock. I'm Seth Blaylock's brother. Now you gents know where I can find him or not?"

At that all three men guffawed. The gunhand slapped his knee.

"We was just funnin' with you, Charlie," the oldest one said, still laughing.

"Yeah?" Charlie asked. "Well, what's so all-fired amusin'?"

The oldest one wiped a tear from his eye and said, "Seth told our boss you were coming." He chuckled again.

"Who's your boss? What'd Seth tell him?"

The gunhand said, "Seems you sent your telegram to the wrong town, Charlie. Your brother lives up near Reno—almost thirty miles back up the line. He works for Mr. Lucian McIntosh up there."

Charlie was thoroughly befuddled. He felt his ears grow warm. "I thought my brother worked for hisself up here."

"No," the third man said. "Seth works for Mr. Lucian McIntosh. And we work for Mr. Lucian's brother, Mr. Thaddeus McIntosh."

"I never heard of either Mr. McIntosh," Charlie said. He began to fear the legends of Seth's wealth and power might be just that—myths, stories, corral dust.

"Oh? Well, you'll hear plenty enough about them from now on. Thaddeus McIntosh practically runs Carson City," the third man said.

"And Thaddeus McIntosh works for his brother, Lucian McIntosh," the oldest fellow said. "Man practically runs Reno."

"So the McIntoshes run this whole stretch," Charlie said. "Practically."

The three men nodded.

"And my brother Seth works for the big boss," he added.

"That's right," the gunhand said.

Charlie breathed easier. He didn't want to admit that they had frightened the deuce out of him. Growing up, he'd been in enough scraps to know that the pack will often turn on the weakling. And he'd shown himself weak for a second. But he'd recovered.

"So what kind of business do the McIntoshes run? What's my brother do for 'em?" he asked.

"You'll learn about all that soon enough," the oldest one said. "Let's get you up to Reno and squared away."

"C'mon with us." The gunslick turned and motioned for him to join them.

Charlie picked up his belongings and fell in behind them, half fearing that in reality Seth might be nothing more than some rich fellow's errand boy. It sounded to him like these McIntosh men were the real powers-that-be up in these parts. And if they were, he'd have to find a way to come under their good graces like Seth had. Whatever else he might be looking for up here in Nevada, he needed somebody to help keep those Texas law dogs from ever getting their muzzles on him.

CHAPTER ELEVEN

Two days later, the train carrying Emmett, Juanito, and Sikes chugged its way into Virginia City—the biggest city in Nevada. Nearly fifteen thousand souls and still going strong some twenty-two years after the first big silver strike.

You could see it all and hear it all in Virginia City. Churches just a couple of blocks from the terminus of the Virginia and Truckee Railroad. Breweries, saloons, and brothels over on C Street. Banks. Claims offices. The works.

As Emmett took it all in, he said, "I'm not in Virginia City for sporting, sightseeing, or striking it rich. But you've gotta admit—if a man's looking for opportunity, this town's got it."

Juanito gave a low whistle. "Never seen anything like it."

The train had arrived late in the day. Emmett wanted to find suitable accommodations for at least one night. While they scouted the streets for an acceptable hotel, clusters of miners made their way in from the nearby mountains. Shops were crowded with folks making end-of-the-day purchases. Piano, banjo, and fiddle music drifted into the streets from the open front doors of saloons and gambling parlors.

Ambling along with the crowds, Emmett said to Sikes, "OK, those fellas were speaking English, but not from this side of the pond, I'll wager."

Sikes nodded. "Cornish, if I had to guess. From the mines in the far southwest of England. The silver strike here is fortunate for them. Copper and tin are playing out back home in Cornwall."

They strolled on. Emmett intentionally headed away from C Street. He decided he liked the looks of the Comstock Queen Hotel straight ahead on Washington.

"Those chaps we just passed," Sikes said, "Irishmen, I'm sure you gathered. A clannish lot. Seems like they always go about with a chip on their shoulder. Always spoiling for a fight."

"Well, tread softly around here, gents," Emmett said. "This Texas Ranger badge may not mean much to folks in these parts."

Juanito unpinned his badge and tucked it into his vest pocket.

"Doesn't mean you need to be ashamed of it, brother-in-law," Emmett said.

"I'm not ashamed. I'm proud to be a Texian—and a Ranger."

"Then why'd you take it off?"

"I just thought you wanted to begin our hunt for Charlie Blaylock as quiet as possible. No sense in having people announcing for all the world to hear that it's Texas lawmen that are asking around about the Blaylock brothers."

"True enough." Emmett paused and pocketed his badge as well.

The Comstock Queen Hotel looked to be a good choice. Plenty of guests—usually a good sign. Clean. And unlike the hotels over near C Street, it didn't seem as likely that some yahoo might put a bullet or three through the windows during the wee hours of the morning.

The front desk clerk also happened to be the hotel's proprietor. He insisted on having a Chinese fellow run Emmett's and his compadres' bags upstairs to their rooms.

They had spotted some Chinese folk at the railroad depots starting around Sacramento. Those had been the first people of Asian descent that Emmett or Juanito had ever seen in person. Sikes had seen a few Asians in the far south of Africa.

Here in Virginia City, Emmett had noted quite a number of Chinese folk out on the streets. More men than women, but certainly women too. Seeing Chinese women had surprised him, since almost everything he'd heard or read about Chinese in America had had to do with male immigrants. Dangerous and difficult labor on the one hand, laundry, cooking, and housekeeping on the other—Chinese men seemed willing to tackle any job.

Emmett sized up the Chinaman who was supposed to carry his bag up and guessed the man couldn't stand any taller than five feet four. Couldn't weigh a hundred and fifteen pounds sopping wet. It made him feel peculiar to hand their war bags over and let such a small man haul them upstairs.

"You know, we can handle these," Emmett said.

"No, no, no," the proprietor insisted. "It's just a little something extra we do here at the Comstock Queen…to set ourselves apart."

Emmett gave in but didn't much like it. As they ascended the stairs, he noted that although the Chinese man wore ordinary trousers, vest, and shirt, he still maintained a long, plaited queue that hung from beneath his black silk cap.

Once he had stowed the bags in their rooms, the Chinese fellow glanced furtively up and down the hallway. "You like good food? I tell you where you find good restaurant."

"What kind of food?" Juanito asked. "Chinese food?"

"All kind food. Cheap too. Everybody in Virginia City want charge you too much money. Too much money for everything."

Emmett gave his friends a glance and shrugged.

They shrugged back.

"OK," Emmett said. "Where's this good, cheap restaurant?"

The fellow beamed. "Go over there Union Street. Past L Street." He pointed. "Xu's Golden Dragon Café. You like."

Emmett reached into his pocket for a two-bit coin, but the Chinaman held up his hands. "Oh, no. You just tell Yong Xu I send you." He grinned again.

"You sure?"

"I sure."

"And what's your name—so I can tell Yong Xu?"

"Chin. Just tell Yong Xu, 'Chin send me.'"

"Thank you, Chin," Emmett said. "I'll do that."

Chin was all smiles as the men descended the stairs.

Out on the street, Sikes asked, "What do you think?"

"What do I think about what?"

"The little Chinaman is sending us out to the edge of town. Is that where we really want to go?"

"If that's where Yong Xu's restaurant is," Emmett said. "And if Yong Xu is willing to serve some non-Chinese folks, then yes, that's where I want to go."

"Sounds good to me," Juanito said, patting his belly.

"All right then," Sikes said, looking askance. "If it's insects and animal entrails you want…"

Juanito grinned and shook his head. "Add some *pico de gallo*, sounds OK to me."

Emmett gave a faint smile and stepped off toward the restaurant. "Juanito, you were right to tuck the badge away for the time being."

"Still chewing on the same plan?"

"Yep. Even though Charlie Blaylock's telegram went to Carson City, I like the idea of starting on the very edge of Seth Blaylock's territory. If Charlie's brother is in fact some kind of big bug, I don't wanna go plowing straight into the hornet's nest."

Emmett sidestepped to avoid an errand boy in a big hurry. "We show up at the best restaurant in Carson City inquiring about Blaylock, maybe somebody runs off and warns the man before we've learned a single thing about him."

Juanito nodded. "Take it slow and easy."

"Another thing," Sikes said. "Charlie Blaylock may expect us to show up right on his heels. If he doesn't feel us shadowing him, maybe he decides we didn't follow him up here after all. He may let his guard down."

They turned onto Union Street. Lanterns illuminated the boardwalks in front of a number of the avenue's businesses.

"I've got a feeling Charlie Blaylock already supposes he's home free—especially if his brother truly is some kind of kingpin," Emmett said. "Likely figures he's got plenty enough protection up here. Probably believes there's not a Texas lawman that can touch him."

Didn't matter what Charlie thought, though. To Emmett this was the most important fugitive hunt since he chased down the hard case responsible for his wife's death. If Blaylock had protection, he'd just have to outsmart him.

As they continued along, the composition of the traffic on the street changed—more Chinese than any other folks now. Emmett could see the sign for Xu's Golden Dragon Café just ahead.

"Based on past experience," Sikes said, "what are the odds of us taking Charlie Blaylock without a big fight?"

"Slim," Emmett said. "Had to chase an outlaw up into Arkansas once. Even with the local law helping out, it still came down to shooting. Same thing in New Mexico."

Juanito fastened his collar button as they approached the restaurant. "*Big* shootout in New Mexico."

With its signage in both Chinese and English, Xu's Golden Dragon looked much the same as any other establishment on that end of Union Street. Whereas many of the buildings back near the rail station boasted brick facades, most of the structures this far out had only wood siding, some painted, some raw. A porch roof covered the boardwalk in front of Xu's—one feature that did set the café apart. Golden lamplight poured out onto the walkway from windows on either side of the entrance.

Emmett could see diners at several of the tables inside. Most were Chinese. In fact, non-Chinese occupied only one table.

Although the aroma—even from outside—started his mouth watering, for some reason he hesitated with his hand on the door. Then he thought, *Aw, why not?*

The three were hardly inside the cheerfully lighted eatery when a Chinese fellow with a shaved head hurried toward them wearing a broad smile.

"Hello. Welcome," he said. He bowed.

Emmett eyed the man's gray frogged jacket and loose black trousers and recalled sketches of Chinese immigrants he'd seen in the newspapers a few times. "Ah...Chin sent us," he said, striving to match the host's grin.

For a moment the Chinese man's smile wavered. Then he seemed to gather himself. "Well...thank you for coming," he said. "I'm Yong Xu."

"It's OK, isn't it?" Emmett asked, touching his chest, then motioning toward the table of non-Chinese patrons.

"Why, of course. Yes." Yong Xu nodded. "I'll bet you gentlemen would love a nice, thick steak, right?"

Sikes cut his eyes at Emmett. "He said *steak*, correct?"

Before Emmett could respond, Yong Xu chuckled. "Yes, steak. Only the finest."

"Beefsteak?"

"Fresh beef."

Sikes wiped his forehead with the back of his hand. Juanito tried to refrain from laughing aloud. When he failed, the unfortunate results included an embarrassing snort. Other diners looked up from their meals.

With a grin, Emmett said, "Thank you. Steak sounds perfect."

"Li," Yong Xu called out. "Come seat these gentlemen while I throw some more wood on the grill. These men would like beefsteak. I'd like to show them what I learned from the steak masters in San Francisco."

"Yes, Baba," a female voice called from the kitchen.

What Emmett saw next sent electricity to the tips of his fingers and toes.

CHAPTER TWELVE

Emmett stood transfixed near the doorway. The Chinese girl who had emerged from the kitchen, napkins and cutlery in hand, was the most entrancing woman he'd laid eyes on since Gabriela had passed away.

He felt his face flush.

"Hello? Emmett?" he heard Sikes say. "Are you going to join us or just stand there in the doorway all night?"

"Coming," he murmured.

As he made his way to the table, he couldn't take his eyes off the Asian beauty. What she wore amused him. Looked to be boys' clothes. American boys' clothes—slim-fitting dark-blue corduroy trousers and a bib-front shirt in white with narrow, light-blue stripes. The outfit modestly covered but couldn't conceal her subtle feminine curves. She wore her dark, silken hair parted on the side, half held up with an exotic Chinese hairpin, half draping over her shoulder.

At the table he paid no mind to Juanito or Sikes.

She smiled cheerfully as she laid out the tableware.

Just then Yong Xu strode back into the dining room with a meat cleaver in hand and a grin on his face. "Do you ever use chopsticks?"

They glanced at one another and hemmed and hawed until Emmett managed to get out, "No, I can't say that we do."

Forks and knives having already been distributed, Emmett noticed that Li still held in her hands a number of tapered sticks. They looked to be of polished steel, each about nine inches long.

Yong Xu turned to his daughter. "I guess we don't need them then, Li-Li." He winked.

With no wasted motion, Li spun and threw the metal sticks one after another at a sawed-off cross section of tree trunk hanging on the wall near the kitchen door. One, two, three, four, five, six. Each hissed through the air and lodged with a sharp thwack in the wood.

Emmett's jaw dropped. His gaze darted from the target to Li to his compadres. Juanito and Sikes burst into laughter.

Li wore a coy smile as Emmett gawked and slowly began to applaud.

With a wide grin, Yong Xu surveyed his new guests. "What do you think of that?"

But before the men could answer, he himself whirled and released the cleaver. End over end, it whooshed across the room and cracked into the wooden ring.

While the act flabbergasted Emmett and his friends, the other diners had to have seen Li and Yong Xu perform the feat before. They all—including the other non-Chinese guests—simply smiled for a few moments, applauded politely, and continued their meals.

"*Madre mía!*" Juanito wagged his head, still laughing.

Emmett's slack-jawed staring turned into grinning at Yong and Li. Out of the corner of his eye, he caught sight of a middle-aged Chinese woman leaning briefly from the kitchen door. She sighed, exasperated, it would seem.

"I taught my daughter well, didn't I?" Yong Xu said.

"Indeed you did," Emmett agreed. *You taught her very well.*

The Chinese man patted her shoulder. "Li-Li, let's go check on the steaks."

Both walked away smiling.

"Well, if that doesn't beat all!" Sikes said after another round of hearty laughter.

"I didn't expect entertainment," Juanito said.

Sikes held his hands apart. "I didn't expect any of this. I came to Texas. Now I'm on a manhunt in Nevada—in a Chinese restaurant in Nevada—watching a Chinaman and his daughter perform a sensational throwing act. Nowhere else but the Wild West."

When Sikes mentioned the manhunt, Emmett made a hasty, silent plea for his deceased brother's forgiveness. And immediately his thoughts darted back to Li Xu. His mind buzzed with curiosity about her. He wondered what it would be like to enjoy the day-to-day companionship of such a lively and breathtaking woman.

Then he caught himself. Was he actually daydreaming about courting a Chinese girl? He felt a fleeting twinge of guilt and asked himself why. Because Li Xu was of a different race?

Gabriela had been a Texian—by blood as Mexican as anyone. But folks generally didn't think of her that way. Why not? Because she was so beautiful? Because her family had come to Texas and fought for the republic's independence? He wondered whether he had actually married across racial lines. Had anybody ever said so? Aside from Victorio Sanchez—the bastard.

He shook his head and tried to pay attention to Sikes and Juanito. But he couldn't. His mind raced back to the kitchen—or wherever Li Xu had trotted off to—hoping he hadn't seen the last of her.

What did they call them? He tried to remember the word used in the newspaper articles. *Antimisconception…No…Antimiscegenation.* That was the word. Antimiscegenation laws—laws declaring it illegal for men and women of different races to marry.

People had argued heatedly over the matter when he'd been a kid right after the war. But that had been mainly about Negroes and whites. Now all of a sudden it seemed like the newspapers were ginning up all kinds of commotion over antimiscegenation once again. This time mostly in news stories slanted against the Chinese—stories that usually left the reader with the distinct impression that Chinese weren't quite as fully human as other folks.

Sakes alive! If this girl Li Xu wasn't human—and as lovely a human as you'd ever find—then who was? If she didn't seem more full of life than any woman he'd laid eyes on since his Gabriela…

Emmett leaned in his chair, trying to steal a peek into the kitchen. He just wanted to talk to her for a little while, to show himself this was nothing more than infatuation. That's what it had to be—pure and simple. He figured as soon as he found out how different they really were, he'd return to his right mind and move along.

But he did want to talk to her.

He cleared his throat and did his best to concentrate on his *compañeros.* They were still jawing, apparently unaware of his mental absence.

"There was this one girl in Cape Town," Sikes said in a low voice, his hand partially blocking his mouth, his eyes beaming.

This time Emmett followed a little more of their conversation. Before long, though, he found himself considering Kit Carson. A hero. Everybody respected Kit Carson. He had not one, but two Indian wives…and later a Mexican wife. Nobody thought any less of him.

Movement in the kitchen snatched him back to the present. It was Li Xu and her father, each carrying platters of faintly sizzling food. The smoky aroma of the steaks made his mouth water. He hadn't realized how famished he was. Even so, his gaze went to Li Xu's eyes rather than to the food.

Was it hot in here? He felt as though he'd guzzled two, maybe three whiskeys one after the other. And that hadn't happened often.

Her dark eyes met his.

"Your steak," she said with a pleasant smile. The quality of her voice—he loved it. Soft, yet by no means timid.

"Thank you," he said quietly. "Smells delicious."

Glancing quickly around the table, he noticed that his steak was larger by half than Sikes's or Juanito's.

"Would you like egg on top of your steak?" she asked the three. "It's my father's San Francisco specialty."

Yong Xu clasped his hands in front of him. "I recommend it."

Each accepted the suggestion. Sikes and Juanito dug into the meal with eagerness.

Yong Xu beamed. "Enjoy."

Before turning away, Li hesitated just a split second and gave Emmett another glance.

Barely chewing his steak, he watched her go.

"*Hermano*," Juanito said, his fork suspended over his food. "What's this? I haven't seen you look at a woman that way since you first met my sister."

Emmett knew his face was still red. "Shut your big bazoo," he said. What *was* this? He wasn't fifteen any more. He shouldn't be embarrassed about his attraction to a grown woman.

"Well, well, well." Sikes chuckled and elbowed Juanito. "This certainly isn't the Emmett Strong we saw at the saloon down in El Paso, is it? Not even Geneve made him behave this way."

"Saloon girls never were his style," Juanito said. "But in the past five years I've never seen anybody turn his head like this."

Emmett glared at them. "I said keep it down. I don't want folks thinking anything strange about me."

"*Hermano*, there's nothing strange about a man thinking a pretty woman is…well, pretty."

"Yeah, well, you saw 'em both throw those weapons." He nodded toward the section of tree trunk with the still-embedded cleaver and chopsticks. "Papas don't like strangers staring at their daughters…even if their daughters are pretty."

Sikes stabbed another piece of steak. "You know what some folks out here call the Chinese?" he said. "Celestials."

"*Celestiales?*" Juanito asked.

Sikes nodded. "The Chinese refer to their country as the Celestial Kingdom." Then he glanced at Emmett and said, "But in this case perhaps celestial has another connotation."

Both Sikes and Juanito chuckled.

"This conversation is over, gents," Emmett said.

Looking the other way, he saw that the four white Americans were leaving. Chinese customers still occupied three tables—families at two tables, three men around another.

"You want to talk to her?" Juanito asked.

"Didn't I say this conversation was over?"

"*Sí.* Your mouth said it. But your eyes are still talking about her."

Emmett cut him off with a glower. "Now that the other Americans are gone, I wouldn't mind talking to Yong Xu…about the Blaylocks."

"Always work, *hermano*."

"Didn't we come up here for a reason?" Emmett speared a slice of steak.

Li Xu returned to the dining room carrying some kind of Chinese mandolin. Situating herself on a chair in the corner nearest the kitchen, she began to play.

Emmett observed that some of the Chinese customers were nodding in approval. When one of the children pointed at her and began to babble, she smiled back at the little fellow. Emmett's insides fluttered.

Minutes later, Yong Xu came in to collect his cleaver. When he glanced their way, Emmett motioned him over and asked for a word with him.

"Of course," Yong Xu answered.

"I was wondering if you could answer a few questions for me."

Yong Xu put on a businesslike face and pulled a chair over from the adjacent table.

"We've traveled a long way," Emmett began, "and we're not here for silver or adventure." He introduced himself, Juanito, and Sikes by name and told Yong Xu that they were Texas Rangers. He went on to tell the story of how Charlie Blaylock had shot Eli. An account of the shootout at the Blaylock cabin followed, then Timothy's explanation of where Charlie Blaylock had fled to and why. He told his Chinese host what he'd found out from the telegraph operator in El Paso. Then he asked, "Can you tell us anything about Blaylock? Is it true what Timothy told us—that Seth Blaylock is a very wealthy and influential man in these parts? We've heard he practically runs Carson City."

Li Xu's music continued in the background, lyrical and mysterious.

"First of all, there are many wealthy and powerful men in the Comstock country," Yong Xu said. "Plenty of them in Virginia City."

"What about Carson City?" Emmett asked.

"I have friends there, and it's a little different. The McIntosh family runs Carson City. No one dares to go against Thaddeus McIntosh."

"So it's not Seth Blaylock that runs Carson City. Have you heard of Seth Blaylock?"

Yong Xu pinched his lip and thought for a moment. Shaking his head slowly, he said, "I don't think so. But I can ask around."

"Be careful about that," Emmett said. "We ought to be able to approach the local law about my brother's murderer ourselves. But sometimes the very wealthy make certain it's their own people who hold office as marshals and sheriffs. When men like that wear the badge, guilt and innocence can become slippery ideas."

Yong Xu's eyes narrowed as he nodded. "From what I understand, that is exactly how it is in Carson City. McIntosh tells the town officials what to do. And they do it."

Emmett eyed his pardners.

Juanito thumbed his mustache. "Good to know."

"Yong Xu," Emmett said, "if you don't mind, go ahead and ask your friends about Seth and Charlie Blaylock for us. Just be sure they're friends you can trust. Friends who won't go running their mouths in the street."

"Give me a day or two," Yong Xu said. "I'll be very careful."

Li Xu leaned her mandolin against the wall in the corner and disappeared into the kitchen. Emmett heard female voices speaking Chinese. Then Li came out carrying four buckets.

As she neared the table on the way to the door, she gave Emmett an innocent smile.

Before he knew it, he was asking aloud, "Going to fetch water?"

She broke her stride and lingered. "Yes. For washing dishes."

Sikes began speaking to the girl's father. "Yong Xu," he said, "with Her Majesty's army I've traveled extensively, all around the world. But I've never been to China." He placed his hand on the man's shoulder. "I'd be fascinated to hear about your ancestral home."

"Really?" Yong Xu asked.

"Yes, absolutely."

Beneath the table, Sikes toed Emmett's boot. When Emmett frowned at him, he tossed his head subtly toward Li Xu. And toward the door.

Yong Xu enthusiastically embarked on a description of China as it had been back in the 1850s.

Blazes! Emmett thought. *What've I got to lose?*

Carefully he slid back his chair. As Yong Xu delved into his recollections, Emmett rose to his feet. He reached out and attempted to gently pry the buckets from Li Xu's hands.

She resisted. "I don't need help," she said softly. "But thank you anyway." Her polite smile faded while her gaze remained locked on his.

Had he misunderstood the subtle cues? Or had he only imagined them?

"No, I insist," he said, easing the buckets from her grasp.

Her smile this time was sheepish, but she yielded and led the way to the door.

I hope I don't regret this, he thought.

CHAPTER THIRTEEN

Charlie Blaylock had been waiting three days for his brother, Seth, to return from some sort of business trip. He had no idea yet exactly what kind of business had made his brother so all-fired rich, but it was plain to see Seth Blaylock had money…and plenty of it.

There was a cook and a full-time live-in maid at the big Blaylock house just outside of Reno. It was a two-story place with a porch that wrapped all the way around the first floor. Fully painted on the outside. Fancy trim too.

Inside, Seth's home was finished with fine wallpapers and—in some rooms—rich wood paneling. There was even a built-in bathtub. Paintings of hunting scenes hung on several walls. And Seth had books—lots of books on wooden shelves in his personal parlor. That's the room Seth's maid lady had told Charlie he should make himself at home in when he wasn't out on the porch.

Charlie expected Seth to arrive any minute now, according to what the cook had said. Even though he was clean shaved, and even though the maid lady had washed—and even ironed—the clothes he was wearing, when he looked down at their threadbare condition and considered that they were the best clothes he owned, he felt self-conscious. One quick look would bear testimony that his story was different from Seth's. It bothered him that the notion even entered his mind, but he couldn't help worrying that money might possibly have made his brother…well, uppity.

Other than that, Charlie was looking forward to seeing Seth. It had been seven years. Thomas's death at Adobe Walls had sent the brothers off in two different directions. He was anxious to tell Seth how he'd finally settled the score, at last paying back the man he held most responsible for Thomas's premature demise. He hoped that accomplishment alone would please Seth enough to earn him a welcome spot in his younger brother's home. He hoped it would make Seth just as proud of him as he was of Seth. And truthfully he was very proud of his brother for coming up here to Nevada all by his lonesome—with nothing whatsoever in his hands—and turning his tale into one of luxury and power and influence. He could hardly wait to hear how Seth had done it all.

Seth's got to be smart as all get-out, he thought. *And more'n a little lucky. Nobody gets this rich without some luck.* He figured the silver mines must've gotten Seth started, but from everybody's reactions, he was pretty sure Seth was no longer directly involved in the mining business.

Charlie's heartbeat picked up when he heard a small ruckus at the front door. Sounded like the maid letting folks in. Charlie stood, straightened his vest, and mopped his hair back with both hands before striding anxiously out into the hallway.

And suddenly, there they were. For just a second, the two stood there staring at one another, neither saying a word.

Charlie sized up his brother—a man, not a kid. Dirty-blond hair, a little on the long side, but handsomely groomed. And my, oh my, what clothes! A regular Belvidere stood before him: dark-blue patterned silk vest, crisp shirt, creased trousers. Charlie figured if he looked down, he'd be able to see himself in the sheen of Seth's fine boots.

The one item that caught Charlie's eye above all others, though, was his brother's gun rig. Sweet Molly! That soft, dark leather had to have been custom engraved. And then there were the ivory grips of Seth's Schofield revolver. Those weren't cheap either.

At last he said, "Looks like time's been good to you, Seth Blaylock. I'm real proud."

A subtle smile bowed Seth's lips. "Well, it's mighty fine to see you too, Charlie Blaylock."

Seth edged aside as someone else slipped through the doorway and immediately stole the spotlight. She too wore trousers, a vest, and a shirt—high quality—and a gun rig every bit as impressive as Seth's. But they fit her unlike anything he'd ever seen on a lady. He'd met strong women before. None so petite and feminine, though. Dark hair braided tightly on both sides of her head joined into one plait at the back. Her deep-brown eyes shone in the lamplight.

It was the whole person that captivated Charlie, not any one feature. Never had he imagined such beauty and perhaps such…deadliness bound up in one person. He felt as though a mountain lioness had just slinked into the hall and poised beside Seth. Could this be his brother's wife?

"Charlie, I'd like you to meet my dear friend Ettie," Seth said. "Ettie's my conscience. She helps me keep from strayin'."

Ettie gave a warmer-than-expected smile but said nothing as she adjusted her fine paisley neckerchief.

"Come along, big brother," Seth said as he set off toward the parlor. "Let's enjoy a whiskey before dinner. You've got to tell me about your trip." He handed his gloves and hat to the maid lady without giving her so much as a passing glance.

Seth slid the parlor door shut, fetched a cut crystal decanter, and poured for Ettie, Charlie, and himself.

"Sit, please." Seth motioned to a leather armchair. Meanwhile, he perched on the edge of his desk.

Charlie noted that Seth carried himself with pride and confidence. "I know it's been too long, brother," he said. "But I didn't feel I could come up here till I settled that ol' score down in Texas. Finally did, Seth. Finally sent Eli Strong to the undertaker and straight on down to hell." His eyes darted to Ettie. "Sorry, ma'am."

Seth nodded unenthusiastically. "Now Eli Strong…That was the lieutenant who failed to take his troopers up to Adobe Walls back when Thomas and the other buffalo hunters were in trouble up there, right?"

Charlie blinked several times. How could Seth treat this as if it was practically nothing? "Yes. Eli Strong's the one who, like a coward, wouldn't attack Quanah Parker and all them Comanches while they was busy slaughtering our brother. He was as much a murderer as them damn Indians." His eyes shot to Ettie again. "Sorry, ma'am," he said. "Don't mean to keep cussin' in front of you."

Ettie nodded. "Not a problem." Her voice was smooth as silk.

When Seth failed to respond right away, Charlie continued, "And then when the whole affair was over, he personally went and settled Chief Quanah Parker on a big ol' farm up in Indian Territory. Meanwhile, it was up to the families to go retrieve the bleached bones of their brothers and fathers from Adobe Walls—if they dared."

"I'm sorry, Charlie," Seth said. "I'm sorry I left you to carry all that burden by yourself. I'm afraid once I arrived up here in minin' country, I put all that behind me. Maybe I shouldn't have."

Charlie stared. After a pause he said, "Well, maybe that's what big brothers are for—to take care of matters so the younger ones don't have to face the ugly business."

"Well, thank you, big brother. Now maybe you can rest and find a place in the new life I've made for myself up here in Nevada."

Charlie couldn't decide whether Seth was talking down to him or not.

"So how'd it go down?" Seth asked. "How'd you finally take Eli Strong?"

Suddenly Charlie felt a fresh wind of righteous indignation. He set his whiskey tumbler on the side table, tugged on the legs of his trousers, and spoke as much with his hands as with his words. "That Eli Strong went on to become somebody big down in Texas. Went on to win hisself a spot in the Texas state senate."

Seth nearly spewed his drink. "Hell, Charlie, don't tell me you waited till the man became a senator before you beefed him!"

"Never had the chance before that, Seth," Charlie said, clenching his fists. "Man always had a passel of soldiers or some other armed men around him."

"So where'd you do the deed? In front of a crowd?"

"It weren't a crowd exactly. More like a few friends."

"Where? Where'd it go down?" Seth clomped his tumbler down on the desk and leaned toward Charlie.

"In the street. Front of a restaurant in Austin."

"And you got away clean?"

"Sure did," Charlie said. "I had it all planned out. I was already in the saddle. Let him have it in the belly so he'd die good and slow, but die for certain. And then I hightailed it outta town. Never saw not one lawman behind me the whole way out here."

Seth rubbed his upper lip and glanced at Ettie. She stood, leaning coolly against the wall, ankles crossed, one thumb hooked in her vest pocket.

"So why'd you come here, Charlie? Really now. To find out how your brother's doin'? Or to lay low from the Texas Rangers?"

Charlie shuffled. "Maybe a bit of both," he mumbled.

Seth raked his fingers through his hair. He slowly blew out a stream of air. "It's all right. It's all right, brother. They won't come all the way up here. And if they do…" He gazed at Ettie.

She gave a wry smile.

Seth chuckled. "If any Texas lawmen are dumb enough to come sniffin' around here for you, why, I believe they'll find a bit more trouble than they ever bargained for."

Just as swiftly as storm clouds had swept into the room, sunshine broke through on Seth's face again. One more long exhalation and he looked every bit as calm and confident as when they'd first come into the parlor.

With arms held wide, he said, "I've done well for myself up here, Charlie. So forget Texas now. This is Nevada—the Silver State." He grinned broadly.

Charlie wiped his nose, then grinned too. "So silver. Is that how you got your start up here, little brother? 'Cause I wouldn't mind rollin' up my sleeves. Find my own self a piece of the wealth."

Seth and Ettie eyed one another.

"Silver?" Seth said. "Only indirectly."

"Well, what do you do then?" Charlie asked. "You in the cattle business?"

Again Seth peeked at Ettie. She now peered at the floor.

"Yeah, you might say I'm in livestock," Seth said.

"Looks like it's goin' well for you," Charlie said. "Can you use a hand? I don't expect to be treated no different than any other employee, but I'd appreciate you findin' somethin' for me to do for hire…if you can."

Seth rose from the corner of the desk. "I'm sure I can put you to work, Charlie. We'll find a place for you."

Charlie fidgeted and cleared his throat. "I'm sorry, Seth. 'Specially sorry if by accident I brought some Texas law dogs up here followin' me."

"I can assure you," Seth said, touching Ettie's shoulder and starting for the door, "it would be a mistake of monumental proportions for any Texas lawmen to come lookin' for you while you're under my protection. Let's go get some dinner."

Is that what it is? It suddenly struck Charlie. He wasn't just lying low or relocating. He was under his little brother's protection now. The notion chafed his pride. But it was the truth.

71

He grabbed Seth's arm. "As long as we're on the subject, I got just one other concern."

Seth and Ettie stopped in place.

"Ain't none of them Texas men worries me," Charlie said. "Except maybe Eli Strong's little brother. Emmett Strong used to have quite the reputation as a pistolero. Reputation's lost some of its shine lately. But I hear he's still mighty good."

Seth looked Charlie in the eye. "Wasn't too bright of you to do it how you did it, Charlie. But don't you worry. You're safe here. We're used to makin' lawmen do what we aim for 'em to do." He clapped him on the shoulder. "Anyway, I'll bet even Ettie here can take that Emmett Strong if he comes nosin' around."

CHAPTER FOURTEEN

Emmett wanted his curiosity about Li Xu satisfied, that was all. Who was this rare beauty who had caught him so completely off guard—this astonishing, multitalented blend of feminine decorum and disarming self-confidence?

He carried the four water pails. She led him to the well at the end of the boardwalk.

"Why did you want to help with the water?" she asked.

Taken aback by the straightforwardness of her question, he struggled for an appropriate reply—one that wouldn't slam the door in his face. Before he could formulate another answer, the words, "You're a fascinating woman," tumbled out of his mouth.

"Fascinating?" She bit her lip and kept her eyes on the well pump.

He hung one of the pails from the spigot and began to work the pump handle. "Well, I didn't expect an entire variety show when I took your father's friend's advice to come eat here."

"Oh? Which of my father's friends do you know?"

"A fella named Chin. I don't really know him. He carries folks' baggage upstairs for them at the Comstock Queen Hotel—the place where we're staying."

"Chin."

He thought he caught her rolling her eyes. "Yep."

The pipe gurgled and belched sporadic splashes of water into the pail.

Her gaze rose to meet his, and she tilted her head a little. "So you didn't expect a show. What did you expect?"

The water flowed freely now.

"I don't know...Good food?"

"Was it good?"

"Best I've had in a while," he said, smiling more comfortably now.

"My parents do know cooking," she said. Her accent was slight, her voice smooth and melodic. "All kinds of foods—North Chinese, South Chinese, American."

He was eager for her to like him. Even if he never saw her again. "They're not the only ones in your family with talent. I liked your music. You play that instrument well. What do you call it?"

"It's a *pipa*—very ancient, very traditional." She reached for the first full bucket. "A lot of fun, for me at least."

"Chinese too, right?"

"Yes, Chinese."

She handed another pail to Emmett.

"Where are you from in China?" he said and right away added, "Although I don't know why I'm asking. I don't know Hong Kong from Peking."

At that, Li Xu smiled. "I'm from right here. I've lived in Virginia City my whole life."

Emmett figured confusion must have been written all over his face because she started laughing.

"Both my parents came here in 1860—the year after everybody found out about the Comstock Lode. Their parents had already been in California almost ten years. Anyway, my father and mother married right after they got here, and I was born the next year in a little house right over there." She pointed away from the center of town, off beyond the café.

"So you're twenty years old then," Emmett said, pleased to have the answer to one of the questions tumbling around in his mind.

"Nineteen," she said. "I don't turn twenty until November."

"Where'd you and your father learn how to throw weapons like that?" He grinned.

Her face took on a mischievous expression. "Just playing around behind the restaurant after we finished our work."

"Chopsticks?" he asked.

She shook her head. "Similar. My father's father had some Korean chopsticks—they sometimes use metal ones. He experimented with those when he was young. Later, just for fun, he made some sticks specifically for throwing."

Emmett pondered whether folks up here let the Chinese own guns. *Good that a man can defend his family with something.* A couple of anti-Chinese news stories flashed through his mind, and he hoped Li and Yong would only ever need their throwing skills to amuse guests.

It occurred to him once again that prior to passing through California a couple days ago, he'd never actually seen an Asian before. He'd only read about them.

He stole another glance at Li Xu. She waited patiently for him to finish filling another pail. *A Celestial.* Not an hour ago, assuming it impossible, he had longed to talk with her, if only briefly. Now it was happening. So what was the verdict? Mere infatuation after all?

Their conversation stalled before the fourth container was full.

"Two and two?" she asked, reaching for a pair of buckets.

"Sounds fair," he said, lifting the other two. "Would've been heavy for one little lady."

She glowered over her shoulder.

"Although I'm sure it'd be nothing for you," he hurried to say. The frown seemed playful, but it was just convincing enough to make him wonder.

Before reaching the café door, she said, "Are you and your friends going to be staying in Virginia City very long?"

He wondered why exactly she asked. "We're looking for someone—a man who ran away from a serious crime he committed down in Texas. Your father seems willing to help us find out something we need to know. So whether we stay here or not, there's a good chance we'll be back to talk with him again."

Directly in front of the door, she turned to face him. He liked the shape of her face and the bow of her lips. "What's my father going to find out for you?"

Emmett wavered over telling her more. But something about the look in her eyes convinced him she truly wanted to know who he was and why he'd come to Nevada. And suddenly it became important to him to tell her—just in case this adventure ended badly for him.

"A man named Charlie Blaylock murdered my brother," he said. "Charlie Blaylock's brother, Seth, is supposed to be a big and dangerous man around here. I think Charlie came here to hide behind his brother. Your father said he'd ask around about where this Seth Blaylock lives and just how powerful he is."

She delayed responding. "I'm sorry about your brother," she finally said. "And I hope my father can help somehow. But I'm curious…"

"About what?"

"Of all the people you could go to for help in the search for your brother's murderer, why a Chinese man? Why a simple restaurant owner?"

"It wasn't something I planned. It just sorta happened."

He reached for the door handle, but she didn't step aside.

His heartbeat picked up.

"You haven't told me your name," she said.

"Emmett," he said. "Emmett Strong. I heard your father call you Li."

She nodded and gave a polite smile, allowing him room to take the door handle now. "Thanks for your help with the water, Emmett."

He returned the smile and gave a single nod while his heart kept thumping a notch faster than usual. Stealing one last moment to etch the details of her face on his memory, he shifted both buckets to one hand and let her take the lead across the threshold.

Dammit! he chided himself. *You're more than infatuated.*

He had a job to do. Distracted like this, he could wind up dead—especially if Blaylock's brother really did turn out to be a big gun. And dead simply wouldn't do…not when life was just starting to become so interesting again.

—∞—

From the shadows between two shops across the street, Chin watched. His eyes burned. This, he thought, was not why he'd sent this cowboy over here.

How could this be? Yong Xu was fine with letting his daughter go out alone with a stranger—a white man, after dark. But he wouldn't let her have time alone with him—a Chinese man. Why not? Because he didn't have enough money? Because his English wasn't good? Yong Xu was clearly becoming too proud. Too American.

And why was Li Xu always so impolite to him? Yes, she was beautiful—perhaps the most beautiful of all the pretty girls in Chinatown. But why had she stopped speaking to him? OK, except for a formal hello or good-bye. Did she think so much of her own beauty? Or did she think she was special because her father was a community leader?

He had tried to impress both Li Xu and her father. That was over now. This was the last insult he would take from either one of them.

Gritting his teeth, he swabbed his eyes with his sleeve. After one last glance at Xu's Golden Dragon, he spun and padded off into the darkness.

CHAPTER FIFTEEN

Almost noon, the sun floated high in the cloudless blue. A chilly edge wouldn't release its grip on the springtime air.

Emmett, Juanito, and Sikes had ridden out of Virginia City at daybreak, having paid to leave their mule and a few of their belongings back at the livery stable. They wanted to travel light in case they had to beat a path out of Carson City.

"You got your role down, Juanito?" Emmett asked.

"*Sí, yo lo tengo.*"

"OK then. Go to it, amigo. You'll find Sikes and me down at the statehouse when you're done."

He nodded. "See you there."

Juanito walked his horse toward the railroad station, while Emmett and Sikes continued straight ahead toward the Nevada capitol building.

"I wish I'd gotten a look at Charlie Blaylock back in Austin," Sikes said.

"Yeah, well…I'll have to keep my eyes shucked for the both of us," Emmett said. "Just be ready to follow my lead if I happen to spot him."

"This is a bold move, Strong."

"Mainly just reconnoitering."

"You won't nab him if we run across him?"

"Depends. Need to find out where he is first. And what kind of protection his brother's providing."

"You said you wanted to stop in at the statehouse."

"Yep."

"You've played it cautious thus far," Sikes said. "Knocking on the statehouse door to ask about Seth Blaylock hardly seems cautious."

"It's not like I'll be out on the front steps, yammering on about Charlie or Seth for all the world to hear."

Sikes shrugged.

In the center of the city, with Emmett still scouring the boardwalks for Charlie Blaylock, the two set about looking for the town marshal's office. It seemed they must've searched both sides of every street and avenue twice and still hadn't located the place.

Emmett drew up, planted his fist on his thigh, and panned the street. "Now what kind of town doesn't put the marshal's office right in the middle where everybody can find it? Juanito's gonna be back here before we've accomplished a thing."

Sikes reined his horse to the side of the street to catch up with a potbellied fellow wearing a bowler and a fine suit hurrying along the boardwalk. "Excuse me, sir," he said. "My friend and I are looking for the town marshal's office. We've covered practically the whole of Carson City and still can't seem to find it."

The man in the bowler stopped, grasped the lapels of his suit coat, and squinted up at Sikes. "Town doesn't exactly have a marshal's office. That'd be why you haven't found one."

Emmett joined them. "No marshal's office?"

The man gave Emmett and Sikes the once-over. "No need for one when there's no marshal."

Emmett pushed his hat back a little. "Peculiar—a city this size with no marshal. Who's your local law?"

"Mr. McIntosh and his boys look out for the town well enough."

Yong Xu's words about Thaddeus McIntosh echoed in Emmett's mind. He glanced at Sikes, who raised his eyebrows knowingly.

"They look out for the town," Emmett said, "in some sort of official capacity?"

The man let go of his lapels. His eyes narrowed. "If you really want an answer to that question, I think you're going to have to ask Mr. McIntosh directly." He looked from Emmett to Sikes and back again. "Good day, sirs," he said, already pivoting to continue on his way.

"Curious," Sikes murmured, leaning on his saddle horn.

Emmett followed the man with his gaze. "Very."

At the next street corner, the fellow approached and spoke to two men wearing gun belts. Though he didn't point back at Emmett and Sikes, he jerked his head in their direction more than once.

After a fashion, the armed men shoved off the lamppost they had been leaning against and began to swagger toward them.

"I expect we're about to meet a couple of McIntosh boys right now," Emmett said. "Looking out for the town, so to speak."

"Appears so," Sikes said. "How do you want to handle this?"

"Head on."

Emmett chirked and lightly touched his pinto's flanks. He walked the horse right up to the pair. "Good afternoon, gentlemen."

"Mr. Farley says there's somethin' you want to ask Mr. McIntosh," the one on the left said. "Is that so?"

Emmett pursed his lips, then said, "No, I don't believe Mr. Farley got that right. I'll be glad to talk to the county sheriff or to any other duly elected or appointed official. But I don't think I need to trouble Mr. McIntosh."

The two men eyed one another. A plug of tobacco distended the cheek of the fellow on the right. He spat a stream of brown saliva to within inches of Emmett's horse's front hoof.

Emmett took pains to remain placid.

"You even know who Mr. McIntosh is, stranger?" the one with no tobacco said.

"Heard his name once before," Emmett said.

"And?"

"And I never heard anybody say Marshal McIntosh, Sheriff McIntosh, or even Mayor McIntosh."

"All them things you said—marshal, sheriff, mayor—you wanna talk about any of them things, you gonna have to talk to Mr. McIntosh."

Emmett nodded. "And when the citizens of this burg want to talk about any of those things, do they have to talk to Mr. McIntosh?"

"Citizens 'round here don't much wanna talk about such things."

About then Emmett spied Mr. Farley again, at the mouth of a side street a couple of blocks ahead. This time the pudgy magpie pointed, and a welcoming committee of a half dozen heeled men fanned out into the street and began to head in their direction.

"A pleasure to meet you gents," Emmett said to the pair directly in front of him. "I think our question's been answered."

"Naw, you ain't leavin' yet," the one with the tobacco said. "We got some questions for you. What're you—"

Emmett cut him off. "Thanks for the welcome. Adios." He touched his hat and wheeled his horse.

Sikes followed suit.

"Hey," the McIntosh man called out, "I said we got questions for you."

They rode away at a trot.

"I get the feeling that even if we talk to McIntosh directly we won't get any help arresting Charlie Blaylock," Sikes said.

"Just a feeling, huh?"

"Think they'll shoot us in the back?"

"Not just yet."

Sikes started to look over his shoulder.

"Uh-uh," Emmett said, keeping his gaze straight ahead. "You look back, you lose."

Several blocks away Emmett and Sikes dismounted and entered the cool, dimly lit lobby of the statehouse. A man in a black suit sat at a desk off to one side.

"Help you gents?" he said, rising from his station. His voice reverberated in the spacious foyer.

"If there was a federal marshal in this fine city, where would we find him?"

The man scratched his thinning hair. He glanced toward the door where Emmett and Sikes had come in. "You bring trouble with you?"

Emmett closed his eyes and shook his head. "Do I look troubled?"

Sikes smiled.

"No, don't reckon you do," the government man said. "You're lucky to catch him in town today. He doesn't spend a great deal of time here." He pointed. "Exit on the other side of the lobby there. Door directly across the street. Won't see a sign, though."

"Didn't figure we would," Emmett said. "Much obliged."

When Emmett opened the door to the federal marshal's office, its sole occupant—his back to them—flinched visibly. Glass clinked on glass and two faint clunks followed. The man pivoted in place.

"Help you?" Thin and hollow-cheeked, the fellow looked as if he'd break in two if he so much as sneezed.

"Where's your badge, Marshal?" Emmett said.

The man absently touched the left side of his blue suit coat. "Reckon I forgot it. Who're you?"

Emmett pulled the Texas Ranger star from his pocket and affixed it to his vest. "Don't know that this means much up here in Nevada." He patted the badge. "Name's Emmett Strong. This is my pardner Granville Sikes."

"Yes?" the marshal said.

"Fugitive flees across state lines, do you suppose it might be within the purview of a US marshal to help give chase?"

The marshal cleared his throat, sniffed, and said, "You chasin' a fugitive?"

"Yep."

"All the way up from Texas?"

"Yep."

"What'd he do?"

"Shot a Texas state senator right in the stomach. In cold blood. Left a young widow to mourn all alone in Texas."

The marshal rubbed his whiskers. "How do you know he came up here?"

Sikes shifted his weight.

"Telegraph office," Emmett said. "Fugitive sent a telegram ahead." He paused for emphasis. "To tell his brother he was coming."

"Fugitive's brother's in Carson City?" The marshal's gaze darted from Emmett to Sikes, then to the door.

Emmett placed both hands on the lawman's desk and leaned forward. "That's something I'm hoping you can tell me."

The marshal edged back, and the wood flooring creaked.

"The fugitive's name is Blaylock. Charlie Blaylock—the brother of Nevada resident Seth Blaylock," Emmett said.

The marshal's face drained of color.

"So you're familiar with Seth Blaylock," Emmett said.

"You don't want to go messin' with Mr. Blaylock." The marshal stumbled over his words. "Not unless you want to end up just like that Texas state senator."

"What do you propose then?"

"Believe me, you two should just saddle up and head on back to Texas. Tell whoever sent you that Charlie Blaylock gave you the slip. Trail went cold."

Emmett pounded the desk. "That Texas state senator was my brother!" he barked. Then almost in a whisper, he continued, "You still think I should just turn around and go home?"

The marshal fidgeted with the blotter on his desk.

Emmett stared at him. "Are you gonna help me out here?"

"I-I don't want nothin' to do with them Blaylocks," he said.

"Then, dagnabbit, tell me where Seth Blaylock lives. We'll go get him ourselves."

"I can't tell you nothin'." The man was trembling visibly by this point.

"Who the blazes are the Blaylocks and the McIntoshes anyway that everybody up here is so thundering petrified of them?" Emmett demanded. "What do they do?"

The marshal turned and grasped the glass of whiskey he had poured. With no apparent qualms remaining, he drained it in one swig.

After he caught his breath, he said, "This is all I'll tell you—and it's probably too much: The McIntoshes and Blaylock, they run a string of saloons, gambling parlors, and bed houses from San Francisco to Genoa. A whole lot of outlaws have gravitated to them. They've got what amounts to their own private army. If people leave them alone, they generally do the same in return. Seth Blaylock…well, he don't live in Carson City. Now that's all you're gonna get outta me. I don't care if you pistol-whip me."

"Why don't you do yourself a favor," Emmett said, his voice low. "Turn in your badge. Quit pretending you're a lawman. Looks like your nerves could use some mending."

The marshal fumbled again for the whiskey decanter. "Ranger, your attitude's gonna get you killed a whole lot faster than my nerves are gonna do me in."

Emmett glared at the wreck of a lawman for several long moments, then turned and headed for the door.

Just across from the Virginia and Truckee depot, Juanito dismounted, tethered his horse to a hitching post, and began to play the fool. He almost never wore a serape. Yet there were times when it came in handy, not only to ward off the chill, but also to play off of misconceptions some people had about Mexicans…or Texans, or Texians.

He slowed his gait and shuffled just a bit more as he walked. Before stepping up onto the boardwalk in front of the telegraph office, he stretched, scratched his belly, and yawned aloud. "*Ay, madre mía,*" he whined.

Once inside the telegraph office, he took off his hat and clutched it with both hands, just above waist level. He scuffled to the counter.

The man behind the desk turned and wrinkled his nose. "How can I help you?"

"*Ay,* Mister," Juanito said in an exaggerated accent. "I have become—how you say?—separated from my boss."

"Yeah," the telegraph man said, nose still wrinkled, brow now furrowed. "Well, how exactly can I help you?"

"It's just that Mr. Charlie, he was going to see his brother, Mr. Seth. He was in such a hurry, he left me behind." Juanito scratched his head and stared.

The telegraph operator cocked his head. "Do you need to send a telegram or what? Because I'm a very busy man, and I've got to—"

"Oh no, Señor. I just need you to tell me where I go to find Mr. Seth Blaylock. That's the brother of my boss."

For a moment the telegraph operator looked dubious. Then he sighed. "You," he said, "are in the wrong town for Mr. Seth Blaylock. Seems you folk from down Texas way keep getting that mixed up this week. First Charlie Blaylock himself. Now you. Lucky for you I'm the one that made sure your boss got squared away. You follow what I'm saying so far? *Comprende?*"

"*Sí.* I mean, yes. I understand."

"Mr. McIntosh's boys have already taken your boss on up to Reno. That's where your boss's brother, Mr. Seth Blaylock, lives."

Juanito palmed his head. "In Reno?"

"Yes."

"*Ayyy,* so far already."

"I'm afraid you'll have to go just a little farther."

"OK, Señor. Well, *muchas gracias*. Thank you."

Juanito turned and shuffled out, mumbling and moaning as he went.

—◊—

Five minutes later, from an alley behind the statehouse, Emmett watched Juanito jog his horse up the street. Somewhere along the line, his brother-in-law had slipped off his serape, rolled it up, and stowed it behind the cantle of his saddle. Reins in one hand, he rode upright, no longer slouched as when he had been playacting. He had flattened his broad hat brim once again and replaced the sombrero at a jaunty angle.

Emmett stepped out to meet him. "Any luck on your side of town?"

Juanito nodded. "He's in Reno."

CHAPTER SIXTEEN

More than a dozen men stood or squatted around a snapping campfire on a hill just outside Virginia City. Ettie was there, too. Charlie Blaylock listened quietly from just outside the circle. He felt a lump in his throat and a heaviness in his chest. He was learning on the fly what his brother Seth did to earn so much money up here in Nevada.

In the deepening darkness, Seth addressed his hired hands. "So everybody listen to Buck Tanner here. He's gonna tell you what he's seen firsthand. It's important that we all get it. We wanna get into Chinatown and out again before anybody else ever knows we're there." He nodded. "Go ahead, Buck."

The buttons of Buck Tanner's faded brown suit coat strained against their buttonholes. He sniffed and began. "You all know it's my job to come here to Virginia City regularly, to sit in the saloons and bars and listen. Then I tell Mr. Seth and Mr. Lucian about whatever little bits of news I pick up from folks around here—whatever might be of business interest to them."

He cleared his throat. "Well, one night a fella over at the Comstock Queen Hotel told me how it might be worth my trouble to take a ride out around the edge of town. Told me to take a look through the windows of a certain restaurant. And sure enough, what I come across caught my eye—in a businesslike sense, of course." Tanner glanced at Seth as though he wondered whether he was doing OK.

Seth crossed his arms. "Go on."

This was all news to Charlie. He hadn't been privy to the meeting between Tanner and Seth and Ettie. His brother had told him to wait outside on the porch, then closed the parlor doors.

Tanner continued. "Well, where this man from the hotel sent me, turns out it was a Chinese restaurant. Not for white folks and all, like some of 'em.

This one was for Chinese only. It had lots of windows across the front, and so I could see in real clear."

"Aw my gawd! Chinese? Really?" one of the men across the campfire said. He tossed a stick he had between whittling into the fire.

Seth shot him a look that told him to shut up and pay attention—which he did.

"Anyway," Tanner said, "you know I seen Chinese girls that's all ugly and Chinese girls that's all pretty. Damn, if these ain't six or seven of the prettiest China girls I ever seen before! I thought to myself these'd be just the type Mr. McIntosh would be real pleased to have for his businesses."

"Chinese?" another of the hands dared to whine. "Most China girls is so ugly they'd back a buzzard off a gut wagon."

Several of the bunch laughed openly.

"I'm tellin' you," Tanner said, "I know Chinese girls don't fit every man's taste, but some fellas like 'em. And these is as pretty as any I ever seen."

Seth stepped forward into the glow of the campfire. "Buck Tanner found out these same girls get together every Tuesday night at the same place—some kind of Chinese girls' club or somethin'. He's gonna lead us on in. It's on the edge of town. It's Chinatown. But we still don't wanna wake up the dead. Aside from the fact that Virginia City's not too partial to Mr. McIntosh, as always, keepin' it a secret who we are—that trumps everything else." His gaze went from man to man all the way around the campfire. "Understand?"

Each man in turn nodded.

He waved his left hand. "You all on this side are gonna split off to the back." He pointed to a gunhand directly across the circle. "From Zeke over to my right, all the rest of you are gonna take the front."

Charlie watched his brother—so refined in his nice clothes, light from the campfire reflecting off the silk of his dark-blue vest and the polished leather of his boot shanks. He recalled his brother chuckling, answering him, "Yeah, you might say I'm in livestock." So this is what he meant, huh? He felt all tangled up inside. One part of him really wanted a piece of the rich life Seth had found. Another part of him was troubled about kidnapping young women for some big boss's hookshop—even if they were only China girls.

Seth finished giving instructions to his gang and told them all to saddle up.

Charlie eyed Ettie and wondered what she thought of all this. Sure, she was dressed just as fancy as Seth. Probably turning a nice profit for her part in this whole business. Yet it puzzled him. How could a woman be OK with doing this to other women?

Before Charlie could step into his stirrup, Seth clutched his arm. "You steady enough to handle this kind of action, brother?" Seth asked, his eyes like a wolf's.

After a brief hesitation, Charlie said, "'Course I am."

"You don't have to do anything except cover the back door with that shotgun." Seth tossed his chin. "Anybody that's not one of us approaches, you just let them have it—especially if it's some Chinese girl's pa or big brother. OK?"

Charlie nodded.

Seth clapped him on the shoulder. "You'll get paid handsome, brother. Believe me."

CHAPTER SEVENTEEN

Gazing beyond the campfire out over Washoe Lake, not far from Carson City, Emmett took a swallow of bitter coffee to wash down his last bite of hard biscuit. That and a few strips of jerky had constituted his supper. After rendezvousing near the statehouse, he, Juanito, and Sikes had cleared out of town fast. They didn't want to stumble into any more McIntosh or Blaylock sympathizers before they had a chance to sit down and talk over what they were learning.

Sikes stood facing the lake, one hand holding a cigar, the other hand behind his back. "Thaddeus McIntosh has got that town wound up tighter than a clock."

"From that Farley fella to the US marshal," Emmett said.

Juanito sat, smoothing the brim of his hat. "Yong Xu wasn't exaggerating about McIntosh, was he?"

"How can McIntosh maintain such a pall of fear over Carson City when it's the state capital?" Sikes asked. "It's obvious to anyone with eyes and ears. Why don't higher officials rein him in?"

Juanito gave a cynical chuckle. "You said it yourself down in El Paso, amigo: people making big fortunes, paying officials to look the other way."

"Seems to me there's got to be *someone* with scruples enough to reestablish the rule of law."

A crisp breeze rustled the nearby trees, prompting Emmett to stoke the campfire. Holding his palms over the embers, he said, "Law in this part of the country is a developing thing, Mr. Sikes. Lot of folks know how it oughta go. But there's a lot of territory to oversee and not enough authorities to do the overseeing. Leaves just enough wiggle room for bosses like McIntosh to run things as they please."

"So what do you expect up in Reno, *hermano*?" Juanito asked.

"If there's another McIntosh up there, more of the same."

"A McIntosh, plus Blaylock's brother," Sikes said. "Could be even tighter there than where we just came from."

"Tighter'n a brand-new pair of mail-order shoes."

"And how far did we get in Carson City before we began to feel the squeeze?"

Juanito pulled his serape around his shoulders. "So we're three lawmen, a long way from home—"

"Since when did I become a lawman?" Sikes said. "I'm not even a citizen."

"Two lawmen and a vigilante." Juanito raised an eyebrow as he turned to Sikes. "Better?"

"Vigilante. Why, I don't know…"

"Anyway," Juanito resumed, "we're outgunned and undersupplied. We have no support from the local law. How do we make a reasonable run at taking Charlie Blaylock back to Texas?"

Emmett stared at the fire, rubbing his chin.

Sikes tossed the stub of his cigar into the low flames. "Operating in enemy territory…Based on my countrymen's recent disaster in Africa, I'll tell you this: Courage and audacity don't guarantee anything. Neither does marksmanship."

Emmett leaned forward. "You were heavily outnumbered in Africa, right?"

Sikes nodded. "Ridiculously."

"Thought firepower would win the day."

"An arrogant assumption with humiliating results, yes."

"Arrogant." Emmett looked from Sikes to Juanito. "Well, who's behaving all arrogant up here?"

"Hmm," Sikes said. "Perhaps the Achilles' heel of the McIntoshes and the Blaylocks?"

"And something we need to avoid at all costs," Juanito said.

Emmett leaned back against his saddle. "So is it arrogant for us to make a careful trip into Reno tomorrow?"

"*Careful* would have to be the key," Sikes said.

"Might be less conspicuous if I ride in alone," Emmett said. "You two can both wait in Virginia City, if you like."

"Uh-uh. No, *hermano*. You're not going in alone."

"Word'll be getting out that an odd trio—a Texan, a Mexican, and an Englishman—are riding around up here, asking some delicate questions about powerful people."

"A Texian," Juanito said.

"Not as far as they're concerned."

"They won't know I'm British unless I open my mouth," Sikes said.

"Odds are you'll say something." Emmett grinned. "Besides, some of McIntosh's boys saw us together in Carson City today."

"OK," Juanito said. "So we ride together to someplace just outside of Reno. Sikes and I wait for you while you go in for a look around. What then?"

Emmett grabbed a few pieces of dead branch and tossed them onto the fire. "That's something I won't know till I get there."

Juanito and Sikes glanced at one another.

"If anything looks peculiar," Emmett said, "I'll cut out three ways from Sunday."

"Like Sikes said, *careful's* the word then, *hermano*."

Emmett nodded. "Who knows? Might catch a fortunate break."

Sikes dumped out the rest of his coffee. "Or they might catch you."

CHAPTER EIGHTEEN

The tables and chairs had all been moved to the edges of the dining room inside Zhang's Restaurant in Virginia City. As Li Xu plucked and strummed her *pipa*, she watched her friends dance. Their giggles brought a smile to her face.

The eleven Chinese girls—all in their middle to late teens—had each dressed in traditional clothes that night, as they did each Tuesday night. All wore wide-legged trousers beneath loose-fitting, thigh-length smocks, most with frogged closures. The colors and patterns varied but tended toward deep reds and burgundies, trimmed with black, gold, or both. Li Xu found the palette pleasant to the eyes.

She still wore her hair partly down and partly pinned up, but most of the girls wore a pair of braids or twists pinned high on the sides of their heads. *Very elegant.*

At the end of the tune, everyone laughed and clapped. The handful of mothers chaperoning the weekly event sat in one corner sipping tea, gossiping, and paying little attention to their daughters.

While several of the girls streamed off into the kitchen to bring out tea and sweet pastries, Li Xu remained seated in the corner opposite the mothers. Her friend Ping scurried over and sat beside her. Before long they plunged into one of their most frequent topics of conversation: turning twenty and facing an arranged marriage.

"Li-Li, why don't you trust your parents?" Ping said. "They're the best. I wish my parents were half as fun as yours."

"I trust them about most things," she said.

"Then trust them now. They'll find you a good man."

Li Xu rolled her eyes. *Here we go again.* "Ping, I'm glad you're confident about the outcome of your parents' arrangements, but honestly, I don't know of a Chinese man in Virginia City that I'd want to marry."

"There are a thousand of us here in this one town, Li. There's got to be at least one…"

Li shook her head slowly. "Anyway, I'd rather choose—when I'm ready."

"It doesn't work that way, and you know it."

"Did my mother send you over here to spoil my night?" she asked, glowering playfully.

Ping laughed. "No, I'm just sad for you."

"Don't be," she said. "I'm perfectly fine."

"What if your parents could find you a husband who's not from around here?"

Li loved Ping to death. But she was growing tired of the persistent pressure to quietly accept any marriage arrangements her parents might come up with. She decided it would be fun to get a fresh reaction out of Ping. Looking up and away, she said, "I wouldn't mind considering a husband who's not from around here."

Ping shifted in her chair for a better view of Li's face. She covered her mouth, then glanced toward the chaperones and back again. "Li-Li," she whispered, "I'm your best friend. I know you. You've got someone particular in mind, don't you?"

Li nearly let a laugh slip. Her friend was so eager for a juicy story. "What if I did?" She bit her lip.

Ping dropped her voice even lower. "Who is he? Is he from Dayton? From Truckee?"

Li shook her head. She too stole a glance at the cluster of mothers in the far corner. "From farther away." She was enjoying the game.

"From China?"

"Uh-uh." For some reason, her thoughts flew to Emmett Strong. Again. "From America."

Ping frowned. "Are you telling me you've got your eyes on an American? On an English American?"

The other girls were coming out of the kitchen with refreshments. Li couldn't decide how long to keep the deceit going. "All I can say is that I met this beautiful American man at the café the other night."

Ping's jaw dropped.

Before her friend could say anything else, Li put a finger to her lips. He *was* handsome, she thought. But this was just a game, right? She and an American?

It would never work. For now, though, it was fun to see Ping getting so worked up.

"He wasn't loud," Li said. "He was very polite. But at the same time he seemed very strong." Then she looked Ping in the eyes. "And somehow very sad too." That much was true.

"You can never defy your parents that way, Li Xu. It's the one thing you cannot do."

Li squeezed Ping's arm. The game wasn't quite over. "Promise me you won't say a word."

"But—"

Peering sternly into her friend's eyes, Li insisted, "Not a word, Ping."

Everyone else was gathering for pastries and tea now. It was time to join them. Later that night she might tell her friend that she had only been teasing. Or maybe not.

Li rose to set her *pipa* on a vacant table.

At that very moment, the front door exploded into hundreds of shards of wood and glass. Another crash sounded from the back of the kitchen. Women and girls screamed as masked men pointing guns poured into the restaurant from both doors.

Several of the men were shouting. A tall one in a blue vest waved a pistol and yelled, "Shut up! All of you, shut up right now!"

The chaperones dashed from their table to put themselves between the invaders and the panicked girls. They shouted back in Mandarin and broken English.

Li's heart pounded as never before in her entire life. She huddled next to Ping and their friends.

Four of the masked men took up spots in the corners of the room, pointing shotguns menacingly. The rest herded the girls and women into the center of the room.

Two of the Chinese women tried to pummel the intruders with their fists. They were instantly pistol-whipped, and they dropped to the floor, blood seeping from their heads.

Now there was more crying than yelling from the Chinese girls and their mothers.

The tall masked man in the dark-blue vest stepped forward. "Line up the girls," he said to his gang. "Side by side."

A smaller man wearing a long black duster, filthy boots, and a beat-up, broad-brimmed hat stood next to him.

One of the teens—a sweet girl named Yan—wriggled free from her captor and sprinted for the kitchen. A terrifying bang filled the air, and Yan stumbled to the floor, the back of her smock already glistening deep red.

A new wave of screaming and wailing erupted.

The man with the blue silk vest yelled, "I told you no shootin' unless the men came runnin', dammit!"

He strode to within a foot of the line of girls. His brow furrowed above the black bandanna that covered his nose and mouth. "You wanna live?" He shook his own revolver in the girls' faces. "You stay put and keep your mouths shut."

Then he turned to his own people. "Time's tickin'. Let's get this done."

He flicked a gloved hand, signaling those of his men who were restraining the chaperones. In response, they struck the women with the butts of their pistols. One by one the chaperones slumped to the floor, unconscious.

Li shivered, crying silently.

The smaller man in the black duster looked at the one in the blue vest.

"Well," the blue-vested one said. "Get on with it. The six best ones."

The man in the black duster swaggered forward. He peered up and down the line of Chinese girls. Silently he pointed a worn glove at one of them—at Min.

Two of the masked men pulled Min out of line. One forced a thick strip of cloth into her mouth and tied it behind her head, while the other one roughly grasped her wrists and bound them with cord. Tears flowing down her cheeks, Min's fragile efforts to writhe free changed nothing.

Li's heart pounded even harder when they slipped a black cloth bag over Min's head and escorted her out through the kitchen. What were these men planning to do to her?

The one in the black duster was still staring at the kitchen, even after the other two had led Min out.

Grasping the small man's shoulder, the one with the blue vest said in a hoarse whisper, "We don't have time for this. Hurry up and pick five more."

The choosing process was repeated. Ping was taken. Xia was chosen.

Li could hear her own pulse rushing in her ears. She felt as if she might pass out, but she hung on. Then the man pointed to her.

"Nooo," she moaned softly, tears running down her cheeks. Leather cord bit into her wrists as they bound her. Panic gripped her as the itchy black sack dropped over her head. A vice-like hand clamped the back of her neck and guided her through the kitchen out into the cool night air.

She sensed she was right beside a horse. Somebody grasped her foot. For an instant she was tempted to kick. But suddenly the image of Yan lying on the floor bleeding was all she could see.

Numbly she allowed one man to place her foot in a stirrup while another lifted her. When his hand slid to her rump, she hurried to sit in the saddle. Even more tears flowed.

The other girls were crying softly nearby.

Someone snagged her bound hands and lashed them to the saddle horn. She was now unquestionably their captive—powerless to fight back.

Another sound cut through her racing thoughts, faint at first, but growing louder—the sound of animated voices. Men speaking Mandarin. Was there any chance? Could they somehow overpower this gang of kidnappers?

She jumped involuntarily at the cough of first one shotgun, then another.

Several more shots rang out.

Shouts turned to screams and groans. The shooting stopped.

All around her, men rustled, hurrying, she gathered, to mount their horses. The horse next to her brushed her leg. With a jolt her own mount set off at a brisk walk. Apparently the whole band was now in motion. Rhythmic hoof-beats and creaking saddle leather were the only sounds remaining as she and her helpless friends were led away into the night.

CHAPTER NINETEEN

Emmett rode into Reno at that hour of the afternoon when the first few men begin to drift into their favorite watering holes to wash down the dust from a hard day's work. He wanted to size up the town, wanted to know whether Reno lay suffocating under the same blanket of fear that smothered Carson City.

The transcontinental railroad ran through Reno. Railroads themselves tended to make certain folk rich and influential. With that in mind, Emmett figured McIntosh and Blaylock couldn't be the only big men in town—powerful as they might be, running a string of high-end bed houses, saloons, and gaming parlors.

From first impressions, he considered the general appearance of Reno to be a little healthier than that of Carson City. Lots of folks were out along the streets. A man and a woman, arms loaded, were coming out of a dry goods store. Looked to be husband and wife. Comfortable with one another. An old codger was heading into a barber shop. Probably full of all kinds of vinegar. Three men in suits were standing on the front porch of a lawyer's office. The Smithson Hotel just ahead looked nice.

Not wanting to draw attention to himself by making the same block multiple times, Emmett tried to take in as much as he could on the first pass down each street. As he scanned the boardwalks for any familiar faces, one particular visage remained imprinted on his mind—Charlie Blaylock's.

A couple of riders coming up the street from the opposite direction gave him the once-over. Judging from their expressions and the way they carried themselves, they must've decided he was just another stranger passing through.

That's why I don't believe in dressing fancy, he thought. *Good boots and a reasonably new hat. But beyond that, ordinary works best.*

Emmett noted that, unlike Carson City, Reno had a sheriff's office. And he found a town marshal's office too, just two blocks farther down the same street. As far as he could see—and he was trying hard to see just about everything—there were no roving bands of gunslicks swaggering around Reno like the ones he'd encountered down in the capital. Lucian McIntosh and Seth Blaylock must've preferred to keep their protection closer to their homesteads.

He'd just about made up his mind to ride out of the city and report back to his compadres when a fellow loping along the boardwalk caught his attention.

His chest tightened. *Looks an awful lot like Charlie Blaylock. And he's by himself.*

Emmett angled his horse toward a scene of everyday activity on the opposite side of the street. A store clerk and his customer were loading supplies from the mercantile onto a buckboard wagon. Emmett dismounted as close to the pair as he could without being in their way and tossed his horse's reins around the hitching rail.

The whole time he kept his gaze fixed on the man he thought might be Blaylock. Walking as briskly as he could manage without calling undue attention to himself, he hurried up the street parallel to the man in brown. The hat sure looked a lot like the one Blaylock wore the day of the shooting down in Austin.

Now Emmett could see the fellow's profile. He was clean-shaven, not whiskered as Charlie Blaylock had been when he had bushwhacked Eli.

Emmett scanned the avenue in both directions. No bad eggs that he could spot.

He cut back across the street, now making a beeline for the suspect. Just about then, the fellow turned his gaze into the traffic. Not directly at Emmett— just a bit ahead of him. That was enough. No question—it was Charlie Blaylock.

A wave of guarded optimism swept over Emmett.

Blaylock trudged on along a stretch of boardwalk that led to the Hyperion Saloon. The saloon had to be Charlie's destination. Not much time to catch up to him before he'd pass through the swinging doors at the next street corner.

Emmett rested his hand on the grip of his Colt. He snatched a quick look around and picked up his pace.

Just a dozen steps more and he could discreetly shove the barrel of his revolver into the murderer's ribs. His heart raced.

Then Charlie Blaylock glanced over. Did a double-take. His jaw went slack, and he began to fumble for his own gun.

Emmett's was already drawn, but Charlie was only a step away from the saloon doors. Rather than face Emmett, he whirled and ducked into the Hyperion.

Dang it! Taking a shot at Blaylock as he turned his back would've been a bad choice. To some folks that might've looked like murder.

Pistol still in hand, Emmett pressed against the exterior wall of the saloon and eased over to the window. Before peering in, he stole another quick look at the street. No dithering now.

Through the window he spotted Charlie at the bar, Schofield in hand. His indistinct shouting spilled out of the nearby doors. The barkeeper—a burly fellow—pulled a shotgun from beneath the counter and turned for the front exit. On his way he waved to somebody Emmett couldn't see at that angle.

From Emmett's blind side, a hand clamped onto his shoulder. He recoiled and spun, ready to shoot.

It was a smallish fellow wearing spectacles. He let go of Emmett and showed his empty hands. "Come with me!" he said. "Quick!"

There was little time to weigh options. Emmett nodded once. "Lead on."

He followed hard on the man's heels as he dashed first down the alley between the Hyperion and a tobacco shop, then down another alley that ran the length of that city block.

At the far end, the wiry, spectacled man pushed open the back door to a tidy, white clapboard building. Emmett slipped in behind him and shut the door. Newspapers hung all around the room. Others lay folded on tables. Still others filled floor-to-ceiling shelves.

Emmett's rescuer wiped his forehead, took a few deep breaths, then said, "Welcome to the *Reno Register*—best newspaper in town."

Before Emmett could respond, the fellow added, "Mister, you pull something like that again in Reno, and you'll likely be cut down in about two shakes."

"Where'd you come from? Why'd you stop me?" Emmett asked.

The man took off his glasses and wiped them with a handkerchief while he talked. "I just dropped off a stack of the afternoon edition at Dick Kimble's mercantile. I came out just in time to see you lighting off, following somebody at quite a clip."

So much for being discreet, Emmett thought.

The *Reno Register* man continued, "The reporter in me said to follow you for a bit. See what you were up to. Along the way, I spotted Charlie Blaylock across the street."

"Wait a minute. You know Charlie Blaylock? He's only been here a few days at most."

The newspaperman nodded. "Saw Seth Blaylock giving him the grand tour of town. Overheard him introducing Charlie to some friends as his brother. So just now when I noticed it was Seth Blaylock's brother you were after—"

"You risked your neck to pull me out of the line of fire. But how'd you know I wouldn't shoot you before turning my gun on Charlie?"

"History's taught me," the newspaperman said, "if somebody's in cahoots with a Blaylock, he's probably on the wrong side of the law. You chasing down Charlie'd put you on the right side of the law…most likely."

Emmett pulled back the lapel of his vest and showed the newspaper fellow the Texas Ranger badge pinned to his shirt.

"Had a hunch you might be wearing one of those…from one jurisdiction or another."

"Charlie Blaylock's a fugitive—a murderer."

"I'm not surprised. Seems to run in the family."

"Knowing as much, you took a big gamble."

"No love lost between me and Seth Blaylock—nor between me and Lucian McIntosh. By the bye, Stanley Cromarty's the name." He stuck out his hand.

"Emmett Strong. Much obliged, Mr. Cromarty."

They shook.

Emmett glanced through the doorway leading to the front office. "If anybody saw you pull me away from that little exchange out there—"

"Yep," Cromarty said. "This is just a quick stop. I'm going to send you packing now that you've caught your breath."

"Even so, won't they show up here any minute? And won't they come down on you with a heavy hand?"

"Nope, they won't touch me. I'm a regular thorn in their side."

Emmett tilted his head. "Now that's a story I'd like to hear."

"Wish we had time, Mr. Strong, but I'm afraid you need to move along now."

"Left my horse over by the mercantile."

"I'll send someone for it. Deliver it to you over at the livery stable. You'll be safe there till nightfall. Then you'd best hightail it out of town."

"I don't suppose you could meet me outside of Reno somewhere to fill me in on the Blaylocks. I don't have any business with McIntosh."

Cromarty seemed to ignore Emmett's request. He stepped to the back door, cracked it open, and strained to see what he could. "Looks OK, but give me a second." He slipped outside.

When he came back in he said, "You just hurry along the alley to your left. You'll likely smell the livery stable before you get there. Let yourself in through the back gate. Look for a big redheaded fellow—goes by Bridger. Tell him I sent you."

"What about filling me in on the Blaylocks?" Emmett asked, hand on the door.

"I'll get you an answer by nightfall."

Emmett tugged on the brim of his hat, then dashed out and down the alley.

—⁓—

Bridger himself, the strapping fellow who ran the livery stable, went and fetched Emmett's horse.

"They're crawlin' all over town, still tryin' to find you," Bridger said. "Asked me a dozen times whose horse this was and why I was takin' it over here to the stable."

"What'd you tell 'em?" Emmett asked.

"Said it belonged to a miner from Virginia City, a fella who was late for his train to San Francisco a couple hours ago."

Emmett glanced at the big barn door on the street side of the building. "I was really hoping to hear something from Mr. Cromarty before I cut dirt."

Bridger rubbed the mustang's muzzle and handed the reins to Emmett. "Oh, I saw him."

"Everything OK?"

"Oddly enough, he don't think anybody saw him pull you into the alley—not anybody that matters anyway."

"That's good news. By any chance did he give you a message for me?"

Bridger said, "Matter of fact…" He pulled a piece of folded newsprint from his shirt pocket. "You best tuck that away and read it later."

Emmett took the paper. "I'm beholden to you, Bridger."

The big man shook his head. "Not at all."

Emmett stepped into the stirrup.

"Now when I throw that big door open," Bridger said, "you'd better ride like hell—straight out the street in front of you. Don't look back till you've put a good two miles behind you. I know this paint can do it." He grabbed the door handle and nodded. "Good luck."

Bridger drew back the barn door, and Emmett gave his gelding the spurs. He reined left into the street, ready to run the pinto like a bat outta hell, when who should he spot straight ahead but Charlie Blaylock and two other seedy hombres.

CHAPTER TWENTY

O nly a block ahead, Charlie and his amigos were crossing the street on foot, pistols drawn, bobbing to catch a glimpse through the window of some shop or office.

Emmett pulled back on the reins. He kept his gaze on the trio as he wheeled his horse.

One of the three—a fellow with a thick mustache—looked Emmett's way. "Hey!" he shouted, jabbing his weapon up the street. "Is that him?"

Charlie spun. "Sure 'nough. Get him."

Emmett gave his mount the rowels—going the wrong direction, but that was of little concern at the moment.

Three shots sounded before he could turn a corner. Once he did, he rose in his stirrups and yelled into his horse's ear, "C'mon, Gordo. Gimme all you've got." The pinto dug in and lit a shuck down the street. Emmett didn't look back.

—m—

It took an extra two hours for Emmett to put some distance between himself and town and then to pick his way south and east to where he'd left Juanito and Sikes. He did his best to ride over rock or through water where he could—anything to slow down those who might try to cut sign and follow him.

At last he arrived at his compadres' campfire.

"Beginning to wonder about you," Sikes said.

"You won't believe this," Emmett said as he swung down. "But I ended up having not one but two brushes with Charlie Blaylock himself."

Juanito's eyes widened. "What?"

Emmett summarized the missed opportunity to nab Charlie right outside the Hyperion Saloon, the newspaperman's intervention, and getting shot at by Blaylock and his two pardners on the way out of Reno.

"So close, *hermano.*"

Emmett shrugged. "It's a start. Laid eyes on Charlie. Maybe found us an ally. Speaking of which…" He pulled the folded piece of newsprint from his vest pocket. "When I asked for word on the Blaylocks, Cromarty—the newspaper fella—gave me this."

"You suppose we have enough time to take a look at it now?" Sikes asked. "Or should we put more distance between ourselves and Reno first?"

"Let's take a quick peek. May help us decide whether to stay close or fall back."

It turned out there were two sheets of paper from Cromarty—a piece of printed newspaper folded around a sheet of plain white paper. On the plain white paper, Cromarty had sketched a crude map of the area from San Francisco to Virginia City and down to the town of Genoa, several miles south of Carson City. To make out the details, Emmett held the map as near to the fire as he dared. "Interesting," he said.

"Well, don't be so mysterious about it, man," Sikes said. "What's it say?"

"It looks like he's listed—burg by burg—the names of the saloons, gaming parlors, and brothels the McIntoshes own."

"What's that got to do with us?" Juanito asked.

Emmett shook his head. "There are question marks beside some of them. Maybe Cromarty's not sure for a fact who owns those."

On the other side of the campfire, Sikes paced back and forth. "I agree with Juanito. This doesn't seem especially helpful—thus far, anyway."

"Over here on the edge of the paper, he made a little chart. Lucian McIntosh at the top, parentheses, Reno. Beneath that is Thaddeus McIntosh, parentheses, Carson City—"

"And that, we already know," Sikes said.

"Will you give me a goll-darn minute, Sikes?" Emmett snapped. He muttered to himself over the paper for a bit, then said, "OK, Cromarty put Seth Blaylock's name just below and to the side of Lucian McIntosh. There's a line connecting the two. And beside Seth Blaylock, it says in parentheses 'procurement,' with another question mark."

Grit crunched beneath Sikes's feet as he continued his pacing.

"Anything about Charlie Blaylock?" Juanito asked, his voice tentative.

Again Emmett shook his head. "I'm obliged to Cromarty for collaring me this afternoon. May have saved my hide. But I thought the little newspaperman was gonna offer me something useful—information that might help us make another run at Eli's murderer." He looked up and sighed. "So you're both right. If we were here to police the doings of the McIntoshes and Seth Blaylock, all this might be helpful. But that's not why we've put a thousand miles between ourselves and Texas, is it?" He folded the papers as they had been and tucked them back into his pocket.

"If I may…" Sikes said, now rocking on his heels.

Emmett spread his hands and nodded.

"Perhaps the newspaperman believes the only way we're going to take Charlie Blaylock away from here is to first bring down the McIntoshes and Seth Blaylock."

"Plan on buying land and settling here in Nevada? Because bringing down men like McIntosh and Seth Blaylock takes time."

Juanito rubbed his eyes. "And bed houses are popular places with hombres like miners—lonely men far away from home. They would probably take Blaylock and McIntosh's side. Join the fight against us."

"Perhaps," Sikes added, "Cromarty understands that there's no real law in Reno—only the token sheriff and marshal that McIntosh appoints."

"And he hopes we'll stay and play the role of the real law?" Emmett said. "No, thanks."

The only sound for a few moments was the snap and pop of the campfire.

"So what now?" Juanito asked.

"We can't stay in Reno," Emmett said. "By now Charlie Blaylock will have let Seth know I've followed him up here. Only a matter of time before the Blaylocks, the Reno McIntoshes, and the Carson City McIntoshes get to talking. Once they compare notes, they'll all realize I'm not up here alone."

"After yesterday we can't stay in Carson City either."

"Or that little town down beside Washoe Lake," Sikes added.

Emmett stood up and stretched his saddle-weary back. "So we fall back to Virginia City, make a new plan, and try one more time."

Sikes cocked his head. "Just one more time?"

"Each attempt has got to count. The more shots we take, the more we expose ourselves to the Blaylocks and McIntoshes. And we didn't exactly bring along an army."

Sikes untied his horse's reins. "If we use up all our chances and still haven't caught Blaylock, I have a feeling you'll always regret coming such a long way for nothing."

"It won't be for nothing."

"That's right," Juanito said as he stepped into his stirrup. "There's that pretty little Chinese girl in Virginia City, the one that—"

"Like I told you before, Juanito, shut your big bazoo, would you? That's not what I meant."

Juanito chuckled and winked.

Emmett threw the stirrup up onto the seat of his saddle. "When it comes to justice, all we can do is plan well and try hard. Pray for the good Lord to bring about the right results."

"Strong," Sikes said, "you always talk about justice. It never gets personal for you? Even when it's got to do with your own brother? Your own wife? You don't ever hanker for good old-fashioned revenge?"

Emmett paused from cinching up his saddle. "Believe me, temptation arises often enough."

CHAPTER TWENTY-ONE

The leather wingback chair Lucian McIntosh occupied groaned as he shifted his weight. He exhaled a cloud of cigar smoke and turned back to Seth Blaylock, shaking his head.

"How many did you take, son?" Incredulity darkened his tone.

"Six, sir," Seth answered.

McIntosh threw his arms wide. "Well, why didn't you go on and take every damn female in Chinatown? What's that? Maybe two, three hundred?"

Seth stood, hands clasped behind his back, in the center of the plush Oriental rug that filled most of McIntosh's study.

"One or two at a time," McIntosh said. "Out-of-the-way towns. That's our style."

"That's what I usually do," Seth said, his face tinged red. "You know that, sir."

McIntosh shook a finger. He took a breath, about to speak, but he stopped. After reconsidering his words, he started again. "You must've made one hell of a racket. How many of our men in the raidin' party?"

"Fifteen, sir."

"Fifteen!" McIntosh felt his neck tighten beneath his crisp white collar. "You took fifteen men ridin' right into Virginia City. Did you lose your mind, son? Must've sounded for all the world like Sherman's March to the Sea."

Again Seth was silent.

"And nobody saw you?"

"Only ones saw us were some Chinese when we were just fixin' to ride out again. Had to shoot 'em, sir."

"Just Chinese fellas."

"Yes, sir."

"Well, at least you got that part right." McIntosh brooded. He struggled to bridle his anger. Even if Seth was a favorite, McIntosh didn't appreciate carelessness.

"Seth, I don't know how else to put it. That raid was too audacious. In too big a city. And too damn close to home.

"It won't happen again, Mr. McIntosh."

"You're damn right it won't. You're better'n that, son." He modulated his tone down a notch. "You've got a lot of years of experience doin' this."

Seth ran the back of his hand across the tip of his nose. "Yes, sir."

The grandfather clock ticked loudly in the heavy silence.

"Well, go ahead and pour yourself a brandy," McIntosh said. "You ain't lost your standin' with me because of this one bad decision. But I want you to know I sure as hell ain't pleased."

Seth picked up the decanter from the mahogany side table and poured himself a half snifter.

"You're well aware that these things don't always go the way we plan 'em. Had but one little thing gone wrong, you'd have been knee-deep in cow pies— even if it was only Chinese girls you took. Virginia City don't take kindly to our organization. It's the one town out here that don't."

Drink in hand, Seth returned to the carpet. McIntosh gestured for him to take the matching wingback chair. A window draped in deep-green velvet separated them.

"Mr. McIntosh, maybe that's why I decided to do somethin' so boldfaced. Maybe it's because the big bugs in Virginia City are the only ones that don't give us—you, rather—the respect you deserve."

McIntosh waved his hand. "I don't need their approval."

"You've done just as well for yourself as any of them dandies down there," Seth said. "Better'n most. Don't seem right that they won't treat you as an equal."

"Scared of the competition, son," McIntosh said. "Nothin' more than that. They're just scared I'll run better establishments than they do and eventually drive 'em out of business." He coughed hard. "But that ain't the point. We go irritatin' Virginia City now, and they might not leave well enough alone. Before you know it, we'll have a little war goin' on between us—a shootin' war. And we don't need that right now."

"Yes, sir. But you're not worried about the Chinese retaliatin', are you, sir?"

"'Course not." McIntosh adjusted his necktie. "Chinese ain't got no legal standin'. Might be mad as hornets, but they'd be too scared to strike back—even if they knew who to strike back at. Afraid it'd bring the government down on 'em."

"There's that too, sir. They ain't got a clue who we are."

"Just the same," McIntosh said. "You're gonna have to resume exercisin' the kind of caution and judgment that made you as good as you are at what you do. Are we clear on this?"

Seth nodded sharply. "Yes, sir."

"Well then, let's see them China girls. I wanna inspect the merchandise. See if it was worth the gamble—just this once."

"Yes, sir." Seth got up and headed to the door.

Ettie was waiting just outside. "Bring 'em on in," he told her.

Seconds later, Ettie and Seth had the six young women standing side by side on the carpet in the middle of Lucian McIntosh's study.

Lucian rose from his chair and walked up and down the line, eyeing each girl head to toe. The Chinese beauties, most still sniffling, looked down at the floor. McIntosh stopped in front of the third in line and lifted her chin with his thumb and forefinger.

"This one's real pretty, ain't she? Delicate like."

Seth and Ettie remained silent.

"A lot of China girls are too skinny, but I think some of these're fillin' out real nice…though it's hard to tell, their clothes bein' so loose fittin' and all."

"You want 'em stripped?" Seth asked coolly.

At that, all but one of the girls began to cry openly, holding their arms across their chests, clutching their sleeves, doing what little they could to avoid being disrobed and exposed. The only one not openly weeping still kept her arms tightly folded. She wouldn't meet McIntosh's gaze.

"No," he said. "Don't need to strip 'em just now. I can see they'll do fine."

He turned to Ettie. "You can give 'em a thorough look-over in private. Be sure none of 'em has any injuries…or, heaven forbid, defects."

"Yes, Mr. McIntosh," she said.

McIntosh moved to the one who wasn't sobbing aloud, though tears did glimmer on her cheeks. She alone wore her hair down—at least on one side.

"My, oh my," he said. "Even considerin' all the different exotics we try to provide for our clients, I'm not so sure I've ever seen one any prettier than this little devil."

He asked her, "You speaky English? Hmm?"

She turned her head to the side.

"What's your name? Hmm?"

She sniffed and tugged her black-and-gold smock tighter. "I speak English," she said. "My name is Li Xu."

McIntosh looked up at Seth, then at Ettie. "I wanna keep this one for myself."

Looking back at Li Xu, he said, "How's that sound, darlin'? Take good care of you here in the big house?"

Tears began to flow down her flushed cheeks. She put her hands to her face. Her shoulders shook as she wept silently.

McIntosh took a step back, then methodically eyed each of the six girls once again, pausing a little longer on one or another. "My, oh my," he repeated, nodding and chuckling quietly.

"OK, Ettie," he said, "take these girls to the guest house out back. Except maybe these two." He put his hands on the shoulders of Li Xu and the girl standing next to her. "Take these two up to the room by mine."

Ettie nodded. She and Seth guided the girls out into the hallway where two McIntosh gunmen waited.

"Seth, stay behind just a minute, would you?" McIntosh said. "And Ettie, you come right on back as soon as them girls are squared away. Tell Margaret to get 'em all some food, too."

Seth closed the door once again. "Yes, Mr. McIntosh."

"Son," McIntosh said, "I don't want to say anything that you might take as encouragement to ever try anything like this again." He drew on his cigar and exhaled. "But damn if they ain't the finest lookin' batch of doves a man could come up with in one haul."

"I thought you'd like 'em, sir."

"I've got a notion I may sell the four I'm not gonna keep for myself. They'll fetch top dollar from some of my business associates. Ought to be right popular over in some of the cow towns out along the railroad."

"Any special instructions then? Until you decide?"

Sweeping his arm toward the south-facing window, McIntosh said, "I'd like you to take 'em to the Gilded Lily down in Genoa."

"All right, sir."

"Tuck 'em away out of sight—whole time you're movin' 'em and once you get 'em there, too. I don't want 'em used down there. Not by Frank Martin. Not by nobody. Understood?"

"Yes, sir."

"These're strictly for sale by me…or until I decide otherwise."

"Understood, sir."

"And I want you and Ettie to stay down there in Genoa with 'em for a few days," he said. "Want you to lay low for a bit till we see how things settle out. If all remains quiet in relation to Virginia City, I'll send for you."

"Will do."

"Oh, and Seth, take the back road. West of Washoe Lake, west of Minden. Stay off the main roads."

"I will, sir. Want me to leave tomorrow?"

"The day after," McIntosh said, tossing the butt of his cigar into the fireplace. "In case I decide to send the other two on down with 'em."

Just then someone knocked.

McIntosh nodded. Seth went to the door. It was Ettie.

"That'll be all then, Seth," McIntosh said. "Let me have a word with Ettie."

Once he and Ettie were alone, he said, "They may not feel much like eatin', but I'd like you to encourage the two upstairs to take a little nourishment."

Ettie met McIntosh's gaze. He found her as lovely in form and face as any female he'd ever encountered. Yet for some reason he'd always been content to leave her alone. His feelings toward her were unique—somehow vaguely paternal.

He sometimes found it difficult to read Ettie. She didn't seem to fear him as many women did. And never did she try using her feminine wiles to advance her standing with him. She usually remained cool and aloof. But loyal…trustworthy. Like Seth. He was glad Seth and Ettie had each other.

"After they've had somethin' to eat," he said, "see to it that they get a good bath. If they look clean to you, I'll probably be enjoyin' their company tonight."

She compressed her lips and nodded. "Yes, sir," she said softly, breaking off her gaze.

"That'll be all, then."

CHAPTER TWENTY-TWO

The sound of the door locking and the key being removed seemed so final to Li Xu, as though her fate were sealed. The room where she had been left was dimly lit but well appointed: one narrow bed, a dresser with a wash basin, soft carpet, and the same dark-green velvet curtains that she had seen in the big room downstairs.

As comforting as it was to have Ping with her, she'd rather have suffered this nightmare alone if only her best friend could be free.

Ping stood, arms folded tightly across her chest, nearly frozen by fear.

Li took her by the shoulders and looked her in the eye. "I will not let that man have us tonight, Ping. Do you hear me? I promise you that."

Quivering, Ping clung to Li.

"Did you hear me, Ping?"

She nodded. After a few minutes' crying, she managed to ask, "How...will you stop him?"

Li wiped away her own tears, then took stock of the room for anything she might use as an improvised weapon. Perhaps the curtain cord. But how far would she and Ping get once she'd strangled that McIntosh beast?

She gave Ping a squeeze, then had her sit on the bed while she checked the dresser drawers. They were empty. She looked under the bed. Nothing.

Frustrated, she lifted her hand habitually to her head—and touched her ornamental hairpin. She could jam its sharp tip into that fat man's neck if he tried to have her. But that still wouldn't get her and Ping out of the house and home free.

Suddenly another desperate thought came to her. She sat beside her friend.

"Ping," she whispered. "Do men want a woman when..."

Ping tilted her head and waited. "When what?"

"You know, when we're having our womanly troubles."

Ping's face still showed confusion. Then her eyes widened. "Oh, that...But I'm not having mine right now. Are you?"

Li Xu shook her head. "But nobody here knows that."

She pulled the pin from her hair. It was about four inches long, a quarter inch in diameter, and fairly sharp at the point. As quickly as she could, she loosened her wide-legged trousers and lowered them.

Ping grasped Li's wrist. "Li, what in the world are you—"

"Shhh! We need blood. We're desperate here." As Li slipped off her underwear, she said, "I'm sorry to do this in front of you."

Carefully she arranged the underwear on the bed and then sat on them. She glanced at Ping, who had put her hand to her heart and averted her eyes.

"Don't," Ping hissed. She turned back and tried to grab Li's wrists again. "It's not worth this."

"Let go," Li said. "It's not what you think."

Her friend at last sat still, though she looked at Li dubiously.

Li grasped a pinch of flesh midway up her inner thigh, drew a deep breath, and then pushed the hairpin deep into it and all the way through.

Ping gasped and gripped Li's sleeve.

Tears came to Li's eyes. She bit her lip, refusing to cry out.

The blood that came out from the two pencil-thick holes ran down onto the underwear she was sitting on—right where it might have gone had she been caught unprepared for the onset of her monthly troubles. *Just a little more*, she thought. Then she clamped her hand onto her thigh to trap the flow.

"Ping, quick," she said, "give me your underwear, too. Hurry."

Even in the dim candlelight her friend's face was pale. But she followed Li Xu's instructions.

"Now," Li said, "pull the waist cord out of my underwear, so I can tie it around where I'm bleeding."

Ping hurriedly extracted not only Li's waist tape but also her own, and tied both snugly around the wounds.

Once both women's undergarments had been stained with Li's blood, they hastily pulled them and their trousers back on.

Li swallowed. She felt woozy.

"What happens if they see the punctures?" Ping asked.

"This is all I could think of to do. Don't ask me how I even thought to do this."

Ping hugged her. "Thank you, Li-Li. I would have died already if not for you."

Several minutes later, the key rattled in the lock and the door eased open. The attractive woman in men's clothing let herself in.

Li Xu squeezed Ping and prayed that their ruse would work.

The woman closed the door behind her. Much to Li's surprise, she didn't begin with a string of cold instructions. Instead, squatting beside the bed she placed a hand on Ping's knee and said, "I know how frightened you must be." The corners of her mouth were downturned.

She's not simply acting, Li thought.

"Nevertheless," the woman said, "we can't fight Mr. McIntosh...not now."

The woman stared at the floor for several silent moments, then said, "My name is Ettie. I'm to be sure you get cleaned up." She finally met Li's gaze.

"Miss Ettie," Li said, shaking her head and speaking softly. "That man can't have us tonight."

Ettie squeezed Li's hand. "I'm afraid he *will* have you, if that's what he decides he wants. That's the way of it."

Li still shook her head, "I don't think he will want us tonight. Both Ping and I, we have started our womanly troubles, and...it's a lot. I think it's the fright that's making it so much."

Ettie frowned. "You're not making this up, are you?" She looked each girl full in the face. "Because if you are, it'll only make things far worse for you both—believe me."

Li said, "May I stand up for a moment?"

Ettie stood and took a step back.

When Li Xu got up, there was blood on the bedcover. "It started when I was on the horse. I was afraid I would get some on the man's rug downstairs. I'm sorry."

Ettie put her hands on her hips and glanced toward the door and back. She shook her head. "He'll want proof."

Ping spoke timidly, "If you'll turn around, I will take off my underclothes and give them for proof."

"I'm sorry," Ettie said. "I can't turn around. For me to go tell this to Mr. McIntosh…I'm very sorry, but I have to see for certain." She bit her lip and put her hand to her forehead.

Li and Ping looked at one another, turned back to back, and lowered their trousers. Li made sure to let one pants leg drop lower than the other. She grasped the waist of her trousers just where the drawstrings bound her pierced thigh.

"OK," Ettie said, "Enough. You can pull them up."

When Li looked at her, Ettie's eyes were red and tear rimmed.

"I'll tell Mr. McIntosh," Ettie said. "If he demands proof, I'll have to come back for your bloomers. Meanwhile, you wait here. I'll send Margaret with some soup for you. You should eat. And I'll send Sarah Ann with water and towels so you can wash."

She turned and faced the window for several seconds. Li thought she heard a sniff before Ettie marched out of the room and locked the door behind her.

Ping turned to Li Xu and hugged her tight.

—⁓—

No sooner had Ettie gotten to the landing at the base of the stairs than a tremendous commotion arose at the front door.

"Well, tell him I've got to speak to him directly," came a man's troubled voice. Ettie peeked into the entryway and saw that it was Charlie Blaylock.

"I'll get him," she told the two gunhands in the foyer.

She hurried to the parlor door and knocked firmly.

"Come!" boomed Lucian McIntosh's voice.

Ettie barely had the door ajar when McIntosh roared, "What the hell is all that pandemonium?"

She looked straight at Seth. "It's Charlie. Says he needs to talk to you immediately."

Seth furrowed his brows.

McIntosh rose and glowered at Seth. "I swear! That brother of yours!"

The men tromped out to the entryway, one behind the other.

Before either could say a word, Charlie began sputtering. "He's here, Seth. In Reno. Nearly shot me in the back. Right outside the Hyperion."

Seth opened his mouth to speak, but McIntosh growled, "Who're you talkin' about, Charlie?"

"Damn Texas law dog, that's who."

Just then two of McIntosh's hands stepped in through the open front door. The shorter one with the brushy mustache said, "We combed the town for him, Mr. McIntosh. Three solid hours. Had him in our sights at the end, but he was already on his horse. Gave us the slip."

"Hell's bells," McIntosh fumed. "It's always somethin' with this brother of yours, Seth."

"Why'd you come here and disturb Mr. McIntosh like this, Charlie?" Seth asked, clearly perturbed.

"Went to your place first, Seth. But o' course you weren't there."

"How many did you say there were?" McIntosh asked Charlie.

"I just saw the one. But he's that damned fast gun, and he was right there in my face before I turned around good. I got myself inside the saloon, and Ted Toler grabbed his scattergun. Zeke here"—Charlie tossed his chin toward the fellow with the brushy mustache—"he come runnin' to help, too. But he was gone by the time we got back out in the street."

"Looked for him a good three hours—"

McIntosh shoved a hand in Zeke's face. "Yes, yes, you told me. Three hours, then he got away."

Seth drew a breath to speak, but again McIntosh held out both arms. "Everybody just shut up!" He glared at Seth. "Take this brother of yours. Hide him at your place. And then when you go to Genoa day after tomorrow, take him with you. You, Ettie, Charlie—all three of you lay low down there a while."

Ettie felt a knot in her stomach. If telling McIntosh about the China girls was already going to be chancy, it might cost her skin now. She stared at Charlie—a hayseed next to McIntosh in his grand black suit and starched white shirt, and next to Seth in his new pinstriped trousers and silk vest. The thought of taking him with them down to Genoa made her cringe. Still, she could hardly wait to get away from Reno for several days.

McIntosh turned to Seth. "Go on. Take your brother home. Now."

Seth settled his hat on his head and gave a simple, "Yes, sir." He wasted no time in grabbing Charlie by the arm and pulling him out the front door.

McIntosh told Zeke and the others in the foyer, "Tomorrow mornin' early, let's get some men out on the streets. See what we can find out about that Texas lawman."

Each man mumbled, "Yes, sir!" in response.

By the time he turned to Ettie, McIntosh looked worn out. There were bags under his dark eyes. "Don't tell me you got trouble, too."

She stepped close to her boss and whispered what she had discovered about the Chinese girls.

His face reddened as he glared at her. He shook his head and proceeded to stomp his way up the stairs, all the while spouting about fornicating this and fornicating that.

At the top of the stairs, he paused and roared, "I'm goin' to try to get some sleep and put this fornicatin' day behind me. Don't nobody disturb me unless the fornicatin' house is on fire. And I damn well mean it!" He slammed his bedroom door behind him, rattling the entire wall.

CHAPTER TWENTY-THREE

The whole way from Reno back to Virginia City, Sikes and Juanito grew increasingly bold in their puckish provocation of Emmett.

He sighed and shook his head as they turned their horses onto Union Street and headed for Xu's Golden Dragon. "Gents, we came up here to arrest Charlie Blaylock, right?"

"Right," Sikes said.

"And the town where Charlie is—and those towns close by, too—have turned out to be less than hospitable, right?"

"Right."

"So we're pulling back to someplace safe."

Sikes was still grinning. "Makes sense. No place on earth safer than Virginia City."

"Except maybe Chinatown in Virginia City," Juanito said, matching Sikes's mischievous smile.

Emmett cut his eyes at his brother-in-law, then at the Englishman. "You hungry, Sikes?"

"Hungry as a Highland black bear."

"Have to eat somewhere. Why not Xu's?"

Juanito jumped back in. "Xu's magnificent San Francisco steaks. So that's the real reason we're coming back here, eh, *hermano*?"

"Safe place to reconsider how to take down Charlie Blaylock. Mouthwatering food. Should be answer enough. But there is one other thing."

Juanito leaned in his saddle so he could peer wide-eyed at Sikes. "Finally. He's going to admit the truth now."

"If you'll recall," Emmett said, his gaze fixed on the restaurant up the street, "Yong Xu was going to ask around about Seth Blaylock for us. Remember?"

"Right, that." Sikes turned to Juanito and knitted his eyebrows. "What do you suppose, amigo? Yong's going to fill us in, isn't he? The precise time and place where we can find the Blaylock brothers unarmed and unguarded. Next Thursday night. Taking tea and cake with the Methodist Ladies' Society." He gave a hearty laugh.

"*Ay, sí,*" Juanito said. "So we can walk right in and join them. Offer Charlie a cordial invitation to come along with us back to Texas."

Emmett rolled his eyes.

"*Hermano,*" Juanito said, now laughing aloud, "it just does my heart good to see you alive again."

They were almost to the Golden Dragon. Emmett frowned. "Strange," he said, sniffing the air.

"What?" Juanito asked.

"Wind's blowing our way, but there's no smell of cooking. First time we came, I distinctly remember smelling the food before we even got here."

"Sign in the window." Juanito pointed.

Emmett swung down and read the heavy paper notice—at least the part in English: CLOSED UNTIL FURTHER NOTICE.

He went to the window. Through the glass he saw Yong Xu and his wife alone, side by side at a table, weeping. His eyes swept the dining room for Li, but he saw no sign of her. A sense of dread came over him.

Glancing back at Sikes and Juanito, he said, "Trouble of some kind for Yong and his wife."

Juanito's demeanor was sober now. "Should we…?"

Emmett rapped lightly on the window.

Yong Xu looked up. Recognizing Emmett, he rose from the table, drying his eyes with his sleeve. His wife scurried away to the kitchen, head lowered.

Juanito and Sikes swung down and tethered their horses.

Yong Xu didn't open the door wide. He didn't invite the men in. His caution at the door and the pained expression on his face stood in stark contrast to the affable exuberance he had displayed the last time they'd met.

"We hate to trouble you at a bad time," Emmett said. "Is there anything we can do? Or should we come back another day?"

Their Chinese friend was slow to answer. He glanced at Juanito and Sikes, then studied Emmett's face. Drawing his sleeve across his eyes again, he said, "Yes, come in, please." He held out a hand toward a table. "Have a seat."

Emmett, Juanito, and Sikes took off their hats and sat. Awkward silence followed.

"Yong...what happened?" Emmett finally asked.

The Chinese gentleman looked up and away, his eyes puffy and red. He sniffed and began slowly. "The night before last...our daughters were gathered over at Zhang's Restaurant. Just like every Tuesday night..."

Emmett's blood ran cold. Something had happened to Li Xu.

"From what the girls' mothers said," Yong Xu continued, "it must have been twenty men. They kicked in the doors. They shot Yan Wu in the back... lovely Yan Wu." He fought back tears.

Emmett could now hear Mrs. Xu wailing in the kitchen. He swallowed hard and fought back his own tears.

Once Yong Xu had regained his composure, he said, "They left Yan to die. They struck the girls' mothers in the head and left them unconscious. And they stole..." His tears now flowed bitterly.

Emmett couldn't look at Juanito or Sikes. Something between fury and despair was ripping at his chest. He forced a calm, steady voice. "Take your time, Yong Xu."

Yong Xu nodded and through more tears at last said, "They stole Li-Li and five other girls—all beautiful, sweet young women."

"White men? Chinese men?"

"White men."

"Any idea who?"

Yong Xu shook his head.

Emmett gripped the edges of the table. "They just rode in, took the girls, and rode out with them?"

"A few of our men tried to stop them out behind Zhang's place. The kidnappers had shotguns. There was nothing our men could do."

"Which way'd they go when they rode out?"

Yong pointed toward the hills to the north.

"What'd the city marshal have to say?" Emmett asked.

"He listened to us." Yong Xu kneaded a napkin and stared at the tabletop. "But he said he couldn't offer much hope for help. I don't think he plans to do anything."

Emmett pictured a cluster of Chinese men standing in the marshal's office, hats in hand. He had to agree with Yong Xu's supposition. They probably wouldn't get any help from the lawmen around here.

"And if your men do anything on their own?"

Yong Xu's gaze met his. "We're not citizens. Everywhere we settle, others—especially other new immigrants—stir up opinion against us. They want us sent away. Everybody thinks we're going to take away their jobs. There's already a rumor that the government is about to cut off all Chinese immigration to America."

From what he had read, Emmett knew Yong Xu wasn't exaggerating.

The Chinaman sighed heavily. "When Chinese in other towns have demanded fair treatment, it has often gone badly. People set fire to the Chinatown up in Truckee—more than once."

"So trying to track down and rescue the girls yourselves…" Emmett said. He was already piecing together ideas about going with the Chinese—or even going by himself—to find Li Xu and get her back.

"Other immigrants will probably twist the story and somehow make it seem that we Chinese are just stirring up trouble, regardless of what truly happened to our daughters. It could lead to suffering for all the Chinese people of Virginia City."

Emmett glanced at Sikes.

"Don't look at me," Sikes said. "I may be new to America, but I'd never…"

"Didn't figure you would," Emmett said.

"I wouldn't put it past a lot of the miners, though." Sikes shifted in his chair. "Desperately struggling to scratch a living in a new land. Banding together, trying to make sure that if anybody loses everything, it won't be them."

What could he do to help rescue the girls? And to curtail any further threat to Yong Xu and his people? Emmett thought about the Texas Ranger badge beneath his vest. It had to be worth something up here. But even if it wasn't…

He grasped Yong Xu's shoulder. "Let me at least go talk to the marshal for you."

Yong Xu lifted his hands and dropped them to the tabletop.

Emmett eyed his pardners. Questions flooded his mind. Chief among them was whether he could put the pursuit of Charlie Blaylock on hold till after he helped Yong Xu get his daughter back. But that wasn't his decision to make alone.

Surveying the empty café and recalling the lively evening he and his friends had enjoyed there just a few nights prior, he now felt an empty space in his chest. The heart of that liveliness—Li Xu—was gone. And he prayed that at that very moment she and her friends were OK.

"I'll be back," he said. "Give me a bit to talk with some folks."

"You don't know this city…this country," Xu protested through tear-rimmed eyes.

"We won't add to your troubles, Yong Xu. I promise."

CHAPTER TWENTY-FOUR

Leaving Xu's place, Emmett and his compañeros made their way over to C Street. Out in front of the Lucky Strike Saloon, they held a quiet pow-wow. Juanito and Sikes would wait at the watering hole while Emmett paid the city marshal a visit. He aimed to find out what, if anything, the local law would do on behalf of the kidnapped girls and their families.

On his way to the marshal's office, it struck him as either odd or admirable that the Presbyterian church in Virginia City was located right there on C Street, mere steps from numerous establishments dedicated to gratifying the various passions of the flesh. He paused in front of the clapboard-sided house of worship and deliberated. After casting a glance in the direction of the marshal's office, he turned and bounded up the church steps, removing his hat and smoothing his hair as he went.

"Hello," he called into the empty sanctuary.

Footsteps resounded from deep within the building. A middle-aged gentleman with a trim beard appeared from a doorway to the left of the pulpit. As he rounded the pews and headed down the center aisle, he adjusted his vest and smiled. "How can I help you?"

"You the pastor here?" Emmett asked.

"I am. Ezra Pine's the name." He extended a hand.

Emmett clasped it and appreciated the firm grip. "I'm Emmett Strong. Do you have a few minutes, Reverend?"

"Sure." He gestured toward the last pew. "Have a seat. What's on your mind?"

The two men sat.

Emmett placed his hat on his knee. He worked its brim between his fingers as he gathered his thoughts. "You've got your work cut out for you, Reverend."

"Meaning?"

"Lot of evil in this world."

"True…" The minister nodded. "But there's a lot of good too. God hasn't lost control of things. Some particular evil troubling you, Mr. Strong?"

Emmett sighed. "Couple items."

"Go on."

"I've got to know where you stand on a matter before I proceed."

"And what matter would that be?"

Emmett looked Reverend Pine in the eye. "God created all people, right?"

"Of course."

"Irish folk, Chinese folk, regular American folk—we're all human beings created in the image of the Almighty, correct?"

Reverend Pine narrowed his eyes. "The thing that's troubling you… It wouldn't have anything to do with the abduction of those Chinese girls, would it?"

Emmett tilted his head. He hadn't expected word to have spread much, if any, outside the Chinese community. This minister certainly had his finger on the pulse of the town. And he read people well too. Both impressed Emmett.

"I have no idea how you divined it, but that's precisely what's troubling me."

"It was all the buzz yesterday," Pine said. "When the Chinese elders went down to the marshal's office, the usual rabble-rousers lost no time getting word out that the Chinamen are up to no good—making unfounded accusations."

"The Chinese've made no accusations at all," Emmett said firmly. "They have no idea who's behind the kidnapping."

"And how would you know that? You're new to town, aren't you, Mr. Strong?"

Emmett placed his hat down on the pew and turned toward the minister. "Like I said a minute ago, before I lay everything out, I need to know where you stand."

Pine showed his palms. "Fair enough. Where I stand on…"

"You said Chinese folk are created in the image of God. Same as you and me?"

"Yes. Absolutely," the minister answered without hesitation.

"Then why can't they get the same consideration—and protection—that people like you and me get?"

This time the reverend didn't answer so quickly. "Now that…is a great evil."

"You seem to know this town well, Reverend Pine. Me going to talk to the marshal about the abduction—a waste of my time?"

The reverend's gaze dropped to the floor. "Probably so, though I could be wrong."

"But in the past…"

"From what I gather," Pine said, "Marshal Pruett has never lifted a finger to help the Chinese. A few times folks have gone in and torn up Chinese restaurants, stores, laundries. Torn them up pretty bad. As far as I know, he's never given a minute of his time to investigate even one of those crimes."

"Any regular citizens ever try to give the Chinese a hand?"

"Once again—best I know—only a little charity here and there. Maybe a little money to help fix up their busted-up places. Maybe a few supplies from the mercantile store."

Emmett nodded. He sat in silence for a long minute, trying to frame his thoughts. Then he leaned forward. "Now I'm gonna get real personal," he said. "I care what the good Lord says about this. And I need to know."

Tilting his head, Pine invited Emmett to go on.

"Is it wrong for a white man to be in love with—maybe even to marry—a woman who's not white? A Chinese woman?"

The reverend looked off toward the gothic window and rubbed his beard. When he looked back he said, "It all goes back to Babel."

"The tower of Babel," Emmett said.

"That's right. Before that, all mankind spoke the same language. There was only one race—the human race."

"And then?"

"Certain men led other men—perhaps most men—to reject God, their maker and sustainer. They wanted a religion of man…to do what they wanted, how they wanted, whenever they wanted. That tower was a fist in God's face. It was a temple to man, a declaration that man was his own god."

"So I've heard," Emmett said.

"So God put the brakes on the building of the tower—"

"Made 'em speak different languages."

"True. But remember this: At first they were all the same kind of people. One race. Just speaking different tongues all of a sudden."

Emmett nodded. "So how'd they get to be Chinese and African and Indian?"

"People of each new language went to live apart from the folks of the other languages. For a long time they intermarried only within their own language group—or pretty much so."

"And?"

"Well, let seven or eight generations go by that way, and all the folks of that language end up with a unique look about them. Similar to each other, yet different from the people of the other language groups. Not to mention developing unique traditions and customs because of where they lived. Their own songs and stories…"

"So that was the start of our so-called races," Emmett said.

The pastor nodded. "As I understand it."

"Well, God sent 'em apart," Emmett said. "Is it wrong for us to try to—you know—cross the line again? Just be human beings? Not this race or that?"

"A lot of folks say we shouldn't cross that line."

"I don't care what folks say. I care what the Good Book says. I want to know whether I'm headed for a moral wrong. In the eyes of God, that is."

Reverend Pine rubbed the bridge of his nose. "The Bible tells us that Moses married an Ethiopian woman. And it seems that when Moses's brother and sister—Aaron and Miriam—went and complained to Moses about him marrying an Ethiopian, God took offense."

"I don't recall that particular account." Emmett cocked his head. "That's in the Bible?"

"Book of Numbers," the reverend said.

"What happened when God took offense?"

"He gave Miriam a case of leprosy. Turned her white as snow."

"Well, I'll be…" Emmett said. "If she wanted white only, looks like God gave it to her."

"God did restore Miriam," Reverend Pine said, "But I think it tells us something about God's views on so-called races."

Emmett gazed intently at the minister. "So it sounds to me like God would be fine with a white fella marrying a Chinese girl then."

The minister heaved a sigh. "There are still the antimiscegenation laws. California, Oregon, several other states have them."

"You mean laws against people of different colors marrying each other."

"That's right. And the Bible does tell us that we need to submit to the government. So it's not so simple."

"But when a law is immoral…when a law is unjust, shouldn't we appeal to a higher law?"

"I can't advise you to break the law, Mr. Strong. That's between you and the Lord."

"I respect that."

Reverend Pine shifted and put his arm on the pew back. "Now may I ask you a question or two?"

Satisfied with what he'd heard from the reverend thus far, Emmett answered, "Don't see why not."

"You're new to Virginia City. Yet you show up troubled about the abduction of several local Chinese girls. What's this got to do with you? Do you know who kidnapped those girls?" The minister searched Emmett's eyes. "You weren't part of their gang, were you? You didn't come down with a sudden case of remorse once one of those girls caught your fancy, did you?"

"No, Reverend. I wish I knew who kidnapped those girls. I stumbled on this situation while here on other business."

"Mind if I ask what kind of business?"

"Not at all." Emmett then related to the minister the full account of the murder of his brother and the pursuit of Charlie Blaylock.

"Seth Blaylock," Reverend Pine said. "Now there's a man sold out to the devil—by all appearances anyway."

Emmett shifted. "You know Blaylock? What can you tell me about him… and Lucian McIntosh, for that matter?"

That question brought a dark expression to the minister's face. "Talk about injustice. Those two are about as evil, ruthless, and proud as any two men in this part of the country. And that's saying a lot in a place where men far from their roots come into money—whether honestly earned or ill-gotten—and spend it hand over fist on any vice you might imagine, with an ever-increasing thirst for more."

"More than one source has told me that they run a string of bed houses from San Francisco down to Genoa," Emmett said. "That's a lot of girls of the line."

"Never seems to be any shortage of women who fall on hard times and end up in the services of men like them. Difficult for women like that ever to find their way out. Meanwhile, the McIntoshes and Blaylocks of the world grow wealthier and wealthier at their expense. But beyond that, Lucian McIntosh's places seem to enjoy a distinct popularity. Rumor is that the girls there don't seem to be the regular down-on-their-luck type."

Emmett frowned. "What do you mean?"

"I hear men say they're prettier. They don't have that wasted look that so many…soiled doves inevitably acquire."

Wait a minute. Emmett frowned and slipped his fingers into his vest pocket. He extracted the papers Cromarty, the newspaperman, had given him in Reno. Searching the sheet of paper with Cromarty's own handwritten notes, his eyes were drawn to the notation *Seth Blaylock (procurement?).*

"What've you got there?" the minister asked.

"Just a moment," Emmett said, holding up a finger.

Then, for the first time, he looked at the portion of newsprint that had been neatly folded around the plain white paper. He turned it over. There was the head-line: BOY FOUND DEAD, YOUNG WOMAN STILL MISSING. It was from the *Sacramento Gazette.* Just above the headline—once again in Cromarty's handwriting—it said, *Seth Blaylock? Procurement?*

Emmett skimmed the story. "An acquaintance in Reno gave me this," he said. "It's a news article telling how a young William Stanton, eighteen years of age, was found with his throat cut ear to ear on the banks of the American River in Sacramento. Seems the young lady who was with William disappeared. Name's Adelle Girard. Age seventeen. My friend seems to wonder whether this sort of thing isn't the way Seth Blaylock supplies pretty, young girls to Lucian McIntosh."

Reverend Pine grew pale. "Nobody's ever made that kind of allegation against McIntosh or Blaylock before. But then again, nobody would—not pub-licly anyway. Not if they want to live."

Ruthless men, Emmett thought. *Ruthless enough and arrogant enough to ride brazenly into Virginia City and simply take what they wanted—a whole group of young women this time. Young women whose families never seem to get fair protection under the law regardless.* He felt anger welling up. *Did Seth Blaylock kidnap Li Xu?*

"You're up here searching for Charlie Blaylock, not Seth Blaylock," the reverend said. "Why do you suppose this newspaperman gave you these notes? How would they help you capture your brother's murderer?"

"Seems Mr. Cromarty believes we have an enemy in common—the man Charlie Blaylock is hiding behind."

Reverend Pine shook his head. "So the newspaperman has strong suspicions about Blaylock's crimes, but probably doesn't have the means to do anything about it—"

Emmett got up and stepped into the aisle. "I believe Cromarty wants us Texas lawmen to do the work the local law won't do."

Reverend Pine rose and followed Emmett.

At the door, Emmett paused. "Bad enough men like Blaylock and McIntosh take advantage of women who volunteer their bodies when they're down on their luck. But if they're kidnapping innocent young women and forcing them into that kind of work…"

"Including, quite possibly," Reverend Pine said, "a young Chinese woman who's captured your affections."

Emmett tugged at his lip as he stared up the aisle to the altar rail at the front of the church. She had captured his affections, hadn't she?

"So can you and your Texas friends take on both tasks—bringing in your brother's murderer and finding out whether Blaylock is in fact the one who kidnapped the Chinese girls?"

With his hand on the door handle, Emmett said, "McIntosh has a small army, Reverend. I only brought two men." An image of Li at the foot of the stairs in a high-dollar saloon flashed through his mind. "What I'm able to do remains to be seen." But he knew already what he had to try to do—and try with all his might.

—∞—

His boot was on the bottom step leading up to the Lucky Strike Saloon when Yong Xu caught up with him.

"Mr. Strong, I'm glad I found you."

After the conversation he'd just had with the minister, Emmett was pleased to see Yong. "How *did* you find me?" he asked.

"I recognized your horse." He nodded toward the fine pinto tethered to the rail. "So I waited here for you."

For no rational reason, a glimmer of hope stirred in Emmett's chest. "Any news about Li?"

Yong Xu's gaze dropped. Hidden only a moment ago, his distress was now evident again. It bunched the skin above and at the corners of his eyes. "No. That's why some of us would appreciate the chance to talk to you. Can you and your friends come back to the Golden Dragon?"

"'Some of us,' you say? Who exactly?"

"Please. Come and see," Yong Xu pleaded.

Regardless of his compadres' answers, Emmett made up his mind. He'd go.

CHAPTER TWENTY-FIVE

When Emmett, Juanito, and Sikes entered the Golden Dragon, six Chinese men rose from where they sat and bowed in unison. Emmett touched the brim of his hat.

Yong Xu spoke in Chinese. The six men nodded.

"These are the fathers of the girls who were stolen," Yong Xu said. "And the father of Yan, the lovely girl who was murdered." He extended his hand toward the man whose loss was irrevocable.

Emmett removed his hat and said to Yan's father, "I'm sorry, sir. Very, very sorry."

The man, dressed entirely in Chinese garb, solemnly bowed again. His eyes looked as though they had no more tears to give.

Yong Xu asked the three from Texas to have a seat and offered them hot tea. They accepted, Sikes expressing special appreciation.

"I speak for these men and for the entire Chinese community of Virginia City," Yong said to the Texans. His gaze rested on Emmett. "I know you are a good man. You too have suffered loss. You have come in search of the evil man who killed your brother. So we have an offer for you, Mr. Strong."

"Emmett."

Yong Xu glanced back at his peers, then said, "Emmett. We have discussed this, and we are prepared to help you capture your brother's killer—whatever the task may cost us, however long it may take us. But we also have something to ask of you."

Emmett anticipated what was coming. "Go on."

"Will you and your friends first help us find and rescue our daughters?"

The seven Chinese fathers waited, to a man fixed on Emmett.

Turning to Juanito and Sikes, Emmett said, "I don't expect you to give an answer until the three of us have had the chance to talk this over in private. But have you heard enough? Or are there other considerations?"

He badly wanted Juanito and Sikes to agree then and there. But he hadn't even had the chance yet to tell them what he and Reverend Pine had deduced from Cromarty's papers.

"I'm still listening," Juanito said.

Sikes took another sip of tea. "Likewise."

"Do you have a plan, Yong Xu?" Emmett asked.

"We Chinese have no recourse on our own. These poor men don't know who else to turn to. They fear that local officials won't do a thing because if they start an investigation, miners and other laborers may start anti-Chinese riots—or that the kidnappers themselves will stir up trouble and then pay the lawmen to look the other way."

"I don't know what—if anything—the Chinese community here can do to help us capture my brother's murderer," Emmett said.

He noticed a subtle drooping of Yong Xu's shoulders.

"But that doesn't mean we won't consider your request," he continued.

The seven fathers focused even more intently on Emmett.

"You must understand. I have to talk this over with Juanito and Sikes. What you're asking…Well, it's a serious departure from what my two friends agreed to come up here to do."

"We understand," Yong Xu said eagerly.

"Then if you'll allow us a few minutes, gentlemen…" Emmett said.

The Chinese rose and bowed. Some spoke in heavily accented English, others with scarcely a trace of foreign inflection. But each thanked the men from Texas on their way out.

Once he was certain they were alone, Emmett recounted a good deal of what he had discussed with Reverend Pine that afternoon, camping heavily on the part about Seth Blaylock and Lucian McIntosh. He spread the papers Stanley Cromarty had given him on the table, then read aloud the entire article from the *Sacramento Gazette*.

"Cromarty seems to believe that Seth Blaylock is getting rich by kidnapping especially pretty girls from all over the area for service in McIntosh's bordellos," Emmett explained. "The reverend thought the suspicion made sense. He said the girls of the line at McIntosh's places have a different reputation than they do at your average hookshop."

"So you think our interests and those of the Chinese intersect," Sikes said.

"I do. And the intersection point is—"

"Seth Blaylock." Juanito tapped the notation Cromarty had made right above the newspaper headline.

Emmett looked back and forth between the two. "That's right."

He couldn't force them to play for new stakes—higher stakes. Yet inside, he struggled. He wanted to plead.

"So looking for Li Xu…" Sikes paused and waited till Emmett's gaze met his. "Trying to rescue her and the other girls doesn't mean we've abandoned tracking down Charlie Blaylock."

"Nope. Not if it pits us against the very man who blocks our way to Charlie Blaylock anyhow."

"But how can we know that's truly the case?" Juanito asked.

Emmett got up and paced to the window and back. "Can we try to meet with Cromarty again? See whether he knows anything else that might help?"

Juanito and Sikes glanced at one another. Both nodded.

But that wasn't enough for Emmett. Without question he still wanted to arrest his brother's murderer. That could wait, though. Because whether or not going after Seth Blaylock was a matter of killing two birds with one stone, Li Xu and her friends were in trouble. And time was crucial. Even while they stood there deliberating, men might be using and abusing them.

He slammed his palm on the table. "To hell with it! Juanito, Sikes, if you stay on with me through all this, I'll be forever beholden to you. If you need more time to think it over, I understand. If you decide to pack it in and go on back to Texas without me, I understand that, too." Both hands on the tabletop now, he leaned forward. "I'm not trying to twist your arms, but my mind's made up. I've gotta do this. I've gotta help Yong Xu find Li and get her back safe—one way or the other. Even if Charlie Blaylock ends up slipping off the hook because of it."

His compañeros sat in silence.

Then Juanito unfolded his arms. Very deliberately, in a low voice, he said, "Damn, you make a good speech, *hermano*." His face erupted in a grin. "And besides, I want to see you and that pretty girl together. I'm in with you."

Sikes lifted his teacup and studied it. "I probably wouldn't do it if the Chinese didn't make such splendid tea." He looked at Emmett. "As long as they keep the kettle on, I suppose I'm at their mercy. Count me in, too."

Emmett blew out a heavy breath. *"Gracias, muchachos."*

"Go on and tell Yong Xu," Juanito said. "Meanwhile, Sikes and I will put our heads together. Try to decide how the Chinese might help us make sure Charlie Blaylock doesn't slip away."

CHAPTER TWENTY-SIX

After thirty-six hours in dreary lamplight, locked up in the same second-floor room at Lucian McIntosh's home, Li Xu waited apprehensively for the inevitable encounter with the big man himself. And it was wearing her down. She had racked her brain for hours at a time trying to come up with a means of escape. Hopelessness would have set in long hours ago were it not for one thing.

A soft thump at the door interrupted her thoughts.

At the sound of the key in the lock, both she and Ping sat up in the narrow bed where they had been lying. It was Ettie.

Of all the kidnappers—or even servants—in this immense, dreadful house, only Ettie had treated them with something other than open disdain or simmering lust.

She stood at the foot of the bed. "I have to leave," she said, her face blank, her voice matter-of-fact. "I'll be gone a few days. Sarah Mae and Margaret will check in on you until…"

Li swallowed and pushed from her mind the image of Lucian McIntosh looming over her. "They're going to sell our friends in some other town," she said. "He wants you to go along, doesn't he?"

Ettie inhaled deeply through her nose and straightened her shoulders. "It can't be helped."

Li wondered what it was that kept Ettie tied to McIntosh and his slavers. "You were the one in the long black coat at Zhang's Restaurant the other night, weren't you? You never spoke. You walked different. Your hat and boots and gloves were different. But it was you, wasn't it?"

After meeting Li's gaze for a long moment, Ettie said, "You're a smart girl. Observant."

"Then you're the one who picked which of us to take and which to leave."

Abruptly Ettie turned for the door. "I have to go."

Li wondered why, after deliberately choosing her and Ping for what she knew would be a living nightmare, Ettie had treated them so sympathetically. Did she suddenly feel guilty?

Just as Ettie touched the doorknob, Sarah Mae barged in. Ettie had to skip out of the way to avoid being bowled over.

The housekeeper was scowling as usual. "What're you doin' back there?" she snapped at Ettie.

Ettie raised her chin. She pivoted and sauntered to the window where she proceeded to pull back the heavy drapes and hook the gold-fringed tiebacks around their hardware.

"Mr. McIntosh doesn't want those curtains opened," Sarah Mae protested.

"Tell him I did it." Ettie glared at the woman. "And don't you close them again until these girls decide they've had enough sunlight for the day. If Mr. McIntosh wants them closed, he can come close them himself."

Sarah Mae huffed. "You may have gotten the curtains open for your little China tramps, but the window glass stays closed—Mr. McIntosh's instructions. You do otherwise, and I'll go straight to him this minute."

"It's going to be hot again today," Ettie said, still glowering.

"Well then, the transom's gonna have to do, because that window will not be opened. Should've left the drapes closed to begin with."

Ettie returned to the doorway, brushing the housekeeper as she passed. She paused there with her hands on her hips. "Don't you be unduly mean to these girls, Sarah Mae. I mean it." After stealing a glance at Li and Ping, she ambled out.

Sarah Mae cut her eyes at Li. "Bad enough I have to pick up after you bleedin' China girls. To have to put up with that uppity princess too…"

She wrinkled her nose as she took hold of the chamber pot. "'Don't you be unduly mean.' Indeed." With a disdainful glare, she waddled out of the room, slamming the door behind her.

Ping whispered in Mandarin, "It's so hard for me not to hate white people. Even their servants treat us like we're some kind of animals, not human beings."

Under the circumstances—abduction, captivity, McIntosh's intentions— Li was tempted to agree. But they weren't all the same. Even though Ettie

136

had handpicked them, Li couldn't bring herself to hate the woman. Whether it was the ruse or something else, Ettie had dealt with her and Ping almost apologetically.

Then there was the Texan. Emmett Strong. For some reason, even as she brainstormed how she might escape, she found herself thinking of him—one white man she was pretty sure she could never hate.

"Not all white people look down on us like that, Ping."

"Well, the ones who have us here do."

"The ones in this house, yes."

Ping climbed out of bed and walked to the window. "Except maybe Ettie."

Li got up and joined her. It came as no surprise that, aside from the men taking care of horses and cattle, most of those she spotted outside looked more like armed guards than ranchers.

"I don't understand Ettie either," Li said. "There were times yesterday when I thought that—if she could—she probably would have let us go free."

Ping turned to her, frowning. "Yes, but I don't know how long she'll keep trying to make things better for us if you keep saying things like you did a few minutes ago."

"Like what?"

"You made it sound as though it was Ettie's idea to sell Min and Xia and Guiying and Jing."

"I was just trying to find out whether I was right—that she doesn't like what's happening here any better than we do." Li leaned against the windowsill. "What do you think?"

Ping was slow to answer. "She's gone now, to do whatever McIntosh wants her to do. Probably what you said—to sell our friends." After peering out the window a short while, she asked, "Anyway, how's your thigh?"

"It hurts...but I'm all right."

Then Ping unexpectedly resumed a conversation they had begun during the middle of the night when a wave of panic had threatened to overwhelm her. "Do you still think that man from Texas is going to be the one to find us and rescue us?"

Li was fearful of nurturing unrealistic expectations—especially the kind that might set them both up for a fall. Regardless, it was critical that they hang on to hope. She spoke barely above a whisper, close to Ping's ear. "You heard all that shouting downstairs the other night. They were saying the very same names downstairs that Emmett, the man from Texas, told me about. He's looking for Charlie Blaylock. And Charlie Blaylock came here—to this very house. When Emmett finds Charlie, he'll find us." She knew that—while factually correct—what she had just voiced was hardly more than a desperate dream. Nevertheless, she clung to it, if for no other reason than to keep despair at bay.

Ping remained close, turning so she could see Li's face. Her eyes were moist. "We can't wait around for somebody from the outside—not even this Texas man—to come find us. Anything could happen to us before then." Tears began to run down her cheeks again. "You're the cleverest person I know, Li. I trust you more than anybody. You have to come up with a plan so we can escape."

Hugging her friend, Li said, "You're right, Ping. I promise. I'll start trying again. We'll think of something."

Ping was quiet for a moment.

What kind of plan could she come up with for the two of them to escape on their own? It seemed impossible. She surveyed the gunmen down below, then glanced at the transom above the door. The only thing she could do was to stay alert for any change, any opportunity, and make the best of it when the moment came.

Taking Ping by the shoulders, she eased her away. But before she got another word out, the now-familiar metallic clack of the key in the lock distracted her. She grimaced at the thought of having to endure more of Sarah Mae's nasty comments.

In the next instant, however, her stomach knotted and her knees nearly buckled.

Lucian McIntosh himself filled the bedroom doorway.

CHAPTER TWENTY-SEVEN

On a little-used road leading to Reno, the wind kicked up a fine spray of dust and grit. Emmett turned his head and pressed on. His amigos—Juanito, Sikes, and Yong Xu—likewise leaned into the stiff breeze with eyes squinched.

"You've got the note I gave you for the newspaperman, right, Yong?" he asked.

Yong patted his vest pocket. "Right here." In lieu of his customary baggy trousers and traditional tunic, Yong wore American trousers, a shirt, and a vest today—although he still kept his light-soled Chinese shoes, and his head was shaded by the shallow cone of a Chinese straw hat.

"Sure hope he agrees to ride out with you," Emmett said.

"If he wants you to do what the local lawmen won't do, why wouldn't he?"

"Not sure. Don't know him that well. Anyway, I appreciate you going in to fetch him."

Yong nodded. "I'll be less conspicuous in Reno than any of you three."

Sikes's horse nearly stumbled. "Whoa! You call this a road, Yong Xu?"

Emmett eyed the deep, weathered wagon ruts and the dry grass that obscured them in places.

"If you want to pass through this country unnoticed..." Yong said. "It's not likely Blaylock or McIntosh will send men to look for the three of you on this road. Only local people use it. And not even them very often."

Once they reached a smoother stretch of the old trail, Emmett resumed mulling over Cromarty's notes and the *Sacramento Gazette* article. The longer he thought about it, the stronger his conviction grew that finding and freeing the Chinese girls would ultimately help him achieve his original goal—locating and dealing with Seth and Charlie Blaylock.

Atop a rise, Juanito pointed to the east. "Does that town look familiar?"

"Certainly does," Sikes said. "And the lake beyond it too."

"We camped on the edge of that lake and then passed through the town the first time we rode up to Reno," Emmett explained to Yong.

"That's Washoe City," Yong said. "And beyond it, Washoe Lake."

"A McIntosh town?" Emmett asked.

"If he wanted it. It's so small, though, I doubt he cares about it."

About a mile farther north, the men reached the top of a higher ridge. Juanito put a hand up, and the four reined in.

He pointed. "We're not the only ones out on this old goat trail today."

Emmett studied the road ahead where the wind twisted and lifted a low cloud of dust. Two slow-moving covered wagons were wending their way toward them. They were accompanied by six mounted men—two riding point, two riding swing, and two eating the dust kicked up by the others.

"Hmm," he said. "It's not like we're out in Indian country. Wonder why they're framing the wagons that way."

"Remember," Yong Xu said. "You're in mining country now. They could be carrying silver ore down to Carson City."

Emmett nodded. "Makes sense. But why not take the main road through Washoe City?"

Yong Xu shrugged.

"Looks like they've spotted us," Sikes said.

The wagons had stopped, along with the swing and drag riders. But the two point men had turned and were loping back toward the cargo.

"We don't know that for a fact," Emmett said. "Let's just stay put for a minute."

—⁜—

At the base of the rise, Seth Blaylock waited for Charlie and the other point rider, Zeke. Ettie eased her horse up alongside him.

"Trouble up ahead?" she asked.

"I doubt it," Seth said. "But I'll take precautions anyway."

The two point riders drew up just in front of Seth.

"Whatcha want us to do?" Charlie asked.

Seth pulled the brim of his hat a little lower over his eyes. "Ride up there and tell 'em to leave this road to us. Tell 'em they're gonna have to cut over cross-country to the Washoe City road."

"And if they won't?" Zeke asked.

"In that case, just ride on back and let me know." Seth scoffed. "If I have to deal with 'em myself, they'll wish they'd simply listened to you." He flicked his gloved hand toward the rise. "Now go on."

Charlie and Zeke nodded and spurred their horses back up the road.

"Water?" Ettie asked.

"No, I'm not thirsty," Seth said.

"I meant for the China girls. As long as we're stopped."

Seth's saddle creaked as he shifted around and looked back. "Might as well."

Ettie walked her horse to the back of the first wagon, lifted the canvas canopy flap, and peered in. Seth watched her pull the stopper from her own canteen and hold it out. A pair of bound hands took it.

"Don't let 'em drink too much," he said. "Don't wanna be stoppin' thirty minutes from now to let 'em piss."

When he turned back toward the rise, what he saw made him purse his lips and shake his head. Charlie and Zeke were roaring back at a full gallop.

Fifty yards out, Charlie started yelling, "It's them! It's that damn Texas law dog!"

Bits of turf flew up as Charlie skidded his horse to a stop. "They got a damn Chinaman with 'em, too," he shouted, spittle flying from his mouth. "How'd they know?"

Seth squinted. "Shut up, Charlie. This is Nevada. There're Chinamen all over the place up here. Havin' a Chinaman with 'em don't mean anything."

"But it's still them," Charlie whined.

"Yeah," Seth said, "Well, it's nice to have 'em all in one place out here in the middle of nowhere so we can finish 'em off and be rid of 'em once and for all."

He pulled the Winchester from his saddle boot and chambered a round. Throwing a glance over his shoulder he yelled, "Cole, Lewis, you two keep them scatterguns ready. We should be able to take care of everything up there on that ridge. But if any of 'em break through and make it down here, let fly."

"Yes, sir," Cole called back from the driver's seat of the front wagon.

Seth waved his arm. "The rest of you, come with me."

—◆—

"You sure that point rider was Charlie Blaylock?" Juanito asked, frowning.

"Didn't you recognize the hat?" Emmett asked. "From that day down in Austin?"

Juanito shook his head and opened his mouth to answer when Emmett cut in again.

"That's right. He was gone by the time you and Sikes got out to the street. But that's him. Besides, why else would those two turn tail and run away like that when all we're doing is sitting saddle up here?"

"We may not need to see Cromarty after all," Sikes said. "It could all come down to what happens right here, right now."

"That it could…depending on who's down there with him."

"Seth in particular?"

Emmett nodded.

Yong leaned forward, straining to see. "I had almost lost faith in fortune."

"What's the plan, Strong?" Sikes said.

Emmett watched what was now going on down near the wagons. They were obviously scrambling to make up their minds just as he was.

"The odds may be better here than they'll be in Reno," Juanito said. "You want to try to take Charlie?"

Just then Emmett noted all six horsemen gigging their mounts at full tilt up the rise.

"This high ground is to our advantage," he said. "Sikes, let's get you on that buffalo gun again."

Sikes was already swinging out of the saddle and unsheathing the heavy rifle.

"Yong, you take the horses down the back slope a little ways, OK?" Emmett glanced at him as he dismounted. "You've got that Colt I gave you this morning. Use it if they come at you. You've gotta pull back the hammer with your thumb. Then just point and squeeze."

The Chinaman patted his holster.

Before Emmett could turn around, the buffalo rifle thundered. He yanked his head toward Sikes.

"Had a shot, and I had to take it."

"Criminy, Sikes! You've gotta let 'em get in range."

The Englishman was reloading. "He was in range. I winged him."

Emmett peered downhill. He spotted Charlie Blaylock. The murderer was clutching his arm, and his horse had dropped out of the charge.

The other five opened fire at Emmett and his compadres. All of their shots were coming in low, kicking up dirt on the front face of the hill.

Yong Xu urged their horses down from the crest. Emmett and Juanito were now prone beside Sikes. A split second before Emmett pulled the trigger of his Winchester, all six riders below looked back toward the wagons. The roll of a shotgun blast carried up the hill.

"Looks like one of the Chinese girls!" Sikes said.

Emmett spotted her. Dark hair, Chinese-style clothing. Running away from the lead wagon toward a broad parcel of ground covered by scrubby mesquite.

Yong Xu came running. "Is it Li-Li?" he yelled, his voice nearly breaking.

"Can't tell from this far away," Emmett said. His heart pounded at the possibility.

When the wagon driver fired a second blast into the air, Charlie Blaylock and his companions wheeled their horses and split up. Four made their way toward the wagons. Two rode for the tract of mesquite.

"What now?" Sikes asked.

Yong Xu didn't wait for an answer. He spun and dashed for his horse.

"Yong," Emmett hollered. "You can't go down there by yourself."

But the man wasn't listening. He mounted and urged his horse up the ridge.

"Yong!" Emmett tried in vain to snag the horse's bridle as it passed.

The Chinaman picked up speed and raced away toward the runaway girl.

"Blazes!" Emmett muttered. "Sikes, you and Juanito stay here. Do what you can to keep those murdering kidnappers pinned down."

Emmett sprinted to his horse.

"Sure you don't want us to come along?" Juanito yelled.

"Just keep an eye on those wagons." Emmett pushed his pinto hard.

CHAPTER TWENTY-EIGHT

L i Xu felt the window frame pressing into her back as Lucian McIntosh stepped into the small bedroom. Ping clung to her arm as though Li were somehow capable of deterring the huge, dark man, whatever his intent.

She didn't like his eyes. They revealed no hint of shame as he leered unapologetically.

Her mind spun, searching frantically for something she might say to make him go away. But what could she say to a man like him...in his own house?

Ping's fingers dug in.

McIntosh closed to within arm's reach, still letting his gaze roam and pause all over her. His cheeks were flushed. His arms hung loosely at his sides.

She thought about the hairpin. The only weapon she had. She might never survive the aftermath of stabbing him with it, but—

"Four or five days, hmm?" he said. He tilted his head.

At first his question made no sense to her. Then she recalled the ploy—the ploy and then the fact that her real monthly troubles had in truth started yesterday morning.

She nodded. "Yes, sir." Her words came out with no voice behind them. "Five days, usually."

Ping had not been so...fortunate. For her, it was still a ruse.

McIntosh now stood so close that she felt his scent might suffocate her. He smelled of cigar—an aroma she ordinarily found surprisingly pleasant. But on him, along with the sickly sweet fragrance of some no-doubt expensive lotion, the odor was repulsive.

He reached out one of his oversized hands and suspended his fingers over her breast. She recoiled, but there was no room left for further retreat.

She was conscious of Ping's anxious breathing—and of her own racing heart and shallow inhalation as well.

Gulping, she worked her fingers, ready to go for the hairpin if he forced himself on her in earnest.

"You're a pretty one," he said in a voice that rumbled like distant thunder. A small upturn tugged at the corner of his mouth.

His fingertips only barely brushed her as he smoothly lifted his hand and rested it on her shoulder.

Turning her face away, she closed her eyes and tried to keep breathing. *The hairpin.*

"I've got time," he chuckled. "You belong to me now…for as long as I care to keep you."

A tear ran down her cheek. *I refuse to cry*, she said to herself. *I refuse to give that power to this man.*

Once she sensed him backing away, she opened her eyes.

From a couple of feet away now, he glanced at Ping. "You're a handsome one, too. A real daisy."

Li feared Ping wouldn't make it through this without fainting—or without lashing out in wild panic. Her friend's breathing was still jagged.

"What's your name, little one?" the heavy man asked Ping, at last lifting his palm from Li's shoulder.

Ping began to wheeze and pressed herself against Li, trying for all she was worth to squeeze in behind her.

Li drew a breath and said, "Her name is Ping. And my name is Li."

"Ping and Li." He gave another deep, soft chuckle.

Giving their names—had it been the right thing to do? It didn't matter, she decided. There was no sense in angering this dangerous man.

He nodded, eyed them both again, then turned for the door.

Li hoped with every fiber of her being that he was leaving them now. She knew what she would do if he closed the door and stayed. Even if it led to her death, she knew what she would do.

Ping still clung to her.

And McIntosh left, locking the heavy, white door behind him.

—⁓—

McIntosh trudged down the hallway. At the top of the stairs, he met Sarah Mae. He clutched the housekeeper's bicep and murmured into her ear, "Find Margaret. Have her start those China girls on laudanum today."

When he drew back, Sarah Mae gave a devilish smile. "Only too happy to, Mr. McIntosh," she said.

He returned the grin and swatted her on the rump as he passed by.

CHAPTER TWENTY-NINE

Leaving the little-used trail to Reno, Emmett raced down the slope in pursuit of Yong. His friend was already halfway to the chaparral the runaway Chinese girl had disappeared into. And he was beginning to draw fire from the suspected kidnappers, most of whom were now gathered around the two wagons.

'Get to the bush, Yong!" Emmett murmured.

His mind was in three places—with Yong, with the girl in the thicket, and with the rest of the abducted girls. All were in grave danger. And for all of them, the difference between danger and death was paper-thin.

Emmett figured the front wagon was the one carrying the other Chinese girls. The wagoner had hopped down and run to the rear where he now stood, aiming his scattergun at the canopy flap.

Meanwhile, two of the kidnappers galloped into the chaparral, obviously intent on retrieving the girl who had gotten away.

Could Li Xu be the one in the thicket? Or was she staring down the barrel of that shotgun at the back of the covered wagon?

Somebody would die here today. Emmett knew it, and his chest tightened.

Reining his horse to the right, he made for the scrub. Bullets whizzed by. He cringed and scrunched down in the saddle until he reached the thicket. Once there he slowed his mount to little more than a walk and peered hard into the foliage.

Motion not far ahead caught his attention. It was the young Chinese woman. Emmett's heart skipped a beat. But it wasn't Li Xu.

The young woman was running toward an arroyo that sliced through a clearing in the chaparral, breathing hard, her pace slowing.

Then Yong Xu came into view between him and the girl. When Yong called out to her in Chinese, her expression lit up, and she altered her course.

A shot rang out. It kicked up dirt mere feet from the front hoof of Yong Xu's mount, causing the horse to leap skittishly. Unable to control the animal, Yong was thrown hard to the ground.

Emmett slid his Winchester back into its boot and drew his Colt. He thumbed back the hammer and scanned the brush as he nudged his horse closer to the arroyo.

He had advanced only a few steps when he had to halt abruptly. One of the kidnappers—a dandy dressed overly fine for chasing and shooting in country like this—emerged from behind a dense cluster of mesquites. Oblivious to Emmett, he raised his pistol and took aim at either Yong or the girl. From that angle Emmett couldn't tell which.

Emmett whipped his Colt up and squeezed the trigger.

Before the Victorio Sanchez incident that ended Gabriela's life, this would've been a potshot. The dandy would already be lying in the dust. As it happened, though, the bullet merely sent the hombre's hat flying.

He spun—Emmett had clearly caught him off guard—and returned fire.

Dammit! Emmett couldn't believe he'd missed at such short range. And the comeback shot had zinged by far too close.

Yong Xu was now half crawling, half stumbling toward the cover of the arroyo. The Chinese girl on the other side was nearly there herself.

Emmett let another round fly to keep the dandy distracted.

The kidnapper flinched but ignored Emmett. He pointed his revolver the other direction and fired again. As though a bare-knuckle boxer had gut-punched her, the young Chinese woman stopping cold in her tracks. She stared straight ahead, her mouth agape. Then she crumpled to the ground—only a couple steps shy of the gully.

No! Rage gripped Emmett.

Another shot sounded from Emmett's left but from beyond the dandy. There was the second kidnapper.

The dandy fired again. Yong Xu cried out and tumbled into the arroyo. Emmett picked up a patch of dark red on his Chinese friend's shoulder as he fell forward.

What he'd give for a shotgun right now. The dandy wheeled his horse toward him. Emmett emptied his Peacemaker in that direction, sending his enemy in search of cover.

He slid off his horse, grabbed the Winchester once again, and raced for the gully—for Yong Xu and the fallen girl. A bullet danced at his feet just before he leapt into the gap.

Slamming hard into the far wall of the arroyo, he winced in pain made worse by his inability to keep his footing on the loose shale. But midair he had glimpsed the second shooter. If only he could scramble to the rim of the arroyo fast enough, he'd have a good angle of fire on that one.

He clambered back up and pressed the rifle stock to his shoulder. There he was, not quite obscured by the mesquite. Emmett snapped off a quick shot. The second abductor's horse nickered in pain and went down.

This wasn't going well.

Though he wished he could check on the girl and Yong Xu, Emmett held his place. It was a good one—a small jag in the lip of the arroyo that gave him good cover. And he could just make out both the dandy and the other kidnapper through the dense lace of mesquite.

The second outlaw was on the move toward his accomplice, stealing through the brush from where his horse had collapsed.

Emmett was now more careful with his aim. He squeezed the trigger once again.

A high-pitched cry came back—not a man's scream. Perhaps another of the Chinese girls had fled into the chaparral, and he'd just inadvertently shot her. His heart thumped with fear. His mouth went dry. No. There had definitely been a second shooter. Somebody on horseback until just a moment ago.

For the next little while, only the occasional shot came from the kidnappers. Meanwhile, in the distance he could hear the report of the Sharps buffalo gun from time to time. Sikes was still at work holding down the rest of the band of abductors. Other rifles answered off to the west. He doubted that anybody except maybe Sikes was having much success out there.

Momentarily taking his gaze off the tangle of brush, he stole a glance at Yong. His friend lay on his back on the floor of the arroyo, eyes closed, mouth open.

Hoofbeats drew his gaze back out into the chaparral. It was the sound of a single horse, trotting away from him. Then all went quiet.

Emmett waited. Heat radiating from the floor and rugged walls of the gully sent sweat running down his back in rivulets.

Finally convinced that the kidnappers had retreated to their wagons, he climbed out of the arroyo and ran to the collapsed Chinese girl. First relief, then shame swept over him. Even if this wasn't Li Xu, surely this sweet girl was just as dear to lots of folks in Chinatown. Kneeling beside her lifeless body, he closed her eyes, squeezed her soft hand, and cursed the dandy who shot her.

He raised his eyes to the clump of brush he'd fired into only a short while ago—the one the feminine scream had come from. Scouting left and right, he stole his way there. Several yards from the collapsed horse, he found spatters of blood in the dirt—and clear evidence that the person he had shot had crawled toward the dandy. Certainly none of the Chinese girls would've done that.

Back in the arroyo, Yong Xu moaned.

CHAPTER THIRTY

Seth Blaylock blinked into the declining sun, trying to decide how risky it would be to make a dash across the hundred yards of open ground between himself and the wagons. Ettie's weight rested against him. His shirt felt wet where her shoulder met his chest. After one last wary glimpse at the rise to his left, he spurred his horse into a hard gallop until he drew up behind the cover of the wagons.

"We're stuck here, Mr. Blaylock," Lewis called out. "Damn buffalo gun got three of our hitched-up horses and one of the spares."

Seth glared at Lewis.

Once Lewis's gaze landed on Ettie, leaning unconscious and bleeding against Seth, he hurried to say, "I'm sorry, Mr. Blaylock. I'm real sorry."

"I'm guessin' the fella on the buffalo gun is out of cartridges," Seth said. He looked around. "Otherwise I suppose all our horses would be dead by now."

Only two things mattered to Seth right now. Above all, he didn't want Ettie to die. Everything else paled by comparison, with one exception—what Lucian McIntosh would think and do once he found out about this mess.

"The China girls?" he asked.

Cole stepped out from behind the other wagon and pointed to where he'd just come from. "Right over here."

"You keep 'em real safe, Cole. I'm puttin' that responsibility on you. You hear?"

"Y-yes, sir," Cole stuttered. "If I may ask, where you goin', Mr. Blaylock?"

Seth deliberated whether he could leave the China girls out here in the open, even if his excuse was to get Ettie to a doctor. He was already on thin ice with Lucian McIntosh. And one China girl out of the four was already dead. He'd had to shoot her, though, on the odd chance that she and that Chinaman had gotten away. He couldn't have either one of them identifying him or his boss. He shook his head and sniffed.

"Gotta get some help for Ettie here, Cole. Don't know how bad she is, but she's bleedin' a lot."

Seth's mind was beginning to clear. He surveyed the scene around the wagons once again. "How many hit? How many dead?"

"Only other one hit's me." It was Charlie.

Seth found Charlie lying on the ground behind the first wagon. He had a neckerchief pressed against his upper arm. A couple more, fairly soaked with blood, were tossed onto the ground nearby.

"You gonna make it?" Seth asked.

"'Spect so," Charlie said. "Hurts like hell, though."

Seth hoped it hurt like hell. As he looked down on Charlie, a slow fuse burned inside. It wasn't the time or place to bring it up, but as far as he was concerned this entire mess could be chalked up to Charlie's stupidity. If he hadn't shot that Texas senator—right there in full sight of his Texas Ranger brother—this attack wouldn't have happened. And Ettie wouldn't be bleeding all over him right now.

"Boys," Seth said, "listen real careful. I've gotta get some help for those that're bleedin'. And I've gotta get us some horses and some reinforcements. Those Texans on the ridge up there are more'n likely out of bullets."

"Why don't we just wait'll after dark? We could hitch up the remainin' horses and head on back to Reno," Zeke said.

"Uh-uh. Mr. McIntosh told us to deliver these China girls to Genoa, and that's where we're damn well gonna deliver 'em. If we don't"—he looked from face to face—"don't reckon any of y'all oughta plan on returnin' to Reno again. Ever."

"Why not? I ain't the cause of all this trouble," Milt Porter said. "'Sides, stealin' them China girls was your idea, not mine."

In a heartbeat, Seth's pistol was shucked and leveled at Milt. "So far none of our crew is dead from this unfortunate turn of events. You wanna be the first?"

Milt held his hands up in front of him and shook his head.

"Besides, it don't matter who first came up with the idea to steal the China girls—Mr. McIntosh is real partial to 'em now. Nevada and California together ain't big enough for you to hide in if you go and mess up Mr. McIntosh's plans. *Comprende?*"

Milt nodded.

"Now you've got plenty of ammunition, food, and water on the supply wagon, so sit tight," Seth said. Then he turned to his brother. "Get on your horse, Charlie. Might as well get you and Ettie to the same doctor."

While he waited for Charlie to climb into the saddle, he turned back to Cole. "The men on that ridge up there'll have to go farther than Carson City to find someplace that'll sell 'em bullets. I can get to Carson City and back long before they take care of their needs."

"What about Washoe City?" Cole asked.

"No doctor in Washoe City," Seth said. "The Texans have a wounded Chinaman with 'em. They'll be lookin' for a doctor. Unless he's dead already."

"I s'pose we got a handle on it then," Cole said.

"Good enough," Seth said, glancing at Charlie. "Once I've got Ettie squared away, I'll be back directly…with fresh horses and a slue of Thaddeus McIntosh's men."

Charlie circled his sorrel and pulled up alongside his brother.

Seth shifted Ettie in his arms, then gigged his horse hard.

Once out of earshot, Charlie asked, "What happens if them Texans overtake 'em while we're gone?"

Seth glowered. "Shut up, Charlie. All you need to worry about is Ettie here. If she don't make it, those Texans'll be the least of your concerns."

CHAPTER THIRTY-ONE

By the time Emmett got back to the arroyo, Yong Xu was conscious again and grimacing in pain.

Emmett recalled what he'd seen just before Yong had tumbled into the gully. "You hurt anywhere other than the shoulder?"

Yong shook his head. "I don't think so." He struggled to sit up.

Emmett helped. "Take it slow."

Yong gripped Emmett's forearm tightly and looked him in the eye. "Guiying?"

"What's that?"

"The girl, Guiying—did she make it?"

A lump in Emmett's throat made it difficult for him to answer. "I'm sorry, Yong. Very, very sorry."

Yong Xu put his hands to his face and wept bitterly. "This just gets worse and worse."

Emmett gave him a moment, then said, "If you can move, we'd better get outta here. They may come back for a second go at us."

―☰―

Safely back on the ridge, Yong hissed in pain as he gingerly let himself down from the saddle. Emmett carefully released the girl's body to Juanito and Sikes. While they in silence arranged the body on the ground, he swung down and headed over to take a better look at Yong's wound.

"Need to get this cleaned up," he said. "I know it hurts like the dickens, but it looks like it just skimmed the muscle—plowed a shallow furrow in that shoulder meat."

154

Yong Xu appeared not to have heard what Emmett said. He shuffled over to the dead girl and dropped to his knees beside her. "Guiying was my close friend Wei's daughter. Losing her is like losing my own." He blotted his eyes and nose.

Emmett squatted beside Yong, remorseful he hadn't hit that dandy back in the chaparral with the first shot. His sorrow was genuine, but so was his relief that the dead girl was not in fact Yong's own daughter. He stared in the direction of the kidnappers' wagons and wondered whether Li might possibly be just that near.

"Would you like a moment alone with her?" Emmett murmured.

Yong nodded.

Emmett clapped his friend on the shoulder, then trudged to the crest of the rise.

Sikes followed him. "Hell of a thing."

Emmett nodded and gazed out at the enemy below. In the last rays of the day's sunlight, he spotted the four horses, motionless on the ground—two in front of one wagon, one in front of the other wagon, the last in between. After a moment, he said, "Good job with the buffalo gun."

"Pretty difficult to hit a man behind cover that far out," Sikes said. "But horses standing still in the open..."

"Wonder why they didn't swap 'em out, use the remaining horses to take the wagons back to where they came from. Unless they're waiting to do it under cover of darkness."

Juanito joined them. "A couple of riders took off a little while ago. Gone for help, I imagine."

"How long ago?"

"Just before you and Yong Xu cleared the chaparral."

"You say a couple of riders?"

"Three actually. Only took two horses though."

"You spot Charlie Blaylock?"

"Charlie was on a horse by himself. A fellow with no hat was doubled up with somebody else on the other horse," Sikes said.

The dandy—Seth Blaylock, I'm willing to bet. With the one I know for sure I shot. Emmett's gaze drifted toward the arroyo. "In the scrub down there I managed to hit one of 'em."

Juanito peered over his shoulder at the now-praying Chinaman. "Speaking of being hit, how bad is Yong Xu?"

"Won't be able to handle that shotgun too well, but I think he'll be OK." Emmett pulled off his hat and ran his fingers through his hair. "Plans, gents. What do we have on our hands here? And what're we gonna do about it?"

"The Chinese girl who ran wasn't the only one in that wagon," Sikes said. "During the heat of battle, they pulled three more out and hid them behind the second wagon. I had to keep that in mind all the while I was shooting."

Emmett's heart lurched. "Only three?" He recalled that a total of six had been abducted.

"Only three. I don't know what's become of the other two."

Emmett chewed on his thumbnail. He couldn't decide whether he liked Li Xu's chances better behind the wagons right there below them—where he might have a shot at rescuing her tonight—or elsewhere, out of the line of gunfire.

"Looks like Cromarty got it right," he said.

Juanito kept his eyes on the wagons as he spoke. "Charlie Blaylock—Seth's brother—just happens to be out here in the middle of nowhere with the same Chinese girls we're looking for. *Sí*, I'd say it's a fair guess. Seth Blaylock's in the business of kidnapping girls for his boss's bordellos."

"I think the one with no hat was him." Emmett kicked a small stone, sending it clattering down the slope.

"Who? Seth?"

"Yep." *And I should've had him.*

After a moment, Sikes asked, "So what do we do, Strong?"

"How're the bullets holding out?"

"No more cartridges for the buffalo rifle," the former British soldier said. "Low on everything else."

"Figured as much."

"I fired more shots than I probably should've," Juanito said. "Just trying to keep them pinned down."

"So in other words," Emmett said, "even though we might gamble our four going up against their five before Seth and Charlie get back, we don't have enough lead to guarantee an acceptable outcome."

"How long do you figure we have till they get back?" Juanito asked.

"I assume they've gone for fresh horses and more men," Sikes said, knocking some of the dust off his shirt and trousers.

"And medical help," Emmett said. "Speaking of which, Yong needs to have somebody clean up that shoulder before it becomes more than just an inconvenience."

"They've probably gone where?" Sikes asked. "Carson City?"

"That's my guess."

"Washoe City's closer. Is that an option for us?"

Emmett shook his head. "Yong said Washoe City is too small for McIntosh to bother with. Might have bullets. Might not. Probably don't have a doctor."

"Then can we chance a visit to Carson City ourselves?"

Hands on his hips, Juanito said, "Thaddeus McIntosh's town? I don't think so."

"Considering the reception we got there the first time," Emmett said, "I doubt we could slip in and out unnoticed. Not with a gunshot Chinaman and the need for a few hundred bullets."

"And if that's where Seth and Charlie have gone, they'll raise the alarm before we get there."

Emmett rubbed the back of his neck. "Probably. So the surest thing for us is to return to Virginia City."

"They'll be back long before we will," Sikes said.

"So we're gonna have to split up. You and Juanito'll have to stay here and keep an eye on 'em."

"And if they come back in force?"

"Stay hidden. In fact, let's make it look like all four of us are leaving. Only you two scout out a fresh vantage point you can watch 'em from."

Sikes cradled the buffalo rifle. "But if they manage to hitch up and leave, you want us to follow, right?"

"Exactly. You'll have to tail 'em…wherever they take those girls." Once again it began to gnaw away at Emmett—not knowing whether Li Xu was among the three captives only a few hundred yards away. "If they take 'em, get a telegram to me in Virginia City somehow. Let me know where to meet up with you. But don't mention the girls in the telegram."

Juanito nodded as the three headed down the back slope toward the horses.

"Yong and I'll get what we need," Emmett said. "And if Yong can't ride back with me, I'll try to get another man who can."

"Just one?" Juanito asked.

Emmett threw up his hands. "I'll do what I can."

They approached Yong Xu, who sat silently beside Guiying's reposed body.

"She sure was pretty," Sikes said softly.

"Very pretty," Yong Xu said.

Emmett stood in silence for a moment, then said, "Did you hear our planning up there, Yong?"

The Chinese man nodded. He met Emmett's gaze. "Tell me the truth. Do you believe Li-Li is down there by the wagons?"

Emmett said softly, "I don't know, my friend. But we want Li back alive. And to be sure that's the way we get her back, you and I really need to go for supplies. Pronto. And—if possible—for more help."

Yong Xu got to his feet. He clenched his fists. "One part of me wants to…"

"I know," Emmett said, putting a hand on Yong's chest. "Juanito and Sikes will keep 'em in sight until we get back. Those men won't hurt her. They want her—" A pang gripped his insides. "Well, they won't hurt her."

That's what he told Yong Xu. But his guts wrenched within him. Unprincipled men like the ones just up the trail might give in to their passions regardless of their boss's instructions. Even if they didn't…He brooded over the nature of Blaylock's business.

CHAPTER THIRTY-TWO

In the carpeted upstairs hallway of Thaddeus McIntosh's opulent Carson City home, Charlie Blaylock shifted his weight from foot to foot. He couldn't have been sweating any more profusely if it were high noon in July under a broiling sun on the Staked Plains of Texas. Weather had nothing to do with his condition, though—it wasn't yet daybreak. But Seth was furious. And he was venting the full heat of his temper on Charlie.

The bedroom door opened, and the doctor stormed out. "That woman in there is in a bad way," he said, his voice a hoarse whisper, blood-tinged droplets of water flying from his fingertips with every gesticulation. "If you two can't keep it down out here, I'm gonna ask Mr. McIntosh to have the both of you removed. Now take your hollerin' elsewhere. Do you understand me?" He glared, beet-faced, before spinning on his heels and returning to the bedroom.

Seth thrust a finger in Charlie's face and hissed, "If Ettie dies, I may damn well kill you myself…before I even beef that damn Texan." If looks could do the deed, it would've already been done. And somebody would already be measuring Charlie's stretched-out body for a pine box. "Now follow me."

Seth marched off down the hall, motioning for Charlie to follow.

Once the two were behind closed doors in Thaddeus's billiard room, Seth laid into his brother again. "To hell with them Texans! How could you have been so stupid, Charlie?"

For the first time since arriving in Nevada, Charlie decided—rich or not— he'd had just about enough of his younger brother lording it over him. He stepped to within inches of the Belvidere. "You blame all this on me. Well, you listen to one thing, Seth: When we was young and our brother Thomas was like a pa to us, when he didn't come home from Adobe Walls, it was me that had to be the man. I'm the one had to go beg that damn Lieutenant Eli Strong to go out and look into the matter. I was the one had to listen to that damn young so-called officer tell me it weren't nothin' more'n rumors about the Comanche up there.

"Our family got ripped apart that day. Thomas dead. You hauled off by a pair of relations we ain't seen in years. Me on my own. How'd I know it'd all work out so pretty for you up here? You didn't have a dime more'n me when you left.

"All I knew was I had a debt to pay. An' I swore I'd pay it. For Thomas. For me. And for you." Now it was Charlie's turn to jab a finger in Seth's chest. "Well, I kept my oath. Took me seven years to do it, but I kept my word. Shootin' down Eli Strong on the street in Austin weren't my first choice. But it was gettin' close to bein' my last chance to do it."

Charlie's heart pounded as he released his pent-up frustration. "Now, I'm real sorry your woman got shot up there today. Real sorry. But all I done was keep my word. Whoever heard of Texas law dogs wanderin' this far from home in search of a man?"

Through all Charlie had said, Seth hadn't budged. Charlie had no idea how his brother was going to react, but that didn't matter. He was done cowering.

Seth narrowed his eyes. His voice was low now. "Why the hell did you have to tell anybody down in Texas you were comin' up here to Nevada?"

Charlie's eye twitched. A shudder ran through him. In a voice aimed at matching his brother's, he said, "'Cause I's so damn proud of all the rumors I'd heard about you and about how well you'd done for yourself up here. That's why. I wanted what few folks I still cared about down in Texas to know I's goin' up to see my little brother what done hisself so proud."

Seth's cheeks flushed.

"Now I kept one oath," Charlie went on. "And I'm gonna make another one right here and now."

"What's that?" Seth folded his arms.

"I'm ready to show you what kind of man I am. I'm gonna take care of that Texas law dog. I'm finished runnin' from him. I swear to you right here and now: that Texas lawman's gonna be dead inside of two days." Charlie's lip quivered. "And I'm gonna do the killin' myself."

"Is that a fact?"

Charlie gave a strong nod. "It is."

"Needs to be done," Seth said, his steely eyes narrowing again, his gaze boring right into Charlie's. "But if Ettie dies, killin' that Texas Ranger still won't atone for the loss of her."

He held Charlie's gaze for several long seconds, then intentionally bumped his shoulder as he walked past him to the door.

— ⁓ —

Thaddeus McIntosh and Seth Blaylock rousted the Carson City telegraph operator out of bed before the roosters had even wiped the sleep from their eyes. They walked him down to the telegraph office in his nightshirt, and now he sat at the desk, pencil in hand, ready to take down their message.

"And this is to go to your brother, Mr. Lucian McIntosh, up in Reno? Correct, sir?" he stammered.

"We've told you that already," Thaddeus said. "Now let's get on with it."

The operator nodded, the pencil quivering in his hand.

"Write this," Seth said. "Wagons ambushed by unidentified enemy near Washoe City. Stop. Had buffalo guns. Stop. Killed our draft horses. Stop. Going back with reinforcements. Stop." He nodded and waved his hand toward the Morse key. "Go on and send that much."

While the operator clicked away at the message, Thaddeus said, "I'm comin' with you, Seth."

Seth turned to him. "You really don't have to do that, sir. I'll take care of Mr. Lucian's business."

"I insist. He told me how impressed he was with those little China girls. And I don't want to see him lose those assets."

Was Thaddeus insinuating, Seth wondered, that he had somehow botched the transfer of the girls? That he might not be up to the task of taking care of Lucian's interests?

That nagging possibility—on top of Ettie's dire situation and Charlie's stupidity—had Seth stewing inside. But this was Lucian's dear brother. It wouldn't do to raise Thaddeus's hackles when he was already in the middle of a dicey situation. Nonetheless, he risked an appeal. "Really, sir. I just need the horses and a few men. You shouldn't trouble yourself."

Thaddeus set his jaw, then said, "I couldn't help but overhear you and Charlie shoutin'. I know it's that Texas bunch that met you on the road. And I know they were lookin' for Charlie."

"Yes, sir," Seth said. "But why should that cause you extra trouble, sir? You know I've always taken care of whatever Mr. Lucian's asked of me."

"A couple of those Texans came through Carson City before they wandered up toward Reno," Thaddeus said. "My boys met 'em on the street. Said they handled themselves like real men."

Before Seth could counter, Thaddeus put up a hand.

"Now we don't know how many they are," he said. "But we're beginnin' to get a feel for how talented and determined they are. So let's just put the kibosh on 'em—one way or another—today."

He cocked his head and paused for Seth to respond.

The telegraph operator had been waiting for a break in their conversation. "Um," he said, waving his hand feebly.

Seth waved him off. "Give us just a minute." Turning to Thaddeus, he said, "Can we step outside, sir?"

Thaddeus's dark brow furrowed. He heaved a breath, then headed through the half-glassed door.

Once on the boardwalk, Seth said, "Mr. Thaddeus, there's one more thing."

"What's that?"

"The Texans had a Chinaman with them."

Thaddeus shrugged. "So what? There are thousands of Chinese around here. Maybe he's their Mary."

"Somehow," Seth said, "in their sniffin' around—for information about Charlie's whereabouts, I suspect—I wonder whether they didn't stumble on *the* Chinese we got those girls from."

"What makes you think that?"

"Because instead of turnin' and runnin' when the shootin' started, that little Chinaman led the charge. Made a beeline straight for that one China girl that tried to get away."

Thaddeus was quiet. "Ain't like Chinamen to lead the charge, is it?"

"Not at all."

"Could be crazy."

"Or could've thought it was his daughter."

Thaddeus tugged at the end of his mustache.

"I shot the Chinaman," Seth said. "Chinaman went down, but he fell into an arroyo. I can't swear he's dead. Might've only winged him."

"So there may be other folks out there—not just the Texans—that've seen you transportin' the China girls."

"I'm sayin' the Chinese could've hired the Texas lawmen to do what the local law wouldn't do—help 'em look for their daughters."

McIntosh laughed. "How the blazes could that happen? You think the Chinese went about postin' signs? Took out an ad in the newspaper? Why, most of 'em are so poor, they can't buy a pot to piss in."

He gazed off down the street. After a moment, he clapped Seth on the shoulder. "Anyway, I wouldn't worry too much about that Chinaman. Like you say, you shot him. He's probably layin' dead in that gulch."

Seth knew the discussion was over. Whether he liked it or not, Thaddeus would go along with him back up to the wagons. He'd check out the situation with the Chinese girls and report it firsthand to Lucian. Seth glanced through the glass at the telegraph operator waiting inside.

"You go on and tell McAfee to get our twelve best men ready," Thaddeus said. "Tell him we'll ride right after breakfast. Meanwhile, I'm gonna go in and pay the telegraph bill. I'll see you up at the house in a minute."

Reluctantly Seth nodded. Twisting his lips, he turned away. He was bothered that he'd told Thaddeus about the Chinaman. Yet he realized that if he hadn't told him and then something further were to go wrong...why, there'd be hell to pay.

As he walked along the street into his own long shadow, his thoughts returned to Ettie. That bullet had ended up in a bad place. The doctor was doing the best he could, but she was in for a lengthy recovery—if she made it at all. And he couldn't remain by her side, where he wanted to be. He had to get those China girls down to Genoa, make sure he maintained Lucian McIntosh's confidence. Right now, it didn't much matter whether his brother was to blame for the predicament.

Ettie, McIntosh, Charlie—it all made him just that much more determined to see the whole bunch from Texas lying by the side of the road in their own blood.

As soon as Seth left, Thaddeus McIntosh went back inside the telegraph office.

"Get back on that telegraph key," he ordered the man in the nightshirt.

"Yes, sir?"

"To my brother, Lucian. A separate telegram, you hear?"

"Yes, sir." He picked up his pencil.

"Know who attacked wagons. Stop. Texans hunting down Charlie Blaylock. Stop. Chinese may have hired Texans. Stop."

Thaddeus turned his back on the operator. "Be sure to send it right away. Put it on my bill."

"Will do, Mr. McIntosh," the operator said as Thaddeus was already stepping out the door.

CHAPTER THIRTY-THREE

Exhausted from riding through the night, Emmett stood rubbing his forehead in front of a packed house. Chinese men filled the dining room and kitchen of Yong Xu's place. More flooded the boardwalk right out front and spilled into the street. Yet another couple dozen crammed themselves into the small lot immediately behind the restaurant. Early though it was, the air inside the crowded café had already taken on a stuffy, suffocating quality.

A pair of older women, experienced in the use of traditional Chinese medicines, had treated Yong's bullet wound, and Yong was now back at the very center of all the activity. Emmett was learning that his new Chinese friend was a man of considerable inner strength and determination.

The same could be said for Wei, who had disappeared only briefly when Emmett and Yong had arrived in the small hours of the morning with the body of his lovely daughter Guiying. Wei was already back among the men in the café.

Emmett held up his hands for quiet.

"So how many of you own a pistol, a rifle, or a shotgun?" he asked once the talk had died down. "Show me your hands."

A low murmuring in Chinese swept through the room. Some were translating his question for their neighbors. A few timid hands went up.

He glanced at Yong Xu, who stood on a chair, counting.

"Only five," Yong said.

Only five? Emmett shook his head slowly. Out of well over a hundred men, only five had firearms. "Does that include the ones outside?"

"I'm afraid so," Yong said. "Most stores won't sell them to us Chinese."

"Two times I ordered a rifle from a catalogue," a nearby man with a wispy mustache said. "Both times, when I went to the post office to pick it up, they told me the package must have gotten lost."

Emmett released a tired sigh. Then he recalled Li and Yong's impressive throwing prowess.

"How about anything else that can be used as a weapon?" he asked. "Yong, I know you can handle a meat cleaver."

Again the room buzzed with chatter. This time it was more animated, a few miming how they might wield some implement or another in combat. Yong gave him a sideways glance as though throwing a cleaver at a human being had never crossed his mind.

"Many of us work in the mines," one fellow in dusty clothes said. "We can use a pick or a shovel."

"OK," Emmett said, his mind at work. "Now, what if we bought a couple of hacksaws and trimmed off one end of a pick to make it lighter and faster?"

Men nodded, answering aloud in both English and Chinese and showing how they might wield a lighter pick.

Yong spoke to the crowd, his expression grim. "You've all got knives of some sort in your houses—for cooking, for fixing things."

As the gruesome reality of what the rescue attempt might actually look like dawned on the Chinamen, the chatter died down. One man after another either stared at Yong with furrowed brows or dropped his gaze to the floor.

"I admit," Emmett said, "it may involve grisly work up there. But your daughters' and your neighbors' daughters' lives are at stake." He tried to make eye contact with as many individuals as possible. "So how many of you would be willing to go back up there with Yong and me to fight those kidnappers and set those girls free?"

Expecting a near-unanimous show of hands, Emmett was flummoxed when a mere fifteen or so volunteered.

Three of the elders rose and faced the crowd. Each in turn berated the men in stinging tones. Emmett didn't need to understand Chinese. Their frowns spoke volumes. Several of the listeners hung their heads but still wouldn't raise their hands. A few answered, their voices matching the elders' in bitterness.

Yong Xu turned to Emmett. "They're afraid of being burned out of their homes. They say the kidnappers were a few bad men from somewhere else. But if Chinese men take the law into their own hands, the people we live among—the men of the mining community—will use it as an excuse to drive us out."

Tang, a tall man in a mandarin cap, stepped forward, eyes glaring. "I don't want white men calling us Chinese a mob of lawless butchers. I don't care what they've done—if you're asking us to hack men up with knives, I'm leaving. It's bad enough around here already."

At that Yong bristled. "You're worried about what our white neighbors may call us? You're worried about your reputation—among people who won't lift a finger to help us? Well, I'm worried about my daughter's life. And so are these men." He motioned toward the other fathers. "What's worth more? Our girls' lives or your reputation?"

"I'm a civilized man," Tang snapped.

"And so are we," Yong countered. "The uncivilized ones are those who shot Yan and Guiying—two harmless young women—in cold blood."

Tang scowled. When he turned and elbowed his way to the door, a half dozen others followed him out.

Emmett glanced at the elders. To a man, their gazes were downcast.

"Tang got one thing right," Emmett said to the crowd. "People may misunderstand our actions. But Yong is right too. The gang that raided Chinatown the other night, they're not gentlemen. They're unprincipled sorts who won't hesitate to shed even more blood."

All eyes were on him now.

"I'd rather bring along five men ready to do whatever it takes to get your daughters back than fifty who don't have the stomach to stand up to bald-faced evil."

Others began to shuffle out. The faces of some suggested that fear rather than morals fueled their decisions.

Emmett and Yong exchanged glances. Yong turned to those who remained, thanked everyone for hearing him out, and then dismissed all but those who had volunteered.

One face in the exiting crowd caught Emmett's attention. He looked familiar. And he wore the same snappish expression Tang had displayed. Emmett frowned. *Chin—the baggage handler from the hotel.*

Once the objectors had cleared out, about two dozen men remained. One of them stood at Yong's elbow, speaking softly, apparently on behalf of the handful of fellows behind him.

Yong said to Emmett, "These eight men say they will come along as porters. But they won't fight."

Emmett nodded to the eight. "Thank you. You're courageous. And your help is welcome."

Stepping over to a table, he opened one of his saddlebags, reached in, and drew out a pouch containing paper money and coins. After thumbing through the bills, he shook his head, wishing it were more.

"Besides those who already own one," Emmett said to his Chinese posse, "who else would be willing to carry a gun if I can manage to purchase a few?"

Four hands flew up immediately.

"Ho!" one of them exclaimed, wide-eyed and drop-jawed.

"It's serious business," Emmett said, his eyebrows knit. "Dangerous and ugly."

Their faces grew somber.

"I do not look forward to killing," the expressive one said. "I am only glad to be able to meet these evil men armed as they are."

The explanation eased Emmett's concern. To his way of thinking, anyone overly eager to use a gun against another human being was a liability. A man did what he had to in that regard. Nothing more.

—m—

Along the way to the Virginia City telegraph office, Emmett realized how badly he hoped Blaylock's wagons were still where he'd last seen them. The rough plans he'd been formulating were far better suited to taking on the kidnappers out in open country than in some town of their choosing. So, when it came to word from Juanito or Sikes, no news would be good news.

As it turned out, no telegram awaited him. That didn't do much to ease his mind after all, though. Anything and everything could change before he and his rescue party got back to the wagons. Charlie and Seth Blaylock could get the wagons moving again. The Blaylocks could bring along an entire army of McIntosh men—armed to the teeth. His inexperienced posse could dissolve in the face of any small setback.

No matter—he had to act on what he knew, with whatever resources he had. Li's life was at stake.

By the time he got back to Yong's restaurant, he had acquired two more shotguns and two used Colt revolvers. He'd spent just about everything else he had on ammunition, counting on Juanito and Sikes to cover their remaining traveling expenses.

Those with impromptu weapons were in the lot behind the Golden Dragon. They'd come up with a collection of knives that would've made Jim Bowie proud. Yet they were having a tough time figuring out the best way to use them to good effect against men armed with guns.

As for those who'd be heeled, Emmett only had time to cover the basics. Target practice was out of the question.

"Just get as close to Blaylock's men as possible before firing," he said.

"How will we get so close?" a younger fellow wearing range clothes and a Chinese straw hat asked.

With a wink that he hoped would bolster their courage, he answered, "I've got a surprise up my sleeve. I'll show you later."

CHAPTER THIRTY-FOUR

Ettie's breathing was labored. Beads of perspiration glistened on her forehead and temples. Seth held her limp hand while the doctor lifted the blood-stained cloth that covered her wound.

"She's gonna make it, isn't she, Doc?" he asked yet again.

The doctor took his time examining the nasty bullet hole in her upper-left abdomen. "Still no sign of infection. That's the good news."

"What's the bad news?" Thaddeus McIntosh asked from where he leaned against the opposite wall.

"Bullet may've nicked her spleen. Or maybe the kidney. Can't tell for sure. Lot of swelling in there."

Seth didn't know much about human organs. But he hung on to what the doc said about no infection. "Think you'll know better in a couple hours?" As he asked, his gaze shifted from the doctor to Thaddeus. He knew Ettie was dear to Lucian. He wasn't so sure Lucian's brother shared the same soft spot in his heart for her. What's more, Thaddeus had already made it clear that he was chomping at the bit to get the replacement horses—as well as his gunhands—out to those stranded wagons and the China girls.

"I'm hoping the fever will subside and that she'll rest better in just a few hours," the doctor said. "Don't worry. I won't leave her side before then."

Thaddeus shifted his weight.

"Texans had to go for more ammunition," Seth said to him. "They won't get back before us, even if we wait two more hours."

"Unless they decided to shave some time off," Thaddeus said.

Seth frowned. "How would they do that?"

"Comin' back by train—at least as far as Carson City."

Seth shot him a sharp look. "Offload their horses right here under your nose? They wouldn't dare."

McIntosh shook his head. "They've shown a lot of gumption. I've got some boys down at the station just in case."

"Well, if you've got boys on it, then we're covered. Right?"

Thaddeus stared back coolly. He shoved off the wall. "Two more hours, Seth. After that I'm ridin'—with or without you. I'll just tell Lucian you were preoccupied."

He ambled out and pulled the bedroom door behind him.

Seth squeezed Ettie's hand. "Don't you go and leave us just yet, you hear, Ettie?"

Doc's expression was somber as his gaze met Seth's.

Me or Charlie—one of us—is gonna be the man to kill that Texan. I got a whole lot more reason to see him dead than Thaddeus does.

CHAPTER THIRTY-FIVE

Marsh covered acre after acre at the north end of Washoe Lake. In a grove just above the marsh, Emmett squatted on his heels, eating a rice ball. "Never figured plain old rice could taste so good," he said.

Although the sun had already set, he could see by the gleam in Yong Xu's eyes that he was proud of his people—the women who had prepared their rice rations no less than the volunteers who had come along.

"We may turn you Chinese yet," he said with a hint of a smile.

Emmett considered what it took for Yong Xu to smile at all, given how little the man knew about the fate of his daughter.

"A spot of fine black tea would finish things off delightfully," Sikes said.

Emmett shook his head. "No fires tonight. No light, no smoke, no smell of food."

The Englishman harrumphed. "Barbarian. Dispensing with tea. Why, even the Zulus delayed hostilities until after we'd had our tea."

"Don't recall reading that they'd given Her Majesty's finest that kind of consideration," Emmett said, standing and adjusting his gun belt. "Anyway, we need to move. We've caught a break. Don't wanna waste it."

The others rose and began readying themselves as well.

Juanito inspected the cylinder of his revolver yet again. "I never imagined we would be doing this before Blaylock got back with reinforcements."

"Yep," Emmett said. "Something seems off. What was the mood out there around the wagons last time you checked?"

"They've got a campfire going. They've got food. I heard them laughing from time to time."

Emmett looked for a reaction from Yong Xu. He hoped the laughs Blaylock's boys were having out there weren't at the expense of the girls.

Yong's fists tightened, but he said nothing.

"Horses?" Juanito asked.

"We'll picket 'em back here," Emmett said. "Go in on foot."

"That's a decision you may regret," Sikes said. "They've got five horses and five men. Three could grab a girl each and ride away into the night. You might never see them again."

Emmett scratched his forehead. "The way I figure it, if they were gonna do that, they'd have gone with Charlie and Seth. Just left the wagons here."

Sikes wore a leery expression. "If there's one thing I learned from the military, it's that if something can go wrong, it probably will. I say you'll regret not bringing the horses."

Emmett's stomach knotted. Sikes might be right, but tonight any premature noise would probably result in a failed rescue attempt. Maybe worse.

"We need to cover that last hundred yards of open ground Apache style— in absolute silence," he said. "Our numbers, plus the element of surprise. Those are our advantages."

He studied his Chinese contingent. Some of them might have been scared, but armed the way they were, they looked as frightening as hell.

"*Hermano,*" Juanito said, tapping Emmett's arm. He took a few steps away from the posse. A grave look came over his face as he searched the dark outline of the ridge to the south.

Emmett frowned and held up a hand for quiet. He squinted toward where the road crested the rise, straining to see and hear what Juanito was listening to.

Blazes! In the dimness he couldn't see them, but he could now faintly hear what Juanito had picked up on—the sound of horses. Plenty of horses.

Juanito glanced at the Chinese volunteers, then leaned in toward Emmett. "I think we may have just lost the advantage of numbers."

Emmett nodded grimly. He turned to the posse. "Gents, the clock just ran out on us."

The apprehension on the faces of the Chinese showed that they too had already heard the distant hoofbeats.

"But even this can work in our favor," Emmett said. "Provided we get moving right away."

Sikes looked at him quizzically.

"Trust me," Emmett said. "They'll let their guard down. They'll think they've got more than enough hot gunhands."

"And won't they?" Sikes said.

Emmett shook his head. "Arrogance."

A half grin creased Sikes's features. "Isandlwana."

Emmett's next remark was for the whole party. "Just don't give up our biggest remaining advantage. They don't know we're here."

Yong motioned for silence.

Emmett marched to his horse and retrieved a gunnysack, then summoned Yong with a wave.

"Once we're in place up there," he said, "pick out the two or three men most experienced in mining. Bring 'em down into the arroyo."

Yong cocked his head.

"I'll fill you in once we're there."

The Chinaman nodded.

It took twenty minutes to reach the dry creek bed where Guiying had fallen. The sad truth that more of them would likely die before the night was over gnawed at Emmett. He only hoped it wouldn't be another of the young women.

Before joining Yong and the miners in the gully, Emmett knelt beside Sikes and Juanito at the edge of the mesquite thicket, no more than a hundred yards from the Conestogas, and surveyed the slavers' camp.

One of the five McIntosh men who had stayed with the Chinese girls used his shotgun to prod the three women back into the canopied wagon.

A moment later, from across the open ground, came a bawdy cry. "About damn time!"

There was laughter and indistinct banter around the wagons as Blaylock's relief column swung down from their saddles. Before long a second campfire was going.

"How many do you count?" Emmett asked.

"They keep moving in and out of the firelight," Juanito said. "It's hard to get an exact number, but I think about twelve new ones arrived."

"Fourteen," Yong Xu said, looking certain.

"Nineteen total then," Juanito said.

Emmett eyed Yong. "Your porters won't fight, huh?"

Yong tightened his lips and shook his head.

Sikes pushed aside some of the brush. "Recalculating the odds?"

"Odds don't matter anymore. Considering any town would be as good as a fort to Blaylock's boys, we have to take 'em here and now. Come with me."

Emmett had the porters remain at the edge of the chaparral to keep watch on the men around the wagons while he took the rest back into the arroyo to explain his plan.

Pulling a stick of dynamite from the burlap sack in his hand, he said, "Any of you miners experienced in the use of this stuff?"

Even in the dark, Emmett could see Yong's eyebrows shoot up. Yong chuckled quietly, then winced and clutched his shoulder.

Emmett grinned.

Three men in a mix of traditional Chinese and Western garb edged forward. "We've worked with dynamite," one of the three said.

"How experienced are you?" Emmett asked. "We can't risk injuring the women."

All eyes were fixed on the miners.

An older man—quite thin—with a sparse beard said, "Very experienced."

"OK then," Emmett said. "We crawl in silence close enough to Blaylock's men for you to throw a few sticks at 'em. And then the rest of us rush 'em like madmen before they know what's happened."

He looked from one miner to the other. "So how many sticks do we need?"

The older man held up three fingers. "Three only," he said. "More too much."

"They can't be thrown too close to the wagon," Emmett said. "They might take a bad bounce and blow the girls to high heaven."

"We will just have to crawl very close," a younger miner said. "Maybe just thirty yards from the wagon. Then light the sticks."

"And you can throw them close enough to shock McIntosh's men, but not so close that the girls are injured?"

The three nodded.

With his fingertips Emmett held the fuse away from the papered explosive. "I don't know dynamite," he said. "But I do know that we can't leave the fuses this long. Either Blaylock's men'll spot us waiting for the fuses to burn down and start shooting or—if we throw 'em with long fuses—they just might scoop 'em up and throw 'em right back."

The older man with the sparse beard said, "We cut fuse very shorter." He turned to his friends. "You two work with short fuse before?"

They both affirmed they had.

"I cut them *very* shorter," he said. "You know fuse. Very tricky. You know. Could blow up self." He pointed two fingers at his own eyes.

The youngest miner looked at the others, then with a resolute jaw said, "We'll take that risk."

At that, Emmett took out three tins of parlor matches. "Thought these would be safer than lucifers."

All three gave a bow of the head.

Emmett clapped the closest two on their shoulders and said, "Let's go rescue your women."

As they clambered out of the arroyo, he muttered softly, "Stay safe, Li Xu. Your friends, too."

CHAPTER THIRTY-SIX

C louds blanketed more of the sky than not. The two campfires the McIntosh gang had made did little to push back the inky darkness of the night. In that blackness, twenty-six men inched forward on their bellies toward the wagons—toward the precious cargo Blaylock's bunch had come to recover.

Seventy yards was a long way to crawl undetected across open ground. Thorns, burrs, and bits of rock weren't making the ordeal any easier. Emmett's forearms and knees were taking the brunt of the abuse—not that the gravel that found its way into his trousers and boots was any treat either.

But each yard he and the posse covered brought them a yard closer to the abducted girls. Closer to Li Xu, he eagerly hoped, so her captivity might end tonight. So he himself could ensure her freedom and safety.

The old Chinese miner to his right hissed softly. Emmett held up his slow crawl and peered that way. The miner nodded.

This would be close enough. The posse lay motionless in a broad arc on either side of Emmett. He glanced right and left trying to see whether they had drawn too close—whether firelight reflecting off their faces might be visible to those guarding the girls.

Though the ground was relatively flat here, the men advancing with him had instinctively sought cover behind even the skimpiest clumps of grass or in the most subtle dips in the terrain.

Indistinct yammering, broken by an occasional round of chortles, drifted from the campfires into the gloom.

Emmett looked to Juanito on his left. His brother-in-law nodded.

Turning again to the old-timer on his right, Emmett breathed, "Whenever you're ready."

The wiry Chinaman looked up and down the line of rescuers, then toward Blaylock's men around the campfires. Rising to his knees, he struck his parlor match.

Only six feet away, Emmett's heart picked up a beat. As he readied himself to scramble to his feet and rush the kidnappers, a thought flashed through his mind: the moment that match touched that snipped-off fuse…the last thing he might ever see on this good earth was one splendiferous blast.

Two more matches flared.

The three dynamite men leapt to their feet and heaved the lit explosives toward the kidnappers. The strongest of them threw for the campfire farthest from the wagons—and the eight or so men lounging in its orange glow. The other two lobbed their sticks to either side of the encampment.

Hoping the latter two explosives wouldn't kill so much as confuse and terrorize men and horses alike, Emmett gritted his teeth.

The concussion from the clustered blasts punched deep into his chest.

One side of the nearer wagon heaved up—two wheels lifting completely off the ground—and dropped violently again to the earth.

From fear of what the explosions might have done to the girls, Emmett's stomach tightened. His ears rang as he staggered to his feet.

Bits of debris and a good deal of sand pelted the wagon's canopy and rained down on everyone. Clumps of dry grass burned on both sides of the Conestogas.

Now the entire posse was up and rushing the camp. They let fly. Along with the booming of shotguns and the cracking of handgun and rifle fire, cries and shouts filled the air. And the initial effect on the McIntosh men was everything Emmett had hoped it would be.

But not for long.

McIntosh's boys began to recover and shoot back. The Chinese miner to Emmett's right staggered and fell.

Several of Yong's volunteer porters raced to the wagon the girls were in. Taking hold of its tongue, they made draft animals of themselves to get the Conestoga rolling away from the shootout. Those armed only with knives and pickaxes took up positions to shield their brother Chinamen.

First one, then another of the straining porters fell to gunfire.

Two McIntosh men rushed the back of the Conestoga, six-guns blazing. Emmett—now directly alongside the wagon—chambered a round, took aim, and dropped one of them.

The second one seemed determined to kill the girls rather than give them up to their rescuers. With little time to think, Emmett swung the butt of his rifle. His uppercut caught the desperado under the chin. The man's head snapped back, and he spun to the ground.

And then Emmett spotted the dandy—the one whose hat he'd shot off down by the arroyo. Had to be Seth Blaylock. He was at the campfire, thumbing and firing his Schofield with a vengeance. Emmett levered the Winchester again, swung it to his shoulder, and squeezed the trigger. Out of cartridges.

His heart pounded.

The dandy paused shooting, reached down, and plucked a chunk of wood from the flames. He reared back and flung it at the wagon the Chinamen were now effectively hauling away. Landing squarely atop the canvas canopy, the burning branch instantly ignited the dry fabric. Screams resounded from within the wagon.

Li might burn.

Torn momentarily, Emmett was relieved to see that the Chinese fighters surrounding the burning wagon were already extracting the girls from the rapidly spreading flames.

He returned his attention to Seth Blaylock. The five or six McIntosh men who remained on their feet rallied around the dandy. And one of them was Charlie.

Still clutching his empty Winchester, Emmett drew his Colt. Just as he took aim, his left hand flew back and the Winchester went flying. Below the little finger his hand burned as though pressed against a branding iron.

More lead rent the air.

Sikes arrived at his side to help. But the Englishman got off only a few rounds before taking a bullet in the leg and going down.

"Saddle up!" Seth Blaylock was shouting as he swung up onto his huge, dark mount.

Charlie turned to follow his brother's lead.

No, you don't. Emmett dashed for the murderer.

With an uncooperative, bandaged arm, Charlie took an extra hop trying to hoist himself into the saddle. He had one boot in the stirrup and both hands on the saddle horn when Emmett collared him. Emmett's own wounded hand screamed in pain.

Charlie sent an elbow flying upside Emmett's head. Willing himself through the stars that danced before his eyes, Emmett coldcocked Charlie with the butt of his Colt. And the outlaw wilted to the ground.

In the melee, Emmett felt a horse wheeling around behind him. Over his shoulder, he glimpsed the other Blaylock, pistol drawn, getting the drop on him.

A shot sounded, and a bullet cut a crimson line across Seth's white shirt-sleeve. His face twisted in pain and rage. Swearing, he gigged his horse and cut dirt into the darkness. Behind him, three other McIntosh men hauled tail into the night.

A few reports sounded from out of the gloom. Then the shooting was over.

Emmett turned to find Juanito right there.

"Couldn't let that *gallo* kill you, *hermano*."

"*Te lo agradezco, cuñado*," Emmett replied without thinking. *I appreciate it, brother-in-law.*

He felt strangely numb…as though everything that had just happened was part of some fever-induced nightmare. But his senses confirmed it was all too real. The comingling of pungent burning smells. The groaning of wounded men. His throbbing hand.

Pivoting in place, he took in the devastation. Both sides had taken losses. Thankfully McIntosh's crew had gotten the worst of it.

"Handle Charlie Blaylock," he mumbled to Juanito.

Without awaiting an answer, he trotted toward the still-burning wagon.

Several yards away, the men who had gotten the girls out were tending to them. One girl cried out in pain, her arm badly burned, her face flecked with droplets of blood where debris had peppered her.

The other two—likewise bloodied and sobbing—clung to their brothers. They seemed to be otherwise unharmed.

Nowhere was Li Xu to be found, though.

Her father squatted beside the young woman with the burns and stared blankly at the ground.

Emmett rested a hand on Yong's shoulder. "Do these girls know what happened to Li?"

Yong nodded. "They said—"

The answer Emmett desperately wanted to hear was cut short by fierce shouting in Chinese near the other wagon. When he spun to see what it was all about, he saw Wei and two other Chinese men attempting to restrain some of their neighbors—men brandishing cleavers and knives as they argued back.

He hurried to the scene.

Wei glanced at Emmett. "These men want to mutilate the kidnappers' bodies for what they did to our daughters," he wailed in English. "And I won't have it. They may deserve it, but we are not dogs." He glowered at the men with blades.

Arms hanging loosely at his sides, blood dripping from his left hand, Emmett suddenly felt spent. Seeing his expression, the clamoring Chinamen gave up their struggle. Those who only a moment before had been set on revenge now dropped to the ground and began to sob.

CHAPTER THIRTY-SEVEN

Emmett gripped his bandaged left hand. "How many casualties?"

"Fourteen McIntosh men dead," Juanito said. "That first dynamite blast must've killed half that number."

Charlie Blaylock, bound hand and foot, sat on the ground at Juanito's feet. The Texian nudged him with the toe of his boot. "One alive here. Four got away."

Scowling deeply, Blaylock studied his captors in silence.

Emmett glared back at his brother's murderer. Having Charlie Blaylock in hand should've given him a sense of satisfaction. It should've left him with little more to do than escort the outlaw back home for trial. But the game had changed. This murderer had gotten himself attached to a band of kidnapping slavers. And one of the women they had abducted was beginning to mean a whole lot more to Emmett than he would've ever thought possible.

Yes, he was glad Charlie Blaylock's hide was in his hands. What he would do with it, however, was no longer so cut-and-dried.

"Wounded or killed on our side?" Emmett asked Juanito.

"Four dead. Seven wounded, not counting the girls."

Having done what he could for the young women, an older Chinese man was now pouring water from a canteen over the bullet wound in Sikes's leg.

"You gonna be OK, Sikes?" Emmett asked.

Sikes bobbed his head. "I don't think I'll be putting much weight on it anytime soon, but after a good cleaning it should mend well enough." In the dying firelight, beads of sweat glistened on his face.

Emmett eyed Juanito, who in turn pursed his lips and nodded.

Yong Xu stood close by, one hand hanging from his belt, close to the holster. Wei was at his side.

"What can I do?" Wei asked.

Yong seemed lost in thought.

After surveying the scene once again, Emmett said, "Let's get the injured into one wagon, hitch up some horses, and get moving for Virginia City." He pointed his thumb back toward the supply wagon. "Bring along any water they had. And any spare ammunition. Leave the rest."

"I'll see to it," Wei said solemnly. He patted Yong Xu on the back as he walked past him.

Emmett stepped over to Yong. "Can I have a word with you, my friend?"

The two ambled out of earshot of the rest of the crowd.

"I'm sorely disappointed, too," Emmett said. He peered at Yong's dejected face. "I wanted Li to be back in your arms by now."

Yong tightened his lips but still said nothing.

"We may not have accomplished everything we hoped to here tonight, but you and your men...You did yourselves proud. You saved three girls we'd never have seen again."

Yong's gaze finally met his.

Emmett went on. "And we have Charlie Blaylock as a bargaining chip. Seth'll want his brother back. I'm pretty sure he'll talk McIntosh into negotiating with us."

When Yong Xu finally spoke, his throat sounded dry. "Min, one of the girls we rescued tonight, told me that monster McIntosh has kept Li-Li for himself. He may already be..." He choked back his emotions, then wiped his sleeve across his mouth. "That filthy man...using my precious daughter."

Emmett's eyes burned. Kept her for himself...Anger roiled within him. He shook his head to clear away images of that McIntosh bastard having his way with Li.

"I'll get her back," he muttered.

Yong began to pace. "What if McIntosh won't give her back? What if he doesn't care about Charlie Blaylock?"

"He'll give her back." Emmett set his jaw and stared into the darkness toward Reno. Getting Li Xu back alive had just become his life's sole mission.

Yong faced Emmett. "And you're actually going to give up the man who shot your brother? The man you chased all the way from Texas?"

"Tonight wasn't about capturing my brother's murderer, Yong. It was about freeing those girls. The good Lord just gave us an unexpected bonus."

Though Yong Xu was trembling, his eyes revealed a glimmer of hope.

"Charlie Blaylock…" Emmett went on. "Convicting and hanging that no-good skeezicks won't bring my brother back from the dead. But if his worthless life can be traded to redeem Li and the other girl, then hell yes—I'll give him up. And I'll consider my trip all the way up here from Texas more than worthwhile." He clapped his friend on his good shoulder.

Yong got ahold of himself enough to say, "I swear an oath to you, Emmett Strong. If McIntosh won't take your offer, I myself will avenge your brother's death. I'll make both Blaylock and McIntosh wish—for the rest of their miserable lives—that they had exchanged Li for Charlie."

Emmett shook his head. "Lucian McIntosh will deal. On my terms."

CHAPTER THIRTY-EIGHT

The brisk breeze that whipped across the open stretch of road fluttered Lucian McIntosh's dark-gray sack coat. Seth Blaylock stood behind his boss, surveying the carnage from the previous night's attack. How in the world had he let himself get caught so flat-footed? He'd underestimated the Texans, their abilities, and their determination. Badly. Had it been his preoccupation with Ettie?

The sight of Thaddeus McIntosh's corpse lying in a most unnatural position, eyes still open, set him on edge. He cast a glance at the cluster of gunhands near the charred wagon frame, then his gaze returned to his boss. His stomach tensed. Seth didn't fear anybody—anybody except a livid Lucian McIntosh, that is.

McIntosh looked up from his slain brother. Hands on his hips, the huge, dark mountain of a man turned. His lips curled back. "To hell with all Texans," he snarled. "Damn bunch of Mexicans. Comin' up here, stirrin' up the damn Chinese against white folk. Slaughterin' my brother..." Clenching his jaw, he inhaled deeply.

He poked a thick finger into the center of Seth's chest. "I want that Texas lawman dead, you hear?"

Seth gave a sharp nod. He'd learned long ago that when the boss was fuming like this, you kept your head down.

McIntosh scuffed a charred spot of ground with his boot. "Dynamite. Who the hell has the gall to come at Lucian McIntosh with dynamite?"

Hardly was the question out of his mouth when he wheeled and snapped at the gunhands over by the wagon, "Will somebody please show a little respect? Get a blanket and cover my dead brother's body. Now!"

He turned back to Seth. "Who the hell would've ever figured it? Texans allyin' themselves with the Chinese? The filthy johnnies!"

Seth tensed for another tirade—a lecture on how he never should've raided Virginia City's Chinatown to begin with.

"To hell with all Chinese!" Lucian spat out. "Why, I oughta use them two China girls back home but good…and then when I'm done, take 'em and leave their dead bodies right there in the middle of Chinatown. Teach them damn johnnies they'd damn well better *never* interfere with the likes of Lucian McIntosh again." He glared. "Who the hell do they think they are anyway? Chinamen!"

Seth sensed a chance to deflect his boss's fury. He put on his most determined face. Narrowing his eyes, he said, "I assure you, sir—them Chinese are gonna get what's coming to 'em. They got no business acting like a white man's equals."

McIntosh met Seth's gaze, his expression hard as granite. Several seconds passed when the only sound to be heard was the rustle of the wind through the scrub grass.

"Bottom line, you know who I blame for this entire mess?" the boss asked.

"Sir," Seth ventured, "let me repeat myself. I made it clear to Mr. Thaddeus that he shouldn't dirty his own hands with this affair. I tried to convince him to stay in Carson City. To let me lead the men back up here."

McIntosh waved his hand dismissively. "I lost my brother on account of that damn Texan. And you don't know if Ettie's gonna pull through yet. I don't blame you. You didn't lead them Texans up here. As much as anybody, I blame Charlie. Now how bad do you want that good-for-nothin' brother of yours back?"

The question was unexpected. And it was surprisingly difficult to answer. To Seth it seemed as though Charlie had arrived with a whole trainload of trouble hitched to him, plus a caboose full of bad luck. On the other hand, letting that Texas lawman determine his brother's fate…That'd constitute an insult to his blood and a blow his own reputation.

He answered his boss cautiously, "Don't wanna let that Texan have the final say about both our brothers."

"What if your brother gets beefed in the process of us takin' down the Texan?"

Seth shrugged. "You have somethin' particular in mind?"

McIntosh stared across the landscape. "Virginia City is the one town around here that can match my resources and my influence. Can't go ridin' into Virginia City demandin' they turn over the Texans and the Chinese that did all this. Hell, the way things are goin', I wouldn't be surprised if somebody in Virginia City—somebody already nursin' a grudge against me—actually gives them Chinese a hearin' and accuses me and Thaddeus of thievin' their girls."

"So what do we do?"

"What do you think, son? You think them Texans are satisfied? Are they gonna pick up and leave now? Take Charlie back south for justice and leave the Chinese to finish business with us all on their own?"

Seth thought about it for a minute. Why wouldn't they? It's what they came here for to begin with. They'd save themselves a whole lot of trouble.

"I don't know about you," McIntosh said, "but I've got an inklin'."

Seth watched Lucian's gunslicks hoist and carry away another dead body. "What kind of inklin'?"

"That them Texans have gone and gotten themselves all righteous for a cause all of a sudden. I expect they'll come callin' on us real soon, wantin' to make a trade. Just may wanna offer up your brother Charlie for them last two China girls."

"You think so?"

"Like I said—just an inklin'."

"Based on?"

"Based on the way they went and pulled together that little Chinese army. I'll bet they cut themselves a deal with the only folks around here stupid enough to go toe-to-toe against us McIntoshes like that."

Seth nodded. "They help the Chinese get their little girls back if the Chinese help them jump Charlie Blaylock. Damn! That's like makin' allies of Indians."

McIntosh pulled a cigar from his inside coat pocket. "Long history of white men usin' one tribe against another when it served their purposes."

The gunhands had gathered all the corpses and laid them out side by side. Only one body had been placed in the wagon. The fine boots sticking out from the end of the blanket told Seth it was Thaddeus's remains.

"Just in case the Texans don't have a deal with the Chinese," Seth said, "or just in case they ain't so righteous…Maybe now that they've got Charlie, they break with the Chinese and try to head on home. I think we oughta have men watchin' the rail stations round about."

McIntosh nodded. "Meanwhile, we sit back a day or two and wait for 'em to come offerin' us a trade." He started toward the wagon.

"And you'll make the trade?" Seth asked, following along.

"Of course. And of course we'll also set an ambush between Reno and Virginia City." The dark gleam came back to McIntosh's eyes. "We'll teach them Texans a lesson. And them Chinese, too. We'll ravish those girls top to bottom right in front of their eyes. Then put a bullet in the belly of every one of their blasted Mexican and Chinese friends. Let 'em die slow and painful."

"Be done with the whole lot of them," Seth said with a smirk.

"Except the China girls," McIntosh said. "We keep them alive. Bring 'em back with us to keep or to sell. All depends on my mood by the time we're finished with all this blasted folderol."

"Just let me be the one to put the bullet in that law dog's belly," Seth said. "He's the one responsible for sendin' Ettie to death's doorstep."

McIntosh flicked cigar ashes. "For Ettie? Yeah, I'll let you finish him off for Ettie. But not before we make him pay dearly for what he did to my brother."

They were now beside the wagon. Lucian reached over the sideboard and rested his big hand on the blanket. He was silent for a long while. Then he murmured, "Don't you worry, Thaddeus. They'll bleed for doin' this to you."

CHAPTER THIRTY-NINE

"Ettie…Miss Main. It's OK. It's just a dream."

Whose voice? She struggled to make sense of everything. *So much blood. So terrible. All the blood. That poor girl.* She heard herself moaning.

"Ettie, it's just a dream. It's me—Doc Monroe. I'm still here."

She felt the cool, damp cloth mopping her forehead. The left side of her abdomen hurt something awful. But why? Her eyes fluttered. She turned her head side to side, searching. Where was the girl? And Seth?

"You're due for another dose of laudanum. Here you go."

A bitter medicinal scent assaulted her nose. She winced. "No. I don't…"

"It'll ease that pain. Help you sleep."

Sleep. Have I been asleep? The poor girl. A bullet in the back. So much blood.

"Here, drink."

Ettie's eyes were fully open now. They focused on Doc Monroe. The smell of the medicine made her shudder. "No, Doc. Not right now, please." Her own voice sounded strange to her.

"OK then, Ettie. For now we'll wait. You feeling a little better?"

She didn't answer. The pain was bad, but at the moment, the things she had just seen were more upsetting. So vivid. And Seth's reaction…

It dawned on Ettie that she was in a bedroom at Thaddeus McIntosh's place. In Carson City. She'd spent a night or two here before. With Seth.

When she closed her eyes again, there was that unfortunate girl once more. An unbelievably huge, gaping bullet hole in her back. Blood that wouldn't stop flowing. Pooling on the hardwood floor. The girl still trying to get up. People yelling and screaming. A deafening blast and a flash. Ettie jumped, her eyes flying open.

It was daylight now. The doctor was gone.

She was thirsty. The pain wasn't quite as bad. But she couldn't get the rest of the vision out of her mind—Seth, smoking Schofield revolver in his gloved hand, laughing. Laughing!

"China girls. Damn fun sport, ain't it Ettie?" That's what he'd said.

Had he really said that? Back at that Chinese restaurant maybe? Or was it only in the nightmare?

Ettie licked her dry lips. No more laudanum for a while. She needed to think.

She envisioned the real Chinese girl at the restaurant. The bullet hole was much smaller. There was less blood. But she was no less dead. Ettie saw the girl's youthful face, soft and lovely, eyes still open.

One part of her wanted to push it all out of her mind. But she couldn't. Not yet. She forced herself to recall that night.

Seth hadn't shot that girl. "No shootin' unless the Chinamen come runnin'," he'd said.

On the other hand, she remembered his eyes. With the Chinese girl lying dead only steps away, they had shown not an ounce of remorse. "You wanna live? You stay put and keep your mouths shut," he'd snarled at the rest of the petrified girls.

A tear rolled down Ettie's cheek. How had she become so inured to this kind of life—to this man?

In her mind's eye, she saw another Chinese girl—beautiful costume, shining hair—running toward the arroyo. Stopped cold by a bullet to the stomach. Seth's bullet.

Ettie's hand moved carefully over her own punctured abdomen. She deserved this, didn't she? That pretty Chinese girl didn't.

As her gaze drifted to the cord that tied back the luxurious burgundy curtains, she recalled her last minutes with Li and Ping—the girls Lucian McIntosh had decided to keep for himself. Wasn't that the way it had started for her? Kidnapped four years ago. A deal between Seth and Lucian so Seth could keep her for himself instead of sending her to one of the big man's bed houses. A chill swept through her as she relived the terror. Just like the China girls.

She wiped away another tear. *I did try to run away from all this. Once.*

Only once. McIntosh had had too many men. When they'd caught her and left her alone with Seth again, that had been the turning point. With his knife at her throat, she had determined to survive and make the best of it. That night she had become an actress.

She remembered—becoming resigned to her fate, burying her feelings a hundred times a day.

It had taken more than a year to gain Seth's trust. He had begun to buy her nice things—things she'd never dreamed of owning as a struggling eighteen-year-old waitress with no family. Another year and she had learned to carry herself with the same cool, ruthless air that he projected. She had refused to let herself think about the pain—hers or their captives'.

Till just recently.

Kidnapping was deeply wrong. Slavery was a darker evil yet. But senseless, cold-blooded murder on top of it all…Her heart and soul could no longer bury what she knew.

Lately Seth had become something worse than a kidnapping slaver. Killing no longer seemed to trouble him. It used to be rare—never when she was around. He used to be patient, waiting for just the right moment to kidnap an unsuspecting young woman. But lately…She thought of the boy, William, down by the river with Adelle.

After staring for a long moment at the dust particles floating in the shaft of sunlight that fell across the room just beyond the foot of the bed, she attempted to prop herself up on her pillow. A stab of pain stopped her short.

If she died from this bullet wound, she'd be free from Seth. But she wasn't ready to die. Not yet. She was, however, ready to be free again—from Seth and from this corrupt life.

Eyes squeezed shut, she decided, *If I survive this, I'm leaving. I'll plan it carefully this time. And I'll do it. Somehow.*

CHAPTER FORTY

Emmett's Chinese friends forced the last few stones into place, sealing off the abandoned mine's sole exit. A decade ago some poor hombre—stricken with silver fever—must've slaved long hours here, searching for his piece of the pie. The dig hadn't panned out so well for him, but the tunnel he'd left behind made an ideal hoosegow today.

"I'll yell," Charlie shouted through the one small hole they'd left in the rock wall. "I'll yell and scream till somebody comes down here and sees what you and these johnnies done to me, Strong." He began to howl like a coyote.

Emmett figured the yelping must have sounded far more intimidating to Charlie inside the cave than it did to anyone on the outside. "Shut it, Charlie," he said through the opening. "I can close up the one hole we've left for you just about as easy as not."

Charlie put his scowling face right up to the hole. "Why'd you put me in here anyway? They got a jail in Virginia City. You can leave me there till you're ready to take me back to Texas—unless you ain't figurin' on takin' me back to Texas."

"We'll get you some food and water directly," Emmett said. "Unless you go back to that lunkheaded howling."

"That's it, ain't it, Strong? You ain't plannin' on bringin' me back to Texas, are you?"

"Quit your yammerin'."

"You better not let these johnnies kill me. My brother'll burn down Chinatown. He'll burn 'em, I tell you."

Emmett turned his back on Charlie, crossed the gully, and clambered up to a vantage point opposite the makeshift jail. He plopped down and rubbed his eyes. How long had it been since he'd slept? Forty-eight hours? More?

A rush of wind drove a dirt devil through the ravine near the mine entrance. The Chinese men were busy gathering their belongings. Two of them dropped their tools into a wheelbarrow, picked up shotguns, and sat down on a pile of rocks, weapons across their knees.

He'd already told Yong Xu that he would gladly trade Charlie Blaylock to get Li and Ping back. But he hadn't yet talked the matter over with Juanito and Sikes. He dragged a sleeve across his forehead, pulled the brim of his hat back down close to his eyes, and hoped they'd back his play once again.

Over at the Comstock Queen Hotel where he'd left Sikes, the Brit was hobbling around on a bad leg now. Emmett glanced at his own bandaged and still-throbbing left hand. He imagined Sikes's leg hurt a great deal worse. How much more could he ask of a man he'd never met until the day Charlie Blaylock shot Eli? Both Sikes and Juanito had certainly done a whole lot more than they'd originally signed on for.

Now he needed to tell them he was giving up the fugitive. And then— when they all got back to Texas—he'd have to tell Eli's wife. Once Nan learned that he'd had her husband's murderer in his grasp but didn't bring him back for trial, she might hate him forever. He wasn't sure how much that even mattered.

There was more than one kind of justice.

Yong Xu returned to the old mine entrance with food and drink for their prisoner. Emmett understood completely why Yong was working so hard to make sure Blaylock was securely hidden away, well fed, and carefully guarded, day and night. Charlie Blaylock—whether offered to McIntosh in a trade or brought to the local law as a witness—was about the only hope Yong had for getting his precious daughter back.

Emmett wondered how badly Seth Blaylock might want his brother back. Enough to lean hard on his boss to make the exchange happen? Even so, nothing guaranteed that Seth's feelings for Charlie would mean a whole dreadful lot to Lucian McIntosh.

As they often do when a man is bone tired, Emmett's thoughts drifted and shifted like sand in the wind—snagging here for a few moments before taking flight elsewhere in the next—until finally they swirled around Li Xu.

He pictured her just as he'd seen her the night they'd first met. Her slender form. The way she wore her dark, silky hair, one side pinned up, the other falling to her shoulder. Her expressive, deep-brown eyes. Again he was captivated.

As far as he was concerned, his discussion with Reverend Pine had satisfactorily settled the moral question. He could live happily with Li Xu as his wife—if the two of them figured they liked each other enough.

Emmett eyed the two men guarding Charlie Blaylock, shotguns across their laps. Most of the Chinese community here welcomed him as a hero and a friend right now. But if it came down to it, would they ever accept him fully enough to let him marry one of their daughters?

Even if they did permit the marriage, what would people outside of this little community think—either in Nevada or in a place like Texas? Would one or both of them become some kind of pariah with no proper place in society? To be with a woman like Li Xu—amazing though she may be—could he give up everything he'd ever known?

He gently rubbed his aching hand. Shaking his head, he chuckled to himself. What a saphead he was. A pretty girl like Li Xu...She could have her choice of a thousand young Chinese fellows. Her father had probably learned how to throw a cleaver like that just to keep all the boys away from her. Besides—he didn't know—she might already be sweet on one of those boys.

He rose to his feet, dusted his Stetson across his thigh, and reseated it low across his brow. Heading down the slope, he reassured himself that it didn't matter. Whatever Li might think of him, he'd still give up his brother's killer to set her free—if not for himself, then for her family and her people. Even for her Chinese beau. Yep, he'd pose a deal to McIntosh. An exchange—Charlie Blaylock for Li and Ping.

Now he needed to bring Juanito and Sikes on board. They were his pardners. Their considerations counted too.

CHAPTER FORTY-ONE

In many ways, the Silver Nugget Saloon was just like a dozen other places on C Street: housed in a two-story wood-frame structure with a false front. Not the fanciest drinking establishment on the block but no special reputation for rowdiness either. The sun was hanging just above the faro parlor across the way when the three from Texas walked into the saloon and found themselves a corner table.

Sikes was getting around all right. Amazingly enough, one of the women over in Chinatown had found him a real wooden crutch—the kind used in the best big-city hospitals. At the table, he rested his bandaged leg on a vacant chair.

The bartender delivering their beer eyed Emmett's hand and Sikes's leg. "You gents run into a little trouble out there somewhere?"

"Mining accident," Emmett replied.

"Sure 'nough?" the barkeep asked. "Wouldn't have nothin' to do with the big ruckus down by Washoe Lake last night, would it?"

Emmett, Juanito, and Sikes glanced at one another.

"What happened down by Washoe Lake?" Emmett asked.

"Rumors been driftin' in all day," the aproned man said. "Big explosions. A lot of shootin'. Nobody seems to know for a fact who was goin' at it or why."

Sikes hoisted one of the beers. "Humph. That's news to us. Like my friend said, we were busy enough with our own misfortune."

The barkeep scratched his balding head. "If you say so. Only rumors anyway. You gents enjoy your beers."

As the barkeep turned away, a fellow perched on a stool at the end of the bar began to strum a guitar. From the very first chords, it was clear that he possessed far more talent than the average saloon musician.

Juanito peered over his shoulder. "That's a paso doble." He wiggled his eyebrows.

Emmett cut his eyes at Juanito. "I'm from San Antonio, too. You think I don't know a paso doble when I hear one?"

Juanito grinned.

"Beats the tar out of the banjo player over at the Lucky Strike," Sikes said.

"He is good," Emmett agreed. The beer was good too. Smooth and cold.

The guitarist's fingers flew as the music grew in intensity and volume. He had the full attention of the Silver Nugget's dozen or so patrons.

While Emmett was anxious to lay out his cards for Juanito and Sikes, he decided it wasn't often that you stumbled across an entertainer of this caliber—in a saloon or anywhere else. It had cost his compadres a piece of their own hides to achieve what they had thus far. And he was about to ask more of them. So he reckoned he'd let them savor the moment.

The final three chords brought rowdy applause and a buzz of chatter from the occupied tables. The barkeeper smiled.

A grin crept across Emmett's face. *Barkeep knows folks'll linger now. Run up their tabs.*

The guitarist seemed pleased in his own right. After a few bows, he took up a softer, more lyrical tune, still with a Spanish flair.

"Amigos," Emmett said, "you know how much I appreciate you."

Sikes's gaze dropped to his bandaged leg. "That's all I get for this?" He gawked at Emmett. "'I appreciate you.' Is that it?"

Emmett kept a straight face. "That and one more beer."

"One more lousy beer…"

"What do you mean, 'lousy'? This is quality beer."

"Horse swill."

Emmett grinned.

Juanito glanced at Sikes, then said to Emmett, "About this appreciation—are we celebrating what we accomplished last night? Or are you setting the stage for act two?"

"You've known me a long time, Juanito."

"Yes, I have."

"Then you know—"

"That you want to talk about Charlie Blaylock? And about why, all of a sudden, you're not so sure it's absolutely necessary for us to take him back to Texas? Yes, I know."

Emmett studied his brother-in-law. "You know so much, go on."

"That pretty daughter of Yong Xu's still needs rescuing, and you don't really care too much about what happens to Charlie Blaylock anymore. Am I right?"

After a pause, Emmett said, "No, I very much care what happens to Charlie Blaylock."

"How much…in comparison to wanting to free the girl?"

"We made an agreement with the Chinese." He waved for the bartender.

"Yes, we did."

"We'd help them get their girls back. Then they'd help us take care of Charlie Blaylock."

"The situation's changed, though," Sikes said. "We've already got Charlie—"

"Does that change what we promised to do for them?" Emmett leaned forward and rested his elbows on the table. "Like Juanito said, they don't have all their daughters back yet."

"Besides," Juanito said, "without the Chinese helping last night we might not have gotten Charlie Blaylock."

Sikes drummed his fingers on the table, then said, "So what do you suggest, Strong?"

Emmett held a swallow of beer on his tongue a moment, then said, "First, I want you to know I'm not asking either of you to commit to anything beyond what you already have."

"We're in," Sikes said, shifting his wounded leg gingerly. "That much ought to be plain to you."

"Might get shot again before it's all over."

"Getting shot rarely bothers me. Why, at Rorke's Drift—"

Emmett's eyes narrowed. "You weren't at Rorke's Drift. Not if you were left for dead at Isandlwana."

Sikes stared back, then finally winked. "The truth is"—he motioned toward his bandaged leg—"this isn't the first time I've been shot. And as far as I'm concerned, I was shot for a better cause last night than I was at Isandlwana."

"So you agree that freeing the Chinese girls is a worthy cause."

"We came up here chasing one murderer—a crazed killer, acting out of anger and revenge. What he did was wrong. But Seth Blaylock is a cold, calculating slaver…and a murderer of a worse variety. You told us he shot the Chinese girl who was trying to run away. Shot her to keep her from reaching Yong Xu."

As the barkeep drew near with fresh glasses of beer, the three held their thoughts. Once he'd wiped off the table and set out the three full glasses, they thanked him, and the music started up once again.

Emmett's gaze returned to his friends. "So how do we finish this business and go home?"

"Back to Charlie Blaylock," Juanito said. "We can't just give him up. We need to find another way to get those two girls back."

"Well, we can't go storming into Lucian McIntosh's front parlor, guns a-blazing, demanding he let the girls go either."

"Maybe we can come up with a plan…" Sikes struck a match to light his cigar. "A way to somehow make McIntosh think he's trading the girls for Charlie. But we end up with the girls and still keep our outlaw…somehow."

Emmett shook his head. "Stakes are too high. I won't gamble Li's and Ping's lives that way. We can always make another run at Charlie Blaylock after the girls are safely back where they belong."

"And you think McIntosh will let that go unanswered?" Juanito said. "You go back for Charlie a second time, he'll come back for Li and Ping a second time. He'll know that if those girls were important enough to prompt you to give up your own brother's murderer, then that's how he can get back at you—going after them again."

"Sounds like we've only got two choices then," Sikes said.

"Take Charlie and get out of Nevada now," Emmett said, "or give him up to McIntosh once we've assured the girls' safe release. No expectation of getting him back."

"Why don't we take Charlie to the local law?" Juanito asked. "He was part of the kidnapping. Right here in Virginia City."

"If we do that, nobody'll ever see Li and Ping again," Emmett said, rubbing his forehead. "McIntosh'll get rid of 'em quick rather than risk having the law discover that kidnapping is how he's getting calico for his bed houses."

Juanito's lips twisted. "Hadn't thought about that." He stared away for a moment. "So do we wait for Seth Blaylock to come here to Virginia City, demanding we give back his brother? Or do we go to McIntosh and Blaylock and demand that they give back Yong's daughter and her friend?"

Sikes set down his beer. "They may think that with Charlie in hand, we'll cut and run. Leave the Chinese to fend for themselves just like everyone else does."

Emmett nodded. "If I read 'em right, they're not the negotiating kind. They won't come out to talk. They'll be watching the train stations, looking to catch us trying to slip away to Texas with Seth's brother."

"May even jump one of us here in Virginia City," Juanito said. "Stick a pistol in our back and tell us to take them to Charlie pronto."

Emmett swirled the beer in his glass absently. "Then let's show some sand. Capitalize on our victory last night. Let's ride right up to McIntosh's front porch and demand the exchange."

"He won't like it," Sikes said.

"Won't like it at all. But it may throw him off balance. I'd wager he's not accustomed to dealing with other folks on their terms."

With a flourish the guitarist finished another piece.

"So you knew I'd be willing to give up Charlie Blaylock, huh?" Emmett eyed Juanito.

"*Hermano*, you had the Chinese put him in a cave. Why would you do that if you planned to start back for Texas with him tomorrow?"

"However the game unfolds," Emmett said, "you don't show your trump card too soon."

Juanito smiled broadly.

Emmett gave a faint grin. "Charlie's our insurance policy. I only hope the policy's worth enough to cover this venture."

CHAPTER FORTY-TWO

As he and his compañeros rode four abreast on the main road just south of Reno, Emmett reflected on what an amusing picture they would present to the men they were about to call on. Juanito with his broad-brimmed sombrero. Sikes in his Cheyenne saddle, sitting ramrod straight like the Queen's Own Lifeguard. Yong Xu, again wearing Western clothes but with Chinese shoes and a straw hat. And himself? Well, just your average Texan.

Sikes had gotten a new pair of trousers—nice ones with fine charcoal-gray stripes. He'd said he didn't want Blaylock or McIntosh's men to know he was riding injured. His leg—clean and healing nicely—was bandaged beneath the pants.

Emmett paid special attention to Yong Xu, wondering how he would bear up as they neared Lucian McIntosh's place—if they made it that far. How would he handle himself if Seth Blaylock were to parade Li and Ping out at gunpoint?

For that matter, Emmett wondered how he would do. An image of Gabriela in Victorio Sanchez's clutches darted through his mind. He still hadn't recovered the confidence he lost that day. Of course if it came down to shooting today, he and his amigos would be lucky if any of them got away alive, no matter how great his skill with the Colt.

A sudden awareness that someone was trailing them drew Emmett out of his musings. He peered over his shoulder. There they were—a pair of them. Hired guns, no doubt. They had the look.

"Got company," he murmured to his compadres.

The others glanced back discreetly.

They hadn't gone a quarter mile farther when Juanito said, "Two more on the other side."

The same sort, Emmett thought. *A little bolder. No apologies for shadowing us.*

By the time Reno was in sight, a welcome party of eight mounted gunslicks boxed in Emmett, Juanito, Sikes, and Yong.

Emmett signaled to his friends and reined in. Though his heart drummed like mad, he was determined to exude nothing but cool confidence.

He deliberately drew a long, deep breath while he sized up each of the approaching riders. Once they were within a mere thirty yards he flicked his spurs and loped straight for the one who looked to be the boss. Pulling up close, he locked eyes with his opponent.

"I've got a proposal for Seth Blaylock," he said. "Seth's brother, Charlie, would appreciate it if you'd give us safe conduct to his place."

The man's upper lip twitched. "It's Mr. McIntosh you'll have to talk to," he said, his voice like gravel. "You don't talk to Seth Blaylock or anyone else in Reno till Mr. McIntosh says so."

Emmett arched an eyebrow. "If it's McIntosh that holds Seth Blaylock's lead rope, then sure—I'll talk to McIntosh."

The hand snickered. "All right. You're safe until you see Mr. McIntosh. Can't guarantee nothin' after that."

Emmett nodded toward Reno. "Shall we then?"

Lucian McIntosh's house was palatial—a two-and-a-half-story San Francisco–style place with a turret at one corner and dormer windows up top. Armed men waited on either side of the front gate, here and there around the yard, and up on the broad veranda. Emmett didn't know exactly why, but it rattled him for a moment that McIntosh was so obviously expecting him.

They had hardly cleared the front gate when an imposing fellow—had to be the big boss himself—stepped out onto the porch, Seth Blaylock at his elbow. Both men glared silently at Emmett and his friends.

Smug hulk of a man, Emmett thought, taking quick note of McIntosh's fine black suit, stiff white shirt, and broad burgundy tie, but above all noticing the contempt between his jowls. The man looked for all the world as though he'd been weaned on a green persimmon. And Blaylock—the dandy. An Arkansas toothpick trying to pass himself off as a Renaissance-era stiletto.

"You four, get on down outta your saddles," the gravel-voiced escort said.

Emmett glanced at Yong. His Chinese friend appeared to be holding up remarkably well. His eyes were fixed unwaveringly on his daughter's abductor. Emmett knew Juanito and Sikes would be all right.

"Won't be staying long enough to bother," Emmett said, his gaze returning to McIntosh and Blaylock rather than to the gunman who had spoken. "Not on this visit anyway."

A bushy-mustached fellow on the porch raised his rifle just a hair and said, "You come ridin' in here to Mr. McIntosh's place, you pay proper respect, you hear? He wants you to get down, you get down. Else this meetin's over before it starts."

Having discussed the plan beforehand, none of the four budged.

All was silent for several seconds, men from each side sizing one another up. It was a tinderbox of a situation—one wrong move and there'd be a flash and a blaze.

Emmett finally spoke. "Seth Blaylock, are you interested in hearing what I've come to say?"

Seth glared coldly but didn't answer. After a moment, he glanced at his boss.

When McIntosh shifted his weight, the porch's plank flooring creaked. "You Texans have caused a hell of a lot of trouble," he said, his voice level. "I oughta shoot the lot of you here and now." His gaze ran across the four of them. "Charlie Blaylock supposedly killed your brother—"

Emmett interrupted. "Matter of fact, he did kill my brother. He was right in front of me when he did it."

McIntosh snapped back, "Interrupt me again and you'll be joinin' your brother."

Emmett leaned forward in his saddle, his hand on his thigh near his Colt.

McIntosh stepped to the front edge of the porch. "If you wanted to beef your brother's killer, you should've done the job back in Texas. And if you weren't skilled enough to take care of business there, you should've ended your chase at the Texas state line." He glowered at Yong Xu, then looked back at Emmett. "But no. Night before last you and your slant-eyed friends went and killed *my* brother."

Momentary panic jolted through Emmett's core. *What?* This could change the game completely. McIntosh's stake in this whole affair was personal now, not just business. He gathered his courage. "Until this very minute, I had no idea your brother was even out there."

McIntosh curled his lip and pointed a finger. "You should've kept it between you and Charlie Blaylock. Not only did you fail to do that, not only did you shoot my brother dead—for which I oughta drop you right now—but you also shot Seth Blaylock's woman. Could've killed her too—a woman."

Emmett's mind raced. *Wait. What woman did we shoot? Seth's the one that shot a woman. In fact, two women—Yan back in Virginia City and Guiying in the brush near the arroyo.*

Then he recalled the scream he'd heard in that same thicket when he hit the second kidnapper. *So that was Seth's woman.*

Recovering, Emmett said, "Nobody was gunning for her or for your brother. Not the way Charlie Blaylock was gunning for mine. Your brother made a bad choice. Rode out into the night to help a gang of kidnappers haul away a bunch of innocent girls—other men's daughters, no matter what their color."

McIntosh visibly reddened. "Shut up, dammit! You shut up! You and them damn Chinese declared war on my men...on my family."

Now Emmett jabbed his bandaged hand toward McIntosh. "You've got the chronology and the blame all wrong. Seth Blaylock here—who works for you—declared war on the Chinese folk in Virginia City when he kidnapped six of their daughters...after shooting another one."

As McIntosh stood there gnashing his teeth and fuming, Seth spoke up. While his tone was cold, it was clear that he too was smoldering. "Our business up here has nothin' to do with you, Texan. It's betw—"

McIntosh put up a hand. He said to Emmett, "No more back and forth on this. Your business in Nevada all started with Charlie Blaylock. As I understand it, you've already got him. I believe it's time for you to take your fugitive and go home to Texas."

Emmett fixed his gaze on Seth. "I'll ask you again, Blaylock. You want your brother back?"

Seth shrugged. "I'll get him back...before you ever leave Nevada."

"You want him back alive?"

"You threatenin'?"

"I'm offering."

McIntosh snorted. "Offering what?"

"You get Charlie alive. We get the two remaining Chinese girls. Alive and well."

The windmill above the water tank clattered.

McIntosh scowled. "This is my offer, take it or leave it: You come back here by tomorrow noon with Charlie Blaylock unharmed, and I'll give you them two damned China girls…unharmed. Then you get the hell out of Nevada. And I'd better never see your faces again."

Emmett shot a glance at his pardners before returning his gaze to the big boss. "Not here," he said. "A neutral spot."

McIntosh looked right and left at the gunslicks scattered around the yard, then returned to glaring at Emmett. "Just where do you suggest then?"

"Open ground. Same place where your wagons got stranded on the back road."

"Like hell!" McIntosh bellowed. "Same place where you gunned down my brother? To hell with that."

"It'll serve as a reminder that we don't need any more bloodshed."

"So you say. Meanwhile, you can pick off more of my men with that damn buffalo gun. No."

Emmett's gaze drifted from one hired gun to another. "Your men stay hidden. It only takes one man to deliver those two girls." He nodded toward Seth. "And it only takes me to deliver Charlie Blaylock. Each side does what they're supposed to, and there's no need to spill another drop of blood. We say adios and part ways."

He remained motionless in the saddle, his hand still close to his holster.

As he stared down the glowering McIntosh, he was dead certain that Li Xu was locked up less than fifty feet away, somewhere in that big house. He wished he could take her home today, but surrounded by so many of the big man's gunslicks, he was doing well to negotiate what he already had.

"Noon tomorrow then," McIntosh said, head cocked and brows furrowed. "Unarmed…and that's not up for discussion."

Emmett nodded. "Unarmed is even better."

McIntosh stared at Emmett, then at Juanito. He spent several long seconds glaring at Yong Xu. Then, with only a quick glance at Sikes, he turned his back and lumbered toward the front door.

At the last second, he stopped and pivoted. "Your name's Strong, right?"

"That's right. Emmett Strong."

"Charlie Blaylock said you've got a reputation. Some kind of pistolero. Was he right?"

Emmett shrugged.

"Don't matter anyway. You so much as think about double-crossin' me, Mr. Pistolero, and I'll be right behind you all the way back to the Rio Grande. And don't kid yourself. I've got at least a dozen men as quick and deadly as you."

Emmett looked over the McIntosh men, pausing a moment to meet Seth's glare. "You don't need to worry about that," he said. "Double-crossing's not my style."

He touched the brim of his hat. Then he and his compadres wheeled their horses and rode out the front gate at an easy jog.

It took all the self-restraint Emmett could muster to leave without demanding proof that Li Xu and Ping were OK. But he wasn't convinced Yong could handle it. A scene might've led to shooting. And the odds definitely weren't in their favor. Not today.

"Soon now, Yong," he said as they picked up speed. "We'll see her tomorrow."

His expression blank, Yong nodded and tapped his horse's flanks.

—⁓—

As soon as Emmett and his friends had cleared his front gate, McIntosh led Seth inside and closed the door behind them.

"Get the men goin'—the best we've got. The best of Thaddeus's boys too—those that're still alive. Emmett Strong does not live to see tomorrow night. Understood?"

"Yes, sir."

"And he dies empty-handed. You get your brother back. I get the China girls back."

Seth looked his boss in the eye. "I'll see to it. Strong'll never make it back to Virginia City—with or without the girls. I don't care if he brings a hundred of them Chinese bastards fully armed."

"Speakin' of armed," McIntosh said, "I know I told Strong the exchange was to be made with you and him both unheeled. You understand I never intended for you to abide by that?"

"Wasn't thinkin' of it."

McIntosh gave a sharp nod. "And then after the bushwhackin', you go on down to Carson City. Spend some time with Ettie. Bad enough we lost Thaddeus. I can't stand that we almost lost her too."

"Thank you, sir." Seth was anxious to get back to Ettie, to see her through her recovery.

"You know she's almost like a daughter to me," the big man said.

"I'll take good care of her, sir."

McIntosh stood gazing up the stairs. "Tomorrow we'll make Emmett Strong pay the bill. With interest."

CHAPTER FORTY-THREE

A good mile out from McIntosh's place, Juanito reined his dun around to face the others.

Emmett frowned at his stern expression. "What's on your mind?"

"Don't you feel it?" Juanito glanced back toward Reno, then up the ridge to the east. "McIntosh's men were waiting for us on the way in. It feels like somebody's watching us now."

Emmett scanned the surrounding high ground. "What if they are?"

"You know what could happen if they find out where we're holding Charlie."

"You've got a point. If they get Charlie back before tomorrow, there goes our exchange."

Yong's saddle creaked as he shifted back and forth, looking for signs of McIntosh's gunmen.

"We're gonna have to play it smart," Emmett said. "Yong, not even you can go to the mine."

Still scouring the landscape from beneath his conical straw hat, Yong said, "I'll send others to keep watch…and to relay anything our guards need to know."

Emmett nudged his horse into a walk. The others followed.

"Four o'clock tomorrow morning," Emmett said, "have your men gag Blaylock and bring him to us down at American Flats. Skirt the edge of town and avoid being seen. They might wanna keep a gun on him. From the flats we'll all make our way together to the exchange point."

"The same men who volunteered before?"

"If they're willing," Emmett said. "Meanwhile, there's somebody else I'm gonna call on. See if I can't drum up some additional support."

—m—

They got back to Virginia City well after dark. Even though the hour was late, Emmett, Juanito, and Sikes paid Reverend Pine, the Presbyterian minister, a visit.

From his front porch, the trim-bearded preacher extended a hand, inviting the three inside. "Good to see you again, Mr. Strong."

Still sensing that they were being ghosted by McIntosh men, Emmett gave the street a quick and wary once-over, then passed through the minister's doorway.

They were hardly inside when a plump woman with a pretty face and a warm smile stepped from the kitchen into the cozy sitting room.

"Well, who have we here, Reverend Pine?" she asked.

"Three men on a mission, my dear," Pine said. "And a long way from home at that." Then, wrapping an arm around the woman's shoulders, he said to Emmett and his pardners, "Gentlemen, this lovely lady is Mrs. Pine, my sweetheart of nearly twenty years."

Emmett introduced himself, Juanito, and Sikes and thanked Mrs. Pine for letting them intrude without forewarning. The minister's wife pishposhed the bit about intruding and insisted over polite protestations that he and his friends sit down for coffee.

Reverend Pine motioned for them to have a seat, then grabbed his pipe from the rolltop desk and pulled out a chair for himself. "How goes the search for your brother's murderer?" he asked, his gaze fixed on Emmett.

Emmett eyed his pardners. "We know where he is."

"Well, that's progress. And what of the Chinese girls? Have you found out anything more about them?"

Emmett filled in Reverend Pine on the events since their last meeting. Then he said, "Last time we met, you didn't hold out much promise for help from the city marshal."

Pine shook his head. "I sorely doubt he'd enter Washoe County to cover you while you make that exchange. He tends to keep his head down and play things safe."

Leaning forward, hands folded on the table, Emmett said, "Out of your entire congregation, is there anybody you can think of who might have the

208

smallest measure of compassion for these girls? Regardless of color, nobody should let a band of kidnappers force young women into a life of prostitution."

Reverend Pine rubbed his hand over his beard. When he looked up from the table, he said, "As far as finding volunteers, you've got two things working against you. First, you're going up against men with powerful reputations. Anybody who'd go with you would have to know they'd be facing some of the toughest hired guns west of the Rockies. Not to mention the lingering danger of retaliation even if you did manage to get the girls back here safely."

"Anything else working against us?"

"Growing anti-Chinese sentiment. People who have to live and do business here don't want to be ostracized for being overly friendly with the Chinamen."

Emmett pursed his lips. "You don't hold out much hope for us. I guess it's just us three and the handful of Chinese we've found guns for then."

"Well," Reverend Pine said, "you can count on one more. I've done some shooting. Not at people. But in this case I would if I had to."

Juanito leaned back, eyes widened. "You'll do it?"

"Yes."

Just then, Mrs. Pine brought cups and a large coffee pot to the table. It smelled far better than campfire coffee. Emmett knew she'd heard every word. He watched her eyes for a reaction, but her face remained unperturbed.

"Are you OK with your husband doing this, Mrs. Pine?" he asked. "He was right—the danger may not be over for him even if we get back safely tomorrow night."

Without missing a beat, she answered, "I'd be mighty appreciative of any Chinese men who'd do the same for us if the tables were turned and our daughters were abducted in their country."

Emmett spoke softly. "You have children, Mrs. Pine?"

She cast a glance at her husband. "No. I'm just saying…Anyway, Ezra will quietly knock on a few doors after coffee. I've a feeling one or two others will join you with a little persuasion."

Emmett followed her gaze to the reverend.

"I'll go ask a few men," Pine said, nodding. "I can't presume to speak for any of them. But I'll see what I can do. Discreetly, of course."

"Much appreciated," Emmett said. "Would it help for us to come along?"

The minister shook his head. "Best to keep this very quiet. I'll do what I can, then meet you at American Flats at five tomorrow morning—with or without additional help."

"You own a rifle?"

"I do."

"I still hope it doesn't come down to shooting."

"Knowing who we're dealing with, we'd better plan for the worst."

"That's a fact. McIntosh won't be bringing along any choirboys." Emmett set down his coffee cup, wiped his mouth, and stood. "The coffee was delicious, Mrs. Pine."

The preacher's wife wiped her hands on her apron. "It's a noble deed you're doing, gentlemen. And you'll need all the help the Almighty can give you. You can count on my prayers, feeble though they may be."

CHAPTER FORTY-FOUR

E mmett checked his pocket watch. Eleven forty-four. He unbuckled his gun belt—long-barreled Colt still in its slim-jim holster—and handed it to Juanito.

"I hate to see you giving this up," his brother-in-law said. "Especially knowing that Seth Blaylock won't do the same."

Emmett stared hard at Charlie Blaylock. Without the slightest waver, he said, "Sikes, if this goes wrong, put the first round from that Sharps Little Fifty through this man right here." He stabbed a finger at his brother's murderer. He hoped by saying as much aloud that Charlie might intervene should Seth attempt a flimflam.

Sikes conspicuously examined a two-inch-long cartridge before slipping it into the buffalo rifle. "Reserved for Mr. Charlie Blaylock, should he or his brother choose to play dirty."

Under the warm sun, Emmett surveyed his backup. Yong Xu had brought along nine of the men who had fought so valiantly the night they'd rescued the other young women. They wouldn't be much good at long range, but once they got the girls back, they'd defend them or die trying.

And then there was Reverend Pine. Much to Emmett's surprise, the preacher wore a gun belt. And it wasn't borrowed. It didn't strike him as unusual that a minister would own a Henry. Lots of folks in the West had rifles for protection. Wild animals wandered into towns from time to time. And there were still great stretches of the country with no law other than the kind with a trigger. Even a man of peace might need a rifle to protect his home and family. But a pastor with a gun belt and a pistolo—that was noteworthy.

It pleased Emmett that the preacher had scared up three other volunteers, including the Storey County sheriff, Bob Morrison. Sheriff Morrison had made it clear that they were operating in another jurisdiction out here and that he wouldn't take an active part until they'd crossed the line back into his county. On the upside, he'd also said he'd be glad to take the witness stand if the matter were brought before a judge. Not that Emmett believed for a moment that any of this would ever make it to a courtroom.

Emmett pivoted at the sound of gravel crunching behind him—Yong Xu leading horses up the slope. It was time. Emmett stepped up into his saddle.

Sikes tossed him a coiled rope and said, "I agree with Juanito. I think you're making a big mistake abiding by McIntosh's terms. You ought to slip your revolver into the back of your waistband." He peered at their prisoner. "I can take out old Charlie here. But that won't bring you back from the dead if Seth shoots first."

At that, Charlie snapped, "To hell with you, you English bastard!"

Sikes marched to within inches of the outlaw. "I'd backhand you in a heartbeat if it wouldn't leave you dribbling blood and give your brother half a reason to back out of the exchange. So shut your filthy mouth!"

Charlie reddened.

"Same reason I'm leaving my gun here," Emmett said. "Plain and simple, I don't wanna give Seth any excuse to back out. So go on and check Charlie's wrists, and let's get him into the saddle."

Once they had Blaylock on horseback, Emmett tossed a lasso around his arms and pulled the loop tight.

"Charlie, you're gonna lead," he said. "And believe me, if you try anything at all, I'll yank you off that horse and drag you through the grit and gravel all the way back to Virginia City. Buzzards'll starve to death trying to find a scrap of you big enough to fill their gullets."

Charlie glared back at him.

"Now move on up to the top of that ridge and stop there until I tell you to ride on."

Yong Xu brought Emmett the two spare horses and handed him the lead ropes.

From the crest of the rise, Emmett looked out past the patches of burned grass that marked where the battle had taken place the other night. A good hundred yards beyond that, he spied a man sitting saddle and two figures on foot. His heart leapt and thumped away anxiously.

"He's making the girls walk out."

Sikes took up a spot nearby. "And you're surprised by that?"

"Guess not." He panned the horizon. "Anybody see anything else I should pay special attention to?"

Cradling a Winchester in his arm, Juanito said, "Just because we don't see it doesn't mean the danger's not there."

"Don't I know that," Emmett said.

"Hope he hits you right smack 'tween the eyes," Charlie said, letting out a cackle.

Emmett gave the lasso a sharp snap. "You want me to start dragging you now?"

"You wouldn't dare."

Emmett gave another tug, and Charlie teetered in the saddle.

"It's noon, Emmett," Reverend Pine said.

Emmett nodded. He glanced at Sikes. "If it comes down to it, make the first shot count."

Then to Charlie he said, "OK, murderer, move out nice and easy."

Charlie chortled again, gripped the saddle horn, and flicked his heels.

As they descended the slope, Emmett kept an eye on Seth. Since Ping and Li Xu were walking, their advance was slow.

Emmett slowed as well. He didn't want to end up beyond the reach of Sikes's buffalo gun yet within range of McIntosh's rifles. As a consequence the ride out to the middle seemed to take all day.

He strained to see Li's face, to read her expression. Whatever her appearance might tell him, he knew he had to keep a cool head. The girls' lives depended on it.

Seth would goad him. Of that he was sure. And so would Charlie, threats to drag his carcass through the chaparral notwithstanding.

At last, perhaps ten yards apart, both parties halted and stared one another down.

Emmett glanced at Ping. Tears trailed down her cheeks, and her nose was runny from crying. Her narrow shoulders shook beneath the baggy crimson-and-gold Chinese smock.

When his eyes met Li's, he nearly lost his composure. Though her hands were bound, she stood there with amazing courage. Tears on her eyelashes glistened in

213

the midday sunlight. But she held her chin high and kept looking from Emmett to Charlie to Seth and back again. Emmett dug deep down inside, determined for all the world to appear completely in control. He wouldn't let Seth Blaylock rob him of Li Xu the way Victorio Sanchez had robbed him of Gabriela.

He drew a breath and kept his voice low and calm. "You ladies OK?"

Li scowled up at Seth and said, "Yes, once—"

"Let's get this over with," Seth interrupted.

"Once I'm free from him," Li said, finishing her sentence.

As his gaze returned to Seth, Emmett's eyes narrowed. He studied the slaver for any signs of hidden weapons.

Then he said, "Charlie, get off my horse."

Charlie peered back at him. "What?"

"I said get off my horse and walk over to your brother."

Charlie's lip curled. "You ain't even gonna give me a horse to ride outta here on?"

"You can have the one Seth gave these young ladies."

Charlie muttered as he dismounted.

"Come on over here, brother," Seth said, producing a bone-handled knife from behind him.

Emmett locked eyes with Seth. "That'd better be for cutting rope. Nothing more."

Seth sneered.

"Li, Ping," Emmett said coolly, "walk on over here and stand on the other side of the horses."

The girls began to trudge through the dry grass. They'd gone no more than three steps when Seth cocked his knife arm. The blade in his gloved fingertips flashed in the sunlight.

"Get down!" Emmett yelled.

Ping crumpled in place and let out a shrill scream. Li dove on top of her friend and shielded her with her own body. Her black-and-gold smock draped over both of them, almost hiding Ping from sight.

Charlie dashed to the other side of his brother's horse.

Seth burst out laughing. He lowered the knife hand slowly and covered his mouth with the back of the other hand. "I was just testin' you. To see whether you were heeled." A grin peeked out from behind his fist.

His chest pounding, Emmett said, "Testing, or baiting?" His gaze darted here and there, searching for McIntosh's boys with their buffalo rifles. Slowly he walked his horse forward, stopping close enough to reach out and cuff Seth.

"If you'd have thrown that," he said, "it would have been the last act of your senseless life."

"Whoa," Seth said, still smirking, eyes widened in mock fear.

"Go on," Emmett said through clenched teeth. "Your head'll explode like a watermelon if I so much as raise my right hand. *Comprende*, amigo?"

Seth snickered again.

Emmett, on the verge of waving for Sikes to open fire, heard Ping whimper. He got a grip on himself.

"You take your brother and ride on now," Emmett said. "We're done dealing."

Seth tucked away the knife and held out a hand to Charlie, his defiant gaze still locked on Emmett. Once he had pulled his brother up behind the cantle, he wheeled and set off for those waiting for him beyond the clearing. For a number of yards, he and Charlie both kept watching Emmett and the girls, laughing openly as they went.

Judging that they had finally moved away in earnest, Emmett swung out of the saddle and sprinted for the girls. He half expected lead to fly, but none came.

Li Xu rose and ran to meet him. She clutched him tightly and buried her face in his chest. Only then did she too let her tears flow freely.

He held her a long time. Maybe too long under the circumstances. But this moment had taken too long in arriving.

Ping stood a few feet away still sniffling. He held out an arm, hoping that with an embrace he might comfort and reassure her as well. She approached shyly and timidly accepted his hug.

"It's OK now," he murmured. "You're both gonna be OK."

When Emmett released the girls, Li lingered, holding to him a little longer.

Much as he wanted to savor the moment, he took her gently by the shoulders, eased her back enough to look into her eyes, and said, "Let's go home, Li."

She wiped her eyes with the heels of her hands and nodded.

He motioned toward the spare horses. "I need each of you girls to take a lead rope. You can hold each other's hand. Just lead a horse beside you with your free hand."

They both looked at him questioningly.

"See your friends up there on the ridge?" He pointed in that direction. "Each of you walk a horse up to them, OK?"

Li nodded and took a lead rope in her left hand. Ping grabbed one in her right. As the girls began the long walk back, Emmett fell in behind them, leading the other two horses. Although he knew everyone at the top of the ridge had him and the girls covered, he couldn't help taking an occasional glance back toward the Blaylocks and the invisible McIntosh men.

CHAPTER FORTY-FIVE

On the other side of the crest, a mood of restrained celebration prevailed. A teary-eyed Yong Xu ran to Li and caught her up in his arms. As he walked her down the back slope, quiet words in Chinese punctuated their soft sniffling. Ping's father simply stood there holding his daughter tightly, letting her release all her pent-up fear. Tears traced down his cheeks.

Sikes clapped Emmett on the back. "I came a hair from pulling the trigger when I saw the girls hit the ground."

Emmett breathed a sigh of relief. "Glad you exercised some that British discipline instead."

Sikes gave a wry grin.

"You did well, *hermano*," Juanito said, clutching Emmett in a hearty bear hug,

"Yeah, well, the job's not altogether finished yet." The tightness that had gripped his chest for the past half hour was giving way to a pressing sense of urgency.

While he longed to take over where Yong Xu left off and cradle Li in his arms, he was sure McIntosh and Blaylock were already hurrying their band of gunslicks southward, riding hard to recover their losses and exact revenge.

"I hate to break this up," Emmett said to all, "but we need to move. We won't be safe till we're back in Virginia City." He motioned for Juanito to hand him his gun belt.

Sheriff Morrison lowered the field glasses he'd been using and turned to Emmett. "We both know they're going to try to cut us off on our way back home. In my judgment, the safest route back is Mound House. About twelve miles thataway." He pointed. "That'll keep us moving away from Reno."

Emmett cast a questioning glance at Juanito and Sikes as he seated his gun leather the way he liked it.

Juanito shrugged.

"From Mound House we can take the train back up to Virginia City," the sheriff said.

Reverend Pine stepped in, shaking his head. "I disagree, Sheriff. That route will take us dangerously close to Carson City and to more of McIntosh's men."

"But Thaddeus McIntosh is dead," Sikes said, "With him out of the picture, the Carson City McIntoshes should be a bit disorganized."

"Or set on revenge," Emmett said.

The sheriff pulled on his leather gloves. "OK, if passing that close to Carson City seems too risky, then the most direct route back is the same way we got here—the pass between Mount Bullion and Mount Scott."

"If we go that way, you realize we'll be out in the open for a while," Juanito said. "McIntosh will see exactly where we're heading."

"True," the reverend said. "While we cross the valley floor, anyone within a good five or six miles will see our dust."

"Then it's a horserace to get to the pass before McIntosh and Blaylock can get there," Emmett said. "The clock's ticking."

Sikes shook his head. "What if he's already got men stashed in the hills, waiting? They'll rain down death on us."

"What do you like better then, Sikes?" Emmett asked. "'Cause I don't think we can hold a lead twelve miles to Mound House. Not with a dozen unseasoned Chinese riders in tow."

"I just don't like running up into that pass. It's a natural choke point. But if that's what you choose…" He folded his arms and cocked his hip.

Emmett blew out a stream of air and dug his heel into the gritty earth. "Any way we go has risks. Knew that before we rode out. But we're closer to the pass than the Blaylocks are. We just need to ride like death itself is nipping at our backsides. Not give up our lead. So if it's OK with you gents, we'd better cut dirt."

CHAPTER FORTY-SIX

It had been a chore keeping the inexperienced Chinese riders moving at a good lope across the valley floor. The whole way, the McIntosh gang's dust trail had been drawing ever closer. Lucian's men had been distinguishable dots on the horizon just before Emmett and his friends entered the ravine.

Now within the confines of the gorge, ascending through the pass, the column slowed to a walk. Emmett, Sheriff Morrison, and Reverend Pine led. The Chinese were clustered together in the middle. Sikes, Juanito, and the other two from the reverend's congregation brought up the rear.

Emmett couldn't recall ever having been so distracted in the middle of such a dangerous situation. He needed to keep his eyes moving, constantly scouring the hills and mountains ahead. Yet he couldn't stop stealing glances at Li Xu.

Every time he looked back, Li's eyes were waiting for him. Sometimes their gazes remained fixed on one another. Sometimes she looked away quickly— usually when her father or a Chinese neighbor spoke.

"This is about where I start to get worried," Sheriff Morrison said. "If McIntosh did stash any gunhands up here, those rocks just ahead are a prime spot for lying in wait."

Clusters of stubby cedars dotted the brown grass that covered the mountainside. Emmett peered from one cluster to another, then to the rock formations the sheriff had indicated. "If we had more men like you, we could've left a few up there ourselves, to hold the high ground for us."

"Yeah, well, if frogs had wings..."

Other than the restrained noises of their own party—horse hooves, saddle leather, and the occasional few murmured words—all was quiet in the pass. Emmett carried his Winchester across his lap, hand in the lever, ready to go.

219

Emmett. It was Li's voice—in his mind. Not a good time for his attention to be divided. Even so, he snatched a quick glance over his shoulder and found her gaze waiting for his yet again. Her father said something in Chinese, and she broke eye contact.

From somewhere above and to the right, a few rocks tumbled and clattered down the slope. Emmett spun around and hoisted his rifle, tracing a line from the falling rocks up the hillside—boulders, bushes, clumps of taller grass. Nothing out of the ordinary.

"Now I've gone and gotten you all skittish," the sheriff said, his voice low.

"Don't know that I'd call it 'skittish,'" Emmett murmured back, lowering the Winchester.

The temperature was rising. A bead of sweat ran down his back.

"Let's press on," he said.

After another quarter mile of slow ascent, he twisted in the saddle, hoping to check the progress of the riders who had been giving chase across the valley. A hill screened them from view.

He peered back to see how the Chinese were handling the steepening incline. Behind them Sikes looked especially uneasy, his head turning side to side, up, then back.

What if they were in fact dry-gulched and slaughtered up here? McIntosh and Blaylock would have won out on all counts. That'd be a tragedy—especially if McIntosh were to get Li and Ping back.

It just couldn't happen. That's all there was to it.

He peeked at Li. This time, she smiled at him. And her eyes told him that there were things she wanted to say. A flurry of feathers swirled in his stomach. *Soon,* he thought, determined to remain vigilant.

Just ahead, the pass veered around a large fold in the rock, forcing them to make a blind cutback to the left. Emmett signaled for the column to hold up. He walked his horse to the bend and eased around it. From left to right, from top to bottom, he studied the high ground ahead. Nothing moved. Nothing flashed unnaturally. There were no out-of-place colors.

Best I can tell... He drew a breath and waved the group ahead.

The last of the party had ridden only a few yards beyond the bend when a shot exploded from the somewhere directly ahead. Blood sprayed Emmett.

Reverend Pine's horse screamed and fell. Emmett glimpsed a gaping hole in the animal's neck as it went down.

"Back!" he yelled. "Back around the bend."

Reverend Pine grasped Sheriff Morrison's extended hand and jumped up behind the saddle onto his mount.

With horses wheeling this way and that, the band had the look of a stirred-up ant bed. Yet even though handling horses within the tight confines of a mountain pass was new to most of the Chinese, it seemed everyone was going to make it back around the bend safely.

Juanito and Sikes hurried forward.

"One of McIntosh's buffalo guns," Emmett said, pointing up the hillside. "Took an ugly chunk out of that pony's neck."

"We can't go back down," Juanito said. "McIntosh's men will be reaching the mouth of the ravine about now."

Turning to the Chinese, Emmett yelled, "Everybody off your horses. Take cover where you can."

They had just begun to do as he had urged them when a hailstorm of lead began to blow in from above and behind them. The percussion and echo of rifle fire in the pass was deafening. It was impossible to communicate to everyone at once.

One of Yong Xu's volunteers twisted and tumbled from the saddle.

Tarnation! Looked as if his worst fear might come true.

In the instant it took to scan the hillside, he lost track of Li. Bullets rang past him as he wheeled his pinto and searched desperately for her and Ping.

Sikes cried out in pain. He slid from his horse and tried to crawl from the trail to cover. He wasn't making good progress.

Emmett swung out of the saddle and ran to him.

"Dammit!" Sikes grimaced. "Same leg they got me in before."

Right away Emmett could tell that this wound was worse. He grasped his friend by the shoulders and dragged him to a boulder that somewhat shielded both of them. Working feverishly, he pulled off his neckerchief and cinched it around Sikes's leg just above the wound.

"You gonna be OK, Sikes?"

Though a little peaked, the Englishman nodded. "Go shoot somebody." He cursed, then lay back and groaned.

Emmett peered over the boulder. Immediately a bullet struck within feet of his head, sending slivers of rock and a spray of grit into his face. He ducked. But not before he had spotted Li Xu. A gray horse lay dead still on its side. She was wedged as close to its belly as she could get.

She's too exposed there.

He picked out another boulder that offered better shelter for her, then dashed down the slope. His intestines tightened. With each step, he expected a fat piece of lead to smack into him and knock him off his feet. He feared going down only feet from Li—lying there, seeing her hit, being completely powerless to help.

But he reached her side. She jumped at his touch, terror in her eyes.

"Come with me. Quick!" He looped his arm around her waist and lifted her. As they ran, he wasn't sure her toes ever touched the ground.

Nestling her behind the boulder, he said, "Stay put, Li. Please don't go anywhere."

"Ping," she said, her eyes pleading. "Ping's out there."

"I'll get her. I promise." He squeezed her hand.

As Emmett stole glimpses around the boulder, the intensity of the gunfire seemed to reach a crescendo. He had no idea how many had fallen on either side, but he could see that his friends here below were firing back up the hillside relentlessly.

He spied Ping's smock on the ground. Her hands covered her head. She was tight up against a man in western clothes and a mandarin cap. His hands likewise covered his head.

Before running, Emmett took a quick glance up and found that he had his first clear shot at one of McIntosh's boys. He threw the rifle stock to his shoulder and squeezed off a round. It missed. The concussion of a bullet whipping by made him turn his head and cringe instinctively.

Working the lever feverishly and squeezing off three more rounds, Emmett at last sent his target tumbling limply down the hillside. *One less bushwhacker.*

Emmett sprinted to Ping. Something orange or red above and to the right caught his attention. He drew his Colt and snapped off a shot.

When he tried to lift the girl, she stiffened.

"Come on, Ping. It's me—Emmett."

She was conscious but evidently in shock, capable of nothing more than staring and trembling.

With no more time to waste out in the open, Emmett hefted her in his arms and made a run for it. His boots slipped on the steep embankment. Shale gave way beneath his feet. Bullets kicked up dirt far too close. At last he reached the dry grass.

Seconds later he skidded to his knees alongside Li. She had wedged herself as close as possible to the massive rock.

"Li, here's Ping," he said, breathing hard.

Li's head came up. She crawled to Ping's side. "What's wrong with her? Has she been shot?"

"I don't think so. Just overwhelmed by it all, I think. Hold onto her. I'll be back."

Emmett raced back to the man Ping had been lying next to. When he got there, he saw why the fellow was lying so still. He wouldn't recover from that hit.

From the fallen Chinaman, he hurried to check on Sikes and found the Englishman chambering a cartridge into the Sharps.

"You're still alive," Emmett said.

"Alive and giving them as much trouble as I can."

Just then two of the Chinese volunteers ducked behind the rock where he and Sikes sat.

One of the two, Chao, asked, "Do you have any of that dynamite with you?"

Emmett cringed. He realized there were two sticks wrapped in thick, waxed paper in his saddlebag. "Yes," he said. "Why?"

"I think we can make our way up there." Chao pointed toward the source of some of the heavier gunfire. "We can plant some up above McIntosh's men. Bring down an avalanche of rock on them."

"Dreadful dangerous," Emmett said.

Sikes scoffed. "And we're safe right now?"

Emmett glanced at Sikes's leg. He was bleeding badly.

"Stay here," he said.

Emmett scrambled to his feet and ran down the slope to his horse, firing as he went. For a moment the return gunfire slacked off. He reached into his saddlebag and grabbed the dynamite. A trail of bullets followed him back to the boulder.

He pulled a tin of matches from his vest pocket. "Here you go. Wait till I reload and start firing again before you run."

Chao nodded.

"Sikes?"

"Yes?"

"You holding up OK?"

"Yes."

"Have you got a target in mind?"

"Yes."

"Then on 'three,'" Emmett said.

He counted. On "three" he popped up, firing toward the cluster of rocks that seemed to have been producing most of the trouble. Sikes leaned forward and fired off a round.

The big bullet from the Sharps loosened a large rock that had been hiding one of McIntosh's outlaws. When the stone fell away, bouncing and rolling down the slope, Emmett caught sight of the gunhand. He took quick aim and fired. The McIntosh man slumped.

Meanwhile, Chao and the other Chinese gent were well on their way up the slope. They zigged and zagged. First they pulled away from where most of McIntosh's men seemed to be. Then near the summit, they cut back.

Emmett returned his attention to Li and Ping. They were still lying tight against the big boulder.

He now searched for Juanito. He hadn't seen him for a while and couldn't spot him even now.

While his gaze combed the slope, he felt a sudden, forceful pressure in his chest, followed instantly by a tremendous flash and a roar. It seemed as though half the facing hillside turned to gravel and rained down on them.

Dirt darkened the air. His ears were ringing. Through the dust, he saw two McIntosh men rise unsteadily to their feet. A fusillade rose from the bottom of the ravine, and the two crumpled and rolled till their bodies came to rest side by side.

For a few seconds there was no further gunfire.

Then he spotted Chao and his friend stooping, peering cautiously downhill at their handiwork. They stood, waved their arms, and cheered.

There was a single pop, and Chao's friend fell.

"Dammit!" Emmett muttered. He had seen the shooter, but just that fast, the outlaw had taken cover again.

"Sikes?"

"I saw him."

"Got him if he moves?"

"I do."

They waited only an instant.

The buffalo gun thundered. And that was the last shot of the encounter.

CHAPTER FORTY-SEVEN

Studying the doctor's face, Emmett discerned without a word that the news would not be good. The characteristic ruddiness was gone from Sikes's cheeks. Eyes closed, the Englishman moaned softly. One of the older Chinese women took over mopping his face with a cool, damp cloth. The doctor gestured for Emmett and Juanito to follow him out of the room.

On the front porch of the simple frame house, the surgeon shook his head. "I'm trying to save the leg. But if I had to guess right now, I'd say we'll be amputating by morning. Maybe before."

Emmett pounded the porch post, then leaned his weary head against it.

Juanito patted Emmett's arm.

The doctor sighed. "I'm sorry."

"I know, Doc. You're doing your best." Emmett pushed away from the post. "If it was me going under the saw, I couldn't complain. This was my mission."

"*Oye, hermano,*" Juanito said. "Sikes volunteered. He knew what he was getting into. And he did it because he wanted to."

Recalling the volunteers who had lost not only legs but lives, Emmett stared past his brother-in-law.

"He and I talked," Juanito went on. "He did it for you. But he did it for the Chinese people here too. He did it because it was right."

Emmett nodded.

"Go rest for an hour or two," the doctor said. "I'll send for you right away if his condition changes."

"You sure?" Emmett asked wearily.

"Absolutely."

Emmett closed his eyes for just a moment, drew a deep breath, and said, "I need some soup…or something."

"Xu's wife has food ready over at the Golden Dragon," Juanito said. "Go get some." He flicked both hands at Emmett.

"I'm going."

Emmett ambled over to the Golden Dragon feeling completely spent. It hurt to walk. When he saw the yellow lamplight spilling out of the café's front windows, he stopped in his tracks. His heart fluttered.

Was all of this about to be over? The long chase of Charlie Blaylock? The daydreams about a lively, breathtaking Chinese girl? Sikes could no longer help. Sheriff Morrison had done all he could. And Emmett wouldn't ask the Chinese for more.

With his hand on the door handle, he hesitated. He wondered whether when he headed back to Texas in just a few days it would be without Charlie Blaylock in handcuffs. Without this mesmerizing new girl in his life. Without his new friend, Sikes. If so, why had all this happened?

When he opened the door, every pair of eyes in the room turned to him. What was it he read on their faces? It eluded him…until Yong Xu's wife hurried over to his side.

"Mr. Strong," she said, taking his arm. "You come eat. Hot pork dumplings. Hot tea. Then you sleep. You must be very tired." She smiled softly.

"I am, ma'am."

"Then you come sit down."

In seconds, there must've been five Chinese mothers waiting on him, bringing him food and drink. One even pulled off his boots and brought a pillow for him to rest his feet on.

"Thank you, ma'am," he said. As he looked around the dining room, he recognized some of the men who had ridden out to help bring back Li and Ping. They were seated with neighbors who had stayed behind. Women carrying heaping platters of savory-smelling food scurried between the kitchen and the exhausted, famished men.

He supposed Li Xu was at home in her own room, asleep. That was good—best for her. But he wished he could see her now, for at least a little while.

He ate a few dumplings and thought they were about the best thing he'd ever put in his mouth.

When they brought him more tea, he said, "May I have water, please? I'm parched. I just want something cool."

"You drink tea," a grandmother insisted. "Help you rest."

He gave in.

And rest he did. The next hour was a blur. Someone—he never would recall who—guided him to a tiny room in a tiny house where he fell into bed. All consciousness escaped him.

CHAPTER FORTY-EIGHT

Lucian McIntosh's dark form seemed to absorb the light from the campfire. He and the band of gunmen standing behind him had ridden hard.

Hands on his hips and feet planted wide, he leaned in. Only his white shirt and his face showed color—and his face was as red as Seth had ever seen it.

"You couldn't hold 'em down another ten minutes?" he roared. "And how the hell did them Chinamen get up above you on that hill?" He pointed toward the spot where the dynamite had been detonated.

Only two of his gunslicks had survived the shootout with Emmett Strong's party. They were rough men—men who had seen a great deal of violence. But they had never been part of a bushwhacking gone so bad.

"Buck Tanner was on the buffalo rifle," one of the two said, a bloody bandanna tied around his head, covering one eye. "Once they got him, we didn't have no more cover from that side. But there was so much gunfire comin' up from the trail that we didn't even know Buck was gone till after it was too late."

McIntosh turned on Seth. Spittle spewed from his mouth as he vented. "They had one Sharps rifle the day this all started. I gave you four of 'em. They used dynamite on you the night they kidnapped Charlie. Do I have to give everybody dynamite every time we go out to take care of business now?"

Seth seethed inside. "Sir, you know we needed those Sharps out there for the exchange today."

"Why?" McIntosh bellowed. "So they wouldn't shoot your sorry backside?"

Never before had Lucian McIntosh shown such low regard for his loyalty and talents. He gritted his teeth, wanting to defend himself. But he held back.

"Now are we gonna stay two steps behind Emmett Strong till he decides he's wreaked all the havoc he cares to up here?" McIntosh said. "Or are we gonna get the jump on them damn Texans?"

Seth drew a breath to answer, but McIntosh jammed his hand to within a foot of his face.

The big boss glared from Seth to Charlie and back. "You got your brother back today, but we still lost. I aimed to have Emmett Strong and them damn Chinese witness me takin' those girls right back. And then I wanted that whole batch of 'em to die. Maybe leave one Chinaman to go back over to the other side of this mountain and tell folks never to mess with Lucian McIntosh again. Ever." He turned to the two ambush survivors. "Instead, what do you expect everybody over there in Chinatown is sayin' tonight? Huh?"

The campfire popped as a chunk of wood settled, sending up a salvo of yellow-orange sparks.

McIntosh crossed over to the gunhand with the bandanna over his eye, grabbed him by the collar with both fists, and yanked him to his feet. "They're over there boastin' about how Emmett Strong and his Chinaman pardner rode into Lucian McIntosh's own yard and told McIntosh the way things were gonna be. And then they made it happen. Now who gets to do such around here and live to tell about it?"

The gunhand stammered, "N-nobody. But you told us to just keep 'em pinned down till you got here. Told us 'specially not to shoot them China girls. You said—"

Something metallic glinted in the firelight, and the gunhand's eyes went wide. McIntosh's huge hand jerked upward from the middle of the gunslick's belly. The gunman gave a choked grunt. When Lucian withdrew his hand, the blade he clutched dripped blood.

McIntosh shoved the gutted gunman to the ground. "I know what I said. And this is what you get for not doin' it."

For several moments, no one dared speak.

Then Seth said, "Strong's still got to get out of here, sir. He's got to try to get back to Texas. We can take him while he's on his way out."

"You think that's good enough?"

Seth gave a slight shrug. "We can do whatever you want, sir."

"Can you?" The big man peered from one hired hand to another. "Can you do what I want? 'Cause I ain't seen it in a few days now."

Aware of his own precarious standing with Lucian McIntosh at the moment, Seth met his boss's gaze and nodded coolly. "I assure you I can, sir."

"Then this is what I want," McIntosh said, holding up his index finger. "We ain't waitin' for Emmett Strong to dictate terms anymore. We ain't gonna sit back and wait till he's seen enough of Nevada and decides he's ready to go home."

"Understood," Seth said.

"You start by hurtin' him good while he's still here. He came into my country and interfered with my business. Now I expect you to make him regret it. Understand?"

"We'll plan carefully, and we'll take it to him," Seth said resolutely.

Zeke, McIntosh's longtime gunhand, looked side to side, then asked, "But Mr. McIntosh, if them Texans is sittin' tight in Virginia City, what can we do about 'em there?"

"Plenty you can do. Just don't be stupid. Can't ten or twelve of you go about it at one time in plain view."

Seth turned to Zeke. "A pair of us here, a pair of us there, always houndin' him, always remindin' him the day he sets foot outside the city he's all ours. That'll wear a man down."

"Hell, don't settle for wearin' him down. Provoke him," McIntosh said. "Get him to step in it—right there in front of the law. Turn the people of Virginia City against him. Get 'em to run him outta town right into our waitin' arms."

"Chinamen might even turn out to be a help on that count," Seth said to Zeke and the others.

McIntosh scanned the scene of the failed ambush. "If Emmett Strong thinks this is over, he's sorely mistaken. By the end of it all, I expect you boys to make that damn Texan regret the day he crossed into Comstock country."

CHAPTER FORTY-NINE

When the sound of Juanito's voice finally began to make sense to him, Emmett opened his eyes. For several seconds, his gaze darted from corner to corner of the small, dimly lit bedroom. He studied the curtains. Nothing here was familiar to him. And he was dreadful thirsty.

"Where are we, Juanito?" he asked, his voice croaky.

"With Chinese friends in Virginia City. You've been asleep about twenty hours."

Emmett bolted upright. "Twenty hours?" He ran the fingers of both hands through his hair. "What—"

Juanito held up a palm. As he crossed the room he said, "Somebody wants to give you some good news." He opened the door and with a wave invited the visitor in.

Li Xu paused with her hand on the doorframe.

Emmett's heart quickened. *Tarnation! I must look like the hindquarters of bad luck. And here comes this—What did Sikes say they're called? Ah, yes—this Celestial.*

And that's the way she appeared to Emmett. She had obviously rested. Her hair was freshly combed and styled the way it'd been the first time he'd seen her—one part pinned up, the rest draping her shoulder. She was in boys' clothes again…but the look of her was anything but boyish. Her face was radiant.

She knelt beside the bed where he sat. "How are you?" she asked.

That voice—like velvet, yet somehow still full of strength. It finally occurred to him he should answer. "I'm OK. What about you? And Ping?"

She smiled warmly. "We're OK. Thanks to you." She kept her eyes on his. "I wanted to be the one to give you the good news."

232

He glanced up at Juanito, who was now leaning on the doorframe, facing away. Looking at Li again, he said, "I could use some good news."

"The doctor told me Mr. Sikes will not lose his leg after all."

"That's great news. It's…"

"He's going to have to stay here in Virginia City at least two weeks before getting on a train back to Texas," she said. "That's what the doctor told me anyway."

To Emmett the news was good on two counts: Sikes was going to be OK. And the doctor's orders meant he too would be staying put for a while. Right away he hoped to spend as much of that time as possible getting to know Li.

"I'll bet Sikes would like to see you," she said. "Can I take you to him?"

"Sure," he said. This was a good start. He might get to spend the evening with her. "Can I wash up a bit before going over, though?"

She smiled and rose to her feet. "Just a moment."

In no time she left the tiny bedroom and came right back with a towel and a basin of steaming water. "I thought you might want these. I'll wait right outside." She glanced at him over her shoulder as she bustled out.

"I'll be outside too," Juanito said with a slight grin.

When Emmett stepped out into the evening air he felt very much alive. The fog of deep sleep had faded away. The thrill of being in Li's company was growing moment by moment.

Li led him and Juanito across the street and down two blocks to another small frame house. She knocked, and an older man with a wispy, gray beard opened the door.

"Welcome," he said with a broad smile. "Your friend will be happy to see you."

Emmett took off his hat as he entered. Right there in the main room was a bed. Sikes, wearing only a long nightshirt, was in it, propped up on two pillows, his twice-injured leg sticking out from beneath the sheets. From midthigh down to the knee, the leg was deep purple.

"Good to see you've still got that limb," Emmett said. "Even if it is ugly."

Sikes frowned. "I told you we should've gone down to Mound House and caught the train back up here," he growled softly. "But no, you had to take the mountain pass."

Li spoke up. "Now why have you spoken so kindly to me and saved all your harsh words for Emmett?"

Sikes looked at Li. "You, my dear, were kidnapped. We need to treat you gently. Meanwhile, this rascal…" He turned his head back to Emmett. "He nearly got us all killed."

"Nearly," Emmett said. "And I'm sorry. Had I indeed gotten us all killed, I don't think I ever could've lived with myself."

Sikes tried to maintain a scowl but failed, a chuckle escaping and a weak smile finding a place on his face.

Juanito and Li both laughed along with him.

Emmett stepped up to the bedside and held out a hand. "Thank you, Sikes. I'm indebted."

Sikes waved. "Not at all." Then he clasped and shook Emmett's hand.

"So I understand we're here for a couple of weeks," Emmett said. He looked to Sikes's host and back. "Will that be all right with you?"

The older Chinese gentleman bowed. "It will be my honor. You Texas men have done for our community what no one else would have done. And we are grateful."

And that's the way it was for the next several days. The Chinese treated the Texans as heroes.

Funerals for Yan and Guiying—the two girls who had been shot—and for those who had fallen trying to rescue the rest took place on the second day. Even on that day, there was an easing of the customary rituals of mourning especially for Emmett and his pardners, and for Li Xu and the other girls who had suffered through the kidnapping.

Throughout the following days, when Li and Emmett strolled together in the cool of the early morning and in the fading light right after sundown, the folks of Chinatown bowed in polite greeting or waved appreciatively. Many offered kind words. No one let Emmett or Juanito buy a meal. They were fed well in the neighborhood's homes, cafés, and restaurants. They were forbidden from getting rooms in a hotel, instead remaining guests in the modest but clean homes that had taken them in following the rescue.

Juanito wandered over to the Lucky Strike Saloon a few times to catch up on news, but Emmett remained as close to Li as each day's activities permitted.

Yong Xu and Li's mother, Xiulan, gave the girl very light responsibilities those first few days, wanting her to recover well from the trauma she had endured.

As far as Emmett could tell, things were going well between him and Li Xu. They spoke freely. Given the circumstances that had brought them together, he ventured to ask her things he might otherwise have considered impertinent—improper for the brief time they had known one another. Yet late one afternoon as they strolled alone, he struggled to find just the right words to ask something that had been needling away at him ever since the exchange.

"Li, I know everyone says you're OK, but I need to know…Did Lucian McIntosh…" He cleared his throat. "Did he, uh, touch you…while he had you in his home?"

She bit her lip, looked down, and shook her head.

"Ping?"

"No," Li said, "but I don't know how to explain to you what I did to stop him."

He frowned. "I don't want to push you."

"It's not like that," she said. "It's just that it has to do with womanly things."

Womanly things…Oh. Emmett gave a slight nod. "I understand. You don't have to say anything more." He pulled his hat off and raked his fingers through his hair. "Haven't thought about womanly things in a while."

She tilted her head. "Why would you ever have to think about womanly things—if we both mean the same…womanly things?"

Before he knew it, the words were out of his mouth. "My wife…"

She stopped in place and faced him. Her cheeks flushed. "You're married?" Her voice sounded thin.

"Oh, no," he said. "Not anymore."

She touched the base of her neck. A gust of wind blew past them.

He looked down. "She died. Five years ago."

Li clutched his arm tenderly. "I'm so very sorry. An illness?"

Turning his gaze back to hers, he shook his head. "Strange. For five years I couldn't get her out of my mind. I thought about her day and night, no matter where I was."

"And then?" she asked.

He looked her eye to eye. "And then…you."

She was quiet for a moment. "Is that OK with you? That I…"

"More than OK."

She gave a faint smile and brushed back the hair that the wind had blown into her face.

"May I tell you?" he asked.

"Please."

"Then let's walk some more."

For the next hour he described how he and Gabriela had met and how they had always felt so natural together—as if they had belonged to one another forever. Then he told the story of the day he lost her.

The next thing he knew, he and Li stood facing one another on the very edge of town in the last rays of the setting sun, a breeze rippling their clothes and hair.

"I killed my wife, Li. I killed my sweet Gabriela."

She looked up the street—back into town and into the direct rays of the sunset. Then taking hold of his arms, she drew him to her and rested her cheek against his chest.

"No, you didn't," she said. "Victorio Sanchez killed her."

When she eased back and peered into his face, tears glimmered on her lashes. "Don't ever say it again, Emmett—that you killed her. You didn't. And I never again want to hear you say that you did." Her scolding was gentle. She bit her lip.

"We'd better go back," she said, keeping hold of his arm.

"The elders," he said.

She only squeezed tighter as she looked straight ahead and walked.

His insides were beginning to feel like melted wax. *How can this be?* he wondered.

CHAPTER FIFTY

"So Seth Blaylock's woman's name is Ettie." Emmett pondered what Li had just told him. He again recalled the shriek he had heard in the mesquite grove when he shot Blaylock's pardner the day Guiying died.

"Yes," Li said as the pair continued their stroll back into Chinatown. "Ping and I were scared of her at first because she's the one who picked out who to kidnap and who to leave behind."

"And somehow you quit being afraid of her?"

Li shook her head. "She seemed like two different people. In Zhang's Restaurant the whole Blaylock gang was so frightening. They were ruthless and violent. Well, she didn't do anything violent, but she was one of the gang. And at that point I wasn't even sure she was a woman—though I had my suspicions."

"Oh?" Emmett turned to see Li's face more fully.

"She had her nose and mouth covered with a black bandanna. She wore a long black coat with the collar up. Leather gloves. And of course a hat. But I could see the eyes."

Her powers of observation impressed him. "And later on? At McIntosh's place?"

"She still wore trousers and a vest—and a pistol. But she was very femi-nine. Her hair was beautifully braided on both sides, close to her head."

They were drawing near her parents' café.

Li went on. "At McIntosh's place, Ettie seemed almost apologetic to us. She tried to comfort Ping."

Emmett considered what—if anything—this news of Ettie might mean.

"Once they told us Ettie would be gone for a few days," she said, "that's when things changed again. The housekeeper and the cook were not kind at all. The cook is the one who started trying to drug Ping and me. They knew we liked tea, so they offered us plenty of it. But they kept putting something in it."

"Like what?"

"I think it was laudanum or something like that."

With a tilt of his head, Emmett said, "And what do you know about laudanum, little girlie?"

She frowned at him. "Little girlie?"

They both broke into smiles.

"Just like any people, there are good Chinese and bad Chinese," she said. "I'm sure you know the reputation some of my people have for smuggling opium from Asia to San Francisco. Then from San Francisco to places all over the West. Mining towns, cow towns, pretty much any town where people suddenly find themselves with more money in their hands than they're accustomed to having."

Emmett understood far too well. There weren't too many opium dens in Texas, but he'd come across them before. And opium was only one side of what went on there. Theft. Prostitution.

"How'd you avoid the laudanum?" he asked.

"It's bitter. Haven't you ever used it?"

"No. I know doctors suggest it for all sorts of problems, but..."

"Well, good thing," she said. "It can make you extremely dull. And it's addictive. We have far better remedies for cramps and colds and diarrhea than laudanum."

"We?"

"Chinese grannies and doctors. Anyway, Ping and I kept dumping it into the chamber pot when they left the room. And we asked for lots of water. We told Margaret—the cook—that her tea made us strangely thirsty."

"Smart girls." He smiled.

Her grin was captivating. "Let's go inside. I'll play the *pipa* for everyone till dinner is ready."

Just before opening the restaurant door, Emmett's attention was drawn to two men lingering in front of a shop a few doors down—in the direction he and Li had just come from. It was a place that sold paper, ink, and such. And the loiterers didn't look much like the type to go home and write poetry. They were heeled and rough cut.

He opened the door for Li. When he again glanced back, he caught the two staring directly at him. One touched the brim of his hat. Then they both turned and sauntered back toward the edge of town. Emmett's stomach tensed.

Quite a crowd filled the café. Juanito was there.

"Just getting some food for Sikes," Juanito said as he made his way toward the door with a basket in hand.

Emmett had seen his British friend a few hours earlier. His progress seemed good. "Tell him I'll stop by after I've had a little grub."

"I'll do that. Everything going OK with Li and you?"

Emmett winked. "I think so."

Juanito raised an eyebrow. "*Muy bien, hermano.*"

After making sure he wouldn't be overheard, Emmett said, "Keep your eyes peeled. I think I just spotted a pair of deuces out there."

"McIntosh men?" Juanito lipped silently.

Emmett nodded.

Juanito waved two fingers in front of his eyes, then away. With that, he turned and headed out.

Emmett pivoted to see where Li had gone. Just as he did so, Yong emerged from the kitchen.

He greeted Emmett, but not with his usual effusive smile. "Let me get you something to eat," he said. "Then you should go visit Mr. Sikes for a while."

"Thank you. I will. Juanito and I were just talking about that."

"Give him plenty of good company. Visit often. He will get well faster." Yong's smile seemed forced.

Li took her customary chair in the corner of the room and began to pluck her Chinese lute. A few heads turned momentarily, but for the most part folks simply continued their table talk.

"Here." Yong Xu motioned toward the kitchen. "I can fix you a plate to take with you. Then you can eat with Sikes. Lift his spirits."

"Uh, sure," Emmett said, eyebrows knit. If he didn't know better it would seem that Yong was deliberately trying to get him out of the café. He wondered whether he'd done something to offend. Or whether he, Juanito, and Sikes might've overstayed their welcome—become an imposition. He didn't for a moment believe the Chinese owed him anything. To the contrary, he'd felt awkward accepting free room and board. He'd done so only because they'd all insisted.

Then he recalled Li's warm embrace on the edge of town at sunset. Maybe someone had seen that and told Yong Xu.

"I don't think I'm very hungry, Yong," Emmett said, though in fact he was famished. "You're right. I think I'll wander over and visit Sikes for a while."

"Very good." Yong nodded enthusiastically, his smile still less than convincing.

—⁂—

Juanito sat on the one simple wooden chair in the room where Sikes lay. Emmett leaned against the doorframe. Mr. Chang, Sikes's host, had stepped out for a while, so at last the men could speak freely.

"Down at the saloon," Juanito said, "people are starting to ask questions. Say things that might provoke some folks."

"Like what?" Sikes asked.

Juanito rubbed the stubble on his chin. "Oh, they say, 'So you're one of those Texans that faced down Lucian McIntosh. Dangerous business. And you did it all for a bunch of China girls?'

"I say, *sí*," he went on, "and they ask again, 'Why would you take that kind of risk just for China girls?'

"I don't have much to tell them, but they ask more. They say, 'How did you even know about those China girls?' and 'What brings you up here from Texas anyway?'"

"It's not polite to be so nosey," Emmett said.

"Oh, some of them say it's a good thing—what we did. Facing down a man like McIntosh. Helping defenseless young women."

"And others?" Emmett asked.

"Not so kind. Seems like some of them want to start something…and not just in the saloon. Even out on the street."

"Start something, huh?"

"They point. Some say it loud because they want me to hear. Others say it soft, but I hear anyway."

"Making threats?" Sikes asked. "Or just running their mouths?"

"I've seen this kind of thing before," Juanito said. "Today they say, 'There goes that damn China lover.' Tomorrow they start the troublemaking. Bumping the shoulder on the way out. Spitting close to the boot instead of in the spittoon."

Sikes adjusted his pillows and sat upright. "I'll bet the Cornish miners—and the Irish—are the worst of the lot."

Juanito said, "It's not just them."

Emmett looked at Sikes, then back at Juanito. "Seems our welcome is wearing thin. And not just out there on the streets."

"Where else?" Sikes asked.

"Even Yong was anxious to get me out of the Golden Dragon tonight."

"Yong?" Sikes frowned.

Juanito shot Emmett a glance that spoke volumes. "That girl likes you. People are beginning to notice. And I don't think Yong wants to let that relationship come to full flower."

All three men stared blankly for a quiet minute.

"Maybe we need to move back to the hotel," Emmett said. "Get outta these people's hair. Give 'em some space."

Sikes drew back the sheet and examined his leg. Above and below the bandage the purple had faded to greenish and yellowish hues.

"You give that leg a try yet?" Emmett asked.

Sikes shook his head. "It feels much better, but I think I'm going to have to rely on that crutch over there in the corner for quite some time yet."

Emmett nodded. "But can we get you over to the hotel? Will you be OK without Chang watching you day and night?"

"I think so. I'll call for the doctor and get his opinion."

"Either way, I think we oughta make the move. Better for everyone," Emmett said.

Juanito pushed his hat back. "But you're still going to want to see the girl every day."

"I will want that," Emmett said.

"And how is that going to end, *hermano*?"

Emmett took a moment to answer. He looked Juanito in the eye. "I truly don't know."

Yet he knew what he wanted to say. He knew what he wanted to happen. He just wasn't sure it was even possible in the world they lived in.

CHAPTER FIFTY-ONE

The next day Emmett and Juanito brought the doctor to take another look at Sikes's leg. He gave the go-ahead to move the Englishman but recommended waiting another few days before making the long trip back to Texas. So with expressions of profuse gratitude to everyone in the Chinese community, the three excused themselves and relocated to the Comstock Queen Hotel.

Still, every day—morning and evening—Emmett made the trip to Chinatown to see Li Xu. And every day he argued with himself along the way. Was he being fair to Li? Was he being selfish? Would the world outside Chinatown ever accept her as his wife? Would people's thoughtless words and actions torment her?

He considered Yong Xu and his wife and deliberated whether it would be cruel for him to have rescued their daughter from Seth Blaylock only to take her away from them and her people forever.

At the end of each day, all the reasoning in the world wouldn't tip the scales. He had to see her yet again, to relish the pure joy of her company.

The third day after the Texans had moved out of Chinatown, when Emmett approached the front porch of Xu's Golden Dragon, Yong was already outside waiting for him. As soon as he spotted Emmett, he dropped the rag he had been using to clean the front windows into a bucket, wiped his hands on the hem of his jacket, and stepped into Emmett's path.

"Let's go talk," he said. No smile. Not even a disingenuous one.

He led Emmett through the side alley to the small lot behind the café and stopped in the shade at the back of the building.

His arms folded, he squared himself to face Emmett. "You know how deeply grateful I am that you saved my daughter, Mr. Strong."

"Emmett."

Yong nodded. "Emmett...The whole Chinese community is indebted to you. You gave up the very thing that brought you to Nevada to begin with. You let a wrong done to you go unpunished so that you could right the wrong that McIntosh and Blaylock did to us."

Here it comes, Emmett thought. *"It's time you leave my daughter alone and go away."*

Yong drew a deep breath. "It can never work between Li-Li and you, Emmett. The world is not ready for that. Not yet. Maybe never."

Emmett tried to be patient, tried to show all the respect due to a community leader. But he wasn't yet ready to accept Yong Xu's open-and-shut conclusion.

"I don't know Texas, Emmett. But I know people. And I have yet to see people who are willing to treat one another as though we are all truly one human race—people with different traditions and languages, but all human beings nonetheless."

"You don't want to see your daughter hurt, Yong. I understand that."

As he spoke, Emmett wasn't even sure how he was supposed to stand: Humbly, hat in hand? Eyes downcast? Or chin up, gaze locked on Yong's? He hadn't faced anything like this since Gabriela's father had called him out ten years earlier. That'd been another cross-cultural confrontation. Yet given their family histories and given that it had happened in Texas between two kinds of Texians, the gap to be bridged hadn't been nearly so wide.

Back then, he was an inexperienced kid. Since then he'd seen so much more of life and human behavior. He knew there was a strong element of truth to what Yong Xu was saying. But then again—he had a strong and growing conviction that if anybody could make this work, he and Li could.

"You're correct, Emmett. I don't want to see Li hurt. But beyond that, we have our customs. We will find her a suitable husband from among her own people. A man of character like you, I hope—only Chinese." His gaze didn't waver.

Emmett wondered whether the compliment was merely a concession, calculated to soften the blow. Or was it sincere? Regardless, he supposed Yong was waiting for him to acknowledge that some things in life simply couldn't be altered—that he should read the handwriting on the wall and let go of Li.

But he wouldn't let go. Not that easily anyway.

"Li's feelings count for nothing then?" he asked.

"Feelings come and go," Yong said. "You will leave in a few days. Li will cry. But by her twentieth birthday her feet will come back to the ground in Chinatown."

Emmett looked around the small yard, then off to the silver-rich hills that had brought folks—including the Chinese—to this place. "Yes, Yong," he said. "I'll be leaving in a few days. But what're you asking of me till then? Am I not to see Li anymore? Are we not to take our strolls or have our talks?"

"You know the answer to that," Yong said. "I wish my door could remain open to you as long or as often as you wanted to come." He clasped his hands behind his back. "But it will be better for both of you to begin to make the separation now. Otherwise you will only continue to nurture a hope that can never be fulfilled."

Emmett's head swam. He wanted to honor Li's father's wishes, but he couldn't bring himself to agree. Even if he and Li were to make a break, the two of them needed to work out how they would let go of one another. They needed to determine how they would remember each other once the train rolled out of Virginia City and life moved forward again.

At last he met Yong's waiting gaze. "I'll think about what you've said. And trust me, Yong—I'll do everything I can to keep Li from being hurt."

Yong Xu bowed from the shoulders. He did not invite Emmett in.

"Suppose I'll be going then," Emmett said, touching the brim of his hat.

With that, he turned and started back up the alley to Union Street.

He'd walked maybe twenty yards up the avenue when he heard a door slam behind him. When he peered over his shoulder, there was Li, dashing his way. She clamped onto his arm and kept walking, taking him along with her. Her eyes were moist.

"Li," he said.

"Shhh! Don't say anything yet."

They turned left at L Street, still arm in arm, marching along in silence. After a few wood-framed buildings played out, the Virginia and Truckee railroad tracks came into view on their right—the same rails that would likely carry Emmett, Juanito, and Sikes out of Virginia City. And possibly out of Li Xu's world.

Once they had gone beyond the last of the buildings, Li stopped and faced him. Color infused her cheeks.

"Please, Emmett,"—her tears flowed freely now—"please take me with you. Promise me you won't leave me behind."

He swallowed hard and tucked a strand of her dark, silky hair behind her ear. What could he say? He wanted to do exactly what she'd just asked. Yet he had to wonder: Would doing so ultimately lead to greater pain and sorrow than Li could possibly imagine? The world was a hard place. Yong Xu could be right.

"I heard everything my father told you," she said. "But if you care for me you won't leave me behind."

The wind whipped her hair into her face once again.

"You turn twenty in a few months," he said softly.

She wiped her eyes with the heels of her hands. "Yes. And my father and mother are already talking about an arranged marriage for me—to Qiang Choi. But Ping loves Qiang Choi. I don't love him."

"So are you asking me to take you away from a marriage you don't want to face? Or are you asking me to take you with me because this is the marriage you want more than any other?"

She nodded urgently, tears sparkling in the sunlight. "I want this marriage."

This was even harder than he'd thought it would be. "A lot of white people won't accept you, Li. Heck, a lot of Chinese people won't accept you. Your own family may reject you," he said, trying to convince himself as much as persuade her.

She hit him on the chest with the side of her fist. "What about you? Are you afraid of what people will say? How they'll treat you if you have a Chinese wife?"

He shook his head. "You know that isn't true. I told you the story of Gabriela. Her death came because some folks just can't accept the fact that brown people and red people and yellow and white are all still people." Cupping her face in his hands, he looked into her deep-brown eyes. "It's not about what people might say to me. It's about the ugly things they might do to you."

She stepped in close and slipped her arms around him.

Dear Lord, how I've fallen for this woman! he thought. *But what's best for her?*

He held her tight and said, "Try as I might, I can't promise I'd be able to protect you."

"You don't have to."

"I would have to."

"Anyway, I've seen enough to know that you can protect me as well as anybody on earth can."

After a few seconds, he said, "You'll miss your mother and father."

She hung onto him and sniffled. "I will. But that's just the way of things."

He stared over her shoulder, taking in the panorama of the town she called home. "Thousands of Chinese here in Nevada. And yet I've never seen a single one in Texas."

"So maybe Texans won't have such hard feelings against me—one lone Chinese girl."

"That's not my point. It's not just your mother and father you'll miss. It's more than that. You've never been in a place where there's absolutely nothing Chinese."

"Emmett, with you there I'll be fine."

He closed his eyes. The feel of her in his arms was too good. He hated this argument. Especially since he wanted everything she was saying to be true. Still, he couldn't be sure...

"If we had kids, what'd happen to them?" he asked. "They might grow up as outcasts from both your world and mine."

At that, she pushed away from him. She opened her mouth to speak but couldn't stanch the tears. Finally she shook her head and managed to blurt out, "How long are you going to do this? It seems like you're trying to find any and every reason why things *can't* work for us."

He tried to unhitch his thoughts from his feelings, but he couldn't. *If you only knew, Li. It's your happiness that matters. It's all about you.*

Neither spoke for a long minute. Then she whirled and traipsed away, back up L Street, wiping tears as she went.

As he watched her go, he threw up his hands and let them drop, wondering whether he had done the right thing.

CHAPTER FIFTY-TWO

It was hardly past noon—far too early in the day, by Emmett's ordinary reckoning, to wind up in a saloon. But today he was finding it difficult to deny himself one beer after another on the way to ending up completely jingled. Then he could just flop into bed and sleep until it was time to go home to Texas.

Sikes had used the crutch to hobble along with Juanito over to the Silver Nugget. For a while they sat and drank quietly, evidently waiting for Emmett to spill his guts—which he wasn't in the mood to do. Somewhere along the line, the two started up their own conversation, speaking in low tones.

Eventually Emmett emerged from his ruminations long enough to realize that his friends were discussing what they'd do once they got back to San Antonio.

"What do you two have up your sleeves now?"

"Oh, so you are listening," Juanito said, crossing his outstretched boots at the ankles.

"Now that you ask," Sikes said, "I believe I've traveled far enough." He patted his wounded leg gingerly. "With this thing likely to give me pain the rest of my life, I don't think I'm fit for day after day in the saddle anymore."

Juanito drew in his legs and leaned forward, elbows on the table. "So that's why Sikes and I have decided to buy a saloon in San Antonio. This will be a nice place. No calico ladies. Just quality beverages—"

"And quality music," Sikes cut in. "Like that chap who played the guitar so impressively here the other day."

Emmett suppressed a belch. "Well, who'd have thought?"

"And that's not all," Juanito said. "Remember that blond girl at the Wild Hog back in El Paso?"

"Vaguely."

Sikes gave a sly smile. "Geneve."

"If you say so."

"Well," Juanito continued, "we spent that evening talking to her, and Sikes and I decided you were right. She doesn't need to spend her life in a place like that. It'll kill her before her time."

"So I've made up my mind," Sikes said, "even if it costs me the rest of what I have, even if she is a 'soiled dove' as some of you fellows so colorfully put it, I want to sweep her off her feet—"

"Believe me," Emmett interrupted, "a lot of fellas wanna do that."

Sikes glared. "That's not what I mean. I want to get her out of that life and be the man to care for her…if she'll have it."

"You gents've done an awful lot of talking. Where've I been?"

Sikes and Juanito looked at one another, then at Emmett.

"Spending all day every day over in Chinatown. Seeing no one except Li Xu," Juanito said.

Emmett waved dismissively.

"Not that there's anything wrong with that," Juanito added.

Emmett shook his head. "That, *mis* amigos, is apparently over."

Juanito frowned. "What? Over? What did you go and do, *hermano*? Step in the mother lode of all prairie pies? Say something stupid to her?"

Before Emmett could answer, a voice rang out from behind him. "They told me I'd find you here."

He twisted in his chair, and there between him and the bar was Cromarty— the newspaperman from Reno.

"Well, look what the bobcat's dragged in," Emmett said. "Good to see you, Cromarty. Pull up a chair."

Of course Sikes and Juanito knew all about Cromarty, but until now they'd not met. Emmett made the introductions.

"Glad you bumped into us," he said. "My Texas compadres and I are just about to wrap up our business here in beautiful Comstock country. About to head back home."

"Without what you came for?" the newsman said.

The bartender approached. "Beer OK for you, sir? Or do you want rotgut?"

"Beer, if it's cold," Cromarty said.

The bartender nodded. "Cold as a witch's bosom. Be right back."

Emmett picked up where Cromarty left off. "Yep, I guess you've seen him out and about in Reno once again. I had to let old Charlie go. Or did you even know we'd nabbed him?"

"Of course I knew—I'm a newspaperman."

"And a mighty fine one, I'm sure."

"So you confirmed my suspicions about Charlie's brother then?"

"Beyond the shadow of a doubt."

Cromarty nodded to the bartender as he set the beer in front of him. "Well, I hate to rub salt in a wound, but your man Charlie Blaylock is up there in his favorite saloon, barking at the moon, night and day."

"In the Hyperion?"

"That's right. He's up there blabbering to anybody who'll listen—and sometimes to folks who won't—about how he bested Emmett Strong, the Texas pistolero, and his law dog friends. 'Got away scot-free,' he keeps saying."

Emmett pursed his lips.

Juanito smacked him on the knee. "Don't let it get to you, *hermano*. You've done a lot of good up here."

"Oh, that's true enough," Cromarty said. "Rumors have drifted as far away as Reno about how a few fellas from Texas rescued some local Chinese girls from a band of notorious kidnappers. Lots of convoluted facts. Lots of speculation. But folks are talking."

"That can't be sitting well with Lucian McIntosh," Sikes said through a fog of cigar smoke.

"No, it's not," Cromarty said. "Not at all."

"Any scuttlebutt up there about McIntosh fixing to retaliate?" Emmett asked.

"That's why I came down here, as a matter of fact."

Emmett tilted his head. "More of Charlie Blaylock's crowing?" From the corner of his eye, he observed Sikes and Juanito leaning in.

"Oh, no. Charlie learned the hard way you don't go throwing McIntosh's name around loosely. Apparently the bartender up at the Hyperion biffed him in the mouth real good the first time he heard him using the boss's name injudiciously. I've got another source. "

"And what's your source say?"

Cromarty lowered his head and his voice. "Word is that McIntosh has been rotating gunslicks through all the major railroad stations round about. Watching for you gents. He doesn't aim to let you leave alive."

"This burg's been good to us," Emmett said. "But I have no intention of spending the rest of my days here." He cast a glance at his pardners.

"Well, you might want to consider some other means of travel for the first leg of your trip. Stay off the railroads."

"Appreciate you coming all the way down here to warn us, Cromarty. Got anything else for us?"

"The day's not over yet, gents," he said. "Who knows? You may end up having something for *me*."

"Like what?"

"Haven't heard word of another kidnapping in a couple of weeks now. Looks like you've effectively applied the brakes to Seth Blaylock's activities, at least for the time being. If you're not careful, you may shut him and McIntosh down completely." He flashed a momentary grin.

"As far as I'm concerned," Emmett said, "my business with that bunch is over."

"Without seeing justice served?"

Emmett took a swallow of beer. "We dished out a bit of justice. Maybe not what we'd planned on to begin with, but…"

"Speaking of the unexpected, what's this ballyhoo Charlie Blaylock keeps going on about—you and your own personal little China monkey, Mr. Strong? Just more of his blathering?"

"It's Emmett."

"Right. Emmett. So what's the true story about the China monkey? You really take a liking to one of those Chinese girls?"

Emmett placed both palms on the table, turned his head, and glared. "First of all, Mr. Cromarty, I'm disappointed to hear you repeating such demeaning phraseology, even if you are quoting Charlie Blaylock. Secondly, yes, I gained the friendship of one of the young women we rescued. But it was just that—an innocent friendship. And it's due to end soon, as my pardners and I must gladly make our way back to Texas."

Cromarty fumbled at straightening his tie. "I-I apologize, Mr.—Emmett. I was in fact quoting Charlie Blaylock. And I admit it was in poor taste."

"Apology accepted."

"Well, then…Main thing I wanted to do was to warn you about the rail-roads. And to advise you about Charlie Blaylock's boastful talk. Now if you don't mind excusing me, I have an appointment with the newspaper editor here in Virginia City." Cromarty stood and fished in his pocket.

"Don't worry about paying for the beer." Emmett patted his own vest pocket. "And Cromarty…"

"Yes?"

"Thanks for the information that led us to the young ladies' kidnappers."

"You're very welcome." He tipped his bowler. "My pleasure. Truly."

Cromarty turned and clacked across the hardwood floors, leaving the half doors swinging on their hinges.

"Good to have the warning," Sikes said.

"Indeed," Emmett said.

Juanito sat silently, elbows on the table and fingers steepled.

"What's on your mind, brother-in-law?" Emmett reached for his beer.

Juanito raised an eyebrow and spoke quietly. "What you said to Cromarty… Are you really giving up on Li Xu?"

"It can't work," Emmett said mechanically.

Juanito shook his head. "In five years, I haven't seen you look so much like the old Emmett Strong—not until I watched that girl light the fire within you once again."

"Yeah, well, it wouldn't be right to her father. To have his daughter stolen away once again. It'd make me as bad as Seth Blaylock."

Juanito scoffed. "Ridiculous. Your motives are nothing like Blaylock's."

Emmett slapped the table and leaned into his brother-in-law.

A few folks around the room turned and stared till they realized they weren't going to get a show.

"Little China monkey," Emmett said, his voice a biting whisper. "How could I be so selfish as to drag her out into a world that'll constantly assault her with ugly words like those?"

"Is that it, Emmett?" Sikes asked. "Is that really it?"

"Charlie Blaylock is a jackass," Juanito said.

"Yeah, well…lot of folks out there just like that," Emmett said.

Sikes matched Emmett's vehemence. "Well, what does Li Xu want? She's a full-grown woman. She can make up her own mind about what she can handle and what she can't."

"She hasn't seen the world like you and me, Sikes. She may be grown, but she's innocent. Besides, they have their customs, their rules. If she—woman that she is—defies her elders, she's finished in her society. It'd be near impossible for her to come back."

"I don't want you to regret this," Juanito said. "Don't make up your mind today, *hermano*. Give it another day or two."

"I thought maybe we'd begin getting ready to leave tomorrow."

This entire time, Emmett had been seated with his back to the door—an arrangement he normally took great pains to avoid.

Out of nowhere something deep inside told him to take a quick look behind him. He attempted to do so discreetly. But as he glanced back, a mustached fellow a few tables over—pretty close to the door—looked straight at him. With a smirk and a gleam in his eye, he raised his glass to Emmett.

Emmett pushed his chair back from the table and pivoted.

The fellow and his pardner—both heeled, both wearing the same cat-just-cornered-the-mouse grin—were now on their feet and ambling over in his direction. They halted just a yard or so away.

"Nice to see y'all again," the one with the brushy mustache said. Then he bent over the table and in a hushed voice added, "Mr. McIntosh and Mr. Blaylock send their greetin's." He touched his hat brim. "We'll be talkin' with y'all some more real soon."

He and his lanky amigo wheeled slowly and sauntered out of the saloon.

"Looks as though the fiesta's not over yet," Juanito said. "I think they both want to sign your dance card, *hermano*."

"Do you recognize them, Emmett?" Sikes asked.

"I recognize 'em."

"I do too—from the day we rode up to Lucian McIntosh's front door."

Juanito stood and watched the two cross the street.

"Yet another reason why I can't bring Li Xu along," Emmett said. "Much as I'd like to."

Sikes shook his head. "Bring her along, leave her behind, they may pay her a call anyway. According to Cromarty, Charlie Blaylock's already declaring the two of you a pair."

Emmett marveled at how careless he had been—wandering around town with Li as though all the world were cloaked in innocence.

CHAPTER FIFTY-THREE

As soon as they left the Silver Nugget, the two McIntosh men hurried toward their next stop—the Comstock Queen Hotel.

Zeke smoothed down his mustache and said to his spindly pardner, "Couldn't hear too much of what that newspaperman said, but it sounded as if he was puttin' them Texans on the alert."

The lanky one's gangly gait was stilted, getting ahead then slowing down to let the shorter-legged Zeke catch up with him. "Maybe Mr. Newspaperman needs to disappear."

"Not till the boss gives the go-ahead."

"People have accidents all the time. Boss can't get all riled up at us if the newspaper fella meets with some kind of accident, can he?"

They were only steps away from the Comstock Queen now.

"Just hold your horses. I'll ask the boss about the newspaper fella. Right now we gotta find that Chinaman. Told me to meet him at the kitchen door somewhere back here."

Zeke took a hurried look up and down the street before leaving the boardwalk and following the alley to the back of the hotel. At the back door he gave a sharp rap. Moments later, Chin—the Chinese fellow who had carried Emmett's baggage upstairs when he, Juanito, and Sikes had first arrived in Virginia City—opened the door cautiously. After a quick glance over his shoulder, he stepped into the back alley.

"You got what we want?" Zeke asked.

Chin looked from Zeke to the other McIntosh man and back. "Yes, I have. But this very dangerous for me."

"Now don't go gettin' yourself all worked up." Zeke drew a small bag of coins from his vest pocket and stuffed it into Chin's hand. "All you gotta do is tell us what rooms them Texas boys're stayin' in."

Chin bounced the purse of coins in his palm, then dropped it into a pocket beneath his apron. "Boss man room number 205. One with bad leg room 206. Mexican room number 207."

"All right. You done good so far now, Ching—"

"Chin, sir," the Chinese man cut in. "Name not Ching. Chin."

The other McIntosh man started laughing, revealing a missing tooth right up front.

Zeke chuckled too. "Yeah, well, Chin, Ching, Ching-a-ling—it's all the same, ain't it? Anyways, you done good so far, but I need you to tell me somethin' else now."

Chin's nostrils flared, but he said nothing.

Zeke dropped his fingers into his other vest pocket and pulled out another bag of coins. He swung it by the drawstring in front of Chin's eyes. "I can promise you, there's more to come if you keep helpin' us out like this."

Chin nodded, keeping his head low. "What else help?"

"Just tell me one more thing: Where can I find that little China girl Emmett Strong is so sweet on? Hmm?"

When Chin lifted his head to meet Zeke's gaze, his eyebrows were knitted. He quickly lowered his eyes again and said, "Don't know who you talk about."

"Oh, you know," Zeke said. "From what I hear, everybody in Chinatown knows her. She was one of the last two to come back. Emmett Strong traded Seth Blaylock's brother to get her back. The feisty little one."

Chin rubbed the side of his nose. "What you do with this Chinese girl?"

"Now look here," the one missing the tooth said, moving his hand to his holster. "Never mind what we do with her. You just spit it out."

Zeke elbowed him and said, "Jim, shut up. I'll handle Mr. Ching here."

He dangled the coin purse in front of Chin again. "So you do know her. C'mon. Where can I find her now? I won't hurt her. Just got some words for her, that's all."

"You just talk to her? That all?"

"That's right. Just talk."

Chin hesitated a moment more, then without looking up snatched the coin purse from Zeke's hand. "Xu's Golden Dragon Café. Over there Union Street. Past L Street."

Zeke elbowed Jim again. "See? You just gotta know how to negotiate with these folks. That's all."

Chin now waved the coin purse. "You think Mr. McIntosh sell me this girl?" He tucked the coins away with the others he'd been given.

"Sell her...to you?" Zeke eyed Jim. "I told you we was just gonna talk to her. What makes you think—"

Without waiting for Zeke to finish, Chin bowed. "We talk later." The Chinaman turned on his heels and rushed inside the hotel.

"You hear that?" Jim guffawed. "That little gopher thinks he's gonna buy a girl Mr. Lucian's got his eye on. Like hell."

Zeke shrugged. "Don't matter what he thinks. We got what we need. Now let's go pay the China girl a little visit before Mr. Emmett Strong decides he's had enough beer for the afternoon."

Jim spat out a stream through the gap where his tooth used to be. "I'm right behind you."

—w—

Minutes later Zeke and Jim pushed their way through the front door of Xu's Golden Dragon. Zeke grinned when he spied Li Xu off to the side spreading a clean tablecloth over a table next to the wall.

When she looked up, she gasped and froze in place.

Just then Yong Xu came hurrying out of the kitchen. He glanced at Li without breaking his stride and stopped only feet from Zeke and Jim.

"I'm sorry," he said, his dark eyes studying the two. "Lunch is over. And we are not ready to serve dinner yet. You can come back later."

Zeke let a grin crawl slowly across his face. "Maybe we don't want dinner. Maybe we just came in for a little snack." He leered at Li.

Jim snickered.

Yong's fists tightened.

"We hear there's some special Chinese cakes that American fellas have takin' a powerful likin' to lately. Thought we might see if we take a likin' to 'em, too."

Yong's gaze remained steeled on Zeke as he spoke firmly to his daughter. "Li, go to the kitchen."

Li had only taken a single step when Jim bounded for the kitchen door to block her way. A table and two chairs toppled and banged to the floor in his wake.

"Come, Li," Yong said, spinning and marching toward the kitchen himself.

Zeke followed closely. Just before the kitchen door, he snagged Yong's arm, whipped him around, and pushed him roughly up against the wall. He leaned on him, one hand on the Chinese man's chest and one on the wall above his shoulder.

"You listen here," Zeke said. "I got a message for you and all your little China friends: when Mr. Lucian McIntosh wants somethin', he gets it."

At that second, a tapered metal stick hissed through the air and embedded itself in the wall only an inch from Zeke's hand.

Zeke pushed Yong into Jim's grasp and spun to face Li. She was still only a step from where she had been. But her arm was poised to release a second metal throwing stick. She gripped several more of the projectiles in her other hand.

"You reckon you're faster with them sticks than I am with my six-gun?" Zeke asked, his tone now gruff, his hand hovering over his holster.

Li said nothing, but her eyes expressed loathing.

Zeke stared for several long seconds. Then he burst out laughing.

"I swannee!" he said. "Jim, you just never know what to expect from these China folks, do ya?"

"Nope," Jim said. "You sure don't."

Zeke patted his holster. "Tell you what, Mr. Chinaman, little China girl, we'll be back in a fashion. Meanwhile, y'all might wanna be extra careful. Oh, and next time you see him, you might wanna tell that Texan, Emmett Strong, it's time for him to go on home."

He eased his way toward the door, keeping his hand right over his six-shooter. "C'mon, Jim," he said. "I got you covered."

Jim shoved Yong Xu hard and grinned. "Like my friend said, we will be back."

CHAPTER FIFTY-FOUR

When Emmett, Sikes, and Juanito stepped out of the Silver Nugget Saloon into the bright white midafternoon glare, Emmett wasn't prepared for what awaited his eyes. There, right next to the hitching rail, arms crossed, stood Li Xu. She was dressed in her Western boys' clothes, but she made Emmett's stomach do a flip-flop.

He had planned to hurry over to Chinatown to speak to her and Yong as soon as he got Sikes squared away back at the hotel. Whether or not her father had advised him to stay away, he had to alert them to new developments involving McIntosh and his men. The last thing he expected was for her to come find him, especially since he had provoked her to the point that she'd run away from him at the end of their conversation that morning.

Clearly she wanted to talk now.

"Where to?" he asked. "Chinatown? Somewhere else?"

Indifferent to what any so-called upstanding citizen might think of him for being sweet on Li, he was still apprehensive for her sake—more so now because of Cromarty's report and the visit from the McIntosh men than because of any social taboo.

Her eyes drifted to Juanito and to Sikes, then back to Emmett. "Can Juanito and Sikes walk with us to where we talked last time? Up L Street?"

Emmett turned to his friends questioningly. He felt bad calling on Sikes to hobble any distance on that crutch, but before he could even ask, the Englishman spoke up.

"I'm tired of sitting and lying down," he said. "It's all I've done for the past two weeks. I'm ready for a walk. How about you, Juanito?"

"*Sí, siempre.*"

"Thank you," Li said, turning toward L Street. She took a couple of steps, then hesitated, waiting for Emmett.

Emmett eyed his friends and nodded thanks to them. Considering the circumstances, he was happy to have them along—packing iron at that. He strode briskly to Li's side and then did something that seemed to catch her by surprise. Ignoring all the folks going about their daily business on Virginia City's busy streets, Emmett took Li's hand and looped it through his arm.

She paused, looked him in the eye, and let a hint of a smile show on her otherwise solemn face. From that point on, he paid no attention to whether the citizenry stared at them, ignored them, or completely missed the fact that he and a Chinese girl were walking down the street arm in arm.

Although they set a slow pace in deference to Sikes's bad leg, they gained several yards on their escorts as they walked along.

"I'm happy to see you," he said softly.

"Me too," she said.

"We had two unexpected visits inside the saloon today."

"Oh?"

He nodded. "The newspaper man from Reno came. He said he has it from a reliable source that McIntosh's men are planning to gun us down as soon as we leave Virginia City."

He felt Li's hand tighten on his arm.

"I'm not surprised," she said.

"And then as soon as the newspaperman left, two of McIntosh's boys had the nerve to walk up and tell us that they'll be seeing us again soon."

She turned to face him. "Did one of them have a bushy mustache? And was the other one missing a tooth in the front?"

Emmett stopped in his tracks. "How'd you know that? How long were you standing outside the saloon?"

"I got there just before you walked out. The same two men came to the Golden Dragon."

"What?" A jolt ran through him. He glanced at Sikes and Juanito, then back at Li.

"They didn't hurt us. It seems like they just wanted to scare us. This time anyway."

Before Emmett could respond, a devilish grin appeared on her face. "I nearly pinned the one named Zeke's hand to the wall," she said. She patted her wrist, and Emmett noticed for the first time that she was wearing a pair of leather cattlemen's cuffs. On the underside of the cuffs, there were custom leather loops to hold in place the metal throwing chopsticks she and her father had made—four per cuff.

"Well, I'll be…" he said. Then he frowned. "And your father?"

"He's OK. He even told me to come find you."

"I'm surprised he didn't come himself."

"He's busy going to the other community leaders to tell them that the McIntosh drama isn't over yet."

Soon they were out past the last of the buildings on L Street. Sikes and Juanito took up watch several yards away.

Emmett faced Li and took both of her hands in his. "It's going to be dangerous getting out of Nevada, but I think it's time for us to go. Today proves it. Us staying here is only going to draw in more trouble from McIntosh and Blaylock."

"None of this changes anything I told you before, Emmett."

He looked away toward Mount Davidson—that huge brown rise just north of where they'd been ambushed. Returning his gaze to Li, he said, "I hope I've proved this much to you: I don't fear anything anybody might say about me being in love with a Chinese woman."

She bit her lip and nodded.

"Once McIntosh finds out I've gone back to Texas, peace and safety may return to Chinatown. I don't know that for a fact. But one thing's for sure—he won't leave you alone as long as Juanito, Sikes, and I stay here."

Li looked at their entwined hands. "That's pretty much what Zeke said."

"So here's what I'm thinking: I don't want to cause your family great pain by taking you away from 'em. If it was just me, I'd take you with me in a heartbeat, but…"

She squeezed his hands tighter and peered deeply into his eyes. "Like I told you, I don't want to marry any of the young men I know of in Virginia City. When my parents try to arrange a marriage for me, I'll refuse. That will cause them pain. So whether I stay or leave, I will cause them pain. I don't like that, but it's just the way it is."

Emmett wanted to concede the argument, kiss Li right there on the spot, and get ready to leave that afternoon. But this decision was big. And it was irreversible.

"You say none of the young Chinese men here catch your eye—"

"It's more than that," she said.

Emmett put up a hand. "Your parents may go to Dayton or Truckee or even to Sacramento to find you a fella if you give 'em a chance. He may be the finest man you ever met."

She stamped her foot. "Emmett Strong, you just told me that if it was up to you, and you alone, you'd take me with you in a heartbeat. Now is that true? Or are you just trying to end it all, saying things to make me believe you love me when in fact you really don't?"

He gazed back at her, admiring her soft, dark hair tossing in the breeze, her flawless skin, and her mysterious, deep-brown eyes. He thought about how courageous and intelligent and talented she was.

"You're only the second woman I've ever loved," he said. "I never dreamed anyone else could capture my heart the way Gabriela did. I don't want to compare the two of you anymore. I just wanna give in to the fact that you have my heart now…completely."

Her eyes grew moist.

"We cannot elope, though, Li. We can't just disappear into the night. It may hurt them, but we have to tell your parents so they'll know for sure where you've gone."

"Emmett, even if they gave me away to Qiang Choi, he could decide to move away any day. Maybe even return to China to do business there. A married woman leaves her parents and goes where her husband goes. They know I may not be nearby forever."

Emmett caressed her cheek with the back of his fingers. "Maybe the visit by the two McIntosh men today will help them accept the decision," he said. "They may take comfort knowing that, for us, escaping Nevada will mean escaping the likes of McIntosh and Blaylock."

She swept her hair from her face. "Maybe so. Just let me be the one to do the talking, OK?"

He nodded, then after staring at her for a moment said, "Let's get going. Don't wanna keep Sikes up on that bad leg too long."

They started toward Juanito and Sikes.

"When will we leave then?" she asked.

"The sooner the better, I think. But there are a couple of things I want to do to make the trip easier on you."

She tilted her head as she looked at him. "Like what?"

He grinned mischievously. "Give some thought to Seth's woman, Ettie."

CHAPTER FIFTY-FIVE

McIntosh's men, Zeke and Jim, watched from across the street. Zeke felt confident the stacked rows of wooden barrels outside the cooper's shop hid them well enough.

Jim leaned out from behind the casks just enough to see the livery stable. "They ain't gettin' their horses now."

"No," Zeke said. "Could be payin' for another week. Could be makin' arrangements to get their things and leave right after supper."

"Think we oughta telegraph Mr. Blaylock?"

Zeke shook his head. "Not just yet. He'd be madder'n a wet cat if we got everybody all geared up for a fight tonight when them Texans ain't leavin' for several more days."

"Chinaman down at the hotel didn't say nothin' about 'em leavin' directly."

"Nope."

The two McIntosh hands shadowed Emmett and Juanito from the livery stable down the busy street for a good thirty minutes. Despite the number of folks out during the last business hour of that warm afternoon, following the Texans unseen wasn't easy.

"Looks like they wanna stop in at half the stores in town," Jim said.

Zeke milled in front of a hardware store. "Maybe we oughta put Seth on alert after all. It's beginnin' to look to me like they are gearin' up for travel."

He wavered, looking up and down the avenue. "Jim, you keep followin' 'em. I'm gonna go back to the Comstock Queen. See if that Chinaman can tell me about any change of plans them Texans might've had. Meet me over at the Lucky Strike in an hour."

Jim nodded. "Easier to go unnoticed alone anyways."

Zeke beat a path back to the hotel. Again he avoided the front entrance. But this time, instead of waiting out back, he let himself in through the kitchen door.

A heavy fellow with a cigarette hanging from his lips stirred a pot of some kind of soup. He eyed Zeke with a frown. "Who you lookin' for?"

"Chinaman that works here. Fella named Ching. You seen him?"

"Chin works up front," the heavy fellow said. "What you want with him?"

Zeke shook his head and pushed through into a hallway. At the far end, he spied Chin rounding the corner.

When the Chinaman spotted him, he held up a finger and hurried to meet him. "I check Emmett Strong's room. Little while after you left," Chin whispered anxiously. "His things all gone."

"And the other rooms?"

Chin shook his head. "All gone, all gone."

"Tarnation!" Zeke said. "Telegraph office. I gotta get there fast."

"Faster out front door. Go left. Over by railroad station."

"Obliged," Zeke said, already on the move.

But by the time Zeke covered the four blocks to the telegraph office, the place was buttoned up tight. Not a soul around.

Blast it! he thought. *If Emmett Strong and his boys get outta here clean tonight, I'd better ride hard for Utah and not look back.*

—m—

The full moon had passed its zenith and was halfway to Mount Davidson. In the deep shadows of the small yard behind the Golden Dragon, Yong Xu and his wife, Xiulan, struggled to stifle their sniffles.

Emmett, arm around Li's shoulders, felt a lump in his throat. "I know it's not what you wanted, Yong," he said.

After a few seconds, Yong wiped his eyes with his shirt cuffs. "No, it's not. But you are a good man, Emmett. I know you will watch over Li. I fear I cannot protect her from men like the ones that came into the café yesterday."

Xiulan could no longer hold back her tears. Li left Emmett's side to embrace her mother once again.

"Shhh," she whispered, "We have to keep quiet, Mama. No one can know we're leaving."

The woman gathered herself and whispered back, "Your father is right. Those men may never leave you alone here. We don't have time to wait and see whether the Choi family will approve your marriage to Qiang. We could all be dead by then." She sniffed again. "This is for the best."

Li squeezed her. "Help look after Ping," she said. "She's the one who's in love with Qiang. Help arrange their marriage. Let them be like a son and daughter to you."

Emmett turned to Yong Xu and extended his hand.

Yong bowed from the shoulders, then clasped Emmett's hand. "The world needs more men like you, Emmett Strong. Thank you for what you did for my people."

"They're our people," Emmett said.

Yong nodded. "Now go. Quickly."

After Li embraced her father one final time, Emmett and she hurried into the alleyway alongside the Golden Dragon.

Just before they reached Union Street, he whispered, "You OK?"

Li sniffed, then nodded.

"Walk beside me now," he said. "And walk like a man—toes out a little, arms loose."

Again she nodded.

Emmett smiled reassuringly. He liked what he and Juanito had bought for her that afternoon. Taking their inspiration from the by-all-accounts-beautiful woman who rode with Seth Blaylock, they'd gotten Li a disguise for traveling. The low-crowned black Stetson and dark-brown duster would transform her silhouette. Beneath the long coat, she wore a new vest, shirt, and trousers—all trim fitting. They were particularly pleased that the new boots had worked out so well. Ill-fitting boots could be crippling. Juanito had guessed right.

And it wouldn't do for her to ride out unarmed. Sikes had chipped in more than he should've to buy her a gun belt. In its holster she carried a Remington Police Model revolver—smaller and with less kick than a Colt.

Emmett and Li walked with purpose as they headed for the livery stable, but not so fast as to look as though they were fleeing. They kept just off the center of the street.

"Do you think we're being watched?" she asked, keeping her voice down.

"Do you feel watched?" He glanced at her out of the corner of his eye as his gaze swept left to right and back again.

"It's probably just my imagination."

"Won't be long now," he said. "Sikes should already be sitting saddle when we get there. Juanito will help us with anything that may come up last minute."

"Maybe my eyes are playing tricks on me," Li said.

"What do you mean?"

"Sometimes the shadows seem to be moving."

He gently grasped her arm and drew her to a stop. Hand near his holster, he made a slow turn, scrutinizing every porch, alley, and even rooftop. He strained to listen for footsteps or even the rustling of clothing.

"Let's go," he murmured.

The big barn door on the street side of the livery stable was open about three feet when they got there. Lamplight poured out onto the dusty street. Once Li ducked inside, Emmett stood with his back to the door, searching the darkness for those moving shadows she had feared.

The stirring of horses, the creaking of saddle leather, and the hushed voices of the stable owner and Juanito inside made it impossible for him to pick up on any sounds that might suggest they were being followed. A dog barked a couple of blocks away.

At last Emmett stepped inside. He shook the stable owner's sizeable hand. "We're much obliged."

"Not at all," the man said in a bass voice. "Glad to help."

Emmett rubbed the nose of the smallish mustang the stable owner had located on short notice for Li. "Healthy-looking animal. Are we all squared away? Everything paid up?"

"All paid." The stable owner looked at Li. "You like him?"

She glanced shyly at Emmett. "Yes. I do."

"I meant the horse." He grinned

Li blushed. "Oh. Yes. I like him too."

Everyone chuckled quietly.

"Guess we'd better ride then," Emmett said.

Juanito grinned. "Good to be going home."

They left in single file with Juanito leading and Emmett bringing up the rear. Moonlight bathed the streets in a soft blue glow—a marked contrast from the blue-black shadows cast by the various businesses and homes. All was quiet except for that same dog persistently barking several blocks back.

Emmett wasn't about to take the same mountain pass where they'd been ambushed. Instead he and his compadres had determined to ride parallel to the railroad tracks, south as far as Mound House. Then they'd cut across the valley to the base of the Sierra Madre.

He touched spur to his horse's flanks and pulled up alongside Li. "They want to gun us down at one of the railroad stations on our way out of Nevada? We just won't catch a train till we're already out of the state."

"How far will we ride then before getting on a train?" she asked.

"At least as far as Truckee."

"How many days is that by horse?"

"Three. Or two hard days. Sikes may not be well enough yet to do it in two, though, so we'll plan on taking it slow. Let me know if you get too tired."

She smiled and nodded.

The foursome made it no more than a hundred yards past the last buildings on the outskirts of Virginia City when Emmett tensed and turned in the saddle. From out of the darkness behind them, hoofbeats were closing in fast and frantic.

CHAPTER FIFTY-SIX

Emmett wheeled his horse and drew his Peacemaker.

"Three riders," he said. "Looks like they mean business."

Juanito neck-reined his horse and rushed to Emmett's side, Winchester in hand.

"Li, stay behind us," Emmett said.

He'd been hesitant to fire—until he saw that the riders wore neckerchiefs over their faces. That was reason enough to sling some lead.

"Where you going?" he yelled, squeezing the trigger. *Don't want any of these fellas telling Seth Blaylock where we're heading.*

His first shot had barely sounded when three shots from their pursuers cracked the air.

He and Juanito both took aim. One of the three pursuers fell. The other two reined in but continued to return fire.

"Stay here," Emmett said to Juanito.

He spurred his horse and charged the two who remained. A few yards out, he fired again. A second pursuer's body jerked before slumping and falling from the saddle. The third rider turned and gigged his horse hard.

No, Emmett didn't want to let him get away to tell Blaylock or McIntosh. But neither did he want to shoot a man in the back. And neither did he want to wake up half of Virginia City. They had been looking for a quiet departure.

When he saw that they were closing fast on the first houses at the edge of town, Emmett decided he had to shoot. In the back or not—it no longer mattered. Li's life was at stake, as were the rest of theirs.

He pointed his pistol across his horse's neck and the Colt kicked in his hand. At just that moment, the rider in front of him yanked the reins and cut his horse hard to the right.

There was no time to waste here. Emmett was now entering the city at a full gallop.

A door opened a few houses ahead. Someone stepped out just enough to see him and to take aim with a rifle. "What's goin' on out here?" the home-owner yelled.

The rider Emmett was chasing cut between two houses and disappeared from sight. Emmett decided he should do the same before one of the locals decided to unload on him. He reined his horse in a loop behind a short row of cabins and then back out onto the road to Mound House. Much to his relief, no shots rang out from behind him.

Once he neared the spot where the second McIntosh man had fallen, he slowed and looked down. Right away he saw that it was the one with the brushy mustache. *OK, so who was the first one I dropped?* He continued on.

Before his horse even stopped, Emmett was already swinging his leg over the saddle. He trotted to the corpse.

Li, Sikes, and Juanito rode up and reined in beside him.

When Emmett rolled the dead man onto his back and pulled off the neck-erchief, Li gasped.

"Well, I'll be," Sikes said.

"Chin!" Emmett said. "The fella from the hotel."

He looked up at Li. "I'm sorry. This man was your father's friend, wasn't he?"

"No," Li said. "He's been trying for a long time to bribe my father to do something my father didn't want to do."

Emmett immediately recalled the odd look Yong Xu had given him the night they had first gone to the Golden Dragon and mentioned that Chin had sent them.

"Once we have time to think it over," Sikes said, "this may provide some answers. But right now we'd better clear out of here."

Emmett mounted up again and looked back toward town.

"Change of plans?" Sikes asked.

"Nope. We just need to ride fast for a while. Get as far away as possible before McIntosh's boy comes back with the law."

"Everybody in Virginia City has heard rumors about McIntosh, Blaylock, and the kidnappings by now," Juanito said. "You really think McIntosh's gun-hand can convince the marshal that we're the lawbreakers?"

"Don't know," Emmett said. "And I don't wanna wait around to find out."

"There's one thing he can do," Li said.

Emmett turned to his bride-to-be.

"As soon as the telegraph office opens," Li continued, "he can let McIntosh and Seth Blaylock know that we have left Virginia City."

Emmett nodded. "And as soon as he does, they'll be out in force, scouting all over the countryside for us. Let's ride while we can."

CHAPTER FIFTY-SEVEN

For Seth Blaylock, this was personal now. It was no longer just about defending Charlie, making sure Lucian McIntosh got his China girls back, or even paying Emmett Strong back for shooting Ettie. Strong had bested him twice. And he'd taken down two more of Mr. McIntosh's men this morning. But it wasn't going to happen again. He'd make sure of that. He rapped sharply on the door to Lucian McIntosh's study.

"Come," bellowed the voice within.

He marched to a spot directly across the desk from his boss. "They're on the move."

That got McIntosh's full attention right away. One eyebrow raised, he said, "You heard from Virginia City this mornin'?"

"Yes, sir." He wanted his facial expression to reflect his resolve.

McIntosh stared, waiting for Seth to go on.

"Strong and the Texans rode out early. While it was still dark. Zeke and Jim took that Chinese fella from the hotel along and tried to stop 'em."

"'Tried to stop 'em.' That mean shootin'?"

"Yes, sir, I'm afraid it did. And they got Zeke…and the Chinaman."

"*Dammit!*" McIntosh pounded the desk. "Did we manage to get any of theirs?"

Seth shook his head. "No sign that we did."

"Figures. Well, let's get goin'. Have the boys double up at the railroad stations. From Truckee to Wadsworth. And have 'em do it fast."

"I don't think we need to worry about the stations that serve the Virginia and Truckee line," Seth said. "They've gotta hop on the Central Pacific if they wanna clear out of Nevada—east or west."

McIntosh's face was blotched red. "And they wouldn't dare ride into Reno, try to catch the Central Pacific right here in my own town."

Seth pulled off his hat and smoothed his hair. "I wouldn't put anything past 'em. But even if they did catch the train here in Reno, wouldn't it be better to take 'em down in Truckee or Wadsworth? Smaller towns. Not right here at home. Train'll stop in both places anyway."

McIntosh rose and lifted his gun belt from the hat rack behind his desk. "Good point. Which one do you want then—Truckee or Wadsworth?" His dark eyes gleamed.

"I know Texas is cattle country. Texans seem more comfortable in the company of cowhand types. You might figure they'd go east and try to drop down through one of the cow towns like Dodge. But for some reason, I've got a notion they'll be goin' out by way of California. I'll take Truckee."

Just then Ettie walked in.

McIntosh's demeanor softened instantly. "Ettie, you're lookin' well today. I haven't seen such nice color in your cheeks in some time."

She smiled politely. "I heard talking. Sounds like something's getting ready to happen."

Seth strolled across the rug and reached out to give her arm a gentle squeeze. She winced at his touch.

Irked, he frowned. "What's this?"

"I'm sorry," she said, her eyes less lively than usual. "Somehow being so close to death has made me jumpy—nervous about everything."

"My apologies," he said, feeling nonetheless snubbed.

"It may be the laudanum they've been givin' her for pain," McIntosh said. "Makes some folks a bit edgy."

Seth nodded, then said to Ettie, "We got word from Virginia City just a few minutes ago. The Texans have moved out. Unfortunately, when Zeke tried to stop 'em they got him."

"But don't you worry, Ettie." McIntosh adjusted his gun belt on his hips. "This time Strong'll pay in blood for what he did to you, to Zeke, and to my brother."

Ettie went to the window. "Which way do you suppose they're headed?"

"We were just speculatin' on that," Seth said. "The more I think about it, the more certain I am they're headin' west. And I think I've got just the plan to trap 'em and deal with all four of 'em—once and for all."

Ettie turned away from the glass. "Four of them?"

"Jim telegraphed that there are four. I'm assumin' they've got that Chinaman with 'em—the one they brought along when they rode up here, demandin' that we exchange the last two girls for Charlie."

"Why would he leave his home and family to go with them?"

Seth shrugged. "The Chinese owe a debt to the Texans. My guess is they're gonna hide out with the johnnies along the way till they decide where to hop on the railroad."

McIntosh gave a low chuckle. "And we all know where the biggest Chinatown along the Central Pacific is."

Seth turned to him. "Truckee. Which is why I'm goin' there—to take care of business personally."

Lucian McIntosh's huge frame stepped out from behind the desk and sauntered up to Seth. Peering into his eyes, he said, "When you're done, don't you let anybody else touch those dead bodies. You haul 'em where you need to. Pay for the undertaker yourself if you have to. But I wanna see the four of them dead. I wanna see 'em with my own eyes."

Seth cracked a smile. "My pleasure."

"And I'll cover Wadsworth myself. Just in case."

CHAPTER FIFTY-EIGHT

Emmett and his friends had made it to the base of the Sierra Nevada southwest of Reno in one day, thanks to Sikes's gritty determination.

After sleeping on the ground under the stars, they broke camp early and made their way onto the Dutch Flat-Donner Lake Wagon Road—the main route for horses and wagons through the Sierra. From some points along the road, Emmett and his compadres could see for miles. In other spots, stands of ponderosa pines—or simply twists and turns around the mountains—limited visibility to less than a hundred yards in any direction.

Under other circumstances the cool, refreshing air might have prompted a cheerful mood among the four. But not today. They were still in dangerous territory, so a sober frame of mind prevailed.

Emmett motioned for Li to ride alongside him. He forced a smile, hoping to offer her assurance that all would turn out OK, despite what he was about to tell her.

"Truckee's a wild town, Li," he said. "Probably wilder than any you've ever experienced—a lot of lawless men."

"Don't worry," she said, giving him a heartening smile of her own. "I'll stay close to you."

"There may be bed houses and even opium dens in Virginia City, but not like the ones in this town. Seems like folks of the vilest sort are drawn to Truckee like flies to a carcass."

Her smile faded.

"I'm not telling you this to frighten you," he said. "But you need to be prepared. I don't exaggerate when I say there are shootings in Truckee pretty much every night. Sometimes for no reason at all."

She glanced at Sikes and Juanito. "Where are we going to stay?"

"All four of us in one room. It may not be the best night's sleep you ever got, but we'll be safer that way."

She nodded.

"Remember to walk like a man. And keep your hat low on your head. Your eyes are a giveaway—pretty as they are." He grinned.

His compliment barely turned the corners of her lips.

"It'll get a whole lot better after Truckee," he said.

"Once we're on the train and heading south?"

"Mm-hmm."

"That will be a relief. We'll be happy, Emmett. I'm sure of it."

He studied the soft features of her face. "We'll need to get married real soon."

That brought a genuine, unstoppable smile.

"I hate to break up this beautiful moment," Juanito said, twisting in his saddle, "but take a look ahead."

Emmett's gaze followed the road's rising grade to find three riders ahead, off to one side. The three sat saddle in silence, observing their approach with hawklike interest.

"We've passed lots of folks on this road. Coming and going," Sikes murmured. "But they've all been moving along, minding their own business."

"Yep," Emmett said. "But these three look like trouble right off. You agree, Juanito?"

"We've seen the type before."

Emmett had no intention of greeting the waiting riders. Something about the way they sat…It didn't look to him as though they were simply resting their horses. They seemed to have been purposely posted to keep an eye on the road.

"They're not even watching in both directions," Juanito said.

"Nope. Looks like they're waiting for somebody in particular coming up from Reno way."

Emmett peered over his shoulder, wanting to be certain no one was boxing them in from downhill. Thankfully the road behind them was empty.

"Li," he said quietly. "Keep Juanito, Sikes, and me between you and those men, you hear?"

She reined her horse behind his.

All three of the waiting riders had the look of hired guns. Up close now Emmett noted their gazes flitting constantly from him to each of his compadres.

None took any pains whatsoever to be discreet in his ogling. One was leaning forward, forearms crossed over his saddle horn. Still looked like he could strike with diamondback speed. Another sat upright, shoulders relaxed, hand on his thigh, just a short distance from his holster—a low-cut rig designed expressly for the quick draw.

No one from either side spoke. No one's hand moved to touch the brim of a hat. You could provoke some folk simply by asking them what they were looking at.

Now parallel to the three, Emmett's pulse throbbed a beat faster than usual. He pondered letting Sikes, Juanito, and Li ride on while he held back to cover them from the rear. Instead he let his horse slow until he took up the drag position. Continuing onward with Li in front of him, he kept glancing over his shoulder.

A few yards ahead, the road was about to take a bend around a copse of pines. They'd lose sight of the suspicious horsemen. Question was, would they follow?

Now far enough from the three to speak in low tones without being over-heard, Emmett asked Juanito and Sikes, "What do you think? More like those three waiting for us farther up the road?"

Juanito leaned out, trying to peer around the bend before they got there. "Want me to scout ahead?"

"Suppose the three back there'll tail us? Close the back door on us?" Emmett asked, trying to determine their best course of action.

Sikes pivoted in his saddle to give the three another look. "I don't think so. Look."

Li, Juanito, and Emmett turned to find that the trio was already moving downhill—away from them—at a trot.

"Kinda suspicious," Emmett said.

"Very," Juanito affirmed.

Just before they disappeared around the bend, all three twisted in their saddles to give Emmett and his friends a final once-over.

Emmett shook his head, told himself it might've been nothing.

The rest of the ride up the wagon road was uneventful. For a minute or two here and there, Emmett and Li basked in the beauty of breathtaking moun-tain vistas, views that momentarily chased away their worries. But once they reached the edge of Truckee—late in the afternoon when shadows were growing long—every idyllic fancy vanished. Apprehension put him back on guard.

Truckee was an ugly town of half-finished buildings. Looked as though nobody had given so much as a thought to completing them. Canvas tenting covered parts of buildings where carpenters had quit, been driven away, or perhaps breathed their last. Piles of lumber and planking lay scattered here and there, some of it burning. Near some of the fires sat lone souls, staring seemingly at nothing in particular. Around other campfires, clusters of dirty, unshaven men were already working on getting good and pickled.

"It's not what I expected," Li said.

Juanito asked her, "What did you expect?"

Emmett observed her scrutinizing the streets and buildings and people, her forehead furrowed.

"I heard Truckee has the biggest Chinese population in this part of California and Nevada. I thought it would be neater and cleaner," she said, "especially after having seen the beauty of the mountains and the forests on the way up here."

"Truckee's Chinatown is over there." Juanito pointed off to the south. "After a big *choque* two years ago, people burned down the old Chinatown and forced the Chinese to move to the other side of the river."

She gazed through the trees near the river for a short while, then turned back to the eyesore that was Truckee.

"There are a hundred reasons why this town is as it is," Emmett said. "We can't change it. We just need to get through it unscathed."

"When does the train come?" Her eyebrows formed a worried arch.

"Nine o'clock tomorrow morning."

"Should we keep riding and stay somewhere else?"

He shook his head. "It'll be dark soon. We won't want to be out on the road after nightfall."

Emmett was glad they'd arrived in this greed-driven town before things began to get as wild as they certainly would. Once workers and loafers alike began to get serious about their drinking, gambling, and womanizing, the place would go nine kinds of loco. They rode up and down only two streets before they decided to take a room at the Dutchman's Inn—an unpainted two-story wood-frame building that at least had curtains in the windows.

"Let me go in to make the arrangements," Emmett said. "You two watch over Li."

They nodded. He patted Li on the knee as he walked by to enter the inn.

It turned out that the place was not too bad. Fairly clean. But since each room was small and had only one bed, the proprietor wouldn't rent one room to four "men." Emmett agreed to pay for two rooms. Once outside again, he explained the situation to the others. Together they decided it'd be smarter—and safer—to occupy only one of the two rooms they'd rented.

"But you two get the bed," Sikes said, shaking a finger at Emmett and Li.

They glanced at one another and then at Juanito.

Emmett shook his head. "You get the bed, Sikes." He turned to the Englishman. "We can't afford to slow down. You need ample opportunity to rest that gimpy leg."

"He's right," Juanito said, nodding.

Sikes stared at Emmett and Li. "But what about…"

Li blushed and turned away.

Emmett raised his eyebrows. "You think anything's gonna happen with you two in the room?"

Juanito chuckled under his breath. "*Ay, ay, ay.*"

As the night wore on, Emmett was glad about their decision to occupy only one room. He slept off and on, mostly sitting up, leaning against the wall that faced the door. Both his Colt and Li's Remington lay on the floor on his gun-hand side. Li curled up on the floor to his left with her head resting on his thigh.

Sure enough, throughout the night their dozing was disrupted time and time again. Yahoos ran and rode up and down the avenues as though they were making the last dash on a cattle drive, hooting and yelling and firing off every kind of handgun, rifle, and shotgun known to the West. Shouting, laced with streams of profanities foul enough to make the old Deluder himself blush, echoed through the streets.

At one point, a glass bottle shattered against the front wall of the Dutchman's Inn. Li jumped in her sleep. Not long afterward, a woman screaming then sobbing bitterly somewhere across the street dragged both Emmett and Li out of their slumber once and for all.

She crawled up beside him and nestled under the protection of his arm.

When her breathing failed to slow into that relaxed, even rhythm that would have told him she'd managed to drift off to sleep again, he whispered, "Are you OK?"

The weeping and moaning from the woman across the street continued.

Li whispered, "That could have been me…if you had not stood up to McIntosh."

He stroked her hair. "Try not to think of that. Let me take you where you'll never have to worry about that again."

She held on to him tightly. "Thank you, Emmett. Thank you for not leaving me."

Even considering all the danger, he was glad he hadn't.

CHAPTER FIFTY-NINE

The next morning Truckee had an entirely different look and feel. It still smelled of burning wood and liquor and human waste. But oddly—as folks would be in any respectable town around the country—ordinary people were up and working as though the only thing heard during the night had been crickets and owls.

The same was true down at the railroad station. There Emmett admired the stalwart locomotive that would pull the westbound Central Pacific railcars over the high sierra: four powerful driver wheels toward the back, four smaller wheels up front, a mushroom-shaped smokestack up top. The big mechanical beast gave an occasional thump or hiss as the engineer, his fireman, and his brakeman clambered about, checking this and that.

Li stood close by Emmett's side. Even as he quietly reminded her to carry herself like a man and to keep her hat brim low, he had to suppress the urge to take her slender hand in his own.

Juanito and Sikes remained vigilant, scanning the platform, eying passengers and passersby alike.

With their tickets purchased and horses loaded, nothing remained but to wait. And it was while waiting that a feeling of disquiet began to descend over Emmett. Rather than drawing comfort from the relative ease of their escape from Nevada, he found himself unsettled that everything had gone as smoothly as it had. Apart from the three suspicious riders out on the wagon road, the only fright had come from the typical nightly horrors of Truckee. He'd expected more trouble. And the fact that it hadn't yet come left him feeling it must still lie ahead. But when? And where?

Just then the train whistle sounded and the bell began to clang. The conductor made the customary "all aboard" call.

Emmett looked down the line at Li, Juanito, and Sikes. "Shall we?"

The locomotive was pulling six cars—the wood fuel car, three passenger cars, a livestock car, and a caboose. Emmett, Li, and company climbed up into the last of the passenger cars, the one just ahead of the livestock car. They took a pair of bench seats that faced each other near the middle of the carriage, Emmett on the aisle beside Li, facing forward, and Juanito on the aisle beside Sikes, facing rearward.

With a last blast of the whistle, the train lurched and began to chug ahead.

Li put a hand to her mouth to cover a giggle.

Inclining his head toward her, Emmett said in a hushed voice, "Manly." He winked. "At least till we get past Sacramento. Then you can be as girly as you want. In fact, I'd like that."

She smiled at him.

"First time on a train?" Sikes asked.

She nodded, and he smiled back.

Emmett made himself comfortable on the bench, but his mind was busy. He wondered how far afield McIntosh and Blaylock would go. Cromarty had told him they would be watching every rail station in the region. Emmett and his companions had cleared not only Nevada, but now also Truckee in California. He found it hard to believe they could have bypassed the threat that easily.

Rubbing his chin, he recalled the railroad map on the wall at the Truckee station. The next stop would be Summit—fourteen miles away up a fairly steep gradient. The train wouldn't move very fast along this stretch. He shifted and adjusted his gun leather, then glanced at Li's waist to see how her holster sat.

What he observed when he looked across at Juanito encouraged him. He had known his brother-in-law long enough to recognize his lawman face—that set jaw that told him Juanito was on the job, ready for action at any moment.

Shifting his gaze to Sikes, he wasn't so sure. He knew the man was in pain day and night. Just how well recovered was he?

As the train achieved about as much speed as it was going to on the climb toward Summit, an unexpected sound caught Emmett's ears.

Juanito's gaze shot to the ceiling of the railcar. Over the clack-clack of metal wheels on sections of rail came the distinct and dissonant clomp of footsteps on the roof.

Emmett leaned forward and said to Juanito, "Does the train crew ever travel from one car to another that way?"

Juanito's hand was already on the grip of his revolver, "I don't think so, *hermano*."

Right then Emmett knew. This was it.

He stood, pistol drawn, and shouted, "Get down! Everyone!"

The eight or ten passengers in the railcar with them turned and gawked, seemingly more puzzled than alarmed.

The car's front and back doors burst open. A rugged fellow with two drawn Remingtons rushed into the front of the car and opened fire.

Emmett didn't think about shooting. He thought only about protecting Li. Out of the corner of his eye, he saw her rising to her feet. With one hand, he pushed her back down. With the other he thumbed back the hammer of his Colt.

He pointed and fired at the gunman with the Remingtons. The man's face jerked to the side, flinging a gory spray. Women screamed.

Emmett felt Sikes behind him. Juanito stepped into the aisle. Both were already shooting.

The next face Emmett saw was Charlie Blaylock's. Charlie struggled to get past the fallen man with the Remingtons. He stumbled, yet even so kept his wide eyes focused on Emmett. As he went down, he managed a shot in Emmett's direction.

Another McIntosh hand had breached the door in Charlie's wake. He too came in with guns blazing. Emmett fired back. Bullets now flew in both directions up and down the railcar. Windows shattered, sending shards of glass stinging through the air.

Suddenly the upper half of a man appeared in the window across from Emmett. Hanging from the roof somehow, the outlaw gritted his teeth, thrust his pistol through the opening, and fired.

Li shrieked. Emmett glanced back at her. She held a hand on her upper arm and stumbled back into the seat where Sikes had been.

Dammit! Emmett fired at the figure in the window. Not waiting to see whether his instincts had been true to him, he twisted toward the door, thumbed back the hammer, and squeezed off a shot at the gunman behind Charlie. A cry from the window told him that shot had found its target. His eyes confirmed he'd hit the one behind Blaylock.

He hazarded another glance at Li. She was fumbling to draw her revolver. "You OK?" he shouted over the melee.

Her eyes widened. In one fluid move, she let go of the handgun, drew one of the metal throwing sticks from her cattleman's cuff, and let it fly.

Emmett spun again to find Charlie Blaylock only steps away, clutching at his own throat. Li's throwing stick was deeply embedded right beside his Adam's apple.

Charlie's tongue flailed in his open mouth. His bulging eyes settled on Emmett. Struggling with one hand to extract the chopstick from his neck, he swung his pistol hand up and fired.

Emmett charged him. He jammed his Colt into Charlie's ribs and pulled the trigger.

Charlie shuddered.

Someone yelled, "You Texas son a of bitch!"

Emmett whirled to find Seth Blaylock clambering up the aisle toward him, his face twisted with rage.

Juanito stepped into the gangway. He took aim at the dandy, but the train jerked on its rails and the bullet went wide. Before he could thumb back the hammer and fire again, Blaylock biffed him with the butt of his Schofield. Juanito reeled and toppled against Emmett.

"Sikes!" Emmett yelled as he and Juanito fell in a tangle. But a momentary glimpse revealed the Englishman was several seats away, grappling hand to hand with another of McIntosh's outlaws.

Emmett clambered from beneath his brother-in-law. Still on his hands and knees, he looked up—and absolute terror gripped him.

Seth had caught sight of Li. Recognition clearly registered in his eyes. Worse yet, the slaver had a clear line of fire at her.

Scrambling over Juanito, Emmett threw himself at his enemy. The Schofield went off. He couldn't see whether or not the bullet hit Li.

All he could do was go after Blaylock with everything he had left. He clenched the outlaw's gunhand and pummeled away at him.

But Seth's fury equaled his own. He shoved and clawed to break free.

Emmett refused to let go, refused to let Blaylock fire another shot.

He punched and jabbed and clung to his enemy until—seemingly right in his ear—a gun discharged. He flinched, and in that instant Blaylock head butted him. Hard.

Sharp pain and sudden dimness and bursting light disoriented him. He shook his head, determined not to drift into unconsciousness. He couldn't leave Li.

Seth had him by the throat now. Fingernails digging in. Grip tightening.

He couldn't breathe.

Just as things were starting to grow dim around the edges, he managed to peel back just one of Blaylock's fingers. And he hung on to that finger. He bent it back and twisted it mercilessly—as though he could tear it off completely.

Blaylock cried out. His grip loosened. Emmett gulped air and lashed out.

Before he knew it, he and Blaylock were trading punches in the doorway at the rear of the railcar. He sensed the train was slowing down. All he could think of was throwing Blaylock overboard before they reached the next station.

At last he got him into a headlock. While Seth threw bruising blows into his stomach and kidneys, Emmett squeezed tighter and tighter. He rammed his enemy's head into the outside wall of the passenger car, then yanked a knee up into his gut.

That did the trick. Finding Blaylock off balance, he gave one final shove and watched the dandy go reeling off the train, rolling over and over on the embankment until he was blocked from view by the livestock car.

Emmett leaned out from between the two railcars. The train was slowing and making a sharp turn on its tracks. He couldn't see where Blaylock had ended up. Twisting the other way toward the locomotive, he saw that the engine was just pulling up to the tiny station in the town of Summit.

Still catching his breath, Emmett stumbled back inside the passenger car. His head throbbed, and the bridge of his nose stung. He dabbed at the spot and found it split and bleeding.

Propped up against one of the benches stood Sikes, revolver recovered and in hand, barrel pointed at the ceiling, hammer cocked. He was covering Juanito, who was making his way down the aisle, pressing a bandanna to the side of his bleeding face, looking things over, seat by seat.

Emmett caught sight of Li Xu—standing right where he had left her—pale but fully alert. Her gaze was fixed on Charlie Blaylock's corpse, sprawled out in the seat directly across the aisle from her. Her throwing stick protruded from his neck, and his side was marked with a deep-red hole surrounded by burnt and bloody shirt cloth.

Just as Emmett reached her, the conductor stepped into the front doorway of the car. Juanito spun toward him. The railroad man's lips parted as he stared past Juanito at the rest of the car. His fingers tightened on the doorframe, and for a moment Emmett thought the fellow was going to retch.

"You're looking at the work of Lucian McIntosh's boys," Emmett said. "A murderous bunch out of Reno."

The conductor blinked several times. "The engineer is afraid we may be overrun by more of these people if we make our regular stop here in Summit. He wants to keep rolling."

"I don't suppose any of these folk would mind putting a little distance between us and the bunch responsible for all this."

The conductor nodded, then turned and hurried for the engine.

After only seconds, the train lunged and strained, grinding its way ahead once more.

"Look!" Juanito pointed.

Emmett bent to get a clear view out of the shot-up railcar windows. It appeared to be three McIntosh men, darting for cover behind a rough timber building.

"Reckon that's all that survived?" He couldn't help but wonder whether that was the last they'd see of the slaver's gang.

"No way of knowing." Juanito kept peering back at the building.

Emmett turned to Li and cupped her face in his hand. Then he lifted her fingers from where she had been pressing them against her upper arm. A bullet appeared to have only just nipped her.

As he examined her wound, he asked, "Anybody happen to see whether Seth Blaylock managed to get up and run after I pushed him off the train?"

Li shook her head.

Sikes eased himself down onto a bench. "I didn't realize you'd thrown him from the train."

"The only McIntosh men I know of off the train," Juanito said, "were the three we just saw running."

"We weren't going all that fast when I pushed him. And he rolled when he hit the ground. Roll might've broken his fall. I couldn't see whether he stayed down or got up and ran."

Having thoroughly inspected Li's arm, Emmett drew her to himself and held her.

"Are you hit anywhere else?" he asked.

"No," she said. "I'm OK."

He stepped back. "Here. Let me see. Just to be sure. Sometimes you don't notice."

Emmett had her turn while he looked her over head to heels. "You look mighty good to me," he whispered in her ear.

She pushed him back and grinned for a second.

Both their grins faded, however, as their gazes settled on the carnage all about them.

Emmett called out. "Anybody else need help?"

At that, an older woman in a fancy deep-violet dress let her tears give way to an audible sob. Li stepped past Emmett and went to sit beside her.

Emmett made his way to Juanito.

Juanito folded the bandanna he'd been pressing to his cheekbone. "Two innocent passengers killed and two more injured, by my count."

"That's more blood on McIntosh's head," Emmett said.

"At least your brother's murderer is dead. I find it a lot easier to go home now, knowing—one way or another—justice was served here."

"One way or another," Emmett said soberly, "it usually is."

CHAPTER SIXTY

The Central Pacific westbound rolled at slow speed through Sacramento. Emmett, like everyone else in the car, stared out the windows in somber silence.

In the hours since they had chugged away from Summit, he and Juanito had moved the dead to the back end of the carriage—Charlie Blaylock and the other McIntosh men on one side of the aisle, the two innocent men caught in the cross fire on the other. Everyone else had taken their things and moved to those seats at the front end that weren't spoiled by blood.

With the train bell clanging in the background, Sikes said, "Looks like lawmen are waiting for us. The stationmaster in Summit must have telegraphed ahead."

Emmett was impressed by the sheer number of them—on the platform, alongside the tracks. Most wore badges—some stars and some shields. A few were mounted, rifles or shotguns across their laps. The rest stood at intervals along the length of the station.

"After our experience in Nevada, I can't help but wonder whether these lawmen are bought and paid for like the ones in Reno," Juanito said.

Emmett frowned. "What? You think they're waiting here to arrest us instead of going after those that stormed the train?"

Juanito shrugged.

"Well, if they are bought and paid for, prospects don't look real good for us. We're heavily outgunned here."

The train jostled to a full stop, the whistle blew, and the locomotive hissed loudly.

Rising to his feet and taking Li's hand, Emmett said, "Time to face the music."

Li met his gaze. "Do you think they're going to blame you?"

He wanted to tell her no, but that wouldn't serve either of them well. The faces they observed outside were grim. He couldn't be sure what their assumptions were. At that moment, more than anything, he wanted to apologize to Li. Though in his gut he knew there was no easy way out of Nevada, he somehow couldn't help believing he could have planned a better getaway if he'd only had more time to think about it.

"Anything could happen," he murmured, giving her hand a squeeze. "Just stay close."

Sikes limped down off the train first, followed by Juanito. Emmett was on the bottom step of the railcar when, from the corner of his eye, he spotted a figure running from the caboose toward the mounted lawman at the far right-hand end of the station.

Hardly had his mind interpreted what he was seeing when a gunshot rang out. Instinctively he blocked the railcar's exit with his body to protect Li. At the same time, his hand flew to his Colt revolver.

In the moment it took for the lawman to flop from his saddle to the ground, the tension on the platform turned into utter pandemonium. Civilians abuzz with curiosity only moments before now fled in panic. Marshals, sheriffs, and deputies with rifles pressed to their shoulders or pistols in hand swept the train and the station for signs of additional gunmen. Several raced toward the caboose end of the rail yard.

Emmett instantly recognized the dark-blue silk vest of the shooter. The question of Seth Blaylock's survival was no longer a mystery. Blaylock was already in the fallen lawman's saddle, firing reckless shots into the crowd and spurring the poor horse mercilessly. Coincidentally, one of his wildly aimed bullets smacked into the side of the railcar no more than a foot from Emmett's hand.

Flinching, Emmett managed to hold himself in the car's doorway as he watched Blaylock gallop madly around the corner.

A few of the lawmen on foot beat a path up the street. A handful raced into alleyways, presumably to cut him off. A half dozen men on horseback took up the pursuit as well.

Blaylock's decision had been desperate. Emmett doubted the man would make it out of Sacramento alive. But then again, this was Seth Blaylock, and it seemed as though he and McIntosh had been beating the odds for quite some time. *Perhaps not this time, though,* Emmett thought.

While several folks attended the downed lawman, a tall, mustached gentleman tromped up and planted himself a few yards away, feet spread, hands on his hips. The badge on his chest read CITY OF SACRAMENTO MARSHAL.

"William McConaghy, city marshal," the lawman said. "You folks'll need to stay put right here until you answer some questions for me."

Emmett stepped onto the platform and discreetly guided Li to stand just behind him and to his left—away from his gun hand.

Sikes hobbled back and took up a spot on the other side of Li. Juanito held up about ten feet away with his back to the railroad car they'd been riding in.

As the marshal's gaze returned to meet his own, Emmett pulled back the lapel of his vest to reveal the Texas Ranger badge pinned to his shirt. "Name's Emmett Strong. Texas Ranger. Gentleman over here to my right is Juan Carlos Galvez. Also a Texas Ranger."

With one hand Juanito pulled the Ranger badge from his pocket and pinned it to his vest, meanwhile keeping his gun hand free.

Marshal McConaghy's manner remained businesslike. "Telegram from Summit said there was a big to-do on this train." He glanced up at the railcar's shot-out windows. "You boys responsible for all this?"

Emmett weighed his thoughts. If Seth Blaylock had pulled the trigger on one of his men, this marshal probably wasn't on Lucian McIntosh's payroll. Then again, back in Virginia City the city marshal had had one idea about Lucian McIntosh while the county sheriff had had another. All the lawmen here couldn't be from the same jurisdiction. So the question remained: Was this yet another McIntosh lackey, looking for someone to take the punishment for one more of the big man's crimes? Or was this man on the up-and-up? He decided to take the bull by the horns.

"Do you know the name Lucian McIntosh?"

The marshal nodded. "A persona non grata around these parts."

Emmett breathed a little easier. But he still had to account for his role in a bloody shootout—one in which innocent citizens had died.

"I understand McIntosh owns some business establishments in this burg," Emmett said, "just as he does in about half the towns from San Francisco to Carson City."

"Did. Doesn't anymore," the marshal said. "Now what's all this got to do with Lucian McIntosh?"

"That was one of his hands—in fact, his *segundo*—that just shot the gent down the way and stole his horse. Man's name is Seth Blaylock."

"Heard that name too. Another person of interest to us here in Sacramento. Go on."

Emmett nodded to his right. "Blaylock's brother Charlie is lying dead in this railcar. He's the reason Juanito and I came all the way up here from Texas. Charlie Blaylock shot a Texas state senator in cold blood down in Austin. Then he fled up here seeking protection under his brother's wings."

By now a pair of deputy marshals had strolled over and taken up positions behind and to either side of their boss. The railroad conductor had followed them from the direction of the caboose.

"Who else is dead up there?" the marshal asked.

The conductor didn't miss a beat. "He can tell you." He pointed to Emmett.

"Unfortunately I can." Emmett nodded. "Six more of the McIntosh and Blaylock bunch...and sadly, two innocent travelers."

"And why the blazes would you get in a shootout with a bunch of gunslicks—McIntosh's or anybody else's—on a train full of, as you yourself put it, innocent travelers?" the sheriff demanded, taking a step forward.

"Self-defense." Emmett held his ground yet was careful not to mirror the marshal's aggressive posturing. "We were on our way home. Wanted nothing more to do with these people nor these parts. They came in— smoke wagons blazing—from both ends of the railcar at once...and from the roof, to boot."

The marshal eyed the conductor.

"These folks," the conductor said, indicating Emmett, Li, Sikes, and Juanito, "they all had tickets just like any other passengers. We didn't sell tickets to that other bunch. They stole their way onto the train."

"You know that for a fact?" the marshal asked.

"For a fact," the conductor said, nodding. "Our brakeman'll be able to testify to that once he gets better."

"Better?"

"Yes, sir. Me and the fireman just found Hicks—our brakeman—in a bad way back in the caboose. Knocked about the head real bad. Little bit we got out of him was that a passel of pistoleros sneaked on and beat him up back there in Truckee."

From only a couple of blocks away, the report of a single gunshot split the air. The deputy marshals whirled that way in tandem as the marshal stayed put and yanked on his six-shooter.

Before the marshal could clear leather, though, Emmett's Colt was out and pointed at the marshal's chest.

"That wasn't us," he was quick to say, jutting his jaw in the direction of the single gunshot. "But you were drawing on me, and I had to protect myself and my party."

His hand still on the grip of his gun, the marshal peered into Emmett's eyes. His deputies wavered behind him.

"Let go of your Schofield there, Marshal, and I'll holster my Colt."

For a tense moment, others on the platform crouched with hands poised to draw.

"He's a good man, Marshal," Li said from behind Emmett. "He won't hurt you."

The marshal blinked repeatedly, evidently taking real note of Li's face only now.

"You can trust him," she said.

Out of the afternoon glare behind the marshal, a very young deputy came running, one arm pumping, the other hand on the crown of his hat. "Marshal, you gotta come see!" he yelled. "Marshal McConaghy, come look!"

After just a beat more, the marshal let his pistol drop back into its holster. "Shall we go take a look together?" he asked Emmett.

Emmett held up his free hand and eased his Colt back into his own holster. He nodded once. "Let's go see."

At a brisk pace the entire knot of lawmen—Californians and Texans alike—set off behind the young deputy. Emmett motioned for Li to join him. She trotted to catch up and took up a quick walk beside him.

When the group rounded a second corner, Emmett spotted what the deputy was so animated about. Sprawled on his back in the dust of the street with a dozen deputies encircling him was Seth Blaylock.

Over the clothes he'd already been wearing was a long black duster. The duster was unbuttoned, exposing his expensive, patterned silk vest. Fastened to the lapel of the vest with a hatpin was a square of paper. On that paper was written one lone word—KIDNAPPER.

Emmett approached the body, cocked his head, and studied what he saw.

Exit wound in the front, he mused.

"I'll bet if you roll him over you'll find that he was shot at point-blank range," he said to the marshal.

After eyeing Emmett for a moment, Marshal McConaghy said to one of his deputies, "Do it."

On the black fabric of the duster it was difficult to notice at a glance, but on closer inspection it was clear. Whoever shot Seth Blaylock had pressed the gun right up against his back.

Emmett looked up and down the street.

CHAPTER SIXTY-ONE

Somewhere South of Sacramento

Emmett and Li sat arm in arm, facing forward on the left side of the train. Since the railcar wasn't very full, Sikes sat sideways on a bench across the aisle, resting his bad leg on the seat cushion. His hat was lowered over his eyes.

Does me good to see him resting, Emmett thought.

The sun's rays fell brightly through the windows on that side of the car. Juanito's seat faced the rear of the car. He stared out the glass, not seeming to mind the blazing afternoon glare.

The rhythmic beat of the carriage moving over the rails had a hypnotic effect. It would have been very easy for Emmett to drift off to sleep. *Not just yet,* he thought.

As warm as it was on the railcar and with danger behind them, Li had shed her duster. In Emmett's opinion the shirt and vest she wore did nothing to diminish her feminine allure. Her dark hair hung in a single braid in back, with a few loose wisps around her face tossing in the breeze.

Their eyes were fixed on one another's now. Until she smiled—which drew his attention to her lips.

He squeezed her hand tenderly and was just about to lean in to give her what promised to be the longest kiss of her nineteen and a half years when he sensed someone approaching in the aisle behind them.

Li's eyes widened and her smile disappeared.

The hair on the back of Emmett's neck stood up.

As the person at his shoulder moved into full view, Emmett's heart jolted.

She was dressed much as Li was—trousers, shirt, vest, but of finer fabrics. All were very costly—custom tailored, no doubt. She too had dark hair and deep-brown eyes. But she wasn't Chinese. Or Oriental at all.

After taking a quick peek at Juanito, who was still staring out the window, and at Sikes, who was still asleep beneath his hat, she bent in close to Emmett and Li.

Emmett felt Li beginning to tremble, which prompted him to smoothly lift the Colt revolver from beside his thigh into the uninvited guest's side. He thumbed back the hammer.

Without flinching, the woman whispered in a silken voice, "Mr. Strong, my name is Ettie Main. I just thought you might like to know—I shot Seth Blaylock. I shot him for that Chinese girl he killed by the arroyo."

Her gaze shifted to Li. Her voice remained hushed. "And I shot him for you."

Then drawing herself upright—all five feet and a smidgen of her—she eyed the couple calmly. "I did it for both of you. Live a happy life together."

She gave a slight smile, turned, and sashayed up the aisle, leaving the car through its front exit.

Keeping his eye on the door, Emmett eased the hammer of his Colt back down and raised Li Xu's hand to his lips.

To the Reader

T hank you for taking time to read *Strong Convictions*. If you enjoyed the book, please consider telling your friends about it or posting a short review. Word of mouth is an author's best friend and is much appreciated.

If you think you'd like to be a part of my "street team" and receive free advance copies of my future books in return for honest reviews, please contact me at author.gphutchinson@gmail.com.

Much obliged.

GP Hutchinson
gphutchinson.com
www.facebook.com/author.gphutchinson
twitter.com/GP_Hutchinson

Coming Soon

Strong Suspicions (Emmett Strong Western #2)
Strong Ambitions (Emmett Strong Western #3)

Also by GP Hutchinson

Sumotori: A 21st Century Samurai Thriller

Acknowledgments

I am tremendously grateful to the Lord God for giving me the imagination and the opportunity to create stories for people's enjoyment. I believe that both the dream and the realization of the dream are gifts from Him.

I can't thank my wife, Carolyn, enough. She is there for me every single day—my sounding board, my encourager, and my friend. As always, I love you, Carolyn.

I have to thank author and writing coach Marg McAlister once again. You helped me gain traction when I didn't quite know where to go next, Marg.

Thank you to the team at CreateSpace for doing such a professional job on every service you've provided. It's always a pleasure to work with you. Your input is priceless.

And finally, to you, the reader, a heartfelt thank-you for picking up this first installment of the Emmett Strong series of Westerns. I hope you've enjoyed the story.

GP Hutchinson
January 2015

About the Author

Former high school teacher GP Hutchinson now turns his attention to the craft of writing. Hutchinson's passion for Westerns started when he was sixteen years old, when he wrote a research paper titled "The Cowboy in American Literature." His influences include artists Frederic Remington and Charles M. Russell, as well as Western author Elmore Leonard. Hutchinson, a father of three and grandfather of eight, lives in the upstate of South Carolina with his wife and one of his daughters. He is a graduate of Louisiana State University and Dallas Theological Seminary who has also lived and studied in Costa Rica and Spain.

84429313R00183

Made in the USA
Columbia, SC
29 December 2017